THE SUN KING RISES

Yves Jégo
Yves Jégo is a member of the French Parliament and spokesman for the UMP party.

Denis Lépée
Denis Lépée is a local politician and environmental adviser. He is the author of books on Ernest Hemingway and Winston Churchill.

Sue Dyson
Sue Dyson has been writing and translating for around twenty years. She is perhaps most widely known as bestselling novelist Zoë Barnes.

THE SUN
KING RISES

YVES JÉGO AND DENIS LÉPÉE

Translated from the French by Sue Dyson

This book is supported by the French Ministry of Foreign Affairs as part of
the Burgess programme run by the Cultural Department of the French
Embassy in London.

www.frenchbooknews.com

Liberté • Égalité • Fraternité

RÉPUBLIQUE FRANÇAISE

A Gallic Book

First published in France as *1661* by *Timée-Éditions*

First published in Great Britain in 2008 by Gallic Books,
134 Lots Road, London SW10 0RJ

A CIP record for this book is available from the British Library

ISBN 978-1-906040-02-4

Typeset in Fournier MT by SX Composing DTP, Rayleigh, Essex
Printed and bound by Creative Print and Design, Wales

2 4 6 8 10 9 7 5 3 1

For Quentin, for Suzanne and Gabrielle.

Experience teaches us that not everything that is unbelievable is untrue.

PAUL DE GONDI, CARDINAL DE RETZ

If I held all the truths in my hand, I would be very careful not to open it and reveal them to mankind.

BERNARD DE FONTENELLE

We encounter our destiny/Often via paths which we take in order to avoid it.

JEAN DE LA FONTAINE

CHAPTER ONE

T HE bells of the Château Saint-Ange were ringing out for all they were worth, announcing the evening service. A silhouetted figure hurried along the wall of the southern tower as if trying to escape the din, then crossed towards the Tiber and disappeared down the stairway which led to the riverbank. Buffeted by gusts of wind and squalls of cold rain, the shadowy willows growing against the wall now covered it almost entirely. François d'Orbay let go of the folds of his rain-soaked grey cloak. He paused for a second at the bottom of the steps, allowing his eyes sufficient time to become accustomed to the half-light, then pulled down his hood to protect his head and started walking again, along the overgrown riverbank. The boat was waiting for him, moored to a ring. Without a word, d'Orbay nodded a greeting to the boatman and jumped on board. The boatman leant across and pushed the boat away from the wall, then took the oars while his passenger settled himself on a wooden plank wedged across the stern. Borne along by the current, the boat made good progress, the boatman's skill keeping it close to the quayside, and almost invisible from the riverbank.

As they were passing Ponte Mazzini, the boatman suddenly lifted his right oar, causing the boat to lurch towards the opposite bank. The boat picked up speed in the current and was heading swiftly for the wall when, at the last moment, the boatman swung it sideways against a stone outcrop just beneath the surface of the water. The hull scraped along the quayside and the boat came to a sudden halt. Plunging his hands into the water, the boatman grabbed hold of a rope and fixed a copper snaphook to it. He signalled to his passenger to duck down.

Guided by the cable, the boat entered a tunnel where there was barely a finger's depth of water beneath the hull. Stretched out in the boat, d'Orbay gazed up at the mossy, vaulted roof, pressing the hood of his cape over his face to protect himself from the stench of sewers that caught in his throat.

As the darkness grew more complete, the boat slowed down. The boatman's voice echoed in the tunnel:

'We are almost there, sir.'

D'Orbay did not reply; he was too busy trying to focus on the glimmer of light which had appeared in front of the boat. The air became lighter as the tunnel broadened out.

He could make out five torches mounted on the wall, and opposite them a quay of white stone with a staircase leading upwards. Leaving his guide there, d'Orbay jumped out of the boat. He walked swiftly, his boots echoing on the stone floor.

Before long he detected the muffled sounds of a conversation. A moment later, pushing aside a heavy curtain of dark velvet, he entered a room whose rich decorations contrasted strongly with the bare underground passageway he had just come through. The bare, damp stone gave way to panelling in precious woods, adorned with paintings and decorated with two large Venetian mirrors reflecting the pale light from the candles.

François d'Orbay let out a sigh of satisfaction as he saw the smiles of the six men present, who had fallen silent as he made his appearance. *Six of the fourteen*, he thought as he passed across the stone threshold. *Six who have come from England, Spain, Italy, Austria and Poland.*

They were seated in large, black-leather armchairs, all identical but one, whose back was crowned with a gilded wooden sun, and whose arms extended to form the claws of a griffon. *Five plus one*, thought d'Orbay, gazing at its occupant with a mixture of affection and respect. Giacomo Del Sarto, a faithful friend and a doctor who was capable of miracles. Giacomo Del Sarto, the great and mysterious master . . .

'I am happy to see you again, Giacomo.'

The tall, thin man he had just addressed did not answer, but signalled to him to sit down. Taking off his cloak, d'Orbay threw it onto a chair and came forward to greet each of his fellow guests.

'A thousand pardons for my lateness, my friends. The journey was not entirely without incident.'

Still without a word, Giacomo gestured that this mattered little, then leant forward to pluck the starched cover from the round table before them. Once this was removed, the marble table revealed at its centre a mosaic motif, featuring the same sun surrounded by fourteen interlinked arches.

'Now that our Brother from Paris has arrived, I propose that we get straight to the point. Some of you are no doubt wondering why I have summoned this extraordinary assembly. Would you enlighten us, François?' he added, turning to d'Orbay.

'Our information regarding Mazarin's health has been confirmed,' he replied. 'This time he really is mortally ill. No matter that his mages predict a prompt recovery; he is close to death, even if he is Chief Minister. The rats are already busying themselves behind the scenes, and Paris is buzzing with talk of his succession, in both financial and political terms. After an unofficial thirty-year reign, Mazarin is at last resolved to die. His henchman, Colbert, is plotting in secret to conceal the origins of the old scoundrel's fortune to endow him with some semblance of honesty . . . But that is not the key issue. What matters is that this can serve our plans: the King's youth, the end of an era, the unclenching of Mazarin's iron fist, all provide us with an exceptional opportunity which may not recur for a very long time. We must therefore take advantage of it.'

D'Orbay paused, struck by a sudden thought. His gaze drifted over the dark wood walls, then stopped at one of the enormous mirrors, as if confronting his own reflection had jolted him back to what he was saying.

'We would of course have preferred less upheaval, but I am confident we will succeed. We must simply ensure that people are not stirred up too much. The recent failure of the revolution that brought down the monarchy in England and the restoration of Charles II to his father's throne mean that things may get out of control. The new King will doubtless wish to avenge his father and track down those who condemned him to death. Those of our Brothers who were involved in that affair believe they were advancing our cause, but now the whole edifice lies in ruins. For the moment that matters little. All that does matter is that this unfortunate failure should not compromise our plans in France.'

One of the participants slid forward in his chair and signalled that he would like to ask a question. With a nod, Giacomo invited him to speak.

'But is it not said that in Paris the rebels are becoming restless?'

D'Orbay frowned.

'I don't believe that for a moment. What do you think stirs the hearts of ordinary people as the Kingdom of France is in the process of changing its master? Why, the theatre, my friends: all of Paris speculates upon the fate of a new play by Monsieur Molière, who is inaugurating the Palais-Royal theatre and has promised a drama to prove his genius! A Chief Minister is dying, yet people are interested only in counting the supporters and detractors of an entertainer . . . Incidentally, I shall take advantage of my presence in Rome to meet one of the former leaders of the Fronde, the exiled Archbishop of Paris, Paul de Gondi. I can easily gain access to him and will try to find out what his former friends and co-conspirators are planning.'

A man with a strong Spanish accent, who had remained silent up to this point, now spoke.

'All the same, should we not fear lest the young King of France seek to increase his personal power as he contemplates his English cousin?'

D'Orbay stood up with a sigh. The wooden floor creaked beneath his riding boots. He paused before a chessboard that lay on a small mahogany gaming table and distractedly picked up an alabaster pawn, rolling it between his fingers.

'Everything is possible where crowned heads are involved . . . Young Louis, however, thinks more of ladies, hunting and music than of power – at least he has until now. He hates only conspiracies and traitors. It is up to us to avoid appearing in either of those roles.'

Replacing the pawn, d'Orbay walked back and stood behind his chair. In the flickering light of the chandeliers, his wet hair, tied back with a velvet ribbon, seemed blacker than jet. Trying to mask his impatience, he waited a moment before continuing:

'In any event, my Brothers, we no longer have a choice. Mazarin's death throes do not leave us enough time to turn back. In fact they dictate that matters must be hastened.'

His voice grew more solemn.

'We cannot risk allowing this opportunity to slip by, nor can we allow any possible public disturbances to undermine us. This is what has prompted my hurried journey from France and our meeting. I ask your pardon for not consulting any of you in advance, but we have seen too many couriers eliminated and too many secret codes broken to entrust any more serious announcements to messengers.'

D'Orbay sat down in his chair, clasped his hands for a moment, then laid them flat on his thighs as he scanned the faces turned towards him and attempted to decipher his companions' thoughts. In the silence a servant entered, drawing aside another hanging which concealed a double door. Without a word, he offered his tray of wine glasses to each man, acknowledging them all with a brief nod. D'Orbay watched him leave, his work done, then turned back to the six men seated around him.

All right, he thought, taking a deep breath, *the time has come*:

'My friends, as our rule demands I have come to request your authorisation for our Brotherhood to transfer the Secret which we guard to the place where we will act . . .'

The Spaniard cut in once again:

'Transferring the Secret is one thing. But what of the key that enables its revelation, the key we have been seeking for so many years? What will happen if we do not find it in time? England has shown us the risks involved when action is taken without it . . . Would it not be better to delay a while longer?'

For a moment, silence fell over the little gathering as its members eyed each other. The only sound was the sputtering of a candle as it was going out. Its flickering light emphasised the Grand Master's hollow features, accentuating the impression of fragility which emanated from his frame.

With a sombre expression, François d'Orbay suppressed an ill-tempered gesture.

'My friends, our Brotherhood has known of the existence of the Secret for more than five hundred years. We possess the manuscript in which it is hidden. Only the means to reveal it to the world slipped through our fingers fifteen years ago, and continues to elude us. If we possessed it, we would be able to convince the King of the legitimacy of our action. That is why we must make every effort to rediscover the key, right up to the last moment. Indeed, that is why the transfer of the coded manuscript from Rome to France is so vital.'

His voice became more impassioned.

'But even if fate were to deny us that achievement, I am

nevertheless certain that we should not draw back. As I have told you, such an opportunity may not come again. The King is still young; he is malleable, and destabilised by the imminent loss of his mentor. He trusts the man we have chosen to further our cause.'

He paused for a moment to judge the effect of his words.

'Throughout all these years, step by step, we have established the conditions for our victory, my Brothers. To delay would be madness: believe me, our Brother Nicolas Fouquet can make the Truth prevail.'

In the profound silence that followed his speech, these last words resounded with the solemn emphasis of a ritual chant:

'Do I have your consent, my Brothers?'

As though summoned by some silent command, a servant appeared, this time carrying a wooden urn with a round hole in it. He placed it on the table and opened a hidden drawer at the base of the urn. From it he took a leather bag, untied its strings and emptied its contents onto a small silver tray. Black and white wooden balls rolled onto the metal with a dull clatter.

The servant went round the gathering, presenting the tray to the seven men so that they could each take one white ball and one black. One by one, each man came forward to the urn and placed inside it one of the balls hidden in his hand. Then Giacomo had the urn brought over to him and opened it, slowly taking out the balls, one at a time. This done, he invited the others to observe the result of the vote. Seven identical white balls lay in a line on the mosaic of the sun.

'So be it,' murmured François d'Orbay. 'The die is cast.'

CHAPTER TWO

Toussaint Roze had been poring over the documents before him for more than two hours. Seated in the armchair given to him by the Queen's mother, Anne of Austria, Jules Mazarin's private secretary had slid out the fine inlaid shelf of the imposing writing desk which stood against the wall, its back towards the window of the Chief Minister's private office. This item of furniture had a secret compartment and had been specially made in Milan a few years earlier. With unfeigned pleasure, Roze had just extracted from it a large, dark-red leather case, stamped with the Cardinal's arms. He caught himself admiring the quality of the leather and the finely worked steel clasp. *Why has His Eminence asked me to bring him these papers as a matter of urgency?* he wondered as he caressed the age-smoothed cover of the magnificent document case. He wondered all the more since, as far as he could recall, and despite being a devoted colleague, he had practically never had access to this desk. The rumours about the Chief Minister's illness went round and round in his mind, like an obsessive litany.

All was calm this cold morning in Mazarin's private apartments – almost more so than usual. Currently the owner preferred to occupy his private rooms in the Louvre, and the servants had for the most part left to join their master or were taking advantage of a day's freedom. Eventually the fires had even gone out in the fireplaces. Was it the cold of these early February days or exhaustion from performing a fastidious task which made Toussaint Roze shiver as he returned to his work?

Concentrated as he was on reading the parchments, the good secretary – who, it must be said, had become a little deaf over the years – did not hear the men who had just entered the hallway of the apartment.

There were five of them, wearing brown leather eye-masks and swathed in voluminous black capes. Having silently closed the oak double doors to the great staircase that led up from the library, they stealthily crossed the room, one behind the other.

Down below in his office, Étienne Baluze, His Eminence's personal librarian, was finishing off a memorandum to his employer that gave an account of his first few weeks of work. The sound of visitors to the neighbouring library had interrupted him in his task several times. The young man was not yet accustomed to this busy day of the week. Moreover, he did not understand why the Cardinal wished to open up his collection once a week to learned Parisians. With a gesture of annoyance, he ran his hand through the thick blond hair which made him such a success with young women, and gave him the look of an angel worthy of the Italian painters whose works filled the Cardinal's collection.

'Help! Fire! Sound the alert!'

These shouts mingled with the racket of falling chairs and running feet that came from the other side of the internal wall.

Étienne Baluze scarcely had time to stand up before thick smoke began to filter underneath his door.

As he entered the great reading room, the librarian saw at once the extent of the conflagration. The smoke made it almost impossible to see the other end of the room. Stunned, he watched as flames licked at a whole row of bookshelves.

'Quickly, water . . . We must have water!' shouted the young man, who seemed not to notice the crowd of people jostling each other in their haste to get outside and escape the flames.

Suddenly, with a terrible crashing sound, one entire wall of the library collapsed into the room, inducing panic in those fleeing. Étienne Baluze's only thought now was to save the fabulous library.

The young librarian struggled to gather his wits. Suddenly it struck him that he could save at least some of the most precious works from destruction if he organised a human chain between the well in the courtyard and the library, where flames danced ever higher.

'Buckets! Go and fetch all the buckets you can find!' Étienne Baluze shouted to the Cardinal's guards, who had seen the smoke and rushed to the door of the great room.

At that moment, puzzled by the noise, Toussaint Roze looked up from his reading. His cry was stifled by the gag stuffed into his mouth by one of the men in black.

'Tie him up securely,' said the man, his tall frame towering over the poor private secretary. 'If need be, knock him out! And search the apartment – there may be other people here. Time is pressing.' Terrified, Toussaint Roze felt his blood turn to ice as the man's strange eyes – one green, the other brown – rested on him.

While his accomplices dispersed throughout the apartments, the leader of the band began to force open the drawers of the imposing Italian desk. Armed with an iron bar, the attacker cared little for the damage he did to the precious wood veneer covering the desk. Like an automaton, he stuffed all the papers filed that morning by Toussaint Roze into a bag hidden beneath his cape. Roze saw with alarm that smoke was now pouring into the apartments from the floor below.

Just then the office door opened and one of the Cardinal's guards entered. The soldier, who had run upstairs to alert the secretary, froze for a moment, petrified by the sight of overturned furniture and the alarming appearance of the intruders. Caught unawares by this unexpected interruption, they stood rooted to the spot, pausing in their search.

'Guards! Over here! Guards . . .' was all the soldier had time to cry out.

Without another word, he collapsed heavily onto the ornate round carpet that covered the middle of the floor, a dagger between his shoulder blades. The assassin – the smallest of the intruders – stood proudly in the doorway, legs apart and hands on hips.

'Thank you, Le Jeune,' said the man with mismatched eyes, as he went on opening the drawers one by one and emptying their contents into his large linen sack.

'It was nothing. The Almighty is protecting us. He guided my hand.' The voice was that of a child, but emerged from the mouth of the individual who had just killed the guard with such incredible precision.

At these words, Toussaint Roze lost consciousness.

'We must go,' said the leader to his men, gathered once more in Mazarin's office. 'We shall take advantage of the confusion to leave the same way we entered. Do not forget to remove your masks as you go down, and turn up the collars of your capes, so that you do not stand out too much in the chaos downstairs.'

Without so much as a glance at Toussaint Roze, who was deathly white and still unconscious, the men in black turned to leave the private apartments and headed down the stairs. But they had scarcely reached the foot of the staircase when they ran into the Cardinal's guards who had formed a human chain and were passing buckets of water from hand to hand. Looking up, the captain of the guard realised that the intruders were emerging from His Eminence's apartments, to which entry was forbidden. Dropping his bucket, he instinctively reached for his sword and unsheathed it.

'Back the way we came,' ordered the intruders' leader as he hurried back up the stairs, followed closely by his four accomplices.

'Guards! Follow me!' barked the captain, ready to rush off in hot pursuit of the fugitives.

'Do not move! I order you not to move! The fire! We must put this fire out . . .' panted Étienne Baluze. 'Continue, I beg you! The Cardinal would never forgive us!'

Complete confusion reigned in the corridor. The guards just stood there, no longer sure whom to obey.

'Three men, come with me! The rest of you, stay and put out

this damned fire,' said the captain, realising that he could not simply abandon the librarian.

But these contradictory orders had given the black-clad intruders a significant start. Without wasting a second they had rushed upstairs, towards the rooftops.

The clock in the tower of the new church of Saint-Roch a few streets away was striking twelve as the five fugitives emerged onto the roof of Mazarin's palace.

'Le Jeune . . . where is Le Jeune?' demanded the leader of the band as he ran, his men making relatively swift progress despite the danger and the height.

Suddenly, the face of the young lad they had outpaced appeared behind them. They slowed down to enable him to catch up. Without a word, he showed them the bulging purse he had casually removed from Toussaint Roze's pocket.

'I found this too,' he said, brandishing the dark-red leather document case. 'It was lying at the old fellow's feet.'

Pleased with his young recruit's boldness, the leader signalled to his companions to make haste and follow him.

'We must hurry. Watch out for the frost, the roof is slippery. We'll go through the Palais-Royal theatre and disappear from sight as we head down towards the Seine. Hurry,' he added, turning towards the distant skylight, a stone's throw away, through which they had hauled themselves onto the roof. 'I can hear the guards.'

The captain's imposing silhouette appeared at that moment, followed rather more clumsily by three soldiers. Managing to maintain their lead, the black-clad men reached a spot above the theatre and began to look for a way down into the building. A terrible crash of breaking glass stopped them in their tracks. Le Jeune had suddenly disappeared through a pane of glass he had inadvertently trodden or perhaps slipped on, having lost his footing on the frozen roof. Leaning over the gaping hole, the leader of the band saw the boy's broken body lying directly below, right in the middle of the large stage of His Majesty's new theatre.

'Hurry, we cannot do anything for him. God has him in his keeping,' he added, crossing himself. 'He has returned to the true Kingdom.'

Without further ceremony, the man with the strange eyes motioned to the group to advance and head in the direction he was indicating. Before the eys of the pursuing guards, they vanished into the darkness of the theatre's attics.

As his accomplices successfully made their escape, the young boy dragged himself towards the edge of the stage onto which he had crashed, his body racked with pain. With one final effort, he found the strength to reach inside his shirt and take out the red leather case he had pinched a few minutes earlier. Gasping for breath and twisted in agony, the boy pushed it to the bottom of the well where the prompter usually sat. Exhausted, he let his head fall back into the pool of blood which was now spreading out across the floorboards of the stage, like a sinister extension of the half-drawn purple curtain.

At that moment, intrigued by the noise, the theatre concierge entered the auditorium. All he saw was the boy's clenched hand falling back onto the apron of the stage. Horrified, the old man rushed into the wings to fetch help.

'Molière,' he yelled, 'Molière, come quickly!'

CHAPTER THREE

Palais du Louvre — Sunday 6 February, two o'clock
in the afternoon

THE curtains were drawn and all candles snuffed out with the exception of two nightlights positioned on either side of the sick man's bed. The massive fire-guard was in place, blocking out everything but a faint red glow from the burning coals. All the furniture in the room was of dark wood. The scene in Cardinal Mazarin's bedchamber had been expertly contrived to remind the few permitted visitors that a man was dying here, and a man of great power at that. The majestic silence was disturbed only by the sick man's irregular breathing and the muffled footsteps of the servant who came at regular intervals to check if His Eminence required anything.

Motionless and propped up on a mountain of pillows, the most powerful man in France, the King's godfather, a minister whose orders were never questioned, appeared to be dozing. All that could be seen of him was his gaunt face, its waxen complexion topped by a Cardinal's red hat and encircled by a crown of white hair, and his hands which lay on the sheets, emerging from the lacy sleeves of an immaculate white shirt.

'My books,' he murmured. 'My books, my papers, just imagine the stench of fire on my books!' he went on in a tired voice curiously tinged with emotion. His hand flapped helplessly. 'And my paintings, Bellini's *Virgin*, the Raphael which arrived last month from Rome . . . Have they at least been accounted for?'

In the ambient silence came a whispered reply:

'Not all of them, Monseigneur. But I am attending to it.'

The breathy voice emanated from a shape hunched on a chair which had been squeezed between two large chests, to the left of the canopied bed. The small, thin man, whose short arms ended in bony hands that looked like claws, melded so intimately with the atmosphere of the place that he was all but invisible. Dressed in a curious suit of ecclesiastical appearance, he was pale-skinned with high cheekbones and a firm chin beneath narrow lips that were pressed together in an expression of contempt. He sat with his hands on his knees, clutching a bundle of documents. His protruding eyes darted towards Mazarin in a look that seemed to express all the tension he was feeling.

'The paintings have been saved, Your Eminence. One frame has some heat damage, but the canvas is intact.'

'Approach, Colbert . . .'

In a single bound the little man was on his feet and bending humbly over the invalid, his head slightly to one side, silent . . .

'Was I asleep for long?'

'No, Monseigneur,' replied the Cardinal's shadowy advisor. 'A few hours have passed since you wished to rest after news of the fire.'

'What has been said about my condition?'

'The truth, Monseigneur: that you are resting.'

The Chief Minister of France gestured in irritation:

'I am not deceived by the hypocritical airs of courtiers, nor by the grand words of doctors.'

He fell silent for a moment, his eyes closed; then he spoke again, this time more softly:

'The former have long since dreamt of burying me, and the latter are afraid to tell me the truth . . . Simoni, my astrologer – bring him to me, Colbert. I have no illusions. I want to know how much time I have left. People say I am ill – what of it! They write about it in lampoons, they make up songs, they draw up far-fetched plans: children's games, all of it. What matters is that for the moment we are in control. Have you read that fable by La Fontaine about the dairymaid and the milk jug, which Fouquet had me listen to a few days ago for my entertainment? Now there's a tale my enemies should meditate upon . . . Did you not keep it, Colbert? I can no longer remember the last verses: can you recall them?'

At the mention of La Fontaine and Fouquet, Colbert stiffened. However, his voice did not betray him as he answered in a steady, even tone, after a moment's rummaging amongst his papers.

'Here we are, Monseigneur, these verses are indeed well observed: "Whose mind does not stray/Who does not build castles in Spain/Picrochole, Pyrrhus, the dairymaid, all of us in fact/As many wise men as fools." Nevertheless, I trust Your Excellency will permit me to express my regret that Monsieur de La Fontaine has not the good taste to limit his irony to these verses, which his protector Nicolas Fouquet abases himself by reading to you.'

Mazarin raised an eyebrow, demanding an explanation:

'Monseigneur, I have here ten sheets of those filthy lampoons to which you have alluded, and in which we find much of Monsieur de La Fontaine's verve . . .'

Mazarin smiled.

'Come, Colbert, for pity's sake don't waste police time on such childish nonsense: what can La Fontaine do if he has talent and is inspired? And do you think that Nicolas Fouquet, Superintendent of His Majesty's finances, is amused by these games?'

Annoyed, Colbert rearranged his papers in silence.

'Returning to what matters most, Colbert, what information do you have about the investigation?'

'It seems that the possibility of an accident has been discounted, Monseigneur. I agree, but I have refrained from telling anyone so, and in the city everyone firmly believes that all that accumulated paper was the source of the fire. The populace has little love for books, Monseigneur. The theory is easy to promote and our friends are eager to spread it. They support it with reference to a partial inventory of the works destroyed . . .'

This word provoked a moan of distress from Mazarin.

'. . . Dante, Herodotus, part of the map collection, the section on medicine, Fathers of the Church, astrology . . .'

Mazarin raised his hand to interrupt the litany. His head rolled from right to left and he mumbled phrases in unintelligible Italian; Colbert tried to convince himself that they were prayers. He began again, cautiously:

'There is another thing, Monseigneur, which I fear is more serious. It seems that the fire was merely a diversion to mask a theft. The fire was started deliberately. A guard was murdered. Your secretary, Monsieur Roze, was attacked, and it is a miracle that he escaped with his life . . .'

The Chief Minister listened in silence. His mouth twisted into a rictus. Colbert thought that his master was in pain, but changed his mind when he heard him speak:

'Who, Colbert?'

'I do not know, Monseigneur, nor do I know why. But I have deployed all my resources and my finest men in order to find out.'

The little man came closer and lowered his voice.

'Far be it from me to importune Your Eminence, but if I utter the name of Nicolas Fouquet, it is because certain disturbing elements concern him indirectly.'

Mazarin's voice became tired and dull.

'Yet again? The facts, Colbert, the facts.'

'We lost track of the assailants in the new Palais-Royal theatre, whose tenant is Monsieur Molière, who – although his troupe bears the fine name of the Théâtre de Monsieur[1] and therefore honours His Majesty's brother – also belongs unofficially to Nicolas Fouquet . . .'

Mazarin clasped his white hands with their long, thin fingers and, bringing them close to his face, deliberately emphasised each word.

'Enough of all this suspicion, Colbert, I want clear leads, names. Quickly. What do the witnesses say?'

'That the assailants talked constantly of Our Lord, saying

[1] Philippe, duc d'Orléans, also known as Monsieur, brother of Louis XIV.

that he holds us in his mercy. In the absence of prisoners, that is all we have. The only man the miserable band left at the scene will not be able to tell us more. He died before we could question him, on the very stage of the theatre where Molière is rehearsing. We couldn't get anything out of him. He was a child, a beggar no doubt, a member of a secret society such as the Cour des Miracles or the Gueule du Chien. He wore a cross around his neck, however, and an olive-wood chaplet at his waist, which is somewhat unusual amongst beggars, whose only religion is sorcery.'

Mazarin sighed.

'This suggests something else to me: fuel for the fanatical pyre. Yes, that is possible. Do we have spies in the religious factions we have dissolved?'

Colbert nodded.

'Activate them. The Jansenists are peaceable, but those . . . Too bad, they will all pay together. Consider summoning a meeting of the assembly of clergy to regulate this affair officially, and cleanse the churches of the sectarians who are lurking within. But first, intensify your investigation. You have a free hand, Colbert,' Mazarin added firmly.

Then, seeing the carnivorous smile which had appeared on his confidant's face:

'On this specific matter, Colbert, you have a free hand. Right, let us come to the subject of the theft. I want to know everything. I must have precise details if I am to have a clear understanding of these infamies.'

Colbert breathed deeply but did not answer.

'Well, Colbert?' demanded Mazarin impatiently.

'The thing is, Monseigneur, there is something even more serious than the fire and that man's criminal character. . .'

Mazarin paled.

'These malefactors, Monseigneur, were not targeting the library, but your own apartments. They entered your apartments,' he specified when he saw the Chief Minister's incredulous expression.

Mazarin grew increasingly angry as he pictured the assailants in his own private rooms, their hands sullying the precious items of furniture he had chosen and accumulated over the years.

'Within my walls!' he roared. 'How far did they go? They did not enter my bedchamber, did they?'

Colbert lowered his eyes.

'Yes they did, Your Eminence. And your office. That is where Roze was when they attacked him.

Mazarin's complexion changed suddenly from pale to deathly white. Alarmed, Colbert thought that the Cardinal had been taken ill, and was about to rise and call for help, but Mazarin indicated that he should remain seated. He recovered his breath.

'Continue. They took papers, did they not?'

Colbert nodded.

'Which ones? From where?'

Mazarin was almost shouting.

'There is great disorder, Your Eminence, and we do not yet know everything, particularly as Roze was filing the papers in accordance with the orders you had given him. But they took a number of accounting documents from the two sealed chests which stand against the wall, of that Toussaint Roze is sure.

Before he lost consciousness, he also saw them breaking open the inlaid writing desk . . .'

Colbert broke off at the Cardinal's ice-cold sigh.

'He mentioned several folders of correspondence, two of beige leather and another dark red . . .'

A long shudder went through the Cardinal's body.

'And also a few coded files. I have asked him to give us a precise inventory as soon as possible.'

The Cardinal did not react and lay still for a long time. Then he sat up a little and shook his head gently.

'Who knows about the deaths and the robbery?'

'Roze, four of your most reliable guards, Molière and a few of his actors. There is nothing to worry about there. The former are trustworthy and we have sufficiently frightened the performers with references to matters of State and the prospect of a trip to the Bastille . . . The premiere of the play is tomorrow, and they would rather keep silent than endanger their show, of that I am sure. Doubtless it will all filter out at some point, but we have a little time before then.'

'Good. Ensure that the troupe also receives a gratuity from me. It can only help to keep their mouths shut. As for the rest, Colbert, leave no stone unturned: this search must be speeded up. I want those papers. Our enemies are many, we know that. They are powerful, all the more so since we do not know who they all are. Nothing must be overlooked, nothing, in the quest for what they have stolen. This is a most perilous time: news of my illness and the robbery itself, these mean that we are no longer safe. Colbert, my interests and therefore yours depend upon the swiftness of our agents. And perhaps a great deal more than that,' murmured Cardinal Mazarin, looking straight at Colbert.

Without a word, Colbert got up and bowed low. Then he walked silently to the door. Calm had already returned to the room when, just as he was opening the door, the Cardinal's voice called him back.

'Colbert!'

'Your Eminence?'

'Go and see Roze, and retrieve the papers from my private desk. Find a totally secure place in which to hide them. Then come back. We must talk again about my will.'

Colbert bowed again and backed out of the room. As he turned away, he looked preoccupied and extremely agitated.

CHAPTER FOUR

Fausse-Repose Forest — Sunday 6 February, two o'clock in the afternoon

'KILL! Kill!'

The young King, excited by the last moments of the hunt, spurred on his mount. Keeping the white horse on a short rein, he directed it to follow the master huntsman who was striding down the slope of a hollow. The wild boar had mistakenly taken refuge there, chased by the dogs, and the slavering pack crowded round the cornered animal, exhausted after a chase that had lasted several hours. It was backed up against a wall of earth studded with the roots of overhanging trees. First one then another of the most foolhardy dogs were dealt violent blows as the beast swung its head right and left. As they fell several metres away, their bellies ripped open and their bodies broken by the boar's razor-sharp tusks, their moans were drowned out by the hoarse barking of other dogs, maddened by the blood. In one movement Louis XIV dismounted and pushed his steed away with a slap to the chest. Three of his companions waited anxiously to see what risks the King was willing to take. The master huntsman came back towards them. Smiling, the King simply stretched out his hand. The man bowed and, holding his large hunting knife by the blade, placed it in the King's palm. Then he withdrew, head still bowed, overwhelmed by the favour the sovereign had just bestowed upon him by deciding to kill the beast with his weapon.

The King unfastened his cape, revealing the leather baldrick that protected his chest.

'Come, Messieurs,' he said to the men surrounding him, 'let us see what the pig has in its belly.'

Thus armed, and followed by men with spears and two others carrying muskets, the King took a few steps forward beneath the cover of frozen branches.

'Take care, Sire, the ground is covered in frost.'

The King smiled disdainfully.

Don't worry, Monsieur d'Artagnan. I may not have sea legs, but I have no problem in the woods of Versailles.'

The wild boar trembled all over, worn out after being harried by the dogs who were now almost touching it, and whose teeth had streaked its bristly pelt with red.

Louis stopped and took a deep breath, smelling the air. The odour of wet foliage and blood seemed enhanced by the cold. The King of France was covered in mud up to his waist, clad and booted in leather; he was bare-headed, his hair tied back by a thick velvet ribbon, and sweat mingled with the earth on his face. But despite his small stature and stiff, upright stance, he exuded a mixture of hauteur and passion.

The image of another hunt came back to him. A small boy, four years old, escaped the hand of the musketeer who was looking after him and ran towards his father with a smile of wonderment, his blond curls flying behind him in the cold morning air, his eyes swollen from too little sleep; a small boy whose heart was filled with a mixture of terror and joy as he saw his father wiping his knife, soiled with dark, almost black blood, on the stag's chest. The clearing resembled those the hunt had just galloped through. The trees were the same, just fifteen years younger.

They had travelled back at a leisurely pace, the boy seated against the pommel of his father's saddle, his face pressed into his glove, which smelt strongly of animals, sweat and blood. He had fallen asleep, only to reawaken on a bench in the hunting lodge to the sound of laughter and loud voices, including that of the Duc d'Épernon which boomed like a drum. On his return, his governess had washed him thoroughly, exclaiming loudly at the sight of the red stains on his little doublet and scarf, which served him as a belt, and even in his hair. And he had laughed as he watched the water flowing over the earthenware of the bathtub, red against its immaculate white.

Versailles was still here, its woods, its smells, the house where the soul of his father dwelt, far from the madness of the city, the hatred of Paris and its populace. Versailles was still here, like a promise to be fulfilled . . .

'Sire, a message from the Louvre.'

Jolted from his reverie, the King glanced disdainfully at the blue uniform marked with a musketeer's cross which had appeared at his side. Then his gaze lighted on the sealed message the man was proffering, as he knelt on one knee before him. Without a word, his jaw clenched in anger, the King signalled to his companion to take the message.

D'Artagnan looked furiously at the messenger, who vanished as quickly as he had come.

'The order came from the Cardinal's house, Sire, and the bearer gave the password which grants safe conduct to Your Majesty without delay . . .' explained the master of the royal hounds who had organised the day, and to whom the messenger had been brought.

'I imagine he did,' the King retorted, 'and I hope the sender has not in any way abused that privilege.'

The King glanced again at the continuing death agonies of the wild beast, then turned back to the captain of his guard:

'So, Monsieur d'Artagnan, what kind of problem is it that demands my immediate attention?'

The sarcasm died in his voice when he saw the look on d'Artagnan's face.

'Sire,' he replied, replacing his knife in the holster on his hip, 'I fear . . .'

'Do not fear, Monsieur, say.'

'A fire has just occurred, Sire, which has ravaged Mazarin's palace. The smoke has blackened the Louvre right up to the windows. There have been several wounded, perhaps some dead.'

The King turned pale.

'The Cardinal . . .'

'. . . is in as good health as the fatigue of recent days allows him to be. His Eminence was not present at the time . . .'

The King cut him short with a wave of his hand and summoned the valet who was holding his cloak. Then he threw the knife to the ground, much to the regret of the master huntsman, who saw his glory fade before his very eyes.

'We must go, Messieurs,' said the King. 'Prepare the carriages with all speed.'

The King and his companions remounted and galloped off to where the carriages had been left and a meal laid out. The horsemen, escorted by thirty musketeers, rode along without a word. Descending the hill, they soon came out onto an avenue lined with poplar trees. In the distance, the pink stone of the Versailles hunting lodge was just visible. The slate roofs sparkled in the winter sunshine.

CHAPTER FIVE

SITTING up in bed, Cardinal Mazarin allowed his thoughts to wander. He had long enjoyed these moments of calm, well before illness had obliged him to rest. They enabled his mind to choose which unexpected subjects to settle on and revealed new ways of seeing things. Annoyingly though, he had to admit that, despite his best efforts, he was finding it difficult to think clearly about the subject which occupied him the most.

Lost accounting papers are vexing, he thought, *and some of them ought not to find their way into enemy hands. But it would be more serious if . . .*

Ice-cold sweat trickled down his pallid brow.

No, the danger would be too great . . .

The sound of running feet on the wooden floor of his antechamber, mingled with snatches of conversation, made him open his eyes. Sitting in the half-light, he heard the footsteps come closer, then the double door crashed open and he was dazzled by light. Blinking, he raised his hand like a visor to shade his eyes. He hesitated for a moment:

'Who's there . . .?'

The shout died in his throat as the radiant figure which had entered his bedchamber grew clearer and acquired the face of the Queen Mother.

The Cardinal smiled as he attempted to control his pounding heart.

'What an entrance, Madame,' he commented, taking the Queen's hand as she stood at his bedside. 'You looked just like a ghost . . .'

The Queen smiled painfully. Her pale complexion, her dark hair scraped back, her severe gown, everything about her exuded fear, hardening the features which had once been so beautiful and soft.

'Come, Madame, your anxiety is out of all proportion. It is not the fire which has forced me to my bed, but rather the lack of fire . . . inner fire,' the Chief Minister joked.

The King's mother shook her head but the air of sadness did not leave her.

'Do not laugh, dear friend, I beg you. I have brought my personal physician; he is waiting in the anteroom. Are you sure that there's no need . . .?'

Still holding her hand, Mazarin indicated that there was not.

'Have no fear. My powers may be waning, but I have not yet uttered my last word and I shall continue to watch over France, that is to say, over you and my godson the King.'

The Cardinal squeezed the Queen's hand a little more tightly when he saw the tears welling up in her eyes. Then he sat up straight and said in a firmer tone:

'Do not be sad, think of all that we have done. We have been France, Madame. All that matters is that our enemies do not take advantage of my weakness in order to destroy us. No one has the right to understand or judge France, its Government or its King. All your energies must now be devoted to one purpose: your son the King needs you to safeguard his throne.'

The Queen nodded silently. She had shared so much fear, so much joy, so many victories and defeats with the minister. And now she saw the whole of her strange life played out in his face. Reluctantly, she had become Queen of a land which for a long time had appeared terrifying; married a King whom she had never known and always feared; been besieged in her own palace, suspected, spied upon and denounced; and then suddenly, in order to save her orphan son's throne, she had transformed herself into a warrior-woman and the leader of a political party, capable of destroying destinies and families . . .

'Jules,' she said softly, her familiar tone indicating the close rapport between them, a friendship without which she would never have found the strength to stand firm.

He stopped her, pressing his fingertips to her lips.

'Go, Madame, I would not wish to impose the sight of my fatigue upon you . . .'

The Queen made a brusque gesture.

'Sleep, dear friend,' she ordered him in a voice which had regained its composure. 'I will only be in the next room.'

With his eyes half closed, the Cardinal watched the majestic silhouette of a Queen of France walk to the door to his private office.

CHAPTER SIX

Palais du Louvre – Sunday 6 February, four o'clock in the afternoon

'THE King!'

Energetic and determined, Louis XIV strode into the room where Cardinal Mazarin lay bedridden. In his anger, the King had not even taken the time to change. He was still wearing his hunting clothes, complete with dirty boots, gloves tucked through his belt and a muddy shirt, as he approached the bed where his all-powerful Chief Minister was dozing, propped up on his pillows. Once again he was struck by the yellowish complexion of the sick man, whose eyes were now acquiring that very distinctive, translucent tinge. A lump came to his throat as he saw how much Mazarin had deteriorated physically. He sat down on the chair which a valet of the bedchamber hastily produced for him, and spent a moment trying to see beneath Mazarin's excess of face paint to determine his exact state of health. As his attention lingered on the old man's whistling breath, Louis could not help remembering the little boy he had once been, standing before Louis XIII on the eve of his death. Like Mazarin, the King had been a silent, almost transparent ghost. But back then, the man lying in the bed today had been at his side. He was the one who had held the small, intimidated boy's hand and pushed him forward towards the sick man with the disturbing appearance and the nauseatingly sweet smell. And it was Mazarin who had been there again that dawn when Louis had had to flee Paris and take refuge at Saint-Germain. He had been so afraid that day, and had only recovered his composure by desperately gripping the Cardinal's hand and refusing to let go of it throughout the journey . . .

The bedchamber was empty and dimly lit, despite the waning daylight. The King realised that his Chief Minister wished to speak to him without witnesses.

'I have come to assure you of my affection, dear godfather. News of the fire was brought to me as I was hunting near Versailles.'

Mazarin managed a faint smile at the sound of this name. Hunting, Versailles: those two words summed up his godson's tastes . . .

'Do you have any more precise information?' continued the young King. 'What is the extent of the damage to your library? What happened to your collection of paintings? What is known about the victims?'

Mazarin stopped the flow of questions with a gesture. He felt too weary to follow the young King's energetic discourse. The minister had to get his breath back before replying.

'Sire, your presence here both honours and comforts me. The worst has come to pass, and today does not bode well for the Kingdom. Colbert has just left having given me a detailed account of the attack.'

'The attack?'

'Yes, Sire, the fire was caused by a band of masked ruffians. Doubtless they were seeking to cause a diversion. My private apartments were broken into, my desk was looted and documents of the highest importance are missing. I was specifically keeping them in that magnificent Italian writing desk you so loved to play on when you were small, Sire. One of my personal bodyguards was murdered, and my private secretary, Roze, was attacked.'

'We will find these murderers and I shall punish them. I will not accept this!' raged the King, disconcerted by his godfather's grievous account.

Unable to control himself, he pushed his chair back roughly and began to stride restlessly about the room.

'How could the guards at your palace allow this to happen without doing anything? I shall have their captain severely punished and . . .'

'Let's forget about that for the moment, Louis, if you will permit it,' said the old man. In the presence of the King he rediscovered the gentle, affectionate tone he had once used to calm the young heir's attacks of rage. 'I must warn you that we have more important things to do, Your Majesty. I implore you to believe me. Please listen to me, Sire. No one must know that this theft was successful, and above all, no one must know that documents of value to me have disappeared.'

During this passionate outburst the Cardinal suddenly sat up. His piercing gaze, accustomed for so many years to penetrating the innermost thoughts of those he met, looked deep into the eyes of the King of France.

At that moment, a tapestry parted gently from the wall behind the Cardinal, and Anne of Austria entered the room.

'I am happy to see you, my son,' she said, with a small curtsey.

'Mother, you are here!'

Louis XIV gazed in surprise at the Queen Mother, who wore a simple black gown and a dazzling pearl necklace which contrasted with her tired complexion. A widow for the past eighteen years, the King's mother bore on her face traces of all the tribulations she had overcome in order to secure her son's power. The look she exchanged with Jules Mazarin was full of compassion and affection. Louis felt reassured, flanked as he now was by the two people he cherished most. Together, they had weathered so many crises! It seemed to him that nothing really serious could happen when they were united like this.

'We have grave decisions to take, my son; ones which may carry heavy consequences.'

'Godfather, I am your sovereign and I must know the contents of the documents. This suddenly seems so dramatic. Have you the slightest idea who could have committed this act of madness, and why?'

The old prince of the Church closed his eyes and took a deep breath before answering in a weak, breathless voice.

'Your Majesty has the right to demand the truth. You are both aware that I have dedicated my life to preserving the Kingdom and providing my King with an untroubled future in a country at peace. But we have no shortage of enemies and I fear that strange coalitions may be forming at this time, doubtless seeking to take advantage of my decline. Death prowls around me and its arrival has unleashed the forces of evil. I am told that our enemies have infiltrated all seats of power, including this palace!'

The Cardinal took another breath and sighed deeply before continuing:

'I kept numerous papers in my private desk relating to the proper organisation of my succession and confirming the sources of my fortune. I also hid a few ancient parchments there which it seems contain important secrets. According to Colbert's report, the murderers took nothing else of any worth from my apartments. From this, I deduce that their only concern was to seize those papers.'

Having paused for a moment to regain his strength, the sick man went on:

'Toussaint Roze heard the guard's killer thanking the Almighty, right there in front of him. The poor man is still trembling at the thought of it, I am told, and seems to feel that these were religious fanatics.'

'If that is the case, Cardinal, we must ensure that you are protected. There is no proof that you yourself were not the target of this insane operation. Whatever the case, you cannot return to your palace. The fire will have rendered your apartments uninhabitable. You shall remain here, and I shall double your guard.'

'Louis, I am not sure that is the solution,' murmured the Queen Mother, moving closer to the King so that Mazarin, who seemed to have fallen asleep again, would not hear them talking.

'According to Colbert, our enemies may even have infiltrated the Louvre. Under these circumstances it seems to me that Vincennes would be more suitable – particularly as I have my own apartments there. The Cardinal will be safer there. The weeks to come will almost certainly be a cruel ordeal for him.'

'So be it! It is undoubtedly more sensible. I shall give orders to d'Artagnan for the musketeers to come to Vincennes, to strengthen the Cardinal's guard around your apartments and those of His Eminence. You must leave swiftly, Madame. I shall use my time now to find out more about this affair. I am to receive Fouquet within the hour,' said the King, who was already on his way out.

On hearing the name of the Superintendent of Finance, Mazarin started. Opening his eyes, he saw the door close upon the young King's vigorous form.

CHAPTER SEVEN

Palais-Royal theatre —Sunday 6 February, mid-afternoon.

'O PRINCE, I know you can, by avenging our rights /
Through your love give voice to a hundred exploits. /
But that cannot equal the price he'd savour / A State's confession, and a brother's favour. / Done Elvire is not . . .'

'No, no, AND NO!'

For the third time since the start of the afternoon rehearsal, Molière leapt out of his seat, interrupting the monologue. Madeleine Béjart looked at him in surprise and disappointedly let go of Dom Garcie's hand, which she had just taken hold of to facilitate the interpretation of this passage from Scene 3. The other actors, who had frozen like statues on the Palais-Royal's stage, also seemed taken aback by the Master's reaction. Admittedly Molière was particularly irascible this Sunday. Was it the macabre discovery of the adolescent who had fallen through the glass roof a few hours earlier, or memories of the stormy reception they had received two nights earlier? Seeming even thinner than usual, and hoarse-voiced, his face twitching beneath the curious little linen bonnet he wore, the actor was flinging his long arms about, as if to lend support to the shaky directions he was voicing.

'My dear, you force me to correct you on yet another point. How many times must I repeat myself? Done Elvire must not show any outward sign of her love for Dom Garcie. That should be obvious! It is the very essence of my work, upon which you seem to be deliberately pouring scorn. Why take hold of Garcie's hand like that? Begin again, Madame,' declared the author, incandescent with rage.

'But, my friend . . .'

'Kindly stop contradicting me. You know very well how much the success of *Dom Garcie de Navarre* means to me. I have not laboured night and day perfecting this script, only to stand idly by as you betray the profound meaning of my play. We will be performing for Monsieur tomorrow, then for every theatre-lover in Paris, perhaps even the King, and I dare not imagine what will come to pass if we continue to be so second-rate. If I have decided to continue our rehearsals today, it is because of your weaknesses and those of your comrades. We are no longer in Pézenas, damn it! Mark this well: our duty is to strive to be worthy of this place and the lofty expectations of our sponsors!

Deeply upset, the actress dissolved into tears and fled into the wings, unable to remain with her colleagues in her shame; shame prompted by the unjust, excessive criticism of a man she loved with all her heart.

'From the beginning!' roared Molière, unconcerned by Madeleine's distress.

Seeing that the other actors did not know what to do without Done Elvire, he turned towards the young man at his side who was busy copying out a letter he had just dictated.

'Rejoice, my young friend. Your hour has come. You are bold enough to want to act? Doubtless you believe you've attained the summit of the art by divine grace alone. Well, Monsieur Secretary, leave your writing-bench and your starched shirt-cuffs! Ascend the stage, take poor Madeleine's place and at long last reveal this talent to us – at least for as long as it takes her to wipe away her tears. We do not have time to waste on the vagaries of feminine moods.'

Gabriel took the manuscript which the master handed him, shivering at the opportunity he was being offered.

At just twenty, the young man was extremely handsome and tall, with brown hair and eyes of a magnificent bright green. He had entered Molière's service a month previously, without any special recommendation. The master had allowed himself to be amused by the enthusiasm and candour of this charming boy, who had approached him one day outside the theatre and told him of his burning desire to join the troupe. The words came readily to his lips as he conjured up memories of a performance he had attended in Anjou a few years earlier. He had been so dazzled as a young boy that he saw this as a vocation. The years had passed, but the fever had not left him.

Molière had recognised this as an opportunity to acquire a private secretary at minimal cost. Gabriel swiftly integrated into the prestigious company where an atmosphere of joyful chaos reigned. The women were won over by his athletic physique and friendly smile. The men were delighted to find in him a helpful and even-tempered friend. As for Molière, every day he appreciated the serious attitude, writing ability and fine education of the boy he knew very little about, apart from the fact that his origins were provincial. Nevertheless, he strongly doubted his vocation as an actor and suspected

Gabriel of being the son of a good family who had fallen out with his parents.

As he swiftly took the stage, Gabriel could feel his heart thudding in his chest. His childhood dream was about to come true. Born into a noble, wealthy family in Amboise, he had been brought up by an uncle in place of his father, who had disappeared when he was very young and about whom he remembered very little. Gabriel de Pontbriand had received an excellent education and been introduced to the best families in Touraine, growing up with a carefree nature and a romantic sensibility derived from the many books he read. That is, until that theatrical performance which had opened his eyes to the possibility that he could have a different life from the one his family had mapped out for him. By fleeing Amboise and the anger of his uncle and tutor to enter the service of the author of *Les Précieuses ridicules*, he had escaped the spell in prison his family had promised him to set him back on the right track and banish his dreams. The mere mention of acting made his uncle grind his teeth and mutter under his breath about 'mad idiots' like his father. Through his daring, Gabriel had also proved how much determination was needed for a twenty-year-old to change the course of his destiny in 1661. He, deprived of his father and raised by a stern uncle, he who had been destined to hold some kind of senior public office, spending his days watching the money roll in from taxation and sending bad debtors to prison, was finally about to accomplish his childhood dream!

Acting, he told himself as he took Madeleine Béjart's place. *I'm acting at last* . . .

'O Prince, I know you can, by avenging our rights /
Through your love give voice to a hundred exploits . . .'

A few moments later, her cheeks still red from weeping,
Madeleine Béjart returned to her place. The rehearsal returned
to normal. Gabriel was aware that he had at least emerged from
this first trial with dignity. A little disappointed nevertheless by
the brevity of his performance, he unobtrusively slid into the
prompter's box to watch the four actors as they played out the
rest of the scene.

'When you can love me as I must be loved,' murmured Done
Elvire.

'And what, alas, can one observe beneath the skies / that
yields not to the ardour inspired by your eyes?' replied the
Prince of the Kingdom of Navarre, as portrayed by Lagrange.

From this point on Molière seemed to be daydreaming,
gazing vaguely at the paintings on the ceiling of the brand new
theatre which the King had placed at his disposal. There were
some nights when this validation brought him out in a cold
sweat. Would he prove worthy of this new honour? Despite the
success of *Le Docteur amoureux* which had won him the favour
of Louis XIV and Monsieur, the King's brother, Molière feared
the consequences should *Dom Garcie de Navarre* prove to be a
failure. After all, the first public performance two nights earlier
had been greeted by a chorus of whistles and cat-calls. And yet
the author had had the strange feeling that they came from an
organised 'claque' of hostile spectators who had been skilfully
positioned around the auditorium. Who would wish to do him
ill in this way? *Unless*, he said to himself, *someone is aiming at
some other target through me?* He then thought of Nicolas

Fouquet, his generous and faithful patron. *Perhaps it is time I considered other forms of protection*, mused Molière as he listened to the end of Act I.

In his refuge, Gabriel was also dreaming, his eyes wide open, his head resting on folded arms at the edge of the stage. As he watched the actors, he felt a subtle mixture of emotion and nostalgia for the exchanges of a few moments before. Just as he was promising himself that he would, at the first opportunity, ask his master for another chance to tread the boards, he felt something flat under his boot. He was intrigued. Kneeling down in the narrow space reserved for the prompter, he discovered an impressive dark-red document case. 'What an odd place to store one's papers', thought Gabriel, picking up the leather case. In the glow of the stage lights, he examined it discreetly and was immediately struck by the sight of Cardinal Mazarin's coat of arms.

Molière's voice tore him away from his discovery:

'Time marches on, my children! If we are to be ready this evening, we must delay no longer!'

In a protective reflex, Gabriel hid the leather pouch under his shirt, resolving to open it somewhere quieter to discover what it contained.

'Come,' said the master to his actors, who were all anxious to know his opinion at the end of the first act. 'That was better! At last my words have had some effect, and you understand the masks which conceal the depths of my characters' souls. Now you must try to reveal their true feelings. We shall resume our rehearsal in one hour. It would be unwise to add the cold to the audience's possible complaints, so we shall make way for the workmen who have come to repair that accursed skylight,' he said, brandishing an angry fist in the direction of the shattered dome.

Happy at the author's new mood, the actors left the massive auditorium to take a short but well-deserved rest in the boxes.

'Stay, Monsieur. We have work to do,' said Molière to his secretary as he nimbly extricated himself from the prompter's box. 'We have to prepare the troupe's accounts as swiftly as possible. I shall have them taken to the Superintendent of Finance first thing tomorrow. With troubled times on the horizon, it is best to strike while the iron is hot!'

CHAPTER EIGHT

THERE was a huge crowd outside the theatre. Joyful and gaudy, it comprised just as many street peddlers, performers and traders of all kinds as it did spectators. Those people, ordinary folk for the most part, awaited a different spectacle: the sight of the aristocracy and members of the Court, whose arrival caused much pushing and jostling as everyone strove to get a glimpse of their clothes and faces. Many secretly hoped that there might be some gesture of generosity, such as coins thrown in amongst the throng. A murmur ran through the crowd, a whisper which came all the way up from the Seine:

'Condé, Condé!'

Then the whispering was drowned out by the bellowing of a ragged little band who had recognised the prince's coat of arms on the Pont du Louvre, and were running alongside his carriage. The movement of the crowd made the people at the front surge forward, piling them up against the colonnade as far as the peristyle, where they collided with officers of the peace who had been stationed there to prevent anyone from entering. The officers drove back the hapless unfortunates with kicks and punches, provoking the beginnings of a scuffle. It stopped as if by magic and a corridor opened through the crowd, secured by two rows of halberdiers who used their weapons like inter-locking guardrails to hold back the inquisitive onlookers. One or two children who had climbed onto the bases of the columns saw a man emerge from the stationary carriage: a giant with a haughty expression, rugged features and a powerful neck. Towering above the crowd by almost a head, the rebel prince – the man who, fifteen years earlier, had dared to defy royal authority – strode forward and vanished into the theatre with-out a glance at the passers-by who chanted his name.

'True to form,' remarked an old woman in a timid whisper from her place in the first row of onlookers. 'He may be Condé, but he'll never behave any differently towards the people of Paris . . . Always haughty, always distant . . .'

But already the attention was shifting to another retinue. The square filled with activity. The bustle of carriages as they set down their passengers and then went to park elsewhere grew ever more intense. Shouts of admiration mingled with jokes, laughter with exclamations.

'Those ragamuffins,' said Mazarin wearily, pulling the curtain across the window in the door of his carriage, which had slid incognito into the procession of vehicles heading for the show. 'Look at them enjoying themselves. What a business, a show staged by street entertainers . . .'

'Come,' Colbert urged his master from the seat beside him. 'We must not delay further, Eminence. The sooner we reach Vincennes, the sooner you will be free from the fatigue of the journey and the noise.'

Mazarin nodded silently, grimacing with pain each time the carriage jolted over the dislocated paving stones. Stretching out his arms, he forced himself to smile at the three young women seated opposite them.

'Farewell, my graces, off to the frivolities with you – it is fitting at your age. Your old uncle has no right to drag you away from life on the pretext that it is leaving him . . .'

His three nieces protested in unison as they bowed their heads to receive the old man's blessing. Beneath his palms their joined heads formed a forest of jet-black hair, whose incredible thickness was emphasised by the centre-parted, looped-back hairstyle they had all chosen that evening.

As Mazarin withdrew his hands, Colbert knocked on the partition behind him to tell the coachman to stop. The door opened onto the colourful bustle of the sightseers, already lit up by the first flaming torches. Mazarin blinked in distress. Hortense was the last to leave the carriage, fleetingly squeezing her uncle's hand and bringing it up to her lips. Then she jumped down to the ground with the aid of the postillion's hand and disappeared, swallowed up by the crowd.

The carriage set off again, preceded by a few guards, and once more wreathed in silence. Soon all they could hear was the echo of the horses' hooves.

'Four months, Colbert. They told me I had four months left. And I myself say four weeks, no more. I know doctors . . . The astrologer said that the danger during this moon was great, and greater still during the next one. I prefer his half-lie to the courtly politeness of those butchers who bleed me time and time again . . . They are too afraid of losing me.'

To Colbert's surprise, Mazarin caught his arm and gripped it forcefully.

'We have no more time. I must think of my glory and of the future. As soon as we reach Vincennes, go and fetch Roze. The time has come to commit our work to paper.'

The old man's fingers relaxed and he appeared to doze off, lulled by the rhythm of the swaying carriage. Colbert closed his eyes too, inwardly smiling at the thought of those frivolous, ridiculous people crammed into that over-heated theatre. *Poor fools*, he thought, *all that time wasted on a show that will not last a week*.

And with this venom-filled thought, he fell asleep.

Of the Cardinal's three nieces, two would still bear the name Mancini for a number of days yet. All three wore gowns which took their inspiration from the same source, differing only in their dominant colour – green for Marie, red for Hortense and gold for Olympe – and with their hair in plaits that framed their oval faces, holding the weight of the style at the napes of their necks, they made an unsettling sight; for at first glance they seemed to be replicas taken from the same mould. It required careful scrutiny to detect the nuances which distinguished them: the gentle features of Marie, the youngest, whose reciprocated passion for the young King Louis XIV had been widely talked about; the elegant sadness of Hortense, the Cardinal's favourite and the least pretty of the three; the determined step, coldness and paler skin of Olympe, whom the whole Court had learned to fear. No one who met her gaze could ever forget the dark fire in her eyes, the flame that burned as she kept a constant watch over the attitudes, looks and smiles around her, and cast glances at her sisters which might be protective or threatening – it was impossible to tell which. As they climbed the front steps, they were greeted with murmurs of admiration followed by an anxious silence in recognition of their closeness to the Chief Minister. With heads held high, they entered the theatre, acknowledging familiar faces but not deviating from the route leading them to the box which their uncle had never occupied. The auditorium was almost full and the tension perceptible. People in other boxes talked in low voices, creating a background hum to which the people in the pit responded with more spontaneous shouts.

'Look, Olympe,' said Hortense, turning to her elder sister, 'who is that young blonde woman wearing that French-blue gown? The one who has just entered Monsieur's box,' she added, with a wave of her fan.

'I see her,' replied Olympe curtly.

The Cardinal's niece was quicker than the people in the pit, who took another second to identify a new presence in the King's brother's box. A murmur ran around the theatre like a sudden shiver, diverting attention even from the red curtain which veiled the front of the stage.

The young blonde girl was quite unaware of the stir she was causing. Her head slightly tilted forward, fingers toying with the dark velvet of her gown, she seemed lost in thought. Her white skin was a striking contrast to the dark red of her lips. With each breath, the flesh quivered at the base of her neck and beneath her shoulders, whose slender curve was followed by the edge of her gown. Her youth was betrayed by high cheekbones set above the hollow cheeks of a child who had grown up too quickly. In the reflections from the silver candelabra fixed to the walls of the boxes, she radiated elegance and vitality. Her blonde hair, drawn back into a large chignon, hung heavy over the nape of her neck, emphasising its slender elegance. Suddenly sensing that all eyes were upon her, she started and reddened slightly. Then she stood up and left the box nimbly, despite a curious, swaying gait, to escape the audience's attention. The moment she disappeared, the atmosphere lost some of its intensity.

Olympe Mancini pouted haughtily as she watched her walk away.

'She's the innocent young thing. Who, by some passing fancy she has been attached to the household of Monsieur's future wife.'

'How beautiful she is,' commented Marie with a smile.

Her elder sister's dark eyes regarded her scornfully.

'And do you know what she is called?' asked Hortense.

Olympe looked exasperated as the three knocks sounded, signalling the start of the performance. Lackeys hurried to snuff out the large chandeliers.

'I am told that her name is Louise de La Vallière,' Olympe consented to reply.

The red curtain quivered and began to rise.

CHAPTER NINE

L ow cloud now veiled the Parisian sky, heralding snow. A bitter cold assailed the theatre-goers as they left the Palais-Royal, hurrying to reach the carriages lined up at the foot of the front steps. A few isolated groups lingered under the peristyle, shivering as they said their hasty farewells. But a group of ten men seemed immune to the cold air and in no hurry to go home. Their roars of laughter echoed along the colonnade, punctuating the speech and gestures of a small, fat man with a curled wig on his round head and deep-set, porcine blue eyes above a curiously upturned nose. His gaily coloured silk clothes and buckled shoes were in sharp contrast to the coarse clothing, boots and soldiers' capes of the men surrounding him.

'Here's to the health of Monsieur Molière!' he declared with an evil chuckle, raising the wine bottle in his hand.

He clinked it against two others that were being passed round amongst his drinking companions, and wiped his mouth on the silk sleeve of his doublet.

'Damn that showman! At least he won't be boring us for much longer with that play,' he muttered, as if talking to himself. 'Here you are, my friends, you've earned your evening's pay.' He felt the weight of a purse attached to his belt, much to the delight of his associates who had been recruited to whistle and generally disrupt the play.

Still laughing heartily, the little group continued on their way through the columns, brazenly staring at passers-by who were hurrying away. At the corner of the theatre, the hired thugs stopped for a moment to discard the empty bottles, then threw their last few rotten apples at the wall in front of them.

The man in the wig watched them from a distance, still darting piercing glances right and left as if in search of a new outlet for his malicious intent.

'Do you dare show your face again?' he demanded mockingly, addressing the figure which had just emerged through the secret door at the back of the building, used by the performers.

The light from a carriage lamp lit up the face of the young woman he had shouted at, bringing a salacious expression to his fat face.

'Don't suppose you've got any other talents, my girl?' he enquired, moving towards her.

Frozen to the spot by the group's menacing advance, the young girl lowered her shawl, drew it about her shoulders and looked anxiously around her.

'You weren't made for that kind of stage! Do you want us to show you a different kind of performance?'

By now the men were almost surrounding the actress, and their cruel smiles brought a flash of panic to her eyes.

'Nobody to walk you home, you poor wretch?' said the fat man in a syrupy voice, rubbing his blubbery hands together. 'And she's shivering, the poor soul! Is it the cold, my pretty one?'

'No, Monsieur, it is the discomfort occasioned by your coarseness.'

The voice made the man in the wig jump. He screwed up his eyes to identify the shadow which had just spoken from the stage doorway.

'What business is it of yours?' he demanded aggressively.

'Come on, Julie,' said Gabriel, moving towards the girl. 'Let's go back inside for a while.'

The man stepped menacingly between them and pushed the end of his walking stick against Gabriel's chest.

'Stop right there, lad. Don't you know it's rude to interrupt a conversation? A yokel like you shouldn't even be speaking to me!'

Gabriel gritted his teeth and caught the girl by the arm, bringing her round behind him. Passers-by hesitated at the sight of the group. Menservants urged their masters to walk away.

'I cannot hear any conversation, only words spoken in drink,' jeered the young secretary. 'And since that is the cause of your odious behaviour, I'm willing to do you a favour and overlook it.'

The man paled and turned angrily to his drinking companions.

'You young scoundrel, I'm going to beat you senseless . . .' he growled, once more face to face with Gabriel.

Nimbly, the young secretary seized the upright cane and tore it from its owner's hand. Whirling it round, he landed a stinging blow on the side of the man's head. The man lurched groggily backwards and found himself sitting on the muddy roadway, whimpering and holding his ear, which was oozing blood onto his now lopsided wig.

The others hesitated for a moment before rushing forward to help him up, clearly worried about the effect this episode might have on the man's generosity. Gabriel took advantage of this to leap towards the shelter of the door, as a parting shot throwing back the cane, which landed on the fat man's belly.

The door slammed. Gabriel's adversary struggled to his feet, pushing away his companions and abusing them in turn.

Through a spyhole, Gabriel watched him limp towards a carriage parked some distance away, a handkerchief clamped to his ear.

'The pig,' he said, turning back to the still-trembling girl.

She smiled at him.

'What a horrible evening . . . Thank you, Gabriel, but you're mad. Don't you know who that man is?'

'All I know is that he's a lout who deserved to be taught a lesson . . .'

She took his hand.

'Little boy from the provinces, playing at being a knight! If you want to be an actor, you'll have to take more care.'

He looked at her in astonishment.

'That man is Berryer, and he's one of Colbert's henchmen. Colbert is secretary to Cardinal Mazarin. He's a man to be feared and a very powerful enemy for a travelling entertainer.'

Gabriel shrugged his shoulders.

'Berryer, you've had a fight with Berryer?'

Molière suddenly appeared in front of his secretary in his

shirt sleeves, looking red-eyed and haggard. He grabbed him by the scruff of the neck and shook him affectionately.

'Poor fool,' he said in a voice somewhere between anger and laughter. 'Do you have any idea who you've just provoked? The leader of the clique responsible for all the whistling tonight. One of those people who've decided that we're going to fail because – in their eyes – we don't belong to the right camp.'

He sighed and let go of Gabriel, giving him a final shake.

'The way things stand . . . I know that Monsieur Colbert's friends have little liking for me. It's not that they dislike my plays, but the money we live on isn't to their taste . . . Come my friends,' he said to the company as a whole, 'we shall think about all this tomorrow. And as for you, Monsieur Secretary: less chivalry and more accountancy, for pity's sake!'

Inside one of the last carriages left in the square, a young woman leant towards her neighbour.

'Louise, what are you dreaming about?'

As she let the curtain fall back over her window, Louise de La Vallière turned away from the little stage door she had been watching throughout the entire episode, closely observing Gabriel's behaviour.

'Oh, nothing,' she replied, shaking her pretty head. 'Nothing at all.'

CHAPTER TEN

Four men, hidden beneath black capes, had been walking for at least an hour along the banks of the Seine towards the walls that marked the boundary between the city and the surrounding countryside. Shivering in the bitter cold and the snow that was now falling in fat flakes, they walked northwards in single file, almost perfectly aligned, in silence. The little group was guided by a tall fellow who was tightly clutching an enormous cloth bag.

'Hey, Your Lordship, where are you off to? I can warm you up if you like,' said a voice that shook with cold.

The voice belonged to the hand, clad in a tattered lace glove, which had just caught hold of the bag and obstructed its passage, the better to intercept the man carrying it.

Without a word being spoken, a dagger's slender blade sliced through the darkness in search of the woman who had halted the group's progress in this way. The muffled thud of a body hitting the ground told the killer that his aim had been true. The poor whore had not even had time to notice the strange green and brown eyes of the man who had just taken her life. The snow would soon hide the girl from sight. The murderer knew that, in Paris, poverty forced so many women to offer their bodies to passers-by that nobody would risk weeping over this death, nor would they claim the frail corpse that lay crumpled on the ground. Still silent, the four men set off again, now striding out towards the Porte Saint-Antoine, where handcarts jostled each other as peasants tried to get out of the suburbs before the snow would prevent them rejoining their families. Whitened by snowflakes, the countryside was illuminated with a new brightness, a reassuring fact for those emerging from the badly lit streets of the city.

'We must hurry,' said the man with the bag, who was still leading the way. 'It would be a pity to make the gentlemen wait.'

Their journey became increasingly difficult as the blanket of snow grew thicker. In the distance, they spotted the outline of Champ-l'Evêque hill, which some also called Mont-aux-Vignes. Little by little, the ultimate destination of their nocturnal walk became visible on the horizon.

'The Regnault folly. There it is!' said the leader of the group, pointing to the magnificent buildings rising up before them.

Thirty-five years previously, the former estate of the wealthy spice merchant Regnault de Wandonne had – after a great deal of work – become a magnificent house of repose and enjoyment for Jesuits. Men of faith came here in large numbers to end their days or to relax in the tranquillity of the countryside. In season, a kitchen garden and orchards provided appreciable sources of revenue and activities for the more able-bodied members of the community. A garden planted with rare species also enabled those Jesuit fathers who were convalescing to find the peace needed for their recovery. This calm and pleasing institution was run by Father de La Chaise. At the height of the Fronde disturbances, when troops armed by the rebel nobles threatened to seize power, Cardinal Mazarin had brought the fourteen-year-old Louis XIV here. From this position overlooking part of Paris, they had observed the violent battles in Faubourg Saint-Antoine. And it was after this visit that the Jesuits had received special permission from the King to call their hill Mont-Louis.

Arriving at the main gate, the nocturnal visitors did not linger to gaze at the landscape, even though it offered a superb view of the capital under snow. They followed the course of the outer wall until they came to the rear of the buildings, where a chapel dedicated to Saint-Côme stood.

'Wait,' ordered the man, increasingly anxious to protect his bag from the snow and damp.

The four accomplices stood with their backs against the wall, to avoid the whirling snowflakes. The men were perfectly motionless, despite the cold and their fatigue. Only an imperceptible movement of their lips betrayed the fact that they were praying.

'*Kyrie eleison, Christe eleison, Kyrie eleison . . .*'

The powerful voices of the Jesuits attending Mass rose towards the vaulted roof of Saint-Côme. Father de La Chaise was conducting the service himself, as he did each day. The congregation was a disparate one: resident Fathers, peasants from the estate and their families. A group of around ten men stood at the far end of the chapel, close to the candle-lit statue of the patron saint. Nobody seemed to pay any attention to this group, absorbed as they were in prayer and reflection.

'*Salve Regina, Mater misericordiae, Vita dulcedo et spes nostra salve . . .*'

As the congregation began to sing the song of devotion to the Virgin, one of the Jesuits left the chapel by a side door and approached the four men, who were still standing with their backs to the outside wall of the building.

'Follow me, it is time.'

Behind the chapel, the men descended three steps leading to a cellar buried beneath the choir of Saint-Côme. The room was vast and lit by large torches, which also had the advantage of warming the place. In the centre, an immense cross-shaped table surrounded by tall chairs constituted the sole item of furniture. A simple olive-wood crucifix hung on the wall. The group from the back of the chapel then entered and arranged themselves in order around the table.

'The cross of Jesus is our only pride.'

This sentence, spoken in vigorous unison, opened the session and gave everyone permission to sit. Only the four men who had come from Paris remained standing, facing the assembly. With extreme care, the leader of the group emptied the contents of his bag onto the table. As the spoils of his burglary spread out before him, a twisted smile appeared on his face.

'Our Lord supported us in our holy mission, Messieurs. Here are the documents taken a few hours ago from His Eminence's office.'

'Thank you,' said the eldest amongst them, his face largely hidden under a black felt hat. 'Nevertheless, I know that you caused blood to flow and that you lost a man. Our Lord has welcomed him to his right hand as a martyr, I am sure of that, but your lack of discretion will cause prejudice against us. This afternoon, at the Louvre, suspicions were already directed at us because of your clumsiness.'

The man with the mismatched eyes paled and hung his head. He had not expected these reproaches.

'I . . . I . . .' he stammered, drawing back.

'Enough, we shall speak of this again,' the other man cut in sharply. 'Simon Pierre, show them out.'

The Jesuit who had led them in nodded and, opening the door, signalled to the four men to leave.

'My Brothers, our struggle is about to acquire a new dimension,' said the eldest man, deeming that from then on, the meeting should continue in complete privacy. 'Mazarin is afraid, and I have the feeling that these documents will confirm my suspicions. He is only concerned about money. He senses that the final judgement is at hand. The cur will do anything to hide his depravity. More than ever, the Almighty calls upon us to cleanse the Kingdom. A little while ago, before leaving the Louvre, I learned that Jules Mazarin would be setting off this very evening to shut himself away at Vincennes. The Queen Mother will follow him there.'

'But must we continue to tolerate what all of Paris derides?' raged one of the conspirators, brandishing a lampoon he had acquired a little earlier in the Île de la Cité.

The text, like numerous others over several years, was a cruel denunciation of the intimate relationship between Jules Mazarin and Anne of Austria.

'Of course not,' cut in the leader of the zealots, 'that is precisely the point of this morning's expedition, to procure absolute proof of this infamy. The contract of their secret marriage is vital to us so that we can open people's eyes and cause a scandal so great that it will justify the elimination of the Italian!'

'And besides, he is proving more and more despotic,' added the man with the hat. 'He now presides over the council of ministers in his bedchamber while he is being shaved!'

'We must act – God commands it,' said another.

Nods and murmurs of agreement ran through those assembled round the impressive cross-shaped table, reinforcing the anger of the men whom the Cardinal had that very afternoon, without knowing who they were, classed as 'fuel for the fanatical pyre'.

'We must make an impression on the people,' continued the man who had just spoken. 'I propose that Mazarin be judged by the standards of Christian morality. He must pay for his crimes. We shall thus demonstrate to the whole Kingdom that the arm of divine justice has the power to strike everyone, even the most powerful. My Brothers, let us follow the example of our elders, who guided the hand of Ravaillac.'[1]

'Everything is possible,' said the eldest man, after a swift perusal of the stolen documents. 'But I fear, having glanced at what has just been delivered to us, that we may lack the essential evidence to initiate a legal case. I cannot find any trace of the marriage contract between Mazarin and Anne of Austria! Our men have completely failed in their holy mission!'

Teeth clenched, he dropped the bundle of documents back onto the table in front of him.

[1] The regicide François Ravaillac, the Catholic zealot, who stabbed Henry IV to death on 14 May 1610 while his carriage was stopped in traffic.

'Go and bring them back, Simon Pierre,' he ordered.

A heavy silence filled the room while the conspirators waited for the henchmen to retrace their steps. At last the door grated open again and the man with the mismatched eyes entered alone. He halted a few yards from the table.

'Cast your mind back and attempt to answer accurately,' instructed the mysterious leader. 'Are you sure that you seized all the documents contained within the inlaid writing desk? Did you search the secret drawers?'

'Not a single piece of wood escaped the search,' he replied without hesitation.

In his eyes there now shone a gleam of defiance, almost of anger. The man with the hat spoke more mildly.

'This is extremely serious, something vital is missing ... Are you absolutely certain you did not forget anything, that nothing was omitted from your account that might explain this absence?'

The man with the mismatched eyes seemed once again thrown off-balance. He searched his memory for a moment, then raised his hand as he groped for the right words.

'Perhaps, yes, when Le Jeune fell ... The one who died, he had a fall,' he went on. 'He had some documents in his hand, a leather document case. Yes, I am sure of it now, he had them in his hand as he ran across the skylight ...'

His interlocutor cut him off with an imperious gesture.

'Go,' said the leader. 'Go and join your Brothers and wait for me to contact you. And on no account make a sound, not one single additional movement that might cause you to be spotted. You have been warned,' he added threateningly.

When the man had left, the leader sat down and looked at his companions.

'There is not a moment to lose. We must continue our search and find the items that were lost today. As for Mazarin, rest assured, he will pay in due course. He and his family of vultures must sooner or later account for the origins of their fortune and their harmful influence on the Court and Kingdom. In the name of our faith, we must continue to toil for the birth of a new age.'

As he spoke these final words, the old man stood up, signalling that the assembly was at an end.

'Let us pray,' he said, joining his hands together. '*Pater noster qui es in coelis . . .* '

While the zealots prayed, Simon Pierre, who had accompanied the four burglars back to the gate of the Mont-Louis estate, put out the torches one by one, gradually plunging the room into darkness. He opened the door, letting in a cold wind. The snow had stopped falling.

'. . . *sed libera nos a malo.*'

The eldest man, his face still half hidden by that strange hat, wished his Brothers a peaceful return journey. And with one voice, the enemies of Cardinal Mazarin repeated their shared pledge:

'The cross of Jesus is our only pride!'

CHAPTER ELEVEN

'COULD you tell me where Monsieur de Pontbriand lives, please?'

The little boy in the torn trousers, sitting on the doorstep of the house in Rue des Lions Saint-Paul, looked up in astonishment. The sight of such a pretty young woman here, just before noon, was most unusual. He brazenly ogled the dress worn by the young lady who had ventured alone and on foot into this modest district, whose boundaries were delineated by Rue Saint-Antoine in the north and the Seine in the south. He blushed as his gaze reached the young woman's face, and she smiled magnificently as she looked into the depths of his eyes.

'Dunno! Best go and look for him around Hôtel Saint-Paul, where the nobility live. All you'll find in this street, princess, are stonemasons, carpenters and joiners – no "Pont-whatsisname"!'

The young lady answered in a sweet voice:

'But I am quite sure of the address. It is very important to me. Are you sure you don't know Gabriel de Pontbriand?

'Oh, Gabriel yes, I know him!' replied the young boy, happy to have recognised the name. 'Of course, everybody round here knows Gabriel. He's an actor with the great Molière's company. At this time of day you'll find him at home. His room is up in the attic. Go up the staircase, right to the top, there's only one door. You can't mistake it.'

'Thank you, charming boy,' said the young girl as she swept into the building, leaving the boy speechless at having discovered his friend Gabriel's noble surname.

Seated at a dark wooden table, Gabriel had just finished examining the papers contained in the red document case he had found the previous day. His reading left him perplexed. The papers were incomprehensible, evidently coded. As he turned over the case to study Cardinal Mazarin's crest, the young man blanched, realising the enormity of the situation. Gabriel went through the parchments one by one, attempting to identify a clue. The only thing he could decipher was the signature at the end of each sheaf of documents. The names of their authors appeared clearly, and in full.

Just then, the young man froze and turned white. Trembling, he murmured the words 'My father'. He had spoken out loud to make the discovery more real. The paper fell from his right hand. He had just read the signature at its foot: *Brother André de Pontbriand*.

At that precise moment someone knocked at the door, forcing Gabriel to pull himself together.

Swiftly concealing the documents under his bed, the young man snatched up the script of the play to give himself an air of composure.

'Come in,' he said at last.

A face appeared in the doorway, and when two white hands pushed back the hood obscuring it, Gabriel exclaimed in amazement:

'Louise!'

'Don't look so shocked, my friend, you're as white as a ghost,' replied Louise de La Vallière teasingly, delighted by the effect of her visit upon the young man she had not seen for seven months.

'Louise de La Vallière! What a surprise,' Gabriel's colour was gradually returning, along with the determination to give a warm welcome to his extremely pretty friend. 'Do please sit down. Try this armchair,' he said, indicating the most comfortable chair he possessed.

The room was modest and unadorned, but reasonably large. The plaster and wooden walls were clean. In one corner, an iron bed stood opposite a small table and two chairs. The only hint of grandeur was provided by an old velvet armchair with a broken leg, propped up on some old books. A wardrobe completed the furniture. Since there was no bookcase, an impressive number of books were scattered all over the place. Gabriel had been living here since his arrival in the autumn of 1660, after he had run away. Optimistic by nature but with a determined, adventurous streak, he had moved directly into this room devoid of luxury or comforts, and he had paid for it with the meagre earnings from his employment with Molière from then on. Fortunately, his natural joviality and infectious enthusiasm had helped him to strike up many friendships, particularly in this humble neighbourhood where he so enjoyed living. His natural charm had also opened the doors to a world that was entirely new to him: the world of pleasure and feminine conquests. An actor at heart, Gabriel enjoyed being charming, delightedly displaying his talent to the only audience he had at present: the young women whose eyes shone when they saw him . . .

'I was the first to be surprised, when I spotted you last night outside the Palais-Royal theatre with the actors from Monsieur Molière's company,' explained Louise. 'I didn't know you were in the capital, and I had no idea that you were living in such destitution,' she remarked, gazing sadly at the sparse room. 'Nor did I realise that you were so chivalrous and such a good fighter,' she added, laughing.

Gabriel smiled in response to her teasing, and at the unexpected pleasure of their reunion: Louise de La Vallière, Louise whom he'd known for ever . . . They had so often roamed the country paths of Touraine with other well-born young folk from Amboise . . . Now, with Louise, he felt as if he had rediscovered his beloved homeland and the sweetness of his childhood at a single stroke.

Although still stunned, he could not help noticing her luxurious outfit, the shimmering fabrics of her gown and the watered silk jacket which she wore carelessly draped over her shoulders. Once again he took in the dazzling clarity of her complexion, the vibrant colour of her eyes, the reflections that played in her hair with each graceful movement of her neck.

'So this morning I went to the theatre,' Louise went on, untroubled by his insistent gaze. 'And I conducted my own investigation. Two smiles and a few coins persuaded the good concierge to give me the information I needed. That is how I found you. But now you owe me some explanations. Why did you leave so suddenly last year? Nobody here seems to know you by anything other than the name Gabriel. Why hide yourself in this room, which even a monk would spurn?'

Gabriel then sat down opposite his friend and gave her a detailed account of the past months. He answered all her questions and hid nothing about his situation. Confiding in her made him calmer. He learned that Louise had arrived at Court in January, to become companion to the future wife of Monsieur, the King's brother. The performance of *Dom Garcie* had been her first outing and she was looking forward to her imminent official presentation to Louis XIV and the Queen. The two friends were delighted as they rediscovered each other, such a long way from their roots. Their conversation went on for a long time, and dwelt on memories of happy childhood moments. Both were orphans who had barely known their fathers: Gabriel had been brought up by his uncle, and Louise by her stepfather, under the warm and watchful eye of King Louis XIII's brother, Gaston d'Orléans, whose patronage had continued to benefit the young girl after his death. After all, it had just opened the gates of Court to her.

'But tell me,' urged Gabriel with growing excitement, 'what have you seen? And what is Court life like?'

Patiently, Louise recounted the splendours and the boredom of her new existence, the moments of idleness and the burden of etiquette. She described a life of hope and uncertainty, grandeur and pettiness.

'Yesterday, we spent four hours sewing and then unpicking some facings planned for the trousseau of Mademoiselle Henrietta of England, because the colours initially chosen were too close to those of the English republican supporters and might have displeased the English Court . . .'

'Are you happy?' Gabriel cut in suddenly, taking her hand.

Louise lowered her eyes as if looking for her slender fingers lost in Gabriel's broad, fidgety hands. Then she looked up and met his gaze.

'I don't know if I'm happy,' she replied. 'But my heart is beating again, I encounter surprise after surprise, and I feel as if anything is possible! You know, it's strange, at night here I sometimes dream of the meadows where we used to walk. And in those dreams I miss them; yet in recent months, before I arrived at Court, they bored me to death.'

Gabriel's eyes followed her as she suddenly got to her feet, a dreamy look on her face.

'I loved those meadows with you, when the field behind your uncle's house seemed like the Americas to us and we told each other stories about the unicorns hiding in the woods around the chateau where I lived. Do you remember? By the time you left, the unicorns were long gone. Well, arriving here, I feel as if I'm again discovering an unknown world. A beautiful world: it's impressive, terrifying sometimes, but wondrous, don't you think?'

'My situation is different, Marquise,' Gabriel answered, teasing her. 'You live in a palace, I live in a hovel . . .'

*

It was almost two o'clock in the afternoon when Louise left. Gabriel accompanied her down to the street, and they promised they would see each other again as soon as possible. As the young man watched her go, filled with emotion, his thoughts returned to the incredible discovery of his own father's signature on the Cardinal's coded papers. Everything was mixed up in his head, making him feel dizzy.

Lost in thought, Gabriel did not notice the man watching him attentively, hidden in the carriage entrance on the other side of Rue des Lions Saint-Paul.

CHAPTER TWELVE

Rome – Tuesday 8 February, eleven o'clock in the morning

Arriving by way of Via Giulia, a little early for his appointment, François d'Orbay took some time examining the outside of the palace where he was to meet the Archbishop of Paris. On a fine sunny morning like this, the Parisian architect could marvel endlessly at the second floor and the cornice designed by Michelangelo himself. He stood outside the building for a while, contemplating the very special harmony of its façade built, it was said, with materials taken from the city's ancient ruins. The largest private palace in Rome exuded an atmosphere that was at once austere and imposing: doubtless a reflection of its first owner, Pope Julian III, thought d'Orbay.

'Kindly inform His Excellency that Monsieur François d'Orbay has arrived,' the visitor told the man in red livery who had just opened the door of the Farnese Palace with a flourish.

'Monsieur is expected,' replied the servant in French, but with a strong Italian accent. 'If Monsieur would be kind enough to follow me . . .'

As he entered the building, d'Orbay once again admired the interior garden, which constituted one of its masterpieces. In the great gallery, he could not resist pausing for a moment, dazzled by the radiant sumptuousness of the vaulted roof, painted a century earlier by Carrache. This baroque design, directly inspired by mythology, shone with a joyous plethora of colours that was in itself fascinating. As he reached the door to Paul de Gondi's office, the architect pulled himself together. He had not come that morning to enjoy the riches of the palace occupied by the Archbishop of Paris.

'Monsieur François d'Orbay,' announced the servant, stepping aside to allow the visitor to pass.

D'Orbay bowed deeply. When he looked up he was impressed, as he always was at their meetings, by his host's alert, almost youthful air. Simply dressed in a cassock, Paul de Gondi stood up to greet his visitor and walked towards him with a broad, welcoming smile on a face lit by dark, penetrating eyes. *It's hard to believe that this is the man who made the King of France tremble, forced Mazarin into exile and almost seized power; the man who inspired the greatest conspiracies of the century; the former prisoner who escaped from the Château de Nantes!* thought d'Orbay. *Nobody would think he's forty-eight years old!*

Exiled to Rome since the failure of the Fronde rebellion, Gondi had retained the noble bearing of those who love to dazzle, despite his many exhausting wanderings during the ensuing years. As a result of assiduously spending time with men of great faith, the former brilliant theology student had also cultivated a suave manner that made him even more charming. The two men had got acquainted through spending time together during the architect's stay in Rome the previous year.

'How happy I am to see you in Rome once again, my dear d'Orbay! When did you arrive? Was your journey a pleasant one? What news is there of our capital?'

The Archbishop vigorously clasped François d'Orbay's

hands in his. A little taken aback by this torrent of words and surprised by the unexpected show of affection, the architect hardly knew which question to answer first.

'A thousand thanks for receiving me this morning, Monseigneur. I too am delighted to see you again in this city, and especially to find you in good health.'

'Please, do take a seat,' said Paul de Gondi, indicating an armchair.

'Monseigneur, as we agreed I have come to show you some sketches for the painted screens which you would like made,' said the architect, reaching into his bag and handing the Archbishop a rolled-up document.

'Excellent, excellent,' said Gondi, carefully examining the charcoal drawings depicting his favourite heroes from ancient Greece. 'You praised your craftsmen's skills very highly to me; when will you be able to set them to work? Now that I have seen these sketches, I am impatient to admire the final result and have them here before me.'

'Monseigneur, your impatience flatters me. I imagine that I shall be able to fulfil your expectations by the summer.'

'Excellent, excellent. I am told that Mazarin is at death's door,' commented the Archbishop, suddenly changing the subject. 'Is there really hope that the Kingdom of France will soon be rid of that villain?'

'Monseigneur, for several days the Chief Minister has not left his bedchamber, and he has ordered his secretariat to put his papers in order . . .'

'The better to conceal the shameful origins of his fortune!' Gondi interrupted with sudden excitement. 'By the grace of

God, I am at last to be avenged for all these years of injustice. Your words confirm my own intelligence. I have maintained strong friendships right up to the doors of the King's apartments, you know.'

The architect told himself that he had been right to request this audience. Despite his exile, the man who had been one of the leaders of the Fronde rebels in 1648 clearly still had eyes and ears all over Paris.

It remains to be seen whether the Archbishop of Paris is capable of hatching a new conspiracy by uniting those still nostalgic for the Fronde, and then coming to upset our plans, thought d'Orbay.

'Nonetheless, I fear that Mazarin may succeed in manipulating destiny one more time,' went on the Archbishop, his expression suddenly anxious. 'That scoundrel will use his last ounce of strength to pillage the State exchequer. You will see: he will make all or part of his immense fortune disappear into his family's pockets. Doubtless he is already destroying the papers which would compromise him.'

He broke off for a moment, as if to reflect upon some intricate point, then changed the subject again:

'My Parisian friends are convinced that the most committed religious networks have already been reactivated. Do you have any information on that subject?'

Prudently, d'Orbay did not answer immediately.

'All Paris is in turmoil, Monseigneur. After all these years, Mazarin's victims are so numerous. It is difficult to determine whether one camp will be able to triumph over the other. As for the Court, it speculates whether the young King has the capability to operate alone once his godfather is dead. In the salons, there is incessant chattering about the profusion of influences which will come to supplant the Italian in the sovereign's mind.'

'And the common people?' Gondi asked again. 'What is their talk of? What are they saying? What are the rumblings?'

'Their mood is difficult to grasp. I believe Mazarin himself no longer perceives the changes of mood in the King of France's subjects with the same precision as before. It is like the end of an era; other aspirations are emerging. Europe has seen more sizeable rebellions in the last twenty years than during the previous hundred. Rebellions that were, moreover, unforeseen – without famine, without excessive taxes. I myself believe that the Kingdom's destiny will depend to an extent upon the ability of future Mazarins to comprehend these developments.'

'And how is the good Monsieur Colbert?'

'As usual, he is putting all his knowledge and skills to the service of his master,' replied François d'Orbay.

The Archbishop nodded and seemed once again lost in thought.

'You are right. Mazarin's death will unleash profound upheavals. Everything depends on who comes to power. The post of Chief Minister will be vacant tomorrow, but there may prove to be many candidates.'

The Archbishop spoke more softly.

'Nicolas Fouquet, for example . . . I am told that he is currently arming troops at his estates on Belle-Île. But doubtless you know more than I do on that subject, my dear d'Orbay, since you are the architect of the chateau being built at Vaux-le-Vicomte by the Superintendent of Finance?'

From this reply, the architect deduced that their conversation about the future of the Kingdom would go no further.

'I fear, Monseigneur, that I have no further information on that subject.'

Clearly, Paul de Gondi had no desire to reveal his opinion on Fouquet, nor for that matter to reveal his intentions for the future. As the conversation moved on to less weighty subjects, the architect told himself that his host had remained faithful to his legendary self: cautious, very well informed, but above all puffed up with pride.

As he left the Farnese Palace just as the bells of Sainte-Béatrice were striking noon, François d'Orbay was convinced that the former Fronde members had no clear strategy as the death of their old Italian enemy approached.

That should simplify our task, he told himself as he turned round to take a last admiring glance at the design of the palace's façade.

CHAPTER THIRTEEN

THE dust raised by the twenty horses of the escort swirled around their riders, obscuring the blue livery of the Light Cavalry. It even clouded the view of the passengers in the carriage, which rattled at breakneck speed along the road to Fontainebleau. Despite this, the man sitting in the place of honour, dressed in a purple and gold cloak and black-leather riding boots, attempted to make out the landscape as he removed his gloves and warmed his hands on a small brazier placed in the middle of the floor.

Seated to the right of Fouquet, François d'Orbay shivered as he felt the crisp morning cold begin to penetrate his shoes and clothing.

'We're almost there,' he whispered, leaning towards his neighbour. 'Look, you can just see the milestones for the old village of Vaux, with Les Jumeaux on the right, and to the left Maison-Rouge and the hill where the old chateau stood; we used its stones for foundations. The estate is very close now.'

Nicolas Fouquet carefully put his gloves back on, wriggling his fingers to ensure that they were absolutely in place.

'It's all right, Monsieur d'Orbay, the cold is not as bitter as all that and I find the journey restful; I know that it will end with a sight that fills me with joy, a welcome change from the worries that make up the daily round.'

For a moment, Fouquet seemed deep in thought, his regular features relaxed and his green eyes half closed.

The silence was broken by his young secretary, who was seated on the bench opposite:

'Robillard, Le Vau and Le Brun are already there, waiting for us. Puget is not – he has gone to take delivery of the marble we discussed earlier . . .'

'Good, good,' cut in the Superintendent of Finance. 'We can see that when we get there and tour the gardens. No news of His Eminence, then?'

'A message will be brought to us at Vaux, Monsieur; I have requested a report on his condition at daybreak to be brought to us without delay. I have also asked that any mail for the King's household be included.'

Fouquet blinked his assent and shivered, then turned smiling towards the architect huddled beside him:

'So, Monsieur d'Orbay, is your snow-palace much further? Monsieur Le Vau, your father-in-law, will be frozen stiff waiting for us to get there!'

The fourth passenger smiled.

'What a wonderful idea of yours it was, Nicolas, this Vaux,' he said plaintively. 'Monsieur d'Orbay, I hear that you would happily have built His Excellency's chateau in New France, in Quebec or Sainte-Louise . . .'

It was Fouquet's turn to smile.

'That's enough, Monsieur de La Fontaine. If you want my advice, Monsieur d'Orbay, avoid the company of poets, or at least don't expect serious conversation from them. For my part, if Monsieur de La Fontaine didn't leave me alone once in a while, I don't know how I would ever fulfil my duties.'

'Make way for the Superintendent, make way!'

The cry went up as the procession suddenly slowed. They could hear jostling, and a horse whinnied. Lifting the curtain that hid the interior of the coach from passers-by and slightly mitigated the icy draughts, Fouquet glanced outside, looking disapprovingly at the cavalry who were barking orders at the crowd.

'It's the stonemasons rolling blocks for the completion of the entrance, Monseigneur,' commented d'Orbay.

'There's no need for all that bellowing. We can surely wait a moment, until they've moved on,' grumbled Fouquet as he dropped the curtain. 'Are we in such a hurry that we must behave so odiously all the time? Really, anyone would think they want to make me unpopular . . .'

The carriage moved slowly through the group of workmen, who cursed under their breath. The little procession was now travelling along a roadway bordered by young chestnut trees, the horses' hooves clattering on newly laid paving stones.

'The trees have grown even taller,' noted Fouquet with satisfaction. 'Even the bad weather does not stop them.'

The secretary seated opposite the Superintendent was about to take advantage of the ensuing silence to speak. Charitably, La Fontaine laid a hand on his arm just as he raised it and opened his mouth to begin. The secretary looked in astonishment at the poet, who indicated with a rueful little smile that he should not make the mistake of talking. In the years he had known the Superintendent, he had learnt to recognise when he would be receptive, and when he was allowing himself one of those rare moments of repose which should not be interrupted on any account. And especially those moments that La Fontaine privately termed 'Dreams of Vaux'. He had seen the man he thought of as a friend rather than a protector lapse into these reveries several times during the regular trips he made from his Saint-Mandé residence to see the progress of work on the chateau. They almost always occurred just as the carriage was slowing before turning right, and then finally stopping, directly in front of the great wrought-iron gate emblazoned with the Superintendent's coat of arms.

Light poured in through the carriage door as the postillion opened it, hurrying to pull down the steps. The dazzled passengers remained seated for a second, then Fouquet half rose and extricated himself from the vehicle. One after another, the four men alighted. La Fontaine, who was last to emerge, felt the cold strike his face. Seeing Fouquet stand motionless, he too turned his gaze towards the magnificent main body of the chateau. Viewed through the thick bars of the gate, the refinement of its construction seemed enhanced to the visitors. Light radiated onto the sculptures on the façade, descending to form a golden halo over the view of the gardens which could just be made out through the immense windows, as though lit from behind. La Fontaine was struck by the wonder of this sight each time he came. He felt his chest contract as he noted the progress, the details that had been added since his last visit. Was it the cold, or was it emotion? Suddenly a shiver ran right through him. Surrounded by cold light, the chateau seemed even more beautiful than he remembered it.

The frenzied scurrying of servants, almost fighting each other to open the gate, contrasted with Fouquet's slow pace. Although accustomed to a life filled with emergencies and constant hurrying, of exhausting his colleagues with questions and new ideas, Fouquet now suddenly seemed bathed in a calm, serene joy. Five years had elapsed since the Superintendent had decided to build a chateau here, contrary to all expectations. Five years in which to recruit the very finest from each profession: the most expert gardeners, the most talented architects, including the young and brilliant d'Orbay. As was his custom, Fouquet had watched his dream coming to fruition, supervising the professionals while allowing their desires free rein. It seemed to La Fontaine that at each stage, Fouquet's obvious joy at being constantly surprised by new ideas was in proportion to his satisfaction at seeing how closely the project resembled his plan. The decision to abandon the classical structure of the central body and the two attached wings, the layout of the gardens and even the strange shape of the dome, which had appeared at the centre of the structure a few days previously, all testified to this.

D'Orbay's voice brought the Superintendent reluctantly back to reality.

'We are about to go through the central entrance. You see, the colonnades are ready to be put into position and there . . . oh! Be careful not to twist your ankle . . . these planks on the ground will be gone shortly, as soon as the green and white marble flooring arrives from Italy.'

'Those weren't there before, were they?' observed the Superintendent, indicating two groups of huts built along the wall of the outhouses.

'A temporary orangery,' explained d'Orbay. 'The real one 'hasn't yet been built. The trees arrived recently and they don't tolerate the cold as well as we do. This way, they are sheltered and the windows provide them with enough light.'

'Ingenious,' murmured Fouquet. 'Is that where all the plants are kept?' he added, lowering his voice and taking d'Orbay by the arm.

The architect nodded.

'Only to help them grow before they are transplanted,' he replied in the same discreet tone. 'I have been able to satisfy myself that all the species we were expecting have arrived.'

They crossed the entrance hall and the ceremonial salons, and headed for the steps leading to the gardens. Fouquet, who had quickened his pace, suddenly stopped.

'Has something changed?' enquired La Fontaine.

'Indeed, Monsieur de La Fontaine,' replied d'Orbay. 'Since His Excellency's last visit, I have worked on site, implementing plans for altering the central structure of the dome. That is the rounded structure you observed just above your head that masks the supporting framework. There are in fact two domes, one on top of the other. I had the idea last year in Rome, inspired by the works of the supreme masters.'

'I would be curious to know the details,' remarked La Fontaine, looking up.

The elegant, rounded dome was thirty feet above their heads. Held aloft by fourteen statues, it already bore pencilled outline sketches of its planned decorations and seemed to be suspended in mid-air.

CHAPTER FOURTEEN

COLBERT gave an exhausted sigh and rubbed his large eyes.
He had been seated at his desk for more than two hours.
With his usual minute attention to detail, he was carefully
examining the accounting documents the Cardinal had handed
him before leaving for Vincennes. The room he worked in was
vast and well lit, thanks to two large windows with superb views
of the gardens. But on this late afternoon in February the daylight was fast fading, and he had called for additional candelabra
to provide light for his work. The fire crackled in the hearth
behind him, spreading gentle warmth across his back. Colbert
was sensitive to the cold, and he was starting to feel numb from
the prolonged inactivity. Although he was a faithful colleague
who had made himself indispensable to His Eminence over the
years, he was well aware that time was no longer on his side.
And what was worse, as the days passed he was increasingly
gripped by an icy fear. *Everything depends on me*, he thought at
intervals, with a feeling of both dread and excitement.

When Mazarin had decided to put his affairs in order in
preparation for death, Colbert had undertaken to see to it all
himself, as usual: exhausting though the work was, he fully
expected to reap numerous benefits by doing it.

Although most people failed to notice it, his ambition was rampant. He had mapped out a swift and audacious route to the summit of State. A decisive stage in his conquest was being played out at the Chief Minister's bedside, of that Colbert was aware. Like a chess player, he calculated his next move. His devotion to the Cardinal was in fact intended to win over the young King.

'Enter,' he said without looking up, when he heard a knock at the door.

'Monsieur Charles Perrault wishes to see you,' announced the servant as he opened it.

'Show him in,' replied Colbert, impatient for news of the investigation he had ordered following the fire in the Cardinal's library two days earlier.

Charles Perrault approached him, bowing several times. The lawyer always displayed great deference, despite a can-tankerous disposition entirely at odds with his acknowledged talent as a writer. Colbert had entrusted him with solving the mystery of the attack and theft as quickly as possible.

'So, Perrault, what is the current situation?' demanded Colbert impatiently.

'Murky, to say the least, but we are making progress on several fronts. First of all, we have identified the young boy found dead on the stage of the Palais-Royal theatre. He was a wretch known as Le Jeune who had no family; he lived more or less at Cour des Miracles and was known for his skill with knives. His accoutrements and religious trinkets incline me to believe that he belonged to a group of zealots.'

'You believe, or you are sure?' Colbert interrupted, irritated by Perrault's lack of precision.

'It is my firm conviction, Monsieur, strengthened moreover by the testimony of Toussaint Roze.'

So, we're back to the zealots, thought Colbert, intrigued.

'Our investigations are concentrating on the Palais-Royal theatre, from which the burglars escaped. I have searched the place from top to bottom, so far without success.'

'Make the theatre employees and those villainous actors talk,' snapped Colbert, becoming increasingly irritated.

'We have spent the last two days questioning them. I have even had several of them followed. In particular a fellow named Gabriel, who works as a secretary. He joined Molière's company only recently, and it seemed to me he was behaving strangely. Yesterday evening, as he was leaving the theatre, he had a public fight with Berryer on a minor pretext.'

Colbert's eyebrows arched upwards at the sound of this name. He knew Berryer extremely well; he had acted for him as an agent in certain delicate – and fruitful – matters. The previous evening, he had personally instructed him, in the utmost secrecy, to attend the premiere of Molière's new play with several accomplices and heckle the performance. By so doing, he hoped to nip the author's ambitions in the bud, as he considered Molière to be one of Fouquet's lackeys. The sudden appearance of his own henchmen in the investigation into the burglary of Mazarin's private office made him uneasy.

'I want to know everything about this man Gabriel. Does he have a surname? Where does he come from? Who are his contacts in Paris? Everything, Perrault,' shouted Colbert. 'Do you hear? Everything!'

'He received a visit from an extremely pretty young woman

at his home in Rue des Lions Saint-Paul,' continued Charles Perrault, without flinching at Colbert's rage. 'It was Louise de La Vallière, Henrietta of England's new companion. She is to be presented to the King in a fortnight's time. She spent more than two hours in the company of this man Gabriel. All that time in such an unsafe district, and what's more in the bedroom of a stranger; it all seems very peculiar for a young girl of good breeding who has only just moved to Paris.'

This information instantly had a calming effect on Colbert. So the investigation was advancing, and his bloodhound had done some rather good work.

'Very well,' said Colbert soberly, 'continue your enquiries. I have a feeling that you are on the right track. I also want to know what our religious friends are saying. Pay your informants handsomely to find out precisely what rumours are in circulation amongst the zealots. And try by the same means to obtain details as to how this little world is linked with the Court, and in particular with the Superintendent, whose influence in those quarters is known. As for this man Gabriel, do not let him out of your sight and report back to me as soon as possible!'

Charles Perrault backed out of the room, executing several obsequious bows.

Deep in thought, Colbert shivered. He stood up to throw a log into the immense fireplace, picked up a crystal decanter from a small table and removed the stopper. As he poured himself a glass of port, he congratulated himself on entrusting this task to young Perrault, who was carrying it out with considerable speed.

How strange that man is, he said to himself, *by day a servile clerk to those in power, willing to commit any excess to extract the truth from the mire. At night, an author of poems and mawkish, insipid tales. At some point I must learn how to make use of his ambiguities.*

Then, thinking through the consequences of what he had just learned, Colbert returned to his table. With a little luck, if everything continued to unfold according to his plans, Fouquet would not survive the process. He returned to his work with a smile, murmuring:

'Well, well, I've enough here to keep me busy all night!'

CHAPTER FIFTEEN

*Château de Vincennes – Tuesday 15 February, ten o'clock
in the morning*

THE snowfall during the night had formed a white carpet over the roof of the keep at Vincennes, and over the whole of the courtyard. It was just possible to make out the shrubs and Anne of Austria's beloved topiary box-trees. Standing by his bedroom window, draped in a dressing gown edged with crimson fur, Cardinal Mazarin silently watched his visitors arrive. Three feet behind him, Colbert was mechanically leafing through the leather document wallet in which he kept the despatches to be examined that morning by the Council of Ministers.

'All is well, Colbert; here is Lionne, always running, always late. Le Tellier has already passed by . . .'

'Only Monsieur Fouquet is missing,' commented Colbert, immersed in his papers.

'Indeed,' said Mazarin, tearing himself away from his contemplation with an enigmatic smile. 'Go, my friend. You need to concentrate on our special affairs.' He winced as he spoke, groping for an armchair to lean upon.

Colbert rushed to his aid, but the Cardinal waved him away.

'Leave me, go downstairs instead. Have the coffers arrived from the library? Yes? Well then, they are more important than what brings these gentlemen here today.'

Seeing that Colbert was reluctant to hand over the document wallet, Mazarin took his secretary by the arm:

'Up here, we will be dealing with everyday matters. Downstairs, you will be helping me with a more complex task, involving much higher stakes for the Kingdom.'

The little man in black felt the grip on his arm tighten.

'You have done a great deal, Colbert. Or rather I should say that we have done a great deal together, you know that. We have still to inscribe it for posterity though, to ensure that no scoundrel can undo what we have fought for, and in so doing sully my memory. The stakes are higher than you think,' he repeated with a weary sigh which signified that he would not accompany his secretary any further. 'I trust you,' he added softly. 'We shall discuss all this later. You will have to meet several people on my behalf . . . But for the moment, devote yourself to putting the accounts in order. I must have peace of mind, Colbert, peace of mind. If you can give me that, you will have no cause to regret it.'

A shiver ran through Colbert as he bowed at these words.

Looking exhausted, Mazarin let himself fall into a large armchair upholstered in green and red velvet, which entirely enveloped his bent form.

With a final gesture to Colbert as he left the room, Mazarin sank deeper into the chair and closed his eyes.

The ministers were shown in one by one and greeted the old man effusively, receiving in return an inaudible word and a vague wave of the hand.

Four of them were now seated around a gaming table: Lionne, Secretary of State for War, looked grave and serious;

Le Tellier, Crown Chancellor, wore an air of superiority which he believed his great age conferred upon him; and finally Nicolas Fouquet, the youngest and most powerful, who could barely contain his desire to begin examining the financial files that were his chief interest. Autocratic as ever, Mazarin allowed the heavy silence to drag on, and none of the ministers dared break it. His excessively made-up face could no longer conceal his weariness. At last he signalled to Le Tellier, inviting him to speak. And the rigmarole of examining the despatches began.

'England, England! That is all you can talk about!'

Scarcely twenty minutes had elapsed when Mazarin suddenly raised his voice, interrupting the fierce debate on the attitude to be adopted towards the new sovereign, now restored to the English throne.

'We must ensure that our boats are in her ports, that our sales and supplies of food are guaranteed. And that we prevent Holland from pressing home her advantage at the English Court by reminding the King that he was welcomed in when only a fugitive. The rest is pointless speculation. England is hostile towards us. She has changed her master, but so what? Would the scoundrels who cut off the father's head be any less capable of cutting off the son's? Let us pray above all that their example does not give anyone else any ideas. Such an example is like blood to a peaceable hunting dog: once it has tasted it, it will seek it out again and again. The common people, Messieurs, fear their masters less and less, and are abandoning all sense! If it were not for fear of burning in Hell for their sin, they would gladly overturn thrones. Think of Ravaillac, think of Clément!'

Mazarin paused without appearing to notice the tremor that passed through Fouquet at these words.

'We must not scatter our forces,' he went on. 'Messieurs, we are no longer at war! The alliances we seek are for the purposes of trading!'

His voice became harsher again as he was carried away by his growing anger:

'The enemies we fight are within our borders, in our own antechambers. The blessed time when monarchies confronted each other as power against power is past: it is the very idea of monarchy that our enemies, nurtured on fantasy, rise up to destroy! Free-thinkers consider us too devout, the devout regard us as libertines, and all of them continue to conspire, year after year, century after century! My God what a burden, what a burden!'

Worn out by this tirade, the Chief Minister sank back into his armchair once again.

'Might we usefully seek credit in England at least?' demanded Fouquet, moving forward to allow Mazarin to hear him more clearly. 'The coffers are proving difficult to fill, Monsieur Cardinal, and it could be a way of putting pressure on our Italian bankers by showing that we can do without them . . .'

'Stop there, Monsieur. I cannot believe that we have less credit in peacetime than we had in time of war.'

A new flame burned in his eyes as he turned towards Nicolas Fouquet.

'You are the one responsible for devising ingenious ways of

meeting the needs of the Crown, which I grant you are great, and in which, I concede, I do not always take the necessary interest because my duties do not leave me sufficient time. Incidentally,' he said, addressing Le Tellier, 'I must speak to you without delay about the need for urgent measures to check the moralistic madness of certain religious groups, which verges on heresy and rebellion. But, as regards financial manoeuvres, I am well aware of your skill,' he turned back to Fouquet, lowering his voice and staring at him sternly. 'I merely expect your best effort to be directed towards the public interest . . .'

To general astonishment, the Superintendent began to speak again.

'On the subject of the financial needs of the Crown, has Your Eminence found the time to study the reports I sent him on the potential of the art trade and on the latest orders for the army? There are, I believe, quite apart from any banking negotiations, potential financial gains that the Crown could legitimately record without delay. And there are economies which I am convinced would offer His Majesty the chance to provide for the needs of his policies, and at the same time limit the drain on his subjects. If they no longer fear their masters, perhaps they might begin to learn to love them?'

Mazarin frowned doubtfully but nodded.

'Yes, yes.'

Then, turning to Le Tellier:

'Monsieur Chancellor, I must inform you about Monsieur Fouquet's reflections on the arts; and we shall talk of weapons again later. As for re-arming: forsooth! What a taste you have for war, Monsieur Superintendent!' the Cardinal declared with false irony. 'All those fortifications you have built on your land at Belle-Île – has the squirrel on your coat of arms turned into a lion? I thought that your India Company was involved in peaceful trade?'

'Indeed it is, Monsieur Cardinal,' Fouquet replied in a neutral tone which scarcely masked his emotion. 'And the fortifications which my enemies like to talk about are warehouses. But those are merely my private interests. And my private interests matter little when I have the honour of maintaining the interests of the Crown.'

Mazarin smiled once more but did not reply, his face inscrutable. When he turned towards Chancellor Le Tellier his expression had turned to one of benevolence, as if to signify that the formal part of the council was to be cut short:

'Well, Monsieur Chancellor, how are the preparations for the marriage of your son Monsieur de Louvois? For my part, I am finding it difficult to involve myself as much as I would like in the nuptials of my nieces Hortense and Marie . . . The poor angels,' he moaned, and tears appeared at the corners of his eyes as he raised them to the heavens.

Pressing his hands together, the Chief Minister murmured a few words in Italian, crossed himself, then stretched out his arms to support himself on the dark wooden arms of his chair and dismissed the ministers, explaining that, if he hoped to disprove his doctors, he must rest again.

When his visitors had left, Mazarin remained motionless for several minutes, savouring the return of silence. Opening his eyes again, he shook the little golden bell with the olive-wood handle which never left his side. The footsteps of his butler grated on the wooden floor. Dreamily, Mazarin said without looking at him:

'Tell Colbert to come up and see me.'

The servant left discreetly and the Chief Minister commented to himself:

'Isn't it funny that after so many years, I still sometimes have difficulty distinguishing deceitfulness from honesty . . . Their outward appearances are so alike!'

Sitting up straight he added with a sigh:

'Sheep, insipid courtiers; and what about him: I can never tell if his impetuosity . . . But I have no more time for daydreams and half measures. More's the pity. No more time.'

CHAPTER SIXTEEN

Palais-Royal Theatre — Tuesday 15 February, eleven o'clock in the morning

'MURDER! Murder! Help! Somebody, help!'

It was Julie's voice. Gabriel, who had just arrived at the theatre, rushed down the corridor in the direction of the shouts and discovered the troupe's concierge on the floor. He was struggling as best he could with two men who had him in their grasp, while the young actress, in tears, looked on in terror. Curled up with his arms wrapped around his head, the old man strove to protect himself from his attackers' blows. Gabriel grabbed one of them by the collar and hauled him upright, smashing his fist full into the man's face with all his youthful strength. The man's nose split open and blood poured out, spattering his white shirt as he crumpled under the violence of the blow.

'Run,' shouted the other man.

Fast as lightning he leapt forward, opened the window and jumped into the void, swiftly followed by Gabriel, who was determined to overpower him. The young actor landed quite well, as the ground-floor window gave directly onto one of the narrow streets that bordered the theatre. The alleyway was crowded with people heading for the nearby vegetable market. The concierge's assailant dodged between the handcarts of the traders, who cursed the mayhem caused by the men's chase. At each street corner, Gabriel feared he would see the fugitive vanish into the mass of people. After at least five breathless minutes chasing at top speed through the capital's maze of narrow, slippery streets, the young man reached the banks of the Seine, panting for breath. The ruffian had seized a boat that had doubtless been moored there by a fisherman who had gone to sell his fish in the market, and he was now speeding off up the river. As there were no other boats available, Molière's secretary realised that he had lost this round. He retraced his steps resolving to force the man left on the floor to talk and strode purposefully back towards the theatre. The blood still pounding in his temples.

'Gabriel, where were you? I was desperately worried,' said Julie when he hove into view.

'Where is that scum? I'm going to wring the truth from him!' raged the young man, still furious at the other's escape.

'He got away; we weren't able to detain him,' said the concierge. 'Thank you, Gabriel. Without you, I would certainly have died,' he murmured, his eyes moist.

The poor man's distraught expression showed how afraid he had been.

As the troupe gathered around them, warmly congratulating Gabriel on his bravery, the concierge sat on a chair to get his breath back and requested a glass of brandy. At the mere sight of the alcohol, colour began to return to the man's face.

'Well, what happened?' Gabriel asked the concierge, who was clearly restored by the drink.

'Ever since I found that scoundrel flattened on the stage, misfortune seems to have dogged our steps,' he lamented. 'First there were those whistles and jeers the other evening, which made good Monsieur Molière ill, and then there were the Cardinal's policemen, who searched the theatre all day yesterday, from the cellars to the attics. Who knows what they were looking for!'

'The Cardinal's police!' Gabriel exclaimed, anxious and incredulous.

'Yes, the very same! They questioned me for three hours about each one of you,' went on the concierge. 'I thought they were going to arrest me and lock me away in those terrible cellars of the Conciergerie. Anyone would think that actors were enemies of the King! They wanted to know everything about the company, including where you live, and the people you associate with. Well, I just told them what I knew. As if I could investigate the private lives of the people who work here! And then this morning, just as I was sweeping the main auditorium, I came face to face with those two bandits. Lord knows where they sprang from.'

'But what on earth are all these men searching for?' said Julie.

'How should I know?' replied the concierge. 'They told me they wanted "their documents". I had barely recovered from the surprise when they jumped on me and shook me violently by the shoulders. By some miracle, I was able to escape their clutches for a moment. But these old legs aren't as supple as they used to be,' he said, slapping his thighs. 'They caught me again just as you arrived, Mademoiselle. The more I told them I didn't know what they meant by documents, the harder they hit me.

They would have killed me, those villains, if you had not intervened, Monsieur Gabriel,' the concierge repeated, pouring himself another glass of brandy.

When he was sure the concierge was restored, the young man considered for a moment. All these people were searching for the documents he had found, whose code he had been unable to break. The presence in the theatre of the Cardinal's police, and now of a band of mysterious attackers, was extremely worrying.

I must be careful not to mention this to anyone, he thought. *Damn it, I won't hand over that document case, even if the Devil himself comes asking for it – not before I've solved the mystery and discovered why my father's signature is on the Cardinal's papers!*

'You seem worried. What are you thinking about, my sweet?' Julie asked him, taking him by the arm to join the rest of the troupe.

'I'm thinking about my father.'

'Your father? But I thought he died a long time ago.'

'So did I,' Gabriel replied, putting his arm round her and leading the way as they hurried towards the main auditorium, where the troupe had assembled.

CHAPTER SEVENTEEN

Château de Fontainebleau – Thursday 17 February, four o'clock in the afternoon

'THE King!'

With a great rustling of fabric, the mass of courtiers crushed into the audience chamber at the Château de Fontainebleau respectfully greeted the King with the ritual dance of bows and curtseys. The men swept off their hats, and the women knelt within the circles of their ample gowns. The King walked slowly across the silent hall, smiling at no one in particular, not even at his wife the Queen, whose full attention was taken up with keeping precisely in step with him. The little Spanish princess had become Queen of France six months earlier, by arrangement between the two powers. Pale, and with that aura of fragility which always surrounded her, she was still nervous about the strange etiquette of the Court, executed as it was in a foreign language; an etiquette whose false simplicity and curious whims she could not understand. The royal couple reached the throne, and the King gestured to the assembly to rise. Then he looked questioningly at his secretary, who held the running order of the session. An ambassador stepped forward, bearing credentials, which Lionne came over to receive in the King's name. The monarch listened with a fixed smile to the formal message, delivered in a strong accent by the

Nordic diplomat. The King's thoughts carried him far from this chamber and from these faces that he knew rather too well but did not trust. He was riding in the forests of Versailles, and carousing, perpetuating the ideal of knightly combat that he so relished, in contrast to the horrors of civilian life. Absorbed in his thoughts, he did not smile, and the Queen feared her husband was annoyed because she did not understand what was expected of her. The father who had just stepped forward to present his daughter officially to the Court thought that he had committed some fatal error. A hush descended. Everyone held their breath. Pulling himself together, the King managed a faint smile and a nod of the head, enabling the ceremony to proceed.

'Mademoiselle d'Épernoy! Mademoiselle de Luynes!'

The names were barked out at the foot of the throne, punctuating the procession of stiff, vaguely frightened-looking girls. *Always the same docile looks, and more often than not, ugly with it*, said the King to himself, once again drifting off into his own thoughts.

How he hated these people and their expectations, and how well he felt he knew their games! As a young boy, he had seen them for what they really were behind their masks, and what he had not been able to see, the Cardinal had patiently taught him how to read, over the years. The young King was overcome by anger and dismay at the thought that not only would his godfather's illness soon deprive him of his protector, but also that certain people dared to conspire against his own authority. To be King, on his own: the thought both terrified and attracted him like some heady fever. He could almost feel the hot blood flowing through his arms and chest. As Mazarin seemed to grow more bloodless with each passing day, his own blood boiled; the protective shelter provided by the Cardinal was wearing away and his lessons were now no more than the murmurings of a powerless old man. *Power, perhaps that is the elixir of life?* thought the King, suddenly intoxicated. He closed his eyes to regain his composure.

'Mademoiselle de La Vallière!'

Opening his eyes again just as she rose from her curtsey, the King met Louise's gaze.

'I am aware of all your accomplishments, Mademoiselle. Madame de Choisy constantly sings your praises and my uncle, God rest his soul, attributed the highest virtues to your family.'

Surprised to hear the King speak to her, Louise remained silent, her blue eyes locked with his. He smiled when Louise, realising how inappropriate her conduct was, blushed and lowered her eyes.

The Queen's sweet voice came to her aid:

'You come from Touraine, Mademoiselle?'

The Queen's words were slow, marked by the intonation of her native language.

'Yes, Your Majesty, through the benevolence of Monsieur d'Orléans I spent my childhood at the Château d'Amboise.'

'It seems that everyone at this French Court is rootless, torn away from childhood dreams,' joked the Queen for the benefit of her husband, who heard the quip but did not smile.

Then to Louise:

'Mademoiselle Henrietta of England, the future wife of the brother of my husband the King, has the good fortune to count you amongst the friends who are to help her as she learns about this new world.'

Louise nodded, curtseyed again and made way for the next girl. As she moved away, she sensed the courtiers looking at her. And in particular, she could still feel the burning traces of the King's gaze.

At the door, a small man dressed in black, with protruding eyes, stood aside to let her pass. She almost ran to her mother, who had been unable to hold back her tears as she heard the royal couple's friendly words, and had taken refuge outside the hall to conceal her emotion.

Still standing beside the door, Colbert watched her suspiciously as she moved away.

CHAPTER EIGHTEEN

Saint-Mandé – Friday 18 February, eight o'clock in the evening

'CHARLES, Armand, Louis! Come and kiss your father! It is time for you to return to your apartments.'

Aged five, four and eight, the sons of the Superintendent of Finance approached in turn to receive a paternal kiss on their foreheads, the prelude to leaving for their bedrooms.

Nicolas Fouquet always enjoyed this ritual, which on that particular evening took place in the great gallery of his library where he had settled himself an hour earlier. His children had joined him with their governess to play for a little while beside him. He liked to withdraw to this imposing room, to enjoy the sight of the twenty-seven thousand works he had accumulated here, the majority of them bound in fawn calf's leather and embossed with the interlaced initials 'NF'. This library, whose collections overflowed into other rooms in the residence, was his pride and joy. He had planned it as a collection of the sum total of universal knowledge and was thinking of opening it to the public, just as Mazarin himself had done. Earlier that evening, he had enjoyed perusing a series of Arabic manuscripts, which he had just acquired at a very high price on the valuable advice of his friend La Fontaine.

'Dinner is served,' announced the white-gloved footman who had come to fetch him.

The Superintendent got to his feet regretfully and, straightening up, fell into step behind his servant, who was armed with a magnificent branched candlestick to light their journey through the long corridors. The immense house in the heart of the village of Saint-Mandé, which gave him so much pleasure, opened onto six courtyards and was in fact made up of several different buildings. Although it looked extremely modest from the outside, inside it was like an elegant palace. They passed through an anteroom decorated with statues of Mercury and Apollo to reach the dining room, whose centrepiece was a white marble fountain surmounted by the figure of a child.

'Where is Madame?' he asked, disappointed to discover the table richly laid but for only one diner.

'Madame has been in bed for two hours. She asks Monsieur to forgive her absence, in consideration of . . . of her condition,' replied the servant, slightly embarrassed even though he had expected this interrogation.

Nicolas Fouquet sighed. Marie-Madeleine's latest pregnancy obliged him to dine alone, something he hated. Just as the servant was about to leave the room, he had an idea.

'Is Monsieur Molière still waiting for me in the gallery?'

'Indeed he is sir. I informed him that he would be granted an audience after supper. He is accompanied by his secretary.'

'Go and fetch them and bring us some glasses. At least they will divert me with their gossip. And I am sure they will be flattered to share the wine from my vineyard at Thomery.'

The gallery where the two guests were waiting opened onto the garden and was decorated with marble gods from Olympus. Two imposing Egyptian sarcophagi arranged on either side of the room completed the decor, one hewn from basalt, the other from limestone. Visitors were always most impressed by these magnificent coffins, which the Superintendent had purchased in Marseilles.

Accustomed to the long waits Fouquet inflicted on those who came begging, and immune to the charms of ancient Egypt, Molière had spent the last hour deep in conversation with Gabriel. The master had asked his secretary to accompany him, as if he needed reassurance after being victimised by the cabal at the premiere of his new play. The prospect of *Dom Garcie* failing was especially worrying in view of Cardinal Mazarin's illness which threatened the stability of the Kingdom and therefore, by implication, the generosity of his patrons.

'You see, my dear Gabriel, these periods of political intrigue are extremely inauspicious for artists like us. We are often hostages to battles for power, which abuse our talent to benefit venal ambitions. Fortunately, I believe that the Superintendent is honest in his dealings with me. What matters is that he guarantees his future at Court,' he said, suddenly lowering his voice as the footman arrived.

'His Excellency will see you now, gentlemen. If you would be so kind as to follow me . . .'

Surprised to find their audience brought forward, Molière stood up, followed by Gabriel who was most excited at being allowed into the private apartments of France's foremost financier.

'Be seated, Messieurs,' said Fouquet, indicating two arm-chairs opposite him, while the footman poured the renowned Thomery wine into Bohemian-crystal glasses.

'As you can see,' he went on, his fingers dripping with butter, 'this evening I am sampling the famous asparagus which Louis XIV so enjoys. My dear Vatel praises this fashionable vegetable highly, and it is indeed very pleasant, even if it would take a wheelbarrow-full to satisfy my appetite. But I imagine, my dear Molière, that your visit is not inspired by gastronomy?'

Clearly embarrassed to find himself a spectator at the Superintendent's dinner table, Molière cleared his throat and drank a mouthful of wine before answering.

'Monseigneur, I have come to report on how I have taken the Palais-Royal Theatre in hand since January. I am also anxious to tell Your Excellency once again how very grateful I am for the trust you showed me on that occasion.'

'I am told,' Fouquet intervened softly, 'that your latest creation is not encountering the success you expected it would, as the opening show of your season. Is this a malicious rumour, or have you lost the touch which made *Les Précieuses* such a triumph?'

He's dropping me, Molière told himself, the shock rendering him unable to articulate the smallest intelligible phrase in response to this provocation from Fouquet. Reading despair in his master's eyes, Gabriel dared the unimaginable.

'Monseigneur, if I may permit myself, you have spoken truly, and like you, Monsieur Molière fears that he is the victim of an odious machination.'

Dumbstruck by this impertinence, even though it was delivered extremely courteously by the young man, the Superintendent stopped chewing the chicken leg he had been devouring. Molière, terrified by his young secretary's audacity, wished that the ground would open and swallow him up.

'That sorry individual Berryer,' went on Gabriel, this time with real assurance, 'came to the premiere with his henchmen, deliberately intending to provoke a disturbance in the audience. Is he not known to be a close associate of certain highly placed individuals who are currently wallowing in intrigue, taking advantage of His Eminence the Cardinal's temporary weakness? My master was just telling me again how honoured he was to count you amongst his most faithful supporters, and above all as a shield, drawing the attacks from Monseigneur's enemies.'

Enchanted now by Gabriel's skill, Molière watched the Superintendent's reaction out of the corner of his eye. Fouquet was stroking his narrow moustache which he had doubtless cultivated in order to balance his rather prominent nose. *This boy has spirit*, he thought.

'Monseigneur knows how much he can count on me in all circumstances,' continued Molière, snapping out of his lethargy, and reassured by the lack of reaction from his host.

'For my part,' replied the Superintendent, emerging from his reverie, 'I will once again demonstrate my trust in you. Monsieur Molière, you know how highly I value the educative virtues of your art. This is not a view shared by many of my contemporaries, and even less by my equals. What can I say? I dream of a world in which the theatre could, for the great majority of people, make up for the lack of education which is so harmful to the Kingdom's future. I am therefore quite willing to renew my support for you in these difficult times. Your allowance will be increased to two thousand livres straightaway. Go and find Monsieur de Gourville first thing tomorrow – he will make the necessary arrangements. I would also like you to compose a new play for me in your style, as a fitting celebration of the end of the works I began several years ago on my land at Vaux. I want a joyous entertainment to cheer the Court this summer. Have it ready in six months!' finished the Superintendent, tucking into another chicken leg with gusto.

Relieved by this outcome, Molière signalled discreetly to Gabriel, and the two men bowed and left.

Nicolas Fouquet was perplexed as he finished his meal. The frankness of that honest-looking young man, whose name he did not even know, had awakened a deeply buried suspicion which now gnawed at him. He, Nicolas Fouquet, was the most powerful and undoubtedly the wealthiest man in the Kingdom after Mazarin; he was the King's loyal servant and the favourite of Anne of Austria; every influential individual in the land owed him a favour. But could he himself be the target of a conspiracy orchestrated by that wretched little accountant Colbert? *No*, he told himself, finishing his glass of wine, *it's impossible and it never will be possible!*

As the carriage taking them back to Paris left the village of Saint-Mandé, Molière let out a sigh and gave Gabriel a sad but affectionate smile.

'Thank you,' he said simply.

The young man did not reply. He gazed out at the cold countryside which still stood between them and the capital and, as he relived that extraordinary evening, he told himself that he was beginning to acquire a taste for the subtle game of power.

CHAPTER NINETEEN

Église des Feuillants —Saturday 19 February, in the afternoon

COLBERT shivered in the biting wind and walked faster so that he would arrive on time for the service. Bitter cold had set in, and a layer of ice now covered the majority of the city's narrow streets, making the uneven paving stones even more treacherous.

For his part, Jacques Bénigne Bossuet was thinking less about his feet than his hands as he entered the pulpit. The cold air in the sacristy of the Église des Feuillants had numbed his joined hands as he meditated until it was time for him to preach. And now he found it impossible to warm them again. He recalled the day in the winter of 1659 when he had climbed into this same pulpit for the very first time, on the occasion of the church's inauguration. How long ago that first day of glory in Paris now seemed, and longer still his years of apprenticeship in Metz! Clenching his teeth, he allowed his gaze to scan the silent ranks of his congregation. He made out a few faces he knew here and there, and a few others that were well known. Turning away, he took a deep breath, set down the thin sheets of paper on which he had penned a few notes, and began . . .

'My brothers, it must seem to come of its own accord, attracted by greatness, and serving as interpreter for the wisdom which speaks . . .'

Colbert gave a start as he realised that he had lost the thread of what was being said. An unpleasant feeling of distrust passed through him. With a sidelong glance, he checked that his neighbours were paying attention to the clear voice of the small thin orator.

'Too delicate,' he grumbled to himself, 'too refined in his reasoning, too angelic . . .'

He could not free his mind of double-entry accounting and the tortuous methods of Mazarin's financial networks, and he was plagued by obsessive thoughts. With a sudden movement, he thrust one hand into his pocket and took out a notebook and a small surveyor's pencil, feverishly noting down three names to check. He noticed with some annoyance that he could not call to mind the theme of the sermon that Bossuet was delivering in that sonorous voice with its ponderous intonations.

'But what is this wisdom?' the orator went on. 'How does the divine spirit open itself to human intelligence? Eloquence enhances the arts, politics and poetry, all human endeavours in which inspiration is imperfect. In what way could this eloquence, designed to dress up the weaknesses of our imperfect reasoning, imagine that it might be of some use in expressing Truth itself, the perfect revelation? Could the work of Our Lord be human because it arrays itself in rags? My brothers, we find the answer to this question by looking at it from the opposite direction: concentrating not on the divine word but on the ear and the eye to which it is addressed. Not only has the divine word no need to adorn itself in finery, but it requires veils so that its dazzling light does not terrify the poor blind creatures to whom it deigns to appear! This is why the Holy Scriptures must be explained: because they are resplendent in their immutable, absolute exactitude. They are the cornerstone upon which everything is built and upon which the magisterium of our Holy Mother Church and the radiance of royalty both prosper. They are their foundations and their legitimacy.'

Satisfied, Colbert put away his notebook. The subject had suddenly come back to him. *That little schemer Bossuet talks to us of 'eloquence in the word of God'. And who does he think he is deceiving?* he thought with a smile, incapable of not projecting his own ambition onto others. *Is he speaking for the Spirit, or are his words directed towards the Queen Mother sitting in the front row?*

Colbert fumed silently, his temper betrayed only by the jerky movements of his leg which he could not control. *Damn you, Monsieur preacher; speak, speak, I am quite happy for you to speak. I am the one counting. And we shall see . . .*

Colbert recovered his composure and, with narrowed eyes, began to follow the rhythm of the words once again.

A lock of blonde hair escaping from a mantilla disturbed his concentration, however. He felt exasperation taking him over once again. The pale hand which pushed back the rebellious lock and a slight movement of the head, revealing a charming profile, confirmed his first impression: it was indeed Louise de La Vallière sitting there on one of the benches to the right of the choir, facing the pulpit. *Little goose*, thought Colbert, who had not missed a word of what the King had said, *she looks as if butter wouldn't melt in her mouth, and . . .* His thoughts faltered . . . *And they're all completely taken in by her. Ah, it's even worse than if she were merely intelligent!* he raged, with a black look at Bossuet. *All the more reason for Perrault to get to the bottom of this for me. That scheming girl and the little actor . . .*

He froze as he felt a hand on his arm.

'Perrault!' He was so startled that he almost cried out. 'Well, what is it?'

'I have news, Monsieur.'

Making a face that was almost a grimace, rolling his eyes and pressing his lips together, Colbert indicated that he did not consider this an appropriate time.

Perrault acted as though he had not noticed:

'Fouquet,' he whispered almost inaudibly, 'it's Monsieur Fouquet, Monsieur . . .'

Colbert froze. He indicated the church porch with his chin.

As they emerged onto the front steps, a gust of icy wind assailed the two men.

'So, Fouquet . . . ?' Colbert prompted.

'. . . this evening, at his home in Saint-Mandé, he met the young man we were talking about.'

Colbert smiled unpleasantly.

'They had a long discussion, apparently about patronage and the theatre. Alas, I was unable to acquire all the details of their exchanges . . .'

With a wave of the hand, Colbert indicated that this mattered little.

'And the boy, who is he?'

'I am still trying to find out, Excellency,' Perrault replied, bowing his head.

As he listened to him, Colbert thought it over again. His

intuition had not failed him! Fouquet was active. Fouquet was trying to find out . . .

'But what?' He ground his teeth in frustration. 'I must know what!'

He clenched his fists, not realising that he was now talking out loud.

'Something is being hidden from me!'

Anxiously Perrault, who had heard only these last words, wondered what to say.

Colbert dismissed him curtly:

'That young man, concentrate on that young man. Go to it!'

He watched Perrault hurry away, trying not to slip on the steps, and disappear round the corner of the church. As he turned back towards the doors, they began to open.

'Amen,' he said, hastily crossing himself.

Then he too hurried away before the first of the faithful emerged.

CHAPTER TWENTY

Rue Saint-Antoine – Monday 21 February, five o'clock in the morning

I N the pre-dawn cold, a man sneaked past the closed shops in Rue Saint-Antoine, his eyes feverish. From time to time, unable to control his anxiety and agitation, he glanced around to check if he really was alone in the frozen streets. He had a mallet in his hand and a linen bag beneath his cape. Every ten or twenty yards he stopped in front of a church door or a wooden shutter to pin up a text taken from his pouch. The man with the mismatched eyes was the author of these lampoons, and he had decided to put them up himself in Paris that night. For several days he had been tortured by the knowledge that he had failed to bring back what his leader had needed, and was dejected that the latter refused to take the radical step of assassinating the Cardinal. His attempts to retrieve the lost documents had been unsuccessful, and he had desperately tried to remember the contents of his incomplete booty. He had skimmed the papers before handing them over, and although he did not fully grasp their meaning, he had seen enough to fuel his anger and justify the irrepressible desire for action which he felt rise within him.

The King will have to submit if Paris rises up when it discovers the extent of the Italian's illegal trafficking, and here is a document which will incite those gentlemen to act, he told himself, furiously nailing his last copy to the door of a cobbler's shop. Without turning round, he threw the empty bag onto the paving stones and hurried away, disappearing round a corner into a narrow alleyway.

When he left his lodgings in rue des Lions Saint-Paul a few hours later that morning, Gabriel de Pontbriand was light-hearted. Louise's regular visits were not entirely unconnected with this state of mind. His childhood friend had visited several times since their reunion, so that they could share memories. She also recounted her discoveries about life at Court. Gabriel was delighted that they had become close again and over-whelmed that he had become her confidant. Molière, whom he regarded as a benefactor, had contributed to his happiness by telling him about the role he had created for him in the play commissioned by Fouquet to celebrate the completion of his chateau, Vaux-le-Vicomte. *So*, he said to himself as he came out of his lodgings, *I am going to become an actor at last and perform in front of the King. My dream is coming true.* This thought made him smile.

'You look cheerful, Monsieur Gabriel,' commented the washerwoman who waited eagerly each day for the handsome young man to emerge from his room. 'But Paris is sad; the city is buzzing with tales of Court intrigue and the news that Cardinal Mazarin will soon be dead. Of course, you'd know more about that than I do, thanks to the company you keep,' added the girl a little perfidiously, alluding to Louise de La Vallière's frequent visits.

'Do not deceive yourself, my dear Ninon, I know nothing and the King does not take me into his confidence! If I am happy, it is at the sight of you,' replied Gabriel charmingly, stroking the washerwoman's scarlet cheek.

The young actor made his way to the cobbler's shop where he had left a pair of old boots in the hope of making them last for a few more months. Gabriel enjoyed strolling along amongst ordinary folk in the noisy, bustling streets of the capital. This contrast between the Court, which he observed in the evenings at the theatre, and the street, in which he felt so at ease, was like a perfect form of alchemy. For him, it was the intoxicating flavour of Paris. Arriving at the cobbler's in Rue Saint-Antoine, he breathed in deeply, savouring the smell of leather which permeated the entire workshop. The shop was vast and extremely well ordered, with several journeymen and apprentices at work. Master Louvet, a renowned craftsman whose customers included the noblest families in Paris, stopped what he was doing when he saw him.

'Monsieur Gabriel, what a pleasure it is to see you this morning! Your boots are ready, but I'm not sure I can guarantee that they'll survive beyond the spring. They're as worn out as the Cardinal's lungs!'

'Thank you all the same,' replied the young man, taking the parcel the cobbler handed him.

'On the subject of the Cardinal, have you seen this lampoon now circulating in the capital?' asked Louvet, presenting him with a sheet of paper. 'I found this one on my own door this morning.'

Gabriel knew that there had been a proliferation of these

kinds of texts at the time of the Fronde, a few years before. Known as Mazarinades, these pamphlets gave voice to those who, with varying degrees of talent, aspired to incriminate their rulers. As he had never come across one before, he was intrigued to see what it was like.

Let us therefore lift up our voices to the Heavens, and cleave the air with the force of our cheering, may birds all fall dead onto tables made ready in the streets, may fountains of Grave, malmsey and hippocras wine be seen at every crossroads. The Sun does not only illuminate the expanses of air, it does not only cause the heat of its rays to be felt on the surface of our Globe, to produce Plants, and to make the animals rejoice, but it also causes its influences to appear in the earth's entrails, and makes known its virtue by generating metals, minerals and precious stones, the production of which is as admirable as its means are unknown and secret to us. Rejoice, Paris, and console yourself now that your Messiah has come back to visit you. His absence had filled you with sadness, and covered you in mourning, his presence will fill you with joy once again, and enrich you with magnificence and glory: the Abundance which walks in his wake will furnish the material for your delights more than ever, the Justice which accompanies him will return the possessions which belong to you and the force which surrounds him will strengthen more than ever the Columns of your peace; and at last his coming will give you the realisation of your most eagerly awaited wishes and the enjoyment of your most passionate desires . . .

In a similarly tortuous style, the remainder of the document announced the arrival of the Messiah who had come 'to punish the powerful who have betrayed their Lord'.

Above all, this long text denounced the 'unprecedented' accumulation of wealth on the part of the Cardinal and the King. The argument rested upon figures and dates notably concerning a purchase of weapons on behalf of the State from the well-known merchant Maximilien Piton. This order, claimed the anonymous message, had given rise to double accounting and to the payment of commissions whose amount inflated the real invoice considerably. With its accusations strangely backed up by a wealth of precise detail, the lampoon went on to say that the operation had apparently involved a network of agents and multiple letters of credit, which had been cashed all over Europe, as a result of which Mazarin had been able to pocket several hundred thousand livres. The lampoon also detailed another murky affair involving land for building in Paris. Since all vacant land in the city was owned by the King, the royal estate had acquired it very cheaply before selling it on in the same state, but at a vastly inflated price. . .

'It was the usual suspects,' whispered the cobbler, 'Berryer, that is to say Colbert and therefore Mazarin . . . This confirms what the common folk have suspected! The author seems well informed, but if I were him I'd watch out for the Cardinal's police. This kind of literature could lose him his head!'

Gabriel, who had started at the name of Berryer, did not reply. Paying for the repair of his boots, he left the shop with a sombre look on his face. He had been overwhelmed by a feeling of foreboding as he read the lampoon. The death of his father, the coded documents hidden in his bedroom, the police searching the theatre, the attack on the old concierge and this accusatory lampoon were all intermingled in his mind; and although he could not establish the precise link between them, he was somehow certain that one existed. On the sill of an open window a kitten was playing with some wool. Gabriel stopped, took the animal in his arms and began to stroke it.

'What do you make of it all?' he asked the animal as it wriggled excitedly.

He allowed the cat to escape from his arms and distractedly watched it scamper off, dragging the tangled skein of wool with it.

'No matter how much I pull at the threads,' he murmured to himself, 'the ball of wool that holds my interest is still as tangled as ever . . .'

CHAPTER TWENTY-ONE

THROUGH the window of his carriage, Nicolas Fouquet gazed idly at the banks of the Seine and the complex manoeuvring of ferries and boats as they narrowly avoided colliding with each other. The Superintendent was so lost in thought that he did not even notice the crowd outside the Église Saint-Germain, gathered round another copy of that curious anti-Mazarin lampoon which was the talk of all Paris. Protected by its escort, the carriage prudently gave the throng a wide berth and headed down Rue Saint-Merry, coming to a halt outside the majestic entrance of a private residence on the corner of Rue Saint-Martin. The massive double gates swung open to let the carriage through, and a manservant hurried forward. Fouquet allowed his mind to wander for a moment longer, then rather regretfully dragged himself away from his reverie.

'Monsieur Superintendent, it is a great honour to receive you!'

The short, thin man who had just spoken came forward to greet his guest, with his hands almost clasped and bowing profusely.

'I am as overwhelmed as I am happy to welcome you,' he added.

His brown, lined skin and hollow cheeks, thin hands and the simplicity of his dark clothing lent him a curiously oriental air softened a little by his deep voice.

Fouquet bowed too and walked a little ahead of his host, who seemed to hover around him as they moved towards the front steps.

'Come, come, Monsieur Jabach, you know how much I have wanted to view your collections so that I can judge if they really are more beautiful than those of the Cardinal . . .'

The little man exclaimed in surprise, his hands flying to his face:

'Are you mocking me, Monsieur Superintendent? It's unkind to make fun of an old man! Rival His Eminence? Me?'

Fouquet appeared not to hear his host's outpouring of excessive modesty.

'If it were not for work, Monsieur, I would have accepted your invitation months ago.'

Jabach swelled with pride.

'Come,' he said, pointing to a stone staircase in the corner of the vestibule, which was tiled in white marble accented with black cabochons.

Nicolas Fouquet pondered the course of the little man's life as he climbed the stairs behind his host, whose short legs obliged him to hasten, making him breathless. Since he had arrived from Naples twenty years earlier, Jabach had amassed a colossal fortune through his unequalled talent for backing the victors in wars and shipping companies whose boats neither sank nor fell victim to piracy. Whereas many like him had allowed themselves to be compromised in causes which had failed because they were championed by losers, Everhard Jabach had never been mistaken, and had never sought to emerge from the shadows where he prospered. Twenty years after he had opened his first business, and ten years after he had received naturalisation papers in return for services rendered, he was now Paris's foremost art collector. *And the most secretive*, thought Fouquet as he crossed the immense ballroom whose walls were hung with dozens of canvases.

'Superb,' he commented simply.

With an enigmatic smile, Jabach indicated that these were not his most impressive paintings and that this was not the place to linger. Then, darting little glances behind him, he led the disconcerted Fouquet towards a door which was concealed in the wall next to a monumental fireplace supported by two black stone colossi.

Opening the door a little way by tripping an invisible mechanism, the man stopped and swung round with his feet together, his smile suddenly fixed.

'Monsieur Superintendent, I am ashamed to speak to you in this way, but for the sake of my family's wellbeing I must ask you, as you enter this place, to promise absolute discretion, which is the only guarantee of my safety. You know how wicked men can be, what people say, the thousand villainies that are perpetrated for no reason, or out of envy,' he went on, inviting his guest to enter the hidden room.

Fouquet's response was amiable but cold.

'Fear not, Monsieur, I do not spread gossip. I have neither the time nor the desire, and even if one day I did display either of those faults, the years I have lived through as a victim of slander would dissuade me forev . . .'

He paused suddenly, rooted to the spot. The most wondrous gallery of paintings and sculpture imaginable stretched out before him, illuminated only by the indirect light from gigantic bronze candelabra.

'God in Heaven . . .'

The man let out a chuckle of pleasure. Titian, Giorgione, Corregio, Raphael, Bellini, Leonardo . . . As the Superintendent walked past the canvases, he felt as if his head were spinning.

'Now you understand the meaning of my words, Monsieur Superintendent. You see also how much I trust you: few men have come in here, entered my paradise. Many see my collection, but hardly anyone sees my treasures. Before your eyes you have my whole life, the quintessence of what pleasure is to me. For the past twenty-five years, ever since the day Van Dyck ushered me through the doors of a similar room in London, my sole ambition has been to acquire one by one the paintings which I consider to be the most beautiful. You see *The Entombment of Christ* and the *Emmaus Pilgrims* by Titian?' He led the Superintendent towards two canvases which gleamed in the half-light. 'I spent years trying to track them down. They belonged to the unfortunate King of England, Charles I. I purchased them before he died upon the scaffold. Can you imagine a beauty more pure?'

Fouquet was speechless for a moment, and moved from one canvas to the next, unable to take his eyes off them.

'Thank you, Monsieur Jabach,' he said at last, turning to his host. 'There is a feeling of energy in this accumulation of beauty, a feeling which warms the heart. Your private gallery is a place of hope for those who have faith in man and in his ability not to yield continually to his baser instincts.'

In a single sweeping movement he gestured to the canvases.

'How can anyone not believe in Truth and its strength when witnessing such a sight? What mind can resist the conviction instilled by such absolute balance and harmony? It may well be that you have chosen the wise path by shunning the madness of public life, and tending your secret garden here.'

There was a glint in Jabach's dark eyes which was at variance with his smile.

'I see that you are a true art lover, and I am persuaded that I have done the right thing in bringing you here. Blessed are those places where the great of this world speak like philosophers! I have a rule, Monsieur Superintendent, which applies only to this room. Since I am invariably alone in this room, it is my custom to be totally frank.'

He looked straight into the Superintendent's questioning eyes.

'Will you consent to play according to this rule, until we leave through that door?' asked the banker, pointing to the heavy wooden door he had pulled shut behind them.

Fouquet nodded his agreement.

'Excellent. So, Monsieur, do you think that I chose this policy of discretion? Not at all. It was imposed on me by my will to survive. I am not well liked, Monsieur Superintendent. People have need of me, my money and my *savoir-faire*. But I do not receive invitations. People may see me in the evening or at a meeting. But they do not "know" me. Who is aware that I knew Rubens as a friend, in Antwerp? Nobody. What can I say? One does not dine with Jabach . . .'

Fouquet made an effort to conceal his unease. Was this the mysterious Jabach's flaw? Did he dream of entering Court society, encouraged by the influence his discretion had earned him?

'You have shown me your secret garden; I shall be happy to show you my own. Would you like to come to Vaux? I am planning a reception there as soon as the works are sufficiently well advanced – I shall let you know the date.'

Jabach bowed and smiled as Fouquet continued.

'I too like the rule you have established for the use of this room. Shall we try to talk for a while about the other subjects that bring me here?'

Jabach's expression took on an element of greed.

'As you wish, Monsieur Superintendent, but is it really advisable to talk openly about business?'

'This deal is so simple that the risk is not great: I need one million livres for my account within eight days.'

Jabach clasped his hands beneath his chin and sighed.

'For your account?' he asked suspiciously. 'Openness demands clarity, Monsieur Superintendent: for your account or for the King's account? For one is good but the other – openness demands this,' he added, indicating the walls and the door '– is less so . . . Having seen loans not repaid, securities guaranteed by Treasury receipts suddenly transformed at a stroke into ordinary securities, that is to say into thin air . . .'

Fouquet felt irritation overtaking him. *He really intends to stick to the rule and he is adept at using it to his advantage*, he thought.

'The money is for my account, Monsieur, and both the guarantee and the repayments will come from my own pocket. But the service for which this money will be used is indeed the King's.'

Jabach looked doubtful.

'You are taking terrible risks, Monsieur Superintendent. A crown is a heavy burden to wear when one is not its owner . . . And as for the gratitude of Kings . . .'

Fouquet cut him short with a wave of the hand.

'Let us leave it there, Monsieur. It is all very well to be frank, but there are some areas which are best left unexplored. Suffice it to say that faithfulness and devotion to a cause do not necessarily render one blind. Besides, I am an old hand at these exercises. Twenty years of practice in financing war have taught me everything I need to know.'

Jabach opened his arms wide and smiled as a sign of acceptance.

'Then so be it, Monsieur Superintendent, you are in command, and God preserve me from knowing any more. You shall have your money. That is to say, the money,' he corrected himself, indicating the door.

As if by magic, the door had just swung open on its hinges.

Fouquet was first to emerge. As he crossed the threshold of the room, he turned back to take one last look at Raphael's *Madonna*.

CHAPTER TWENTY-TWO

Château de Vincennes — Sunday 27 February, ten o'clock
in the morning

Toussaint Roze dipped his quill pen into the inkwell, carefully wiped away the excess ink, and turned to look at the Cardinal, his arm suspended above a sheet already covered with his small, precise handwriting. Jules Mazarin was sitting in his comfortable armchair, which was upholstered in red and green stripes and embossed with his coat of arms. As he dictated, he frantically juggled the few sheets of paper that littered his desk:

'"And we give to the community of the Brothers of the Humility of Christ . . ." Ah, but where are they?' he grumbled.

Colbert, who was standing behind his master, swiftly extracted a sheet buried under a pile and calmly indicated a line which had been crossed out several times.

'Yes, yes.' Mazarin seized the document. 'Note this down, Roze: "we give the sum of one thousand livres, and the enjoyment by full ownership of the benefice attached to the parish of Saint-Fiacre de . . ." Oh, a plague upon the village!' he raged.

Closing his eyes, he let himself fall back, struggling for breath.

'Rabastens,' whispered Colbert, who nodded to Roze's questioning look that he should note down this name.

'Rabastens, that's the one. And now we have finished with the abbeys, have we not?'

Colbert nodded and was about to take away the pile of jumbled papers corresponding to each chapter when Mazarin's hand suddenly stopped him, as though it had received a jolt of energy. His voice grew harder:

'But we have not seen the Châtellerault living, which I have promised to Abbé Soulet, have we?'

Colbert looked sour but did not reply.

'Write, Roze,' said Mazarin icily: '"and as a sign of the friendship, yes, yes, of the friendship we bear towards Abbé Soulet, we give the benefice of the living of the Église Saint-Roch in Châtellerault and the surrounding land, which amounts to . . ." You will have to ask Monsieur Colbert for the overall surface area; he must know it, since he crossed it off the list.'

Without looking at Colbert, Mazarin allowed a second to elapse before he continued frostily:

'I do not know what grievances you hold against him, Colbert, but now is not the time to settle the score. And never forget that no score is settled in this house without my being informed.'

'I thought it pointless to trouble Your Eminence . . .' exclaimed Colbert.

'That is enough,' cut in Mazarin, 'I am not yet in my senile death-throes. And it never wearies me to hear talk of rewards and punishments. In fact, organising their distribution has been one of my life's rare entertainments,' he added, his voice benevolent once again. 'Come, Messieurs, let us move on to the officers of the King.'

The morning dragged on. Roze voiced his concern several

times at the growing fatigue of the Cardinal, who was visibly exhausted after drafting text for four hours without a break.

'All that remains is for me to sign?' asked the Cardinal, his voice barely audible. 'I shall do so later; my trembling hand would leave a signature unworthy of the archives of France. What is the total?' he asked Roze.

The secretary's tongue protruded as, one last time, he mechanically added up in the margin of the drafted will the figures accumulated during the morning and over the past few days.

'Forty-two, three, seven and five make twelve, add . . . Forty-seven million, six hundred and ninety-four thousand two hundred and thirty-three livres, not including the books that have not been valued, and pending a further valuation of the works of art personally owned by Your Eminence and the most valuable gemstones, which are to be bequeathed to the royal family. The "English Rose", a fourteen-carat diamond, for the Queen Mother, a cluster of fifty diamonds for the Queen, thirty-one emeralds for Monsieur . . .'

Mazarin interrupted the tally with a wave of his hand.

'There is no need to go back over it in detail. Simply read me the codicil for the Queen Mother which follows the insertion concerning the diamond. I want to be sure I have worded it correctly . . .'

Roze leafed through the bundle of papers beside him.

'"We give to the Queen . . .",' his slow voice was still searching, '"everything she would like from our palace in Paris." That's it, Eminence.'

'Yes, that is right,' commented Mazarin.

In the ensuing silence, Colbert narrowed his eyes. His two

thumbs linked on his belt toyed mechanically with each other. Mazarin sat motionless, apparently lost in thought.

'All that,' he murmured, 'to be leaving all that . . .'

Then, emerging from his dream with some regret, he turned to Colbert.

'Is the clause regarding secrecy adequate? Is it precise enough?'

'It is, Eminence: no viewing by anyone save the executors, no publication, and no records open to anyone except the King.'

'Good,' commented Mazarin. 'Monsieur Roze,' he said, turning towards his secretary, who was rolling sand across the last page to help it dry more quickly, 'we have worked hard. I shall give you your freedom for the rest of today. Kindly re-read what has been written with great care, and remember that this copy must be seen by no one, nor altered in the future by anyone but me.'

Roze bowed, closed up his writing case, carefully fastened the portfolio containing the documents and left without further ado.

Mazarin got to his feet and approached Colbert.

'What about my business associates? Can you be sure of their silence too?'

'I would swear to it, Eminence, all the more so since these transactions have proved extremely lucrative for them as well.'

'And the total?' he murmured, 'the total figure, Colbert? Is it credible?'

Colbert sighed.

'We have already made a great many adjustments, Eminence . . . And you cannot make gifts without these signs of your generosity being reflected in your assets. But as it stands, yes, I think our inventory is well supported and plausible.'

His pursed his lips, reflecting.

'Unless, of course, the thieves carried off secret papers which might be incriminating,' he remarked. 'The rubbish posted on church doors over the past few days is sufficiently worrying. The source of it is crystal clear: these same burglars have now turned to journalism. Fortunately the unrest has not spread and seems to be dying down . . . for the moment. The people who read the posters were not able to follow the gibberish written on them; Maximilien Piton, who is mentioned in the lampoons, is in Holland on business for several weeks – I shall see him on his return – and your guards have taken down the majority of the notices. They continue to do so, as more appeared in certain districts of the city this very morning . . .'

Mazarin shuddered, then pulled himself together: *Colbert could not know and must not yet know.*

'Of course, of course,' he said evasively. 'But I must have results. Is the investigation progressing?'

'It is making progress, Eminence. But it would help if we knew what we were looking for.'

Mazarin looked annoyed.

'That is not important. It is the thieves who must be found. You said it yourself just now: they are the same people. Wherever they are, there too will be the documents! But to return to our subject: the total sum. It is still a problem.'

'Not if no one is allowed to examine the accounts or transactions of exchange.'

'No one must examine them,' thundered Mazarin. 'No one.'

'Nor will they, Excellency.'

'But what if my enemies should get it into their heads to

contest the will? A will can be nullified: I know that, for I myself nullified the will of the late King Louis XIII! And what if they take their opposition to the Parlement? Not everyone there is a friend of mine!'

The Cardinal paced around the room in silence.

'In fact, they are all my enemies.'

'Monsieur Fouquet is the Procureur General,' said Colbert treacherously.

Mazarin did not respond, but shot him a look of exasperation.

Colbert smiled unpleasantly:

'Eminence, I may perhaps have a way of ridding you of this unbearable doubt, a way which would guarantee the soundness of your will, render it unassailable, prevent any investigation into the origin of the possessions bequeathed, and thus ensure the continuance of your arrangements and, above all, your lineage.'

Mazarin shivered:

'Then speak, Colbert!'

'All you need to do is to make a gift of all your possessions, Eminence. In that way, you will no longer own anything, nobody can take anything away from you, and if someone wishes to initiate a court case, they will have to initiate it against someone else.'

Mazarin, his face ashen, seemed almost to suffocate.

'But . . . you have lost your mind!'

Tottering, he caught hold of the back of his armchair. Colbert offered him an arm and helped him sit down again. Then he brought his large, round head close to the Cardinal's. The cleric's breath was coming in short, wheezing gasps, and there were drops of sweat on his brow; he made a Herculean effort to compose himself.

'Fear not, Eminence, I am never more in control of my mind than when I am thinking of your affairs,' he said unctuously. 'You shall see that this horrible prospect can be changed into a radiant vista, as one might change the scenery at the Théâtre des Italiens!'

Colbert drew even closer.

'The first stage of my proposal does however suffer from two disadvantages: you lose your possessions, and the court case – admittedly against someone else – may still come to pass. What can we do, then, to circumvent these problems? First of all, your recipient must be beyond the reach of a court case, and second, he must be obliged to cede your possessions back to you. Is that not brilliant?'

Colbert's eyes now shone with a strange light.

'Against whom may one not take out legal action? Why, the King, by Jove! And who is not able to accept a legacy from one of his subjects, even if that subject is his godfather and his Chief Minister?'

Straightening up, Colbert walked behind the desk and, placing both fists onto the leather inlay, looked straight into the Cardinal's eyes.

'So, you give all your possessions to the King. As he is unable to accept, he will restore them to you. But the fortune will no longer be yours: it will have passed through his hands and, in so doing, will have become inviolable.'

Only the Cardinal's gasps for breath disturbed the silence. Triumphantly, Colbert saw that his ingenious idea was taking hold in the old man's mind.

The Cardinal sighed; he laid a hand over one of Colbert's as it rested on the desk.

'Dear Colbert . . .' was all he said.

Then, opening his eyes and fixing Colbert with his piercing gaze:

'But are you certain that he will refuse? The coffers are empty . . .'

'I heard that Monsieur Fouquet arranged for a new loan two days ago to cover his immediate needs. And anyway . . . Does the King's pride not outweigh his greed? Louis XIV wants to rule, Eminence: that comes with a price.'

Surprised by the audacity of these words, Mazarin frowned.

'Well then, let us do it, Monsieur Colbert,' he said, resigned. 'I place myself in your hands. Confer with Roze to arrange for a codicil to this effect. I shall sign as soon as my hand has rested.'

Colbert bowed and was about to leave when the Cardinal called him back.

'No, you shall write it yourself, Colbert, no one must know. Only the Queen; she will talk to her son.'

Beaming, Colbert bowed once again.

'As you command, Eminence,' he said with immense gravity.

'Next we shall speak of Hortense's marriage contract, and of Marie's. My God,' he added as if to himself, 'what a burden this is, my God . . .'

The sound of the door closing informed him that Colbert had left.

CHAPTER TWENTY-THREE

Mazarin's palace – Monday 28 February, five o'clock in the afternoon

'AND who is he?'

Julie leant her head towards Gabriel and whispered.

'That man there,' she replied, pointing discreetly, 'is the Prince de Condé, and the lady is the Palatine princess. She has been furious ever since Olympe Mancini started scheming to take over the stewardship of the Queen's house at her expense. See how angry she looks! The lady she's talking to, that's Louise de Gonzague, the wife of the King of Poland and former lady-friend of Cinq-Mars. Oh look, behind her is the Duc de Vendôme. And there's Madame de Chevreuse. How funny this is, all the old supporters of the Fronde reunited at the Cardinal's palace after they've conspired against him for so long.'

Amused by the young girl's excitement, Gabriel looked at her in wonder:

'But how do you know all this?'

'Goodness me, Monsieur Apprentice Actor, in the theatre we perform for the courtiers. And a craftsman who doesn't know a thing about his customers cannot serve them properly. Would you go to a cobbler who didn't know anything about your feet?'

Gabriel smiled and shook his head. Standing in the shadow of a pillar, with their elbows resting on the balustrade which ran all the way around the gallery overlooking the grand vestibule, the two young people watched the procession of guests who had attended the wedding mass in the Cardinal's private chapel, and were now heading for the reception halls.

'What time are the entertainments?' whispered Gabriel, suddenly serious again.

'We have time,' giggled Julie. 'Unless Monsieur Molière comes looking for you,' she added teasingly.

'You're right,' said Gabriel. 'I'll go and see if he needs me.'

And before Julie had time to object, he headed for the stair-case that led to the ground floor.

Downstairs, the sight of so many festive gowns and robes was even more impressive. Everything sparkled with opulence, right down to the livery of the lackeys who circulated amongst the guests to offer refreshments. Gabriel suddenly spotted the newlyweds and flattened himself against the wall in the shadows. Dressed in a sumptuous purple and gold gown which emphasised the fifteen-year-old's radiance, Hortense Mancini was more ostentatiously languid than usual as she took the arm of the man who had been her husband for the past hour: Armand Charles de La Porte de La Meilleraye.

'They signed the contracts this morning in front of the Cardinal himself,' Julie had explained, 'and they took the name of Mazarin. From now on they'll bear it along with the titles of Duc and Duchesse, to secure the Cardinal's lineage. He gave them a gift of more than a million livres, and guaranteed them his collection of antiques and half of his palace,' she'd told him eagerly, as if this largesse might be contagious. 'People are even saying that he might make them his sole legatees.'

Gabriel's silence had not cooled Julie's enthusiasm.

'You know, the Cardinal chose Maréchal de La Meilleraye's son in preference to Charles Edouard de Savoie and even Charles II, the current King of England! Even though he's almost twice her age! And do you know why? Because he's the grand-nephew of Cardinal de Richelieu through his mother, Marie de Cossé. Through him, Mazarin has reunited his family with Richelieu's and assured them a place in history.'

Behind the married couple came one of Hortense's sisters, Marie, who was visibly moved by the marriage, perhaps because her own was fixed for only a few weeks' time.

'See how sad she looks,' Julie had said, moved to pity. 'People say she weeps for the King, because she was desperately in love with him. And loved by him in return,' she had added, emphasising each syllable. 'And now she's leaving for Italy to marry a complete stranger: Onulphe Colonna, Prince of Naples . . .'

Glancing towards the main entrance, all Gabriel could see was an impressive rank of guards. The rumble of conversation drowned the music played by the chamber orchestra, led by a small, nervous man whom Julie had pointed out to him as a very promising Italian composer called Lulli, recently arrived in France.

'Gabriel?'

The exclamation made the young man jump.

'Louise!' he replied happily at the sight of his friend.

'Don't tell me you were looking for me?'

'To tell the truth, no, I'm looking for Molière, but he must be sorting out the playlets for the supper entertainment. I'll probably find him in the main hall.'

The girl touched his arm.

'You can't imagine how pleased I am to see you. You'll never guess what happened: the King spoke to me! It's true, as true as you are standing there! The King of France spoke to me!'

'Child . . .'

Gabriel smiled and replaced a blonde ringlet which had slipped down over the young woman's face, before realising how inappropriate this gesture was. Seeing him start, Louise understood his concern and drew him behind one of the pillars that supported the colonnade.

'Take care, Monsieur! You call yourself an actor, but you're not playing your part very well!'

'Don't joke about it,' Gabriel cut in, his tone serious. 'You know what will happen to me if I am recognised. Fortunately, nobody looks at actors. It's a rather curious paradox. Louise, what's the matter?' he added, noticing that she was no longer listening to him.

Putting his arm round her shoulder, he turned and saw what had attracted her attention.

'The King,' she whispered, blushing.

The royal couple were indeed entering the hall, prompting a wave of movement and a distinctive rustling sound. They walked serenely through the corridor of people which had formed to allow them passage.

'They're on their way to the Cardinal's apartments. He came back from Vincennes this afternoon after the contracts were signed, first to be in his chapel and now here,' murmured a voice very close to them.

Looking up, Gabriel could not identify who had spoken. As he observed the still-dreamy Louise out of the corner of his eye, a liveried lackey from the King's household detached himself from the troupe following the royal pair and suddenly appeared right in front of them.

'Mademoiselle de La Vallière?' he asked in a tone which indicated that he already knew the answer.

When Louise nodded, the man removed an envelope from the left sleeve of his livery, bowed, and handed it to her. Then, without further explanation, he disappeared.

Rooted to the spot, Louise turned to Gabriel and showed him the paper.

'A note from the Duchess no doubt,' he said, laughing in his friend's ear, 'or perhaps a copy of that lampoon against the Cardinal . . .'

She shrugged her shoulders and sighed.

'That's not very amusing,' she said, breaking the seal on the paper.

Thinking that he had spotted Molière at the back of the room, Gabriel stood on tiptoe and saw the familiar figure disappear in the direction of the dining room. Turning back to Louise to tell her that he was off to track down his master, he was struck by the young woman's pallor and the distracted expression on her delicate features.

'Louise,' he said gently, with a frown. 'Louise.'

She stood clasping the letter tightly, but did not respond. Gabriel took her by the arm.

'What is it?'

She raised her blue eyes towards him, infinitely slowly. In them he saw a strange brightness, like excitement mingled with a little fear.

'The King, Gabriel, the King . . .'

'The King?' Gabriel coaxed her, understanding nothing.

'He's the one who had this letter brought to me.'

The young man's eyes widened.

Louise turned crimson and bit her lip.

'I must go,' she said, drawing back.

'But where?' Gabriel asked, following her.

She turned aside again.

'I don't know, to get some air.'

The voice which rang out behind them made them start. They turned to see the Superintendent of Finance's ironic smile.

'Well, well, it's our friend the political actor! Monsieur Molière is sweating profusely at the thought of this evening's spectacle, and here you are enjoying yourself! You see, Monsieur de La Fontaine, this is the young man I spoke to you about the other day. I told you he had spirit; and he must certainly be cherished by Providence, for he seems to have good luck, too,' he said for his companion's benefit, with a small bow to Louise de La Vallière.

Disconcerted, she gave a small curtsey. Gabriel stammered as he introduced her, not realising that Fouquet was poking fun at him, an actor with a taste for high society.

'Go, Monsieur, go and join Monsieur Molière; I have seen how valuable you are to him when he is worried.' The Superintendent smiled. 'As for you, Mademoiselle, our meeting is both a pleasure and a source of concern to me. My friends had in fact told me how much your presence at Court has raised its prestige: but I am disappointed that their description was so much less than the truth, and delighted to be able to correct it with my own eyes.'

Then the Superintendent bowed and, without waiting for a response, continued on his way across the hall, with La Fontaine following in his wake.

Colbert, who had appeared in the doorway to the Cardinal's apartments to estimate the number of revellers, feigned indifference as he watched them pass by. Sweeping the remainder of the room, his piercing gaze lighted on the figures conversing in the shadow cast by the pillar.

'It's them again,' he muttered: 'Fouquet has just left La Vallière and that Gabriel fellow. All three of them together this time. I swear I shall get to the bottom of this.' He raised his voice to address the butler who was with him:

'Come, it is time for everyone to be seated. Go and inform the Cardinal and ensure that the roast meats are prepared. And tell the actors to be ready to start.'

'I have to go,' Gabriel told Louise. 'Are you sure you're better now?'

'Yes go, my friend, go,' Louise reassured him with a small smile that scarcely brightened her now-pallid face. 'I shall go home to rest. I will be in touch.'

Regretfully, the young man went off to the dining room. The doors were now open, allowing glimpses of the immense tables separated by giant candelabra whose light complemented that of the twelve chandeliers suspended from the ceiling. Each table was covered in gold and silver-gilt plates and cutlery, and surrounded by a bustle of liveried lackeys who rushed about bearing silver platters laden with game, meat and fish shaped into pyramids and geometric forms. Motionless, Louise seemed to be watching the revellers who were leaving the room and heading for the wedding supper. The enigmatic note seemed to be burning the palm of her hand. *The King has invited me to Versailles*, she thought, once again feeling her head spin. *To Versailles, and it is a 'secret' which we share, he wrote that word.* She smiled without realising. *I share a secret with His Majesty!*

And, as though terrified by her own thoughts, she hurried towards the exit.

CHAPTER TWENTY-FOUR

Château de Vincennes — Tuesday 1 March, noon

'How sad, he's just like Mascarille!'[1]

'The procession is pitiful and the spectacle ridiculous,' replied the courtier, who nevertheless bowed deeply in deference as the sedan chair bearing His Eminence passed by.

At around eleven o'clock that morning, the Cardinal had demanded to be dressed, powdered and attended by his barber in order to 'show himself to the good common folk'. With infinite difficulty and proceeding cautiously, Jules Mazarin's devoted servants had succeeded first in getting the sick man out of bed, and then dressing him. In order to try and hide his greenish complexion, his cheeks had been rouged. The Cardinal had even insisted on having his hair curled.

Thus attired, the most powerful man in France had taken the air for almost an hour in the gardens of the Château de Vincennes, obliging the numerous visitors and beggars of all kinds to bow each time he passed by.

The sick old man suffered horribly in his chair and cursed 'the damned useless bearers'. At each painful jolt he groaned and threatened them with the gallows. Jules Mazarin had no notion what a grotesque spectacle he presented. He sincerely

---

1 Mascarille was a shrewd servant in Molière's *L'Étourdi*.

thought that he could deceive people by waving a greeting at courtiers as he passed along the sunny pathways.

'Ten years ago,' said the Cardinal out loud, 'ten years ago I was driven from the Kingdom by the same people who bow before me this morning. Well, the Italian is going to show them that he is still very much alive!'

The Cardinal then reached into his pocket for a small gold box. From it he took a fragrant pastille and placed it in his mouth to combat his bad breath, which had become unbearable. Then, dozing off all of a sudden, he dreamt that he was reliving the terrible days of February 1651. That tragic month ten years earlier had begun with Nicolas Fouquet's marriage, after many years as a widower, to the young and beautiful Marie-Madeleine of Castille, who was just fifteen. That same day, 4 February, Parlement had spent from six in the morning until six at night feverishly discussing a decree which would expel him. As he dozed, the Cardinal once again heard the footsteps of those who had been allowed to enter the Louvre during the night of 9 February: the common people of Paris, filing respectfully past the foot of Louis XIV's bed to assure themselves that he was not about to leave them. He remembered the terrible humiliation for the extremely young King, who was traumatised by this nocturnal sight for a long time thereafter. And then he saw himself on the road to Le Havre, alone, leaving for exile in Germany.

'The cards, the cards, the cards must be made to speak!' he declared, suddenly emerging from his dream and demanding to be taken back to his apartments forthwith.

His doctors met him at the entrance to his bedchamber. After suffering for several months from acute nephritis, aggravated by pulmonary oedema, the Cardinal had been declining for several days, a decline doubtless exacerbated by the medications inflicted upon him by the Faculty.

'First a clyster, then bleeding followed by purging,' said the first doctor.

'It is vital that he should also drink this emetic wine,' said the second, pointing to the carafe containing a liquid concoction based on antimony and potassium tartrate.

The arrival of Anne of Austria put an end to the learned gentlemen's debate around their prestigious patient. Out of respect, they left the room. Mazarin smiled, relieved to be rid of those leeches and pleased to see the woman who had brought him so much happiness throughout his life.

'Jules, I have received reports of imprudent behaviour. Did you go out into the gardens this morning?'

Without replying, the old man smiled at the King's mother. He loved to gaze upon the features he knew so well, and to lose himself in the gentle sweetness of those eyes. The silence lasted a long time.

'I have dictated my will. You should know, Madame, that I have decided to bequeath my entire fortune to the King of France,' he said in a weak voice. 'As I prepare to meet God, it seems to me right that I should give back these possessions which, alas, were often improperly acquired!'

'My dear Jules, this act honours you and I regard it as further proof of your constancy in being a true father to my son,' said the Queen Mother, whose eyes had grown misty with tears. 'But you know perfectly well that the King of France cannot accept it,' she sobbed. Thinking that she had wounded the Cardinal, she then added: 'Your legacy is magnificent. You crushed the Fronde, brought back order to our provinces and made peace with Spain. In bringing about this marriage between Louis and the Infanta Maria Theresa, you have also opened up a new era of serenity for the Kingdom of France. This sound foundation, along with everything he has learned from you, will enable our dear child to display his talent in the future by making your conquests bear fruit. If, as you often predict, "he goes further than previous monarchs", such will be your legacy.'

'Well, if Louis refuses my will, so much the better,' replied the Cardinal enigmatically.

Clearly the day's efforts had exhausted the old man. The Queen Mother decided to withdraw, to allow him to rest. As she was leaving the bedchamber, she passed the fortune-teller who had come to read the cards at the Chief Minister's request. This encounter, together with Jules Mazarin's surprising words, aroused her suspicions: *What if illness was causing the Chief Minister to lose his mind?*

CHAPTER TWENTY-FIVE

Église Saint-Roch – Saturday 5 March, five o'clock in the evening

THE Église Saint-Roch was dear to Louis XIV's heart. He had laid the first stone in 1653, and on this late afternoon it was full to bursting. Throughout Paris, prayers were being said for the salvation of the Cardinal who was dying at Vincennes. This was exceptional, for up until then this forty-hour period of prayer had been reserved for those of royal blood. Everyone realised that this was the King's way of demonstrating his great esteem for his godfather.

In Vincennes, the crowd of supplicants at the Chief Minister's bedside was growing by the hour, each hoping to obtain one last favour from His Eminence, or indeed the benefit of a final codicil to his will. As for the ordinary folk of the capital, they had responded to the priests' calls. If the truth be told, Mazarin was not particularly well liked by Parisians, notably because of his foreign roots and the somewhat dubious origins of his wealth. But France recognised his positive role in promoting the unity of the country, and had not forgotten that he had been the architect of peace with Spain.

This atmosphere of collective fervour and sadness had aroused Gabriel's curiosity, so he joined the crowd at Saint-Roch. There, in the calm of the church, he was happy to have found a place where he could reflect on the riddle of his father's signature. His feeling of unease had been heightened by a visit from his washerwoman a few hours earlier. She had come to tell him about the suspicious comings and goings of mysterious strangers around his lodgings. Hiding the documents as best he could, he had decided to step out for some air. *I can't stay here doing nothing, waiting for those criminals to come and find me*, he admonished himself.

So, as sacred music echoed beneath the church's high, vaulted ceiling, the actor was not thinking of the young laundress's charms, although he was not indifferent to them, but of the documents contained in the red leather case. His father's signature gave these papers a precious link to a past which intrigued him. Gabriel had not known his father well; according to his mother, he had died during a journey to London. He had gone there to sell the wine produced on his lands in Touraine. Gabriel had been five years old at the time and was left with nothing but a few fragmented memories of the man he had so missed during his childhood and adolescence. That was why he had decided to keep the papers whatever happened, even if it were to endanger his life. Gabriel was more determined than ever to unlock their secret and find out how his father could be mixed up in a mystery which seemed to concern so many people.

I must find a way of discovering what this is all about. A specialist in codes, that's what I need, he thought. But no matter how much he turned the problem over in his mind, he could think of no one capable of helping him. *Unless* . . . he thought, as he left the church at the end of the service.

*

The outer sanctuary of the church was crowded with worshippers, and Gabriel had to elbow his way through to get down the steps. Just as he reached the street, a firm hand grabbed him by the shoulder. Turning, the young man recognised the bandaged face of the man whose nose he had broken at the theatre, to save the life of the old doorman. Gabriel pulled free of his grip and fled. The sound of running feet in the street behind him told him that at least two people were following him. Running as fast as he could, he managed to weave between the traders crowding the narrow streets of Paris, selling dairy products, sand, rags and a thousand other things.

'Where do I go now?' he wondered, running from one alleyway to another. 'Not to my lodgings, that's for sure: the police are bound to be waiting for me! Louise, I'll go to Louise's apartment. At least I'll be safe there.'

Ten minutes later, he arrived breathless at the door of Louise de La Vallière's residence. Her apartment was on one of the upper floors of a private house belonging to Monsieur, the King's brother. It looked out onto a narrow street with ill-smelling drains.

Gabriel ran up the stairs in a flash.

'Louise, it's me, Gabriel. Open up!' he gasped.

'Whatever is the matter?' exclaimed Louise de La Vallière as she opened the door to her friend.

Her blonde hair had been hastily piled into a chignon, from which strands escaped and hung loose about her cheeks.

'I was getting ready for dinner. But you're out of breath, as if you've been fighting!'

'I'll explain,' he replied, diving inside the apartment.

Simply furnished but decorated with brightly coloured tapestries, Louise's room exuded calm. As he got his breath back, Gabriel savoured the pleasure of seeing how his friend lived. Then he told her what had happened that evening, without mentioning the documents he had discovered at the theatre.

'But at least,' she told him after she had listened attentively, 'you have nothing to fear from the police; they must be watching you and the rest of the actors in Molière's troupe after Mazarin's fire and the discovery of that dead boy you told me about before. As for those men . . .' she trailed off.

'As for those men,' said Gabriel, 'they are pursuing me for something, but I don't know what it is they're after. It's all very worrying, especially since, as you know, I have to be careful.'

'I do,' said Louise. 'Perhaps the men were sent by your uncle?'

'I thought of that, but if that is the case why would they attack the concierge?'

Before Louise could reply, there was another knock at her door. This time it was the connecting door between her apartment and that of Henrietta of England, fiancée of the King's brother, whose companion she was.

'Louise,' moaned a voice punctuated by sobs.

Louise immediately recognised the voice of Henrietta, who was in Paris to prepare for her wedding which was to take place in May. She was astonished by this most unusual intrusion. Before opening the door, she pushed Gabriel into the bathroom:

'Wait for me in here, and whatever you do, don't make a sound. No one must know that you're here with me this evening!'

When she opened the door, Louise found the King of France's future sister-in-law collapsed on the threshold, in tears.

'Madame, please get up, I beg of you! What is wrong?' cried the young woman, disconcerted by her mistress's great sorrow.

She put an affectionate arm around her and helped her to her feet.

'The King's own brother, my future husband,' sobbed Henrietta, struggling to get her breath back to finish her sentence, 'he's being unfaithful to me,' she sniffed. 'I have proof that he's deceiving me with a man!'

CHAPTER TWENTY-SIX

Hôtel d'Orléans – Saturday 5 March, seven o'clock in the evening

Hiding in the bathroom where he had been hurriedly secreted by Louise, Gabriel heard her footsteps moving away across the wooden floor of the bedroom. Then the door closed again, and the young man was plunged into silence. The white-walled room was small and not excessively luxurious, and contained a well-made copper hip-bath as well as an earthenware bowl surmounted by a large mirror framed in gilded wood. Spotting a chair, Gabriel pushed it up against the wall and climbed onto it, bringing his head up to the level of the open skylight. Putting his elbows and chin on the edge, he was able to see the sky and by leaning over a little more and standing on the tips of his toes, he could make out the residence's paved courtyard.

Ah well, he thought, *I'm stuck here now for goodness knows how long. I can only hope that Monsieur's fiancée doesn't go on for too long.*

He was about to get down from his perch when two footmen rushed forward to open the great double gates, which then admitted a coach drawn by four horses. Gabriel saw the outline of a woman descend, walk towards the front steps, and then disappear from his field of vision. Intrigued, he got down and sat on the chair, trying to recite Act I of *Dom Garcie* to himself to pass the time.

His memory exercise was interrupted after a few minutes by the sound of a woman's voice which seemed distant, but distinct. Listening carefully, Gabriel looked around the room to identify the source of the sound.

'. . . to tell you the news without delay,' said the woman.

There was the sound of footsteps and moving furniture, then a few phrases he could not make out. But he thought he heard the name 'La Vallière', and listened twice as intently. Then there was a man's voice, followed by the woman's who said:

'. . . you consider that he was awaiting the King's decision,'

The man's voice thundered:

'Decision! What a grand word! Does my brother think he has taken a decision?'

Recognising the voice of Monsieur, the Duc d'Orléans, Gabriel went over to the corner of the room from where the sound seemed to be coming. He noticed a small grate set into the tiled floor. The room's ventilation shaft was clearly linked to the chimney flue of a fireplace in one of the salons on the floor below, thus offering a channel of indiscretion.

The man's voice was filled with anger:

'Your uncle is far too cunning to have given him the choice. Did he give him a choice in the matter of your sister?'

There was a silence before the woman's voice spoke again, annoyed now:

'Indeed not, Monseigneur, but this minx . . .'

'Olympe Mancini,' murmured Gabriel to himself, recalling the face of the young woman Julie had pointed out to him at Hortense's wedding. 'It must be her, and the sister she is talking about is Marie, the King's first love. But what is she doing here?'

'The rumour has been verified, Monseigneur,' said Olympe Mancini. 'The Cardinal has made a gift of his entire fortune to the Crown. And it is also true that the King has just refused this bequest, returning my dear uncle's possessions to him.'

All Gabriel could hear in the ensuing silence was heavy footsteps, which he imagined belonged to the King's brother. They stopped and his voice went on:

'Well, what an audacious wager! One doesn't give away millions of livres every day, even when one is dying. The Cardinal still has the power to astonish us.'

'For my part, I detect the influence of external advice which I can easily imagine to be Monsieur Colbert's. He hardly leaves my uncle's side now, has assisted him at each stage in drawing up the documents, and has just been appointed the only writer fit to work on the text. And if any further proof of his influence were needed, the fear which gripped my uncle this morning before the King made known his answer to him speaks volumes . . . I thought that his illness was responsible for his grey complexion, but seeing as he recovered as soon as the news was brought by the Queen Mother, it seems the Cardinal really did fear right to the end that his sovereign might take him at his word.'

'Candour obliges me to say that, although this is a triumph for Monsieur Colbert, we must all rejoice that the manoeuvre has succeeded: You are an heir, by Jove, but so am I, if your information is correct. And by the grace of my brother, we are now heirs with the value of our bequests guaranteed. Making him wait three days, three days before giving his answer . . .'

Monsieur's voice took on an amused tone.

'In truth, it is a gesture befitting royalty and my brother is acting in accordance with his office!'

The voice became serious once more.

'All the same, the Cardinal must have been worried if he was moved to dream up such a stratagem! Is his wealth so enormous? Undoubtedly it is.'

'I believe that he was unsettled by the fire the other day. And his staff's concern to cover up the incident sounds curious to me,' replied Olympe.

'So you believe these rumours about papers being stolen?'

'Having heard him when he was delirious the other day, in bed and half asleep, I really do believe that the fire coincided with the loss or the theft of something which was very dear to him . . .'

'Well, Madame, I know you were willing to rush here from Vincennes to bring me this news,' went on the King's brother, 'but what of this other subject you wished to discuss with me which, you say, concerns a companion of my future wife?'

'Mademoiselle de La Vallière, yes, Monseigneur.'

At the sound of Louise's name, Gabriel shivered and went even closer to the grille to hear more clearly.

'I would just like to put you on your guard, Monseigneur. Mademoiselle de La Vallière was presented to the King a few days ago.'

'Well?'

'The King did her the honour of speaking to her. Nothing more than a few pleasantries, you will tell me. What is rather less mundane is the fact that the King has written to her.'

'Written to her?' repeated Monsieur, intrigued.

'Yes, Monseigneur, and if my information is correct, which I have every reason to believe it is, he has written to her in terms which are strongly suggestive of a rendezvous.'

'Interesting, interesting. This is nothing new, although my brother doesn't usually take the trouble to write. Everything depends on what happens next, and also on the young woman's mettle. Is she pretty?' he asked in a cold voice which betrayed his lack of real interest in the subject.

Olympe Mancini replied in a neutral tone that Mademoiselle de La Vallière was fresh and charming.

'Appetising?' enquired the King's brother.

'You could say so.'

'We must keep an eye on the matter, Madame. Times are changing and your uncle's succession will not only bring each of us increased financial security, it will also redraw the maps of power. In this game, each pawn we have on my brother's side will be a useful mechanism to advance our cause. And we must ensure that we take account of everyone's ambitions, and I do mean everyone. So we shall keep an eye on this young girl, just in case.'

'I shall see to it personally, Monseigneur,' replied Olympe.

Gabriel shuddered at the cold, metallic way in which she spoke those words. The prince's voice betrayed annoyance.

'I hope she can also calm the rages of my future wife. Her nonsensical prattling is putting me in an ill-temper . . .'

The voices became more distant, until he could no longer hear them. Then the footsteps died away and a door slammed. For a moment, silence returned. It appeared infinitely long to Gabriel, whose head was pounding. Louise . . . a rendezvous with the King? And threats towards her? How could he defend her without appearing to know anything? He broke into a sweat. And yet another mention of the lost papers and the red leather case which reminded him of his father and represented so many intimate things to him. How was he to decipher the documents? How could he make head or tail of it all?

'Gracious me, dear Gabriel, what an expression – you look as though you've seen a ghost!'

Louise's mischievous face was framed in the half-open door.

CHAPTER TWENTY-SEVEN

Paris, Mademoiselle de Scudéry's salon — Sunday 6 March,
nine o'clock in the evening

As the churches of Paris still echoed with prayers for the soul of Cardinal Mazarin, one of the capital's most fashionable salons was buzzing with its guests' many conversations. Society life stopped for no man; nothing seemed able to interrupt its course. Who was going to succeed as Chief Minister? Would Fouquet and Le Tellier fall into disgrace? And who would replace them? Everyone had their own ideas on the subject, according to their friendships or interests.

Madeleine de Scudéry, mistress of the salon, pirouetted from group to group in search of confidential snippets or the latest news about one or other of the Kingdom's inhabitants. Her loyalty to the Superintendent of Finance was well known. The author of *Clélie, histoire romaine*, she regarded Nicolas Fouquet as a Richelieu-like protector of the arts; in this period of political transition, she continually made strenuous efforts to sing the praises of the lord of Vaux-le-Vicomte. Her salon was one of the most popular and accommodated a random assortment of nobles who lacked any real political role, members of the bourgeoisie in search of recognition, and artists in search of a patron or an admirer. This evening, one of the attractions of the reception was the presence of Blaise Pascal, the genius who had created the arithmetical machine and a brilliant scholar of physics and mathematics. In fact, Pascal scarcely ever went out since his accident at Neuilly, on 24 November 1654. That evening, after his brush with death, Pascal had written a fervent text inspired by his encounter with God. Since that date he had become a brilliant theologian, and spent less and less time in society circles. This man whom everyone admired, and who was already afflicted by illness, was engrossed in conversation with Molière.

'Well, I would wager on Zongo Ondedei. The bishop of Fréjus seems to me to be the man best suited to succeed His Eminence.'

'There is also much talk about the Maréchal de Villeroy,' replied the ever-cautious author of *Les Précieuses ridicules*, who was unwilling to reveal to Pascal the nature of his current links with the Superintendent.

'The truth is,' said the scholar with a sad smile, 'that this question of succession seems to be the only matter that interests anyone in Paris, when the real subject that ought to occupy us, the only one worthy of any interest, is entirely different: it concerns the stability of the Kingdom. You see,' he continued, noticing Molière's expression of surprise as the playwright wondered where Pascal was leading him, 'the common people have been bled dry; civil wars, religious wars, external wars, all these have taken their toll. They are now incapable of determining whether it is more important for them to be subjects of the King of France, or of a local squire who may tyrannise them and have a much more direct influence on their future . . .'

'That is why we must pray that we are given a strong Chief Minister who is capable of combating these local abuses . . .'

'Not a strong Chief Minister,' Pascal corrected him in measured tones, 'a just King. Where does the strength of a sovereign really lie? Not in weapons, but in the natural support of his people.'

'But that is not in question: it derives from the monarchy's sacred origins!' Molière exclaimed.

'I'm pleased to hear you say so,' smiled Pascal. 'But it won't have escaped you that it was in the name of a sacred cause that our sovereign's grandfather, Henri IV, was assassinated. For my part, I am convinced that it will be necessary in the future for a King not to rely solely on the dictates of divine law for his authority, but to complement that with another more prosaic authority based on recognition of the common people's personal and collective happiness. Faith is vital, and it is a powerful driving force in many ways. I am, however, suspicious of it in politics, and more so with each day that passes.'

'"Complement,"' repeated Molière with quiet admiration for such boldness. 'May it please Heaven that no one misinterprets "complement" as "replace", Monsieur . . . it might be your undoing.'

Pascal gave Molière a distant look.

'Possibly. But people like us might be undone for any number of reasons, or who knows, for no reason at all. Much better to understand why things happen to us . . .'

Olympe Mancini, Comtesse de Soissons, was only a few feet away, dressed in a very severe and sober gown; she had arranged for Louise de La Vallière to be introduced to her.

She was trying to obtain information from the girl about the incident which had allegedly occurred the previous day between Henrietta of England and Monsieur, the King's brother.

'How is your mistress this morning?' asked the Cardinal's niece after the usual exchange of compliments. 'Rumour has it that she has been ill since yesterday evening?'

'His Majesty's future sister-in-law will be happy to know of the Comtesse's concern for her health,' replied Louise evasively.

She realised at that moment that everyone in Paris must have found out about poor Henrietta's misfortune.

'The ways of folk in the capital are very strange', she said to herself, thinking again of Louis XIV, who had recently begun to preoccupy her.

In the neighbouring room, Jean de La Fontaine was involved in a debate between Colbert's supporters and Fouquet's. As a faithful friend, the author was energetically defending the Superintendent of Finance.

Meanwhile, as Molière had insisted on bringing him to this salon, Gabriel was trying without success to find someone who might help him to decipher the papers. An idea came to him just as the author was introducing him to his publisher, the voluble Barbin.

'Monsieur,' said the young actor to Barbin, 'I have a great favour to ask of you.'

'Ask away, my young friend, always ask,' replied Molière's publisher, who was also the owner of a well-known bookshop in the capital.

'Monsieur Molière has entrusted me with an extremely complicated task and I should like to ask for your help with it. In order to enrich the plot of his next play, my master has instructed me to write him a coded document, which he will use to write the character of the spy in the play. But you see, I know nothing of the art of code and I fear that my work will be of little use.'

'There's an interesting idea,' replied Barbin, delighted to learn that his author had started writing again. 'You might usefully ask Bernard Barrême for help. He is a renowned mathematician whose friend I am honoured to be. I'm sure he will turn you into a great expert on the art of codes. Come to my shop tomorrow, and I will give you a letter of recommendation.'

Gabriel smiled at this prospect and then bowed, thanking Barbin and asking him not to reveal to Molière this serious gap in his secretary's knowledge.

But when he noticed Louise de La Vallière talking to Olympe Mancini, the young man froze. He had feared for his friend since the previous day. The sincere concern Louise had shown for his situation, and the natural closeness which had sprung up between them once again, made Gabriel feel even more uneasy. His Eminence's niece had been swift to begin the surveillance she had promised the King's brother. But Gabriel, who was not supposed to know the contents of the correspondence between Louise and the young King, could not think how to inform Louise of what he had learned, or how to warn her of Olympe's machinations.

Just as the young girl smiled at him, clearly pleased to see him there, he turned on his heel and left the salon, telling himself that, after all, dear Louise would doubtless pay more attention to the King's compliments than to an apprentice actor's advice to be careful.

CHAPTER TWENTY-EIGHT

Vincennes – Monday 7 March, eleven o'clock in the morning

Abbé Claude Joly was so absorbed in his preaching that he did not understand his beadle's frantic gestures. Admittedly, at ninety yards long, the 'church of a hundred columns' was extremely dark, despite its twenty-five windows. The priest of Saint-Nicolas-des-Champs finished his sermon and left the transept in the pause provided by the playing of a piece on the organ, one of the finest in Paris. A soldier of the King's guards was waiting by the side chapel.

'Father,' he said solemnly, 'the King requests that you come immediately to Vincennes, to the bedside of His Eminence Cardinal Mazarin, in order to administer the last rites.'

'Go and fetch my oils,' the priest told his beadle at once, realising the urgency of this royal request. 'You will have to ask Father Girardon to finish the service. He's in the sacristy,' he added, and left without bothering to take off his chasuble.

The priest followed the musketeer, climbed into the carriage that was waiting for him at the foot of the front steps, and left the area escorted by eight mounted guards.

At that moment, the Cardinal and his trusted colleague were alone in his bedchamber at Vincennes.

'Colbert, I asked for you because I wish to add a certain codicil to my will,' said the Chief Minister, suddenly appearing to recover a little of his strength.

While Colbert prepared to take down his dictation, the Cardinal sat up in bed, wincing with pain.

'My beloved niece, Olympe, Comtesse de Soissons, is to become Superintendent of the Queen's House,' dictated the old man, aware that these were his very last wishes. 'And the Princesse de Conti is to receive the superintendency of the Queen Mother's house,' he breathed, exhausted.

'Will that be all, Monseigneur?' asked Colbert calmly, although he was infuriated by the latest whims of the Cardinal's nieces.

They will strip him of everything, right up until his last breath, he thought.

'In all conscience, Colbert, ought I not to advise the King to dispense with Monsieur Fouquet?' said Mazarin after a long period of reflection.

Colbert was so surprised by this that he dropped the pen he had been using to write the addenda to the will. The evening before, at the end of the council meeting, Mazarin had assembled Le Tellier, Lionne and Fouquet in the presence of Louis XIV and recommended all three to the King. Had he not said of the Superintendent that he 'gave judicious advice on all matters of State, whatever their nature'? Although inwardly jubilant at this change of course, which for weeks he had been hoping for, the devoted Colbert did not display any reaction, and answered as always without apparent emotion.

'Taking account of the Superintendent's numerous financial

manipulations, I can only advise Your Eminence to exercise the greatest caution. Moreover, the number and power of his supporters must be taken into account before any decision of this nature is made. Finally,' Fouquet's sworn enemy added treacherously, 'the considerable forces the Superintendent has assembled at his estates on Belle-Île could endanger the internal peace of the Kingdom, and cast a dark shadow over His Majesty's future.'

'Thank you for your frankness, my good Colbert; as always you reason solely in the interests of the State and your analysis is prudent and correct. Moreover, as my hours are now numbered, I shall not hide from you the fact that I have recommended you to His Majesty, assuring him that you would manage affairs of State as you would a private house,' whispered the dying man. 'The King has consented to the creation of a third appointment, that of Steward of Finance, which will be given to you as a reward for your dedication,' concluded the Chief Minister, fighting for breath. 'I also wanted your merits to be written into this document in black and white. You shall insert these lines,' he said, handing him a small sheet of paper covered with his handwriting, which was more shaky than usual.

Colbert took it without a word and bowed his head as a sign of gratitude. Swiftly he scanned the first lines, his heart thumping faster as he read the document which guaranteed the success of his ambitions. 'Integrity, fidelity and intelligence, of which I am very sure, having witnessed them in an infinite number of encounters . . . , after experiencing the affection and zeal which the said Monsieur Colbert has shown in serving me for almost twelve years, I cannot speak too highly of the satisfaction I have received from him . . . That is why I approve of everything carried out by Monsieur Colbert, both regarding the general exercise of his power of attorney and in following orders he has received verbally . . . desire that Monsieur Colbert's word should be believed as regards everything that has been received, spent and managed at his command, whatever the nature of the matter . . . desire also that all the accounts which concern the affairs of my household remain or are put into the hands of Monsieur Colbert, for his discreet safekeeping.'

The blood was pounding in his temples; he was convinced that this was the first, irreversible step in his quest for power. Henceforth he, Colbert, the industrious and obscure petty accountant, would be on a level with Fouquet.

'The hours to come are going to prove decisive', he told himself, approaching Mazarin's bed in order for him to sign his will. The tension within him was so great at that moment that he started when a voice rang out.

'The King!'

At this announcement, the Cardinal opened his eyes again to see his godson, the King of France, enter his bedchamber. This impromptu visit overturned all the rules of etiquette.

'Your presence honours me, Sire, and warms my heart. Nevertheless it informs me that without a shadow of a doubt the hour of my terrible journey has come. As you can see, Louis, I am ready; I was even about to sign my will. As the Queen

Mother has told me that Your Majesty refuses the bequests to him, I have in fact been forced to make other arrangements. Monsieur Colbert will explain them to you if you wish.'

The King of France sat down on the chair by the side of the minister's bed. Although infinitely sad at the prospect of the inevitable, Louis XIV smiled and took the old man's hand.

'My dear godfather, my visit is guided only by the affection which I feel for you. I sent for Abbé Joly, as you asked, and he is waiting in your antechamber. But after what he wrote about you ten years ago, I am still surprised by your choice. Why him?'

'He is a sincere and brilliant man of the Church. He does not like me, I know that. But at least I have the certainty that his absolution, if he gives it to me, will not be feigned!'

The King nodded in silence. Then, seeing a shiver pass through the old man's body, he turned towards the fireplace and left his seat to poke the fire energetically, watched with emotion by Mazarin.

Having obtained his master's signature on all his last wishes, Colbert left the room, bowing deferentially as his narrowed eyes glinted in the darkness.

'My dear Louis, permit me one last piece of advice,' said Mazarin, taking his godson by the arm. 'I have been reassessing the situation for several hours now. Information in my possession leads me to beg you to be suspicious of the ambitions of our Superintendent of Finance from now on. Of course I do not take back anything I have told you about him; he would be capable of great things if only he could stop thinking about women and architecture. For pity's sake, be circumspect.'

'Your advice in this matter is precious to me, my dear godfather,' the King replied, trying to banish the blush which had appeared on his cheeks at the allusion to Fouquet's tastes for the fairer sex, 'like all the advice I have received from you since the early days of my childhood . . .'

'Sire, I have merely done my duty as a minister and a man. Today I can reveal to you how precious your affection has been to me, first as a small boy and then as a sovereign. My life, my entire life,' said Mazarin, his eyes filling with tears, 'would have been poor and futile without you, my dear Louis.'

After a pause to allow the wave of emotion which had overwhelmed him to subside, the old man continued:

'Be careful in your alliances. Be careful in war; its prospect intoxicates and glorifies, but it can also subdue the most resolute hearts. Be wary of those who conspire in the shadows against your authority . . .'

The King shuddered.

'The threat is everywhere, Sire,' went on Mazarin. 'Royalty maintains its position through honour and fear, but there will always be dreamers imbued with visions of a perfect world. I have devoted my time to keeping them at a distance, Your Majesty. I fought them for years, and with some success I believe,' he added with the shadow of a smile, 'but I was never vain enough to imagine that they had been defeated and eradicated.'

His breathing quickened, the dying man had to pause again to inhale some air.

'Beware, Sire, of these dreamers and their manipulations. Be prudent – not excessively so, but stand firm. Follow Colbert's advice when I am no longer here . . .'

He tightened his grip on the young King's hand.

'If I do not succeed in putting my affairs in order before I pass away, I shall tell him certain things of the highest importance, so important that I thought I would never share them with anyone for fear of harming your interests. You must listen to him . . .'

His voice was no more than a whisper now.

'I owe you everything, Sire. You have refused my fortune, but I believe I am acquitting myself to some extent by giving you Colbert,' added the Cardinal faintly.

Louis XIV did not respond to his Chief Minister, who was suddenly overcome again by the somnolence of the dying. He laid the old man's fleshless hand upon the sheet and left the room without a sound. On his way out, he sombrely asked the priest of Notre-Dame-des-Champs to go to the sick man's bedside without further delay. Then he strode down the stairs and, rejecting his carriage with a wave of his hand as it moved forward, signalled to d'Artagnan to dismount and let him have his horse. Jumping into the saddle, almost knocking over the musketeer who was holding the reins, he furiously spurred the animal into a gallop. As he leant forward over its neck, the King of France felt burning tears running down his cheeks on to the horse's windswept mane.

Just then, in the chateau's darkened bedroom, a dialogue was beginning between the two former enemies as Abbé Joly attended the dying man with great piety. But when he attempted to persuade the Cardinal to tell him about the public monies, the

Italian summoned up his last ounce of strength and found the authority to put the priest in his place.

'Monsieur Abbé, if I have summoned you here it is to talk to me of God. So I beg you to confine yourself to your ministry,' Mazarin told him, thus proving that even in the face of death he remained as determined as he had always been.

Early that afternoon, on 7 March, Cardinal Jules Mazarin received the last sacraments of the Holy Church and was absolved of his sins.

CHAPTER TWENTY-NINE

*Paris, the Conciergerie – Monday 7 March, six o'clock
in the evening*

'FOR the last time, talk. Confess. You were the one who set fire to the Cardinal's library. You looted his office. It was at your home, this morning, that we found these texts that have been posted up all over Paris over the past few days,' barked Charles Perrault, brandishing a bundle of pamphlets under the prisoner's nose.

The interrogation had begun three hours earlier in the damp, cold cellars of the famous Conciergerie prison. The man with the mismatched eyes was called Richard Morin, and he had been arrested that afternoon at his home. And here he was dressed in nothing but his shirt, seated on a stone bench with his wrists chained together. For three long hours the prisoner had refused to answer any questions, either quoting entire passages from the Bible, or mumbling prayers with his lips closed. But the documents found at his address proved that he belonged to the network of religious zealots and was implicated in the recent distribution of a text attacking the Cardinal. Perrault knew perfectly well that the authors of this lampoon had been inspired by the accounting documents stolen during the fire in the Chief Minister's library. He wanted to make Morin confess his link with the theft so that he could then obtain, freely or by force, the names of one or more co-conspirators.

'I'll ask you one last time, Morin, clear your conscience and tell me who you're working for,' Charles Perrault continued, this time in a calmer voice. 'I have the impression that your friends have abandoned you; if not, we would never have discovered your address. Do you not find it strange that this anonymous letter arrived on my desk yesterday naming Monsieur Richard Morin as the author of the lampoons and leader of a band of thieves and arsonists?'

'Lies! Lies!' roared the man, shaking his chains as though to try and rid himself of them.

'It is you who are lying,' retorted Perrault. 'The proof was supplied to me barely an hour ago by Toussaint Roze, the man you attacked in the Cardinal's apartments. He confirmed that he remembers perfectly that his attacker had one green eye and one brown. A description that fits you exactly!'

During this exchange, a musketeer from the Louvre had appeared bearing an urgent letter for Perrault. In it, Colbert asked his police chief to do his utmost to obtain a confession from the prisoner and to find out his exact links with Nicolas Fouquet. 'By any means necessary', concluded the message.

'Ah well, you have brought it upon yourself,' said Perrault. 'Messieurs, it is now your turn!' he added, addressing the three men who had been busying themselves with strange instruments at the back of the room for the past few minutes.

Morin was dragged roughly into the torture chamber and placed upon the 'sellette', a wooden seat where prisoners underwent their final interrogation before the torture itself began.

Morin denied everything once more and begged for divine mercy.

'You will undergo six torments, three times each,' announced the chief torturer in a strong Catalan accent.

'At each stage, you will have the opportunity to confess; if you do not, I shall pass on to the next stage,' Perrault then said, searching for a flicker of panic in the eyes of the accused.

The first ordeal inflicted upon Richard Morin was the boot. A kind of box formed from four pieces of wood was tightened around each leg by means of ropes. Perrault heard the ankle bones break and, three times, saw the zealot withstand the pain without crying out. Next, the unfortunate man was suspended by a rope from a beam more than ten feet above the ground, his hands tied behind his back. The torture consisted of letting him drop back down, the first ten times without additional weight, then with twenty kilos suspended from his feet and finally with a weight of close to fifty kilos. Despite the dislocation of his limbs and the howls of pain which he could no longer contain, the prisoner continued to deny everything, refusing to divulge any information. At each ordeal, Perrault asked the same questions, in vain. The final torment involved a sawhorse. This was a prism-shaped wooden structure resting on four feet. Richard Morin was seated upon it and securely bound to it. The ends of his bonds were then attached to a screw jack, the manipulation of which tore apart the accused man's limbs. His cries became more unbearable as the tearing became more intense.

'He has exceptional resilience,' remarked the chief torturer, untying the bloody body of the prisoner, who had finally lost consciousness. 'I have rarely seen anyone endure these torments to the end without talking,' he added, with a hint of admiration.

While the torturer rested having once again chained Morin's broken body to the stone bench, Perrault fumed at his failure to obtain a confession from his prisoner. As he left the cellars with his henchmen, he promised himself that he would return at the first opportunity the following day, and make this devil of a man talk, at any price.

A few moments after their departure, as Morin was beginning to regain consciousness, an old man swathed in a black cape slipped into the torture chamber.

'The cross of Jesus is our only pride,' he whispered into the unfortunate man's ear.

'Master,' said Morin, who instantly recognised the voice of the zealots' leader, the voice which had humiliated him at Mont-Louis a month earlier by reproaching him for his negligence. 'The love of God has helped me to keep silence, but for pity's sake save me!'

'That is why I am here, my son,' said the man, his face almost touching Morin's. 'You betrayed our trust in taking the initiative to write that lampoon, I know not why. That is why we decided to sacrifice you by denouncing you. Understand that your poor existence, like mine, carries no weight compared to a cause which is greater than any of us. God gave you the strength to resist the pain and keep silent. Be calm. Then he will welcome you into His Kingdom.'

The zealots' leader poured a vial of strong poison into

Richard Morin's mouth, instantaneously putting an end to his sufferings.

'The cross of Jesus is our only pride,' concluded the mysterious visitor, crossing himself before leaving the torture chamber as discreetly as he had come.

CHAPTER THIRTY

Vincennes – Monday 7 March, seven o'clock in the evening

Seeing Colbert slip through the half-open door of the Cardinal's apartments, the tide of visitors waiting in the anteroom and all the way down the staircase rushed towards Mazarin's confidant. Elbowing each other out of the way, trying to avoid being knocked over, they stretched out their arms in the hope that Colbert would notice what they were holding: a piece of paper here, a rosary there, a medal . . . With a thunderous expression, Colbert scanned the heaving crowd in front of him, protected from it by three servants who held it back. He ignored the shouts and calmly tried to identify familiar faces that would be useful to him.

'I have here a letter from the Cardinal,' yelled a man of the Church, sweating and brandishing a parchment.

'Monsieur Colbert!'

'My son, who . . .'

'Make way!'

The voices mingled in an indescribable clamour as Colbert's sharp-eyed gaze moved to the other side of the room. He signalled to the guards positioned along the walls, pointing out three women who were attempting to get through the door. Protests intensified as the crowd realised that soldiers were pushing them aside to allow the newcomers to come through.

'By what right?' demanded the indignant churchman who had come to demand his benefice.

'The right of blood,' replied Olympe Mancini with contempt, pushing back the hood of her cape to reveal her dark hair and eyes.

Resigned now, the courtiers who had come to claim crumbs from the Chief Minister's succession ceased their whining to watch as the Cardinal's three nieces walked past them and straight into the room they so longed to gain entry to. The door closed behind them.

'Hortense, Olympe, Marie . . .'

Moist-eyed, the Cardinal stretched out his hands to his nieces. He blessed them when they approached, tracing the sign of the cross upon their foreheads. Kneeling beside the bed, the three young women remained silent while the old man caressed their lowered faces, tilting up their chins when he lamented that it was the last time he would look into their dear eyes. 'Marie,' he said, wincing, 'I would dearly have loved to be present at your wedding and know that you were in the safe hands of that worthy man Colonna . . . Ah, my angels, how hard it is to leave the people one loves . . . Think from time to time of your old uncle and bear witness that I wanted the best for my loved ones . . . But why are you so silent?' the dying man said in surprise.

Olympe's voice was almost a whisper.

'Uncle, it is sorrow which seals our lips.'

Mazarin looked away, choking back a sob.

'And the fear of tomorrow, Uncle. Who will protect us, who

will guarantee our future and that of our families if we do not have you? You have been so kind, Uncle . . . Deprived of your generosity, who will ensure the future of our children, of your blood?'

Standing at the back of the room, Colbert clenched his teeth. 'A plague upon the family,' he muttered.

Outside, the noise suddenly intensified.

'They have no respect!' exclaimed Colbert loudly, delighted to be able to channel his anger into a less perilous subject, and at the same time interrupting the eldest niece's manipulations.

'What is it, Colbert?' murmured Mazarin, turning his exhausted eyes towards his colleague.

'Undoubtedly visitors impatient to declare their attachment to Your Eminence,' replied Colbert sarcastically, heading for the door.

Mazarin looked unimpressed.

'Tell them to go and pray for my soul at church, not in my palace,' he said, gasping between words.

Then he turned back to his nieces:

'And you, my children, go forth without fear. I have seen to it that nothing may disrupt your future. Colbert is my witness to this.'

With his hand upon the door knob, Colbert silently turned to nod and smile.

With her nostrils quivering, Olympe just managed to hold back her fury at seeing her petition thwarted.

'Go, and remember me,' Mazarin repeated.

*

After they had gone, Colbert re-entered the room with a smile on his lips.

'The noise will not trouble Your Eminence any further. I have had the visitors sent away, inviting them to pray for your recovery, and explaining that their laudable desire to show you their affection would only tire you and delay your recuperation.'

This turn of phrase produced a grunt from Mazarin, who waved the words away, knowing how illusory they were.

'Come Colbert, you may stay. Was there not a single person amongst them who was of sufficient worth for me to see them?'

Colbert shook his head.

As though seized by sudden inspiration, Mazarin sat up in bed and laid his white, trembling hands flat on the purple coverlet.

'What about the Abbaye de Prône, Colbert? Did we deal with it?'

'Do not worry, Eminence, everything is in order.'

Another shadow passed across the Cardinal's exhausted face.

'And what of the stolen papers, Colbert?'

'Alas, Eminence, we arrested one of the attackers, but he had nothing on his person or at his residence, and he has not talked,' Colbert said with anger. 'Perrault is concentrating all his energies on finding the papers.'

Mazarin fell back, shaking his head.

'We have a promising lead, two in fact, and I am hoping to resolve the matter without delay,' Colbert assured him.

'I have hardly any time left,' commented Mazarin.

The door opened to admit the Cardinal's personal valet. Approaching Colbert, he whispered a few words in his ear.

Colbert's face darkened for a second, then he shook his head and dismissed the man. He left with a silent bow.

When the door was closed once again, Mazarin raised a questioning eyebrow.

'It is another visitor, Eminence, insisting that you receive him.'

Mazarin's eyebrow remained raised.

'Superintendent Fouquet, Eminence. I told him that you were resting.'

The Cardinal did not move.

In the ensuing silence, Colbert walked slowly across to the window and parted the curtain which kept the room in darkness. A ray of light pierced the gloom, illuminating the dying man's impassive face.

'One year,' murmured Colbert, 'one year . . .'

His mind filled with memories of his private meeting with the Superintendent a year earlier, the Cardinal's final attempt to reconcile the two men. An hour spent listening to his rival's reproaches, flattering him, putting on a brave face, bowing to that squirrel who treated him like a servant and had dared allude to the grass-snake featured on his coat of arms, seeming to question the veracity of his Scottish ancestors' aristocratic origins . . . He felt renewed anger as he recalled what else Fouquet had said and implied. He had spent a year repeatedly reliving the humiliation of having to defend himself against direct accusations of slander, when all he had done was report back to His Excellency . . . Closing his eyes, Colbert drove away the memory which burned within him. *The time for bitterness and patience is coming to an end*, he thought.

When he opened his eyes again, he saw Fouquet walking swiftly down the front steps of the building.

As he watched the rejected Superintendent walk alone across the garden towards his residence, a smile lit up the face of the little man in black.

CHAPTER THIRTY-ONE

*Saint-Mandé – Tuesday 8 March, four o'clock in
the afternoon*

FRANÇOIS d'Orbay paled when he saw the young man enter the great gallery. Those features, the face and that bearing were so familiar to him that he could scarcely believe his eyes. And yet he did not know him, he was sure of it. Like everyone else present that afternoon, the newcomer was waiting for an audience with the Superintendent of Finance. D'Orbay was so intrigued that he immediately introduced himself.

'My name is François d'Orbay. I am the architect of the Château de Vaux-le-Vicomte,' he said with a smile.

'Charmed to make your acquaintance, Monsieur. I greatly admire your talent. And I,' answered the young man, 'am Monsieur Molière's personal secretary.'

François d'Orbay then pursued the conversation in a discreet attempt to find out more about the young man. But the events of recent days had put Gabriel on his guard, inclining him to remain reserved. He had a talent for being extremely courteous without giving away one jot of information about himself.

'Monsieur d'Orbay,' announced a low, solemn voice. It was the servant responsible for showing the architect into Nicolas Fouquet's office.

'Alas, I am forced to abandon you, Monsieur,' concluded d'Orbay, determined to carry out a swift investigation to discover this boy's identity.

Once the architect had left, Gabriel occupied himself by gazing around the room. He spent a long time scrutinising the famous sarcophagi which had already surprised him during his recent visit with Molière. Louise was the one who had persuaded him to request this private meeting with Fouquet. After his encounter with the thugs, he too had felt it necessary to seek some protection by confiding in one of the Kingdom's senior officials, who might be able to help him. Gabriel admired the Superintendent. In order to obtain the audience, he had used the pretext of various accounting documents for the theatre which required his signature. Gabriel did not know to what extent he would take Fouquet into his confidence, but he trusted him. An hour later, it was the young actor's turn to hear his name called out. He stood up, happy to be moving about after the long wait, and followed the servant through the corridors of the sumptuous residence. On the way he noticed the stucco work by Pietro Sassi which set off the ceilings so magnificently, and gazed admiringly at Veronese's *David and Bathsheba*, which he encountered at a turn in the corridor. Arriving at the door of the Super-intendent's office, Gabriel felt a tinge of anxiety. 'How will he react to what I have to say?' the young man wondered, suddenly unsure whether this meeting was such a good idea after all.

The Superintendent was seated at his desk.

'Please enter, Monsieur,' he said warmly.

The room was not vast, but it had been furnished with care. Its character was entirely attributable to the cabinet-making skills of the famous Jean Lepautre.

'Monseigneur, I have come at Molière's request. He sends you respectful greetings and asks if you will please examine and sign the documents I have brought with me,' said Gabriel, handing the Superintendent a thick bundle of papers.

Nicolas Fouquet gave his visitor a friendly smile, then took the papers, which he examined and began to sign.

'Do you know if Monsieur Molière has found his inspiration, and begun to write the entertainment he has promised me for the summer?' asked the Superintendent.

'He's working hard on it, I can attest to that. I think I am even permitted to tell Monseigneur that the new play will be as great a success as *Les Précienses ridicules* was last year.'

'That is very good news,' replied the Superintendent, still signing the documents. 'I believe you have just made the acquaintance of d'Orbay, the architect of my folly at Vaux. Your troupe must match the standard of the design he has produced, which I devised with him. I want the whole Kingdom to discover the talents of our artists.'

'We shall be equal to it, Monseigneur, and I myself will have the immense honour of acting in the entertainment,' replied Gabriel, encouraged by his host's warmth.

'I'm pleased to hear it,' said the Superintendent, raising his head and looking straight at Gabriel. 'But tell me, my young friend, I hear the Cardinal's police are watching your troupe. Are you suspected of financial irregularities?'

Gabriel was as relieved that Fouquet had given him an

opportunity to broach the subject as he was impressed by the Superintendent's grasp of the situation, and he began to recount everything he knew about the police surveillance. He went into detail about the attack on the old theatre concierge, but wisely did not mention the coded documents.

'I myself was almost abducted three days ago,' concluded the young man, 'by the same men who attacked our concierge. Monseigneur, may I make so bold as to ask for your advice on these strange happenings.'

The Superintendent smoothed down his slender moustache, as he always did when he was thinking. He was both intrigued and amused by this incredible tale, and was beginning to feel warmth towards the young actor. He had realised at their first meeting that Gabriel's manners indicated noble origins. Fouquet told himself that he would like his own sons to be like this young man when they were older.

'I must reveal something to you, Monseigneur,' Gabriel continued, deciding not to hide his personal history from this man who might be able to help him with his research concerning his father.

The Superintendent listened more closely as he told him about his upbringing, his flight from Amboise and his attempts to find out if the men pursuing him had in fact been sent by his family. This idea made Fouquet smile, for he knew the source of all the agitation: the fire in Mazarin's library and the disappearance of documents whose loss seemed to enrage Colbert. Isaac Bartet, an agent in the Cardinal's service who had been playing a double game for several years, had informed the Superintendent about the entire affair. This same man had informed him a few moments earlier that Richard Morin had been arrested that afternoon.

'Whether this is to do with your family or not, you need to take precautions. We must protect you,' said the Superintendent, who had resolved to please the young actor but above all wanted to ensure that he held on to one or two crucial pieces in this chess game where everyone now seemed to be pushing around their pawns.

The Superintendent pretended to think for a moment, then went on:

'I suggest that you leave and spend a few days at Vaux-le-Vicomte to guarantee your safety. When you arrive you will be greeted by La Fontaine, who has withdrawn there to write. I shall come and join you in due course. By then many things will have happened and I shall have had sufficient opportunity to get to the bottom of this affair.'

Delighted at this suggestion, which he almost took to be an order, Gabriel bowed and thanked the Superintendent for his trust.

'Take your signed papers,' said Nicolas Fouquet, 'and go and inform Molière this evening that you have to leave Paris for a few days, due to a bereavement. Don't tell anyone where you are going. Tomorrow morning I shall send a carriage to take you to Vaux-le-Vicomte. Go, young man,' said the Superintendent, suddenly serious again. 'Be off. What is being played out at present is not a farce written by your friend Molière; indeed it may turn out to be a tragedy.'

When Gabriel had bowed repeatedly and left his office, the

Superintendent sat down at his work table and began to stroke his moustache again.

That young devil undoubtedly knows more than he's told me. I must find out why the whole of Paris is looking for him, and above all what scheme Colbert has devised this time!

CHAPTER THIRTY-TWO

Saint-Mandé – Tuesday 8 March, six o'clock in
the evening

FOR the fourth time in only a few minutes, Fouquet looked up from the documents he was annotating and let his gaze stray through the window to linger on the shadows of the waning day. He sighed, set down his bundle of papers on a little side table next to the three-branched candlestick which provided light for his work, and closed his eyes. Was it tiredness that prevented him from working with his usual efficiency?

'Monsieur Superintendent, Monsieur d'Orbay requests an audience.'

Opening his eyes again, Fouquet saw that the servant had entered without a sound and was standing in front of him. He looked at him for a moment, then nodded.

The servant left, closing the door behind him. Surprised, Fouquet closed his inkwell. *D'Orbay, again?*

He had just stood up when the door reopened. The servant stood aside to allow the architect to enter. He took off his cloak and hat, and Fouquet indicated one of the two armchairs which stood beside the fire.

'So, François, here you are again,' said the Superintendent as he sat down. 'Kindly tell me what this is all about instead of jumping around like a lunatic!'

D'Orbay made an obvious effort to calm himself and sat down.

'That lad you saw this afternoon, that lad you saw after I left, the one I met in your waiting room . . .'

Fouquet frowned in puzzlement.

'Molière's secretary?'

'The very same.'

'What terrible thing has he done to bring you back here this evening?'

Fouquet's sarcasm died when he saw the architect's marble-like expression.

'Do you know his name, Nicolas?'

The Superintendent shrugged his shoulders, admitting ignorance.

'Gabriel . . . Gabriel something?'

'Gabriel de Pontbriand, Nicolas, his name is Gabriel de Pontbriand. Does that not mean anything to you?'

Fouquet shook his head.

'Why, should it?'

'What if I were to tell you that it is also the name of a man who calls himself Charles Saint John, and that it was their astounding similarity which caused me to recognise Gabriel?'

Fouquet started.

'What! What are you saying? Are you sure?' he went on in more measured tones.

'Certain,' replied d'Orbay. 'I had a terrible shock when I noticed him in your anteroom. Your Gabriel is the son of our Brother André de Pontbriand, whom you know by the name of Charles Saint John.'

The ensuing silence lasted for quite some time.

'Gabriel de Pontbriand . . .' murmured the Superintendent.

'The coincidence is most disturbing,' said d'Orbay, noting Fouquet's sudden look of dismay, 'and I must confess that the shock I felt this afternoon turned my blood to ice. Our mission is too fragile and its importance too great to ignore such coincidences. That is why I wanted to put you on your guard without delay, even if I am the first person to acknowledge that we must not overreact. We have enough to do without allowing ourselves to be distracted. After all, this young man's parentage may play no part in the troubles he has brought upon himself . . .'

'I'm sure you are right, but all the same we must be vigilant. In any event, you were right to alert me. When I think that I granted him my protection and hospitality, without having an inkling . . . Yes,' nodded the Superintendent in response to d'Orbay's look of surprise, 'he told me of attacks and threats, and gave me such a sincere and romantic account of his flight to Paris, incognito, to escape the mediocre life his protector had in store for him that I invited him to take refuge at Vaux, until things have calmed down.'

'Well, so much the better,' exclaimed the architect. 'At Vaux we shall have him under our control, and it will be easier both to watch over him and to ensure that he does not intend to disrupt our plans. Let us take advantage of this respite to bring his entanglements out into the open and find out why there is so much hostility towards him. That would be the best way to rid ourselves of this disagreeable feeling of doom we both seem to harbour.'

'What exactly does he know, in your opinion?'

D'Orbay frowned sceptically.

'There is no reason why he should know anything. Or be capable of leading our enemies to us, or attract their attention. He knows nothing of his father and has not seen him for fifteen years, we can be certain of that.'

Once again, Fouquet remained silent for a moment.

'Increased activity by Mazarin's agents, Colbert and his police, that burglary . . . and now this ghost returning to haunt us. It's all very worrying.'

He seemed lost in thought, then turned towards the architect.

'When did you say the delivery was to take place?'

'The Secret will leave Rome in a month,' d'Orbay replied, lowering his voice. 'It will be here one month later. And at Vaux a few days after that. Everything will be in place for the summer.'

Fouquet clasped his hands in front of his face.

'Pray Heaven that we find the formula between now and then. Otherwise . . .'

'Otherwise we shall act without it,' d'Orbay interrupted him.

The Superintendent glanced out of the window.

'I know what you're thinking, François. I understand your impatience. I too have confidence in the work we have carried out. I too believe that Vaux can become the temple of a new political era, which may finally re-establish the Truth of things in accordance with the reality of Christ's teaching. But I do not want to overestimate our strength.'

He gazed at the architect and smiled.

'Mine in particular, François.'

D'Orbay picked up his cloak from the armchair where he had left it and threw it over his shoulders.

'Well,' he said, 'we shall talk of this again when the time comes.'

Looking up, he met the Superintendent's shining eyes.

'But fear not: you will persuade him,' he declared, pulling on his gloves. 'You will persuade him, I am sure of it.'

'God willing,' whispered Fouquet when the door had closed behind the architect. 'God willing . . .'

CHAPTER THIRTY-THREE

Château de Vincennes — Tuesday 8 March, seven o'clock
in the evening

'IT is time for us to part, Madame . . .'

The Queen shivered as she heard the thin thread of the Cardinal's voice in which she could now barely detect the musical, melodious tones that had been so dear to her. Anne of Austria had been sitting for a long time in an armchair at the sick man's bedside, absorbed in her prayers, and thought Mazarin was asleep. Forcing herself to smile, her gaze lingered on the emaciated features, yellowish complexion and closed eyes of the sick man. It was almost as if life had abandoned him already. She took his hand but did not reply, fearing that her words would betray her emotion, and chose instead to caress the Chief Minister's cold, motionless fingers.

'How hard it is to leave this world for a better one. And yet my cares are melting away: I no longer think of my paintings or my books. And hardly even about the State. This I dare to tell you, and you alone . . . But do not weep, Madame,' went on the Cardinal in a fading voice, making an effort to open his eyes in the dim light to look at the face of the Queen, who was finding it increasingly difficult to hold back her tears. 'I trust the King's judgement, and his maturity. What is more, I am reassured by the knowledge that you will always be at his side. What better support can a son hope for than that of a loving, experienced mother?'

The Queen could not suppress a sob.

'That of a father,' she whispered with great difficulty.

Mazarin stiffened and closed his eyes again. Freeing his hand, he raised it gently to the Queen's lips as if to silence her.

'There are words, Madame, which must never be spoken for fear that the walls have ears; words that our hearts know to keep as a secret between themselves,' he said slowly but firmly.

Then he relaxed, as if these few words had cost him an excessive effort.

Silence. Sitting perfectly still, Anne of Austria once again allowed herself to consider the madness of that secret which had for years ruled her life as a woman constrained by queenly duties. Slowly it came back to her, in successive waves resurfacing from her past: the memory of her early years of dissembling, which had become an increasing necessity as she faced up to the inexorable attraction drawing her to the young Mazarin. More than thirty years had elapsed since then, and the ambitious young man with the plump face and sparkling gaze had been transformed into this impassive, dying sphinx with hollow cheeks and dead eyes. Yet the spark was still there, uniting the Queen of France and the Chief Minister via a secret, invisible yet indissoluble bond. Anne of Austria relived the days when she had been deeply distressed by the French populace's rejection of her foreign parentage, then by the suspicions of her husband, King Louis XIII, and his Chief Minister, Cardinal de Richelieu. Who had supported her when they accused her of conspiring against her adopted homeland on behalf of her native country? Only Mazarin, also a foreigner, an Italian whose accent people mocked. He had understood her, defended her, helped her. Understood her, and loved her . . . He had never wavered, never once failed her. And the silence which had been imposed upon them, far from driving them apart, had united them in unrivalled complicity, sealed by the sight day after day, month after month, year after year, of a growing boy who was destined to be King of France . . .

Now it was the Cardinal's turn to clasp the Queen's hands in his. He brought his lips close to her ear.

'This secret, Madame, is greater than we are and does not belong to us except in so far as we must ensure it disappears with us. When I still had boundless strength, I was arrogant in omitting to destroy all the clues which might reveal it. I kept the letters you sent me after the birth, Madame, and the contract drawn up between us to bear witness before God that we were committing no sin that He in his mercy could not absolve. I knew that I should destroy them, but I could not bring myself to do it.'

The Cardinal's voice cracked and he remained silent for a moment before continuing:

'I gave my secretary orders to remove those documents from their hiding place in my apartments . . .'

Suddenly realising, the Queen shuddered with terror:

'The theft!'

The Cardinal nodded.

'Yes, Madame. Those papers are amongst the ones that were stolen, for I do not believe they were delivered up to the flames. That is why it is a matter of urgency to retrieve them. I was hoping to carry out that task myself, but we must now face facts. You will have to undertake it, Madame, in our joint names. God be praised, the documents are coded and, I believe, indecipherable.'

With an enormous effort the Cardinal propped himself up on one elbow, his lips almost touching the Queen's ear:

'But no one must know, Madame. Colbert will be invaluable to you, but he cannot know anything about the real content. You alone must bear the secret, which the King himself – the King above all –,' he corrected himself 'must not know. Retrieve the papers and destroy them.'

'How incautious you were, Jules,' murmured the devastated Queen, in a tone of voice that held no hint of reproach.

Then, in a firmer tone:

'Do not worry, I shall protect the Kingdom. You may lay down your burden; I shall carry it for both of us,' she said, gently stroking the dying man's moist brow.

The Cardinal managed a small, painful smile. He parted his lips but this time it was she who placed a finger over his mouth.

'Shh! No more talking; you're tiring yourself. We don't need words any more, do we?' She added in a trembling voice, 'We never *have* needed words, my dear.'

'Alas Madame, that is not all I have to tell you. We lack time, so listen carefully to what I am about to say. Those papers, Madame, were contained in a leather document case with a sheaf of other papers which were also coded, but by other people and in a code I do not know. They contain a secret for which people have already killed, a secret much more terrible perhaps than our own, a secret which could change France's destiny even more radically.'

At these words, the Queen shivered.

'Madame, those papers came into my possession years ago, when the Fronde was setting the country alight and the conspirators thought they were nearing their goal of toppling the State. I know the price that certain of those faction members place upon the papers. The man who was in possession of them, and who was arrested by my police officers, succeeded in escaping, but he abandoned the documents and no one knew where they were. Nobody has yet managed to reveal their secret. I had resolved to destroy them too, in time, convinced that if this secret could not be possessed it must be destroyed. The Devil's beauty must not be gazed upon. Repeat my words to Colbert; make him understand that these papers may place our position and the monarchy in danger, that he must not let anything stand in the way of finding them. Anyone who compromises the search must be pushed aside. Anyone who might appropriate them himself must be rendered incapable of doing harm. Satisfy yourself that he has retrieved and destroyed them, Madame. And then our secret will disappear too. Go, Madame, it is time,' he concluded, pulling the bell-cord to summon his personal valet.

As the valet entered, the white hands of the Queen and the dying man clasped one last time, then the Queen stood up.

'Tell Monsieur Colbert that the Queen wishes to see him in her apartments immediately.'

CHAPTER THIRTY-FOUR

Paris, Bertrand Barrême's residence — Tuesday 8 March,
nine o'clock in the evening

BERTRAND Barrême wrenched the pince-nez from the bridge of his prominent nose. His other hand passed lightly over the four sheets of paper laid out before him, then pulled back as if suddenly burned. Holding the pince-nez between two fingers, the mathematician pointed another finger at Gabriel, who stood motionless on the other side of the table.

'Where the devil did you find this, young man?'

Gabriel stammered but did not reply. The fat man in the tight silk dressing gown impatiently wobbled nearer to him. His face was very close to Gabriel's now, and the young man could see every little line at the corners of his eyes and on the crown of his almost-bald pate. Only his youthful voice betrayed the true age of the thirty-year-old who looked like an old man.

'These papers?' he repeated. 'Who did you get them from?'

'Do they mean anything to you?' Gabriel asked.

Barrême looked at him suspiciously and returned to the table with a grunt.

'Possibly, yes, but they are incomplete . . .'

Putting his pince-nez back on, he bent over the sheets of paper once more, scanning them in the same worried and cautious manner.

'Do you know any mathematics, Monsieur?'

'A little,' ventured Gabriel. 'I know a little geometry and algebra . . .'

'Codes,' interrupted Barrême, 'are a mathematical game. They are also signatures. Hundreds exist, but in the end there are not many families of them, and inventions in the field are very rare. In the twenty years I've been working in this area, I've very rarely had cause to be surprised . . .'

'But you are by this? Is it something you're unfamiliar with?'

Gabriel immediately regretted his words when he saw Barrême's angry expression. He clenched his fists and forced himself to control his impatience.

'No, young man. Do not be in such haste that you make the wrong deduction! I am certainly not in the presence of something I do not know, but on the contrary something which I do know, or rather recognise. I would describe it more as a distant memory.'

Noting Gabriel's impatience, the mathematician remained silent for a moment to add weight to what he was about to say.

'If I ask you where you obtained these documents, it's because I have not seen them for almost fifteen years. I was very young then, and my father had sent me to stay in Tuscany and Rome, to learn accounting techniques and the sciences from the Italian masters. Perhaps the quality of my work attracted attention,' mused the mathematician with undisguised vanity. 'Anyway, one evening, I was summoned to a palace in Rome, in an atmosphere of great secrecy, to work on encoding some documents – this document was one of them,' he specified, extracting one of the four sheets.

'So you know the code?' Gabriel exclaimed, unable to control himself.

A black look from the fat man stopped him short.

'Do you never listen? Barbin told me you were hot-headed, but not to this extent! Monsieur Molière is fortunate that he is an artist and not a geometrician with you by his side . . .'

Gabriel lowered his head and opened his mouth to apologise, but Barrême waved his attempt away; he had been interrupted too often already.

'Well no, I do not know the code. In fact that is why I remember this document: I encoded it, but did not read it . . .'

Gabriel looked utterly lost, which seemed to please Barrême.

'Yes, yes, without reading it, or at least only reading a section that had been extracted from it, rendering its meaning totally incomprehensible. I imagine other coding experts like myself were working on the other parts.'

Disappointment was written all over Gabriel's face.

'This is scarcely going to help you with your play, is it?' the man went on suspiciously. 'But listen to what happened next. After I'd finished my work, I was asked to wait in the same palace for several hours, and then the document was brought back to me so that I could encode it once again. This is the classic technique of the double code, an Italian speciality. What was rather less classic, however, was the nature of the process applied to my first encoding while I was waiting: I had never seen it before and have never seen it since. How can I explain it to you simply?' He looked at Gabriel, pleased with himself. 'That code was not mathematical: it was, you might say, harmonic or aesthetic. That is to say that it was not based, I am certain, on objective mathematical logic but on a subjective perception. That code was beautiful, young man, beautiful in the manner of a cathedral, not beautiful like an equation!'

Still lost for words, Gabriel looked again at the sheets of paper. They told him nothing and seemed to him to be no more than a heap of cabalistic signs and impenetrable figures. While he was looking, longing to see something new, Barrême had come up behind him. Just a few drops of sweat still betrayed his fleeting excitement, and in his eyes there was doubt once again as to the young actor's real intentions.

'There is something else I remember: the appearance of the man who brought the documents that evening, and who paid me handsomely for my trouble.'

Gabriel jumped when he realised that the man was staring intently at him.

'He was just the same size and build as you, with hair like yours and his features, yes, yes, as I recall they were very similar to yours . . .'

White as a sheet, the young man blurted out a few words of thanks and an invitation to the forthcoming play as he feverishly gathered up the documents.

As he watched him leave, Barrême shrugged and took off his pince-nez. Why did the prospect of setting to work on developing the new accounting system ordered by the Cardinal's department suddenly seem so uninspiring? Was it the strange memory which had suddenly reappeared before his eyes, or seeing those features from the past on the face of that young man?

He got to his feet, dressed hurriedly and went out, scarcely taking the time to lock his door.

Twenty minutes later, he was knocking at the door of a private residence in Rue de la Verrerie. As soon as it opened a fraction, he pushed it inwards.

'I must see Monsieur d'Orbay without delay,' he barked. 'Tell Monsieur d'Orbay that I am here!'

CHAPTER THIRTY-FIVE

Château de Vincennes – Wednesday 9 March, two o'clock in the morning

No one slept that night, as death prowled the bedchamber of Jules Mazarin. Both the servants and the members of Court attached to the Cardinal's household remained awake, waiting. This activity, unusual as it was at that hour, gave the chateau a strange atmosphere. Everyone walked about on tiptoe and spoke in hushed voices, as if to avoid attracting ill luck. During the late afternoon of 8 March, the old Cardinal had sunk into a sort of unconsciousness. He no longer recognised anyone and talked deliriously with his eyes wide open, asking for his mother in Italian. Mazarin conversed out loud with Hortensia Bufalini, 'mia Mamma', as he must have done in his early childhood in the Abruzzi. In the evening his breathing had become increasingly irregular. The Chief Minister lay in his bed which now appeared to swamp his emaciated body. The immaculate sheets, changed with zealous affection by his old servants, were wrapped around him like a first attempt at a shroud. Care had been taken to put a little rouge on his cheeks in order to hide the extreme transparency of his face. His hair, which had become sparse as the illness progressed, had been combed. The fire crackled in the fireplace, providing the sole light in the room where His Eminence's confessor stood deep in prayer, as did his doctors. The Queen Mother had remained at the dying man's bedside until midnight. Then, exhausted by the long vigils of recent nights, Anne of Austria had retired to her apartments, giving orders that she was to be informed 'of any sign that destiny was progressing more quickly'. The King had returned the previous day to the Palais du Louvre, where he had rejoined his young wife. In the room next to the Cardinal's bedchamber, Colbert kept vigil along with Lionne and Le Tellier.

On the other side of the wall, the dying man's breathing suddenly became more laboured. Each movement of his chest brought on a hoarse whistling sound. Life was ebbing away from the man whose career had shaped the history of France. The doctors did not have time to inform Anne of Austria before the Cardinal passed away. The Swiss clock on the chimney breast was stopped at the moment when His Eminence's eyes were closed by his confessor for eternity. It was forty minutes past two on the morning of 9 March 1661.

CHAPTER THIRTY-SIX

Palais du Louvre — Wednesday 9 March, four o'clock
in the morning

T HE messenger had just arrived, having exhausted his horse
on the road from the Château de Vincennes. As he handed
over the letter he was carrying to the commander of the palace
guard, the rider related the news already known by everyone
who had served the Chief Minister at Vincennes. The
commander immediately rushed to the steward of the King's
household and woke him to pass on the news and the letter. The
steward pulled on his clothes and went out, preceded by two
servants whose eyes were still swollen with sleep after their
abrupt awakening. They carried candelabra to light the
steward's way through the darkened maze of the Louvre.

His Majesty was with the Queen that night. A year earlier,
Louis XIV had resolved to marry the Spanish Infanta for
obvious reasons of State. This union, ardently desired by
Mazarin, constituted a masterstroke by the old Cardinal which
put an end to the interminable conflicts between the two nations
and at the same time concluded young Louis' dalliance with his
own niece, Marie Mancini. The young married couple, who
were born in the same year, had met for the first time on the Île

des Faisans, on the border between France and Spain, three days before their wedding. The King of France had shown Maria Theresa such consideration during the ceremony, which was celebrated at Saint Jean-de-Luz on 9 June 1660, that she had believed he sincerely loved her. But as soon as he returned to Paris in August of the same year, the young husband had once again displayed his interest in Marie. The Queen Mother, whose affection for her young daughter-in-law was reciprocated, and who kept a weather eye open for trouble, had put the situation to rights by sending the beautiful Marie far away from the young King. But after he had shown interest in his Spanish wife for a few months, Louis XIV had swiftly rediscovered his taste for new conquests . . .

Nevertheless, on the night of 9 March the sovereign had felt moved to spend the whole night with his wife. Was it the imminent demise of his beloved Cardinal that had provoked these moments of tenderness and love, or a sudden desire to become a father at a time when destiny was about to deprive him of his godfather? After this night of love, and despite the late hour, Louis XIV was still awake and deep in thought as he lay with his eyes wide open, watching his sleeping wife beside him.

She is small and plump and her wit hardly sparkles, he told himself, *but I am sure she will give me fine children.*

The King sat up at the sound of footsteps approaching his bedchamber. As he saw the steward bow low before him, he felt his heart race. Suddenly there was a lump in his throat. The letter he was handed was signed by Colbert. Its contents were sober: 'His Eminence Cardinal Mazarin passed away peacefully on this day, 9 March.'

He was gone: the man whom the King of France had admired the most in the world, who had guided him ever since the death of Louis XIII, the man who – along with his mother, Anne of Austria – made up his protective family. Never again would he be there to advise him, or to teach him how to govern. For the first time in his life, the terrible burden of his responsibilities weighed heavy upon his shoulders. At that moment, Louis XIV was strangely torn between grief at the death of his dear godfather, and the jubilation which bubbled inside him at the prospect of at last being sole sovereign of his Kingdom.

'Madame,' the King told Maria Theresa, who had just awoken, 'immense tragedy has struck our nation: we have just lost our Chief Minister. I am going to Vincennes in order to make the necessary arrangements. I shall leave immediately, to ensure that the Queen Mother has the support of her son and the affection of her sovereign at this difficult time.'

The young Queen burst into tears at this announcement, which profoundly touched Louis XIV. It moved him to see his wife express feelings which he, as King of France, would have to hide. To combat the turmoil within him, he demanded his clothes and issued his first orders.

'Steward, send a messenger to Vincennes immediately to announce my imminent arrival. Also, tell Colbert that I wish to convene a meeting of the inner council. Have my carriage and my personal guard ready to leave within the hour!'

As he left the capital that cold night, lulled by the din of the horses' hooves galloping over the flagstones, Louis XIV thought of the hours to come and of how he would now to assume the government of his Kingdom.

The sound of hooves clattering along the paved esplanade alerted the musketeers who were stationed within sight of Vincennes. Louis XIV was in a hurry. In a hurry to embrace the Queen Mother, whose infinite grief he could well imagine. In a hurry also to show everyone what he was capable of, even if, deep inside, the King was less self-assured than he wished to appear. As he entered the palace, he noted that the Cardinal's guards had upended their rifles as a sign of mourning. The King had been joined on his journey from Paris by Marshals Villeroy, Gramont and Noailles, who now walked at his side. Anne of Austria was waiting for him, together with various ministers and Colbert, in the room adjoining the bedchamber where Jules Mazarin's mortal remains lay.

'The King,' barked the sheriff, suddenly throwing open the doors.

The entrance of the sovereign at this hour of night, and in these circumstances, constituted an extraordinary spectacle that combined the pomp of life at Court and the sad simplicity of a family gathered together in mourning. The Queen Mother sat in an armchair beside the fire warming herself with a cup of chocolate spiced with cinnamon. Lionne was conversing in hushed tones with Le Tellier, Brienne and Colbert. Everyone stood to acknowledge the King of France's entrance. The King rushed to his mother, who had already got to her feet to receive her son's kiss. Straightaway he noticed that her eyes were swollen with weeping and fatigue.

'Madame, know that I share your pain,' the King told her affectionately as he took her in his arms. 'I know how much your presence at my godfather's side must have eased his last days.'

'Sire,' said the Queen Mother, unable to hold back her tears, 'the Kingdom has lost its most faithful servant. Your presence brings us comfort and consolation. I am certain that, to his last breath, your godfather thought only of Your Majesty,' added Anne of Austria, her voice jerky with sobs.

'I want to see him,' demanded the King.

This order surprised everyone, for it was quite unimaginable that the King of France should be placed in the presence of death. In the ensuing heavy silence, Louis XIV repeated his order.

'I want to see him!'

The sheriff then opened the door that separated the room containing the sovereign from the room in which the Cardinal's body lay.

Louis stopped in his tracks, suddenly feeling an immense wave of grief wash over him at the sight of his godfather's inert body. He stood there motionless, as though both fascinated and hypnotised by the spectacle of the bed that held the Chief Minister, lit only by the single, flickering flames from the candlesticks arranged around him. Tears flowed down his cheeks. At that moment, Louis relived the most memorable moments of his childhood with his godfather. Once again he heard the voice with its distinctive accent which had taught him so many things, and he became aware of the silence that meant he must now and for ever face his destiny alone.

Anxious not to make a spectacle of his grief, Louis XIV simply gestured to the servants to close the door.

'Messieurs,' the King said solemnly to the group surrounding Lionne and Le Tellier, 'this is a time for prayer. Nevertheless I have asked Monsieur Colbert to summon all the ministers here present to my office, and I invite you to join me there.'

Realising that Louis XIV wished to be alone for a moment with his mother, Michel Le Tellier left the room and took the others with him.

'Madame, in order to spare you the vexing burden of public affairs at this painful time, I have decided to limit this meeting to my ministers alone.'

Stunned by the announcement, the Queen Mother did not know how to respond to this sudden exclusion, which came as a terrible surprise. At that moment, Anne of Austria felt alone and weak. Had she not taken on more than her share of power since the death of Louis XIII, especially during the terrible ordeals of the Fronde? She asked herself what her son could possibly reproach her for, and was particularly stung as his unexpected announcement came only hours after the death of her loving companion.

The King did not take time to concern himself with his mother's reaction. He kissed her on the forehead and left the room. Outraged, Anne of Austria turned on her heel and walked back to her apartments.

'I suspected as much. I suspected that he would be ungrateful and would wish to show his strength,' she muttered as she went.

CHAPTER THIRTY-SEVEN

Vincennes – Wednesday 9 March, eleven o'clock in the morning

QUICKENING his pace as he crossed his gardens and headed for the esplanade at the Château de Vincennes, Nicolas Fouquet was oblivious to the beauty of the frost-covered branches. He clenched his fists in the pockets of his immense coat, his jaw tense with worry.

'Confound my spies and my agents,' he muttered through his teeth. 'They never alerted me, the villains. And why was I not informed about this meeting or the King's arrival? Doubtless an oversight,' he forced himself to believe.

But he could not rid himself of the sombre premonition which gripped him.

The Superintendent greeted the Queen Mother with a bow as she wandered through the great anteroom outside the King's apartments.

'Madame, I have only just heard the sad news.'

The Queen smiled at Fouquet, happy to see a friendly face amid the succession of ordeals that made up this painful day.

'Good day to you, Monsieur Superintendent. The King,' she said, speaking the words with unaccustomed emphasis, 'sent for you, I presume?'

'Indeed not, Madame, I came without any summons to meditate at the deathbed of Monsieur Cardinal. But I am told that the King is holding a council meeting . . .'

'A restricted council, as you and I are both now aware.'

A few yards away, the King stood by the window of his small private office, his eyes fixed on the paved courtyard below. Behind him, Lionne, Séguier, Le Tellier and Colbert listened in silence as he uttered short, sharp sentences interspersed with long silences.

'We shall make the funeral arrangements later. As regards the Cardinal's affairs, the will is to be respected but there will be no widespread publication of its details. Monsieur Colbert, you will assemble the Cardinal's records and give an account of their content to me alone, and without committing anything to paper. As for the appointments which the Cardinal made, I shall make known tomorrow at nine o'clock in council – you will organise the meeting, Chancellor – the new organisational structure which we will adopt.'

The King turned to face the motionless ministers again.

'I thank you. Until tomorrow.'

Still silent, the four men bowed at length and headed for the door.

'Colbert, a further word please,' the King called him back.

Suppressing a smile, Colbert stopped to allow the other three to leave. They didn't so much as a glance at him.

'Sire?'

Louis XIV sat down and softened his tone a little.

'Monsieur, my godfather, may his soul rest in peace, told me how much I would be able to trust you.'

He silenced Colbert's protests with a wave of his hand.

'He told me what you have achieved. He told me what a burden you bore in order to defend us against agitators and those who spoke evil of us. You should know that I remember such things. I want you to share your concerns with me. In addition, you are to inform me personally about the confidential files in your charge. I thought my godfather appeared anxious in his last days, particularly after the fire and the theft by the brigands . . . Do you know anything more about this? Were his worries well founded?'

'Sire, I do not wish to nourish fears which have no basis,' said Colbert. 'Certainly there are dangers, and some people close to the centre of power do dare to harbour questionable ambitions. But with your permission I will reserve my conclusions until I am sure, with proof, names and facts. I shall devote myself to the task.'

'Very well. As the Cardinal will doubtless have informed you, you are to be endowed with the rank of Steward of Finance, to work alongside the Superintendent. I am sure this role will aid you in your investigations,' said the King enigmatically.

Colbert's eyes shone with joy as he bowed to indicate his gratitude.

'Go, you seem tired. Get some rest. I shall have need of all your energy in the weeks to come.'

'Sire, your glory has need of no one,' Colbert said quietly as he backed towards the door, bowing repeatedly.

Raising his prominent eyes just as he passed through the door, the little man saw the sun's rays strike the young man's hair through the glass, creating a halo of light around his arrogant face.

As he passed through the succession of rooms leading to the other wing and the Cardinal's apartments, Colbert's heart beat fast. Lost in his reverie he did not see Nicolas Fouquet, who had lingered in the courtyard after his visit to bow before Mazarin's dead body. As the Superintendent watched the little black-clad man walk by, he felt his stomach knot again.

CHAPTER THIRTY-EIGHT

Mont-Louis – Thursday 10 March, five o'clock in
the morning

Huddled in the shadow of the bushes, Colbert had patiently observed the procession of silhouettes as they moved, one by one, across the space that separated the buildings of Mont-Louis from the adjoining Saint-Côme chapel. A small door was hewn into the chapel's apse. Each time it opened a little way, the light enabled him to count the arrivals one by one. He had grown nervous when the succession of people entering the chapel had ceased for several minutes, but his worry was instantly dispelled with the arrival of the last man, in a state of obvious agitation, escorted by two torch-bearers. Smiling, Colbert pulled his hood down a little further over his face and turned to the soldier who was crouching beside him.

'They are all here. Now remember: at my signal, but only at my signal. Until then, absolute silence – your men must not move a muscle. Remind them that they are only to surround the building closest to us.'

Then, with surprising agility given his sickly appearance, he stood up and headed for the darkened chapel, shivering with each gust of wind.

Not a sound disturbed the night's icy cold, save the whistling wind. Slowly, Colbert crossed the open space to the door. He remained there, motionless. When nothing happened, he half opened the studded wooden door and slipped inside.

'Let us pray to Our Lord to grant us grace amid this turmoil to understand the proper conduct he expects from us.'

Hearing the voice tear through the silence, Colbert froze. All that separated him from the conspirators' meeting was the enormous pillar he found himself behind, which masked the light from the two torches illuminating them. Silence fell once more. Colbert held his breath and strained to hear.

A different voice spoke next.

'One does not weep for the death of a mad dog! Providence has settled our doubts by dispensing with that evil-doer. If there is anything to regret, it is only that we did not arrange the demise of the accursed Cardinal ourselves!'

'Anger is not what Our Lord commands,' went on the first voice. 'I wanted us to meet after the announcement of the Cardinal's death in order to bring our activity to an immediate halt in the face of this new upheaval.'

The voice hardened.

'Morin's example should incline us to greater wisdom, my Brothers. Our poor Brother allowed himself to be overtaken by anger. He almost brought about our downfall by drawing attention to us and attracting the King's anger. What we detested in Mazarin was that he diverted divine royalty from its sole task: that of ensuring the glory of Our Lord on earth. By attacking royal power and invoking the right to rebel, Morin – may God have pity on him – forgot this and perverted our message. It is of little importance that he failed to bring us back the papers proving the monstrous union of Mazarin and the Queen

Mother. All of that died with the Cardinal. What matters now is that we assure ourselves of the King's intentions. For my part . . .'

'As confessor to the King, that's well said, Monsieur!'

Stunned, the assembled men turned to look at the figure who had just emerged from behind the pillar.

'We have been betrayed!'

One of the zealots leapt forward, unsheathing his dagger, but his leader stopped him in his tracks.

'Yes, very wise, King's Confessor,' commented the unexpected guest phlegmatically. 'Indeed, I advise all of you to keep your weapons in their scabbards.'

The dumbstruck zealots watched silently as the man walked down the steps towards them.

'Gentlemen, any resistance is futile unless you wish to die martyrs. Outside, two companies of guards are surrounding the area and they will not allow anyone to leave alive without my safe conduct.'

'Who are you?' demanded the King's confessor.

'A man who is sufficiently well informed to know that you went to see Morin in order to ensure his silence. And to know the names and identities of every one of you. And to have had each one of you constantly watched since your society of zealots was dissolved last September. Sufficiently well informed to have seen you leave the Louvre after the news of the Cardinal's death had been announced to the King. So, my friends, I will reveal myself' he said, pushing back the hood of his cape.

'Colbert!'

'The very same, Monsieur Confessor, the very same.'

Colbert took a chair and sat down.

'So here we all are, present and ready to talk.'

'What do you want?' asked one of the men in a voice heavy with suspicion.

'I want to avoid killing people I am not convinced are my enemies. And the proof of that is that had I wished to kill you, you would all be dead by now, or at the very least on the way to a most disagreeable prison. That this did not happen is because I did not think it necessary and the words I heard before I revealed myself to you incline me to believe that I was right.'

When he saw the questioning looks on the conspirators' faces, Colbert paused for a moment, and then said:

'You detested the Cardinal, so be it. He is dead. You wanted to destroy him by revealing the intimate secret of his links with the Queen Mother, but he has carried that scandal to his tomb. So why go on fighting?'

The man who had produced his dagger leant forward and spat contemptuously:

'Because we respect the sacred cause of Our Lord.'

Colbert fixed him with a weighty gaze.

'And who here is the enemy of the Church? Believe me, no one believes that the King is anything of the sort. On the contrary, the King wishes to strengthen the spiritual order. As we are speaking in confidence, I can tell you what will not be generally known for a little while: in a few days' time, the King will ask the clerical assembly to deal ruthlessly with deviants of all kinds by obliging clerics to sign a Formulary which would guarantee their absolute respect for the authority of our Holy Church and of the King, God's knight upon earth.'

Pushing back his chair, Colbert began to pace up and down the room, staring at the men gathered there.

'Don't deceive yourselves, things are different now. You must serve your cause, but don't mistake your enemies. They are the people who oppose royalty because of the spiritual order on which it is based. I also fear these people greatly, encouraged by the King who personally told me of his suspicions,' he lied, omitting to mention that it had in fact been the Queen Mother. 'Together we can fight these enemies. Do not allow your blindness to deprive Our Lord of the fighters he needs,' he concluded, lowering his eyes with solemn intensity.

As he gradually perceived that he was winning over the men around him, Colbert was filled with an excitement, which shone in his dark eyes.

'You have a choice, my friends: either walk away unfettered, to continue your activities all the more freely since they will be done in accordance with the King's wishes as expressed through me. Or leave here with chains about your ankles, en route for the Bastille tonight and the scaffold tomorrow. It is your turn to speak. Have you nothing to say? Come,' he added as he headed for the door, 'I will go back outside, into the open air. You have ten minutes in which to make up your minds. After that, I will answer for nothing.'

As he arrived at the threshold he paused, as if to correct an oversight.

'Ah! Of course, Father, you will be coming with me. His Majesty has today once again summoned me to Vincennes for the council, and I am certain that you will be exceedingly useful to its members.'

Without waiting for a response, Colbert opened the door and went out.

Silently, the leader of the zealots crossed himself and murmured an unintelligible prayer. Then, putting on his cloak, he too left. When he heard the door creak behind him, Colbert smiled, realising that he had won this round and secured allies who would be all the more loyal because they owed him their survival.

CHAPTER THIRTY-NINE

Vincennes – Thursday 10 March, nine o'clock in the morning

LAYING his hands on the table's green marble top, Colbert savoured the delicious sensation of coolness that emanated from the stone. Out of the corner of his eye, he covertly observed the other eight men assembled in the room for this first council of ministers without the Cardinal: Séguier, the old Chancellor of France, who kept his right hand hidden to mask its uncontrolled tremor; Le Tellier, with his careworn brow; Hugues de Lionne, looking as haughty as ever; La Vrillière, so anxious about any kind of change that his eyes kept darting into every corner of the room; the two Briennes, so insignificant that they were more and more difficult to tell apart; Guénégaud, the epitome of a great lord; and finally Nicolas Fouquet, lost in contemplation of the allegorical painting adorning the mantelpiece.

The door opened suddenly, startling La Vrillière. The two Briennes looked round and Séguier reacted belatedly, when he saw everyone else move.

The King strode briskly in as they got to their feet. Dressed in a bright-blue coat belted with a white silk sash, and a broad-brimmed hat decorated with two white feathers, he halted with his hand thrust forward, resting on the pommel of his ivory cane, and gave the assembled men a searching look from beneath his heavy eyelids.

'Monsieur,' he said, addressing the Chancellor without removing his hat or sitting down, 'I have summoned you here along with my ministers and secretaries of State in order to tell you that until now I have been perfectly content to allow my affairs to be managed by Monsieur Cardinal.'

The cane tapped lightly on the stone floor.

'Now it is time for me to take charge of them myself. There will no longer be a Chief Minister. You will assist me with your counsel, when I request it.'

The nine men bowed solemnly.

'Monsieur de Brienne, you will collaborate with Monsieur de Lionne on all military matters. Monsieur Superintendent, you will benefit from the cooperation of Monsieur Colbert, whom I have made Steward of Finance, a new office especially created for this occasion. Messieurs, you will give reports of your activities directly to me. We shall meet for that purpose in the coming days.'

Colbert attempted a gracious smile, with the addition of a small bow in the direction of the Superintendent, but unable to conceal his excitement, he succeeded only in producing a frightful grimace.

'The face of politics is changing, Chancellor. My principles will be different from the Cardinal's in the government of my State, in the control of my finances and in external negotiations. You know my wishes. It is now up to you, Messieurs, to carry them out.'

The King left the room, deigning to exchange a few words with the courtiers chosen to come and pay homage to the Cardinal. In the front row stood the Archbishop of Rouen, Harlay de Champvallon, president of the clerical assembly.

'Your Majesty ordered me to refer to the Cardinal on all matters,' he began deferentially. 'Now he is dead, to whom does Your Majesty wish me to refer?'

Listening only distractedly but catching the last sentence, the King suddenly turned towards him and looked at him with new interest.

'To me, Monsieur Archbishop. You are to refer to me.'

CHAPTER FORTY

Maincy – Thursday 10 March, noon

'Do not be afraid, Monsieur de Pontbriand. I wish you no harm.'

The man who had just entered the carriage in which Gabriel was sitting was masked. The vehicle, which Fouquet had placed at the young actor's disposal, had come to a halt, and the man had taken advantage of this to briskly open the door and sit down opposite Molière's secretary. Gabriel was disconcerted to hear his family name being spoken.

'What do you want with me? Who are you?' Gabriel cried as the carriage set off again through the narrow, paved streets of the tranquil village of Maincy, a few leagues from the Château de Vaux-le-Vicomte.

'You are Gabriel de Pontbriand, son of André de Pontbriand. When you were five years old, your father left Amboise for England and since then you have had no news of him. Your mother and your uncle told you that he had died in London. You live in Paris on Rue des Lions Saint-Paul,' said the man in a strangely calm voice. 'Your uncle is searching for you and the police are watching you.' Gabriel was thunderstruck.

'But who are you?' demanded the actor angrily.

'My name matters little. I am a friend of your father, whom

you strongly resemble. You are in great danger and I have come to warn you.'

'You knew my father? Why do you speak of him as if he were still alive, and what danger do you wish to warn me about?' Gabriel asked feverishly.

'That is not important now. Today your life is threatened. Monsieur de Pontbriand,' continued the man coolly, 'do not seek to understand, do not try to find out the origin or content of the documents in your possession.'

'What documents?' the young actor demanded in fury.

'Monsieur, time is moving on and we shall soon be arriving at Vaux. Must I really describe to you in detail the coded documents in your possession? Perhaps you'll claim you don't know Monsieur Barrême either. You should stop meddling in all this. The Kingdom is about to experience a period which could prove both crucial and tragic. Extricate yourself from the net in which you have unwittingly been caught. For pity's sake, forget those documents, or give them to Barrême. That would be wise behaviour. They contain secrets that are greater than our own sorry lives!'

The carriage stopped again, this time in the middle of the countryside at the end of the immense driveway bordered with oak trees that ran along the edge of the Superintendent's estate. At that moment the intruder left the vehicle as abruptly as he had entered it.

'We shall meet again, "Cherubino",' he shouted, jumping to the ground and then mounting a horse which was waiting calmly beside a tree. 'Until then, think carefully and be cautious.'

Gabriel sat open-mouthed while he watched the horse gallop away.

'"Cherubino", that's the nickname my dear father used for me! Who is that man? How does he know all this? What was the meaning of that warning?'

The young man asked himself a thousand such questions as the carriage set off along the majestic avenue that led to the steps of the Château de Vaux-le-Vicomte.

Galloping off along the road to Melun, the mysterious coach passenger flung his mask to the ground. He was relieved and happy to have been able to talk to Gabriel.

'The resemblance to André is incredible,' François d'Orbay said to himself. 'Let's hope that my warning at least encourages him to be more cautious!'

CHAPTER FORTY-ONE

Maincy – Friday 11 March, early afternoon

CHARLES Le Brun, the illustrious painter whose task it was to decorate the Château de Vaux-le-Vicomte, stood outside the door of the former Carmelite convent at Melun. He had been waiting stoically in the cold for almost half an hour.

At last the carriage appeared, drawn by four horses from Vaux-le-Vicomte's neighbouring chateau, and stopped in front of the building which Fouquet had reacquired from the nuns of the Carmelite order in 1658. The Superintendent of Finance emerged from the carriage, followed by Jean de La Fontaine and Gabriel.

'So, my dear Le Brun, how is our work progressing?' Fouquet asked, taking the painter by the arm and easing him out of his respectful bow.

'Extremely well, Monseigneur, our heddle setters work miracles every day. Vaux will be decorated just as you wanted it to be. What's more, I have some happy news. Our production rate is at its maximum, which means that I can guarantee here and now that we will meet our deadlines. I can't wait to show it all to you,' added Le Brun.

'Monsieur de La Fontaine, whom you know, and this young man who is with me, are also most eager to visit your hive.

Come, Le Brun, open up your workshops and reveal its wonders to us.'

The four men entered the convent's inner courtyard. Gabriel was stunned by the bustle of activity inside and the methodical organisation which was evident everywhere. The production area was divided into workshops and stores. *It really is a hive; the image is highly appropriate!* thought the young man. In a corner of the courtyard, beneath an awning, lay heaps of bales of uncarded wool from different sheep farms in the Kingdom, which had been commissioned to provide raw material of the highest quality. Le Brun guided them round with a commentary:

'It takes us three days and seven processes in order to treat the wool and transform it. Allow me to tell you, Monseigneur, that from one pound of oiled wool we obtain three thousand feet of double thread which, at the touch of our master heddle setters, turns into the framework and body of the tapestry.'

'Do you have any supply problems?' asked Fouquet.

'When we began, Monseigneur, the mediocre quality of the wool we received obliged us to send back many bales. I must say that now, thanks to your lands on Belle-Île, our raw materials arrive more regularly. Your farmers are dedicated to selecting the finest fleeces,' replied Le Brun.

After they had visited the dyeing workshop, their tour took them to the tapestry designers' studio. Here, the designs were painted onto full-size canvases in reverse. Le Brun was very proud of his Dutch designers; he had brought them over expressly, and they copied his paintings with incredible talent.

'Look, Monseigneur,' the painter declared proudly standing

before an immense design which had been laid flat on the table. 'This will be the portière – I showed you the sketches for it.'

Fouquet bent over the work.

'I admire your talent, Monsieur. That squirrel in the centre has a graceful delicacy that is quite delightful. I cannot wait to see it in silk and cotton, and to admire the effect at Vaux.'

Gabriel was fascinated. Each of the three hundred workers seemed to have a precise understanding of what he had to do. Everything seemed as carefully choreographed as a ballet, in particular the work of the heddle setters whose incredibly agile fingers brought to life the works of art designed by the painter. In the storeroom, Gabriel had the leisure to admire and feel the tapestries accumulating there before their delivery to Vaux. This was the moment Le Brun chose to ask his patron about an embarrassing matter.

'Monseigneur, yesterday I delivered the inventories Monsieur Colbert asked for, but . . .'

'What's that?' Fouquet interrupted him. 'What inventories are you talking about?'

'It seemed strange to me too,' said the painter, relieved to be able to unburden himself. 'Monsieur Colbert asked me for a complete inventory of the production area. I spent two days writing a memorandum, which detailed the exact state of our stocks, a complete list of our workers and master journeymen, their salaries and the number of our machines. I thought you had been informed of this request.'

'Absolutely not!' Fouquet raged. 'What is Colbert up to? This is my home and I fully intend to remain master of it. You should not have acceded to that request without informing me.'

Gabriel, who was only a few feet away, did not miss a single word of the discussion. *So, Colbert continues his machinations: first he tried to sabotage Molière's plays, and now he has a minister under surveillance. He's completely brazen, and he appears to have no scruples*, he thought with a frown of disgust.

'This confirms my suspicions,' said La Fontaine. 'He was supposed to act in the Cardinal's name, but now that His Eminence is dead, you must not tolerate these intrigues any longer. Monsieur Superintendent,' went on the storyteller, leading Fouquet into a more discreet corner of the storeroom, 'when will you finally realise that Colbert, that venomous master of deceit, is engineering your downfall? I am convinced that he has spent the past few weeks trying to pressurise the dying Mazarin into suggesting to the King that the position of Chief Minister should be abolished, with the sole aim of barring your route to power. You are too good-hearted or, if you will allow me, too naïve. You must do something!'

Fouquet was disturbed by Colbert's audacity in daring to give orders in the Superintendent of Finance's own house. *La Fontaine is right*, Gabriel told himself as he stood silently some distance away. His gaze fell on the motif drawn from Fouquet's coat of arms. *A squirrel confronting a snake*, he thought with a sigh.

'My dear Jean, I am sure you are right,' said the Superintendent after a long silence, taking his friend's arm and returning to Le Brun, who was still standing in the centre of the room. 'I shall request an audience with His Majesty without delay, to clear this up. I shall also see the Queen Mother. You know the affection she has for me. In fact I have a sum of money to pay her, and that will give me a pretext to speak of all this and ask her advice.'

Le Brun, still ashamed of his blunder, was waiting somewhat anxiously for the Superintendent.

'In future, try to be less artistic in your management of the production area,' said Fouquet with a smile. 'I shall forgive you on account of the marvels produced here under your direction. You have enchanted us, Monsieur Painter. Still, since the art of the inventory seems to be another of your strengths, you will kindly provide me as swiftly as possible with a memorandum containing all the information you gave to Colbert.'

Le Brun bowed, clearly happy to have emerged so well from the affair.

'Your workers seem underfed,' added the Superintendent of Finance. 'You must be wearing them out with work. To show them my gratitude, you may pay them an additional tenth of their salary from this week on. What is it, Gabriel?' he turned to the young man.

'I . . . I was wondering where all these people live, all these workers and artists: is there a building allocated to them?'

Le Brun's expression soured. Then, when Fouquet gestured that he would welcome an answer to this question himself, he replied, scowling at Gabriel.

'Well . . .' he began, 'we have of course been concentrating our efforts on production . . . Not all the additional building works have yet been finished and . . .'

Fouquet cut him off in a voice that was suddenly icy.

'I had forgotten this matter. Thank you, Gabriel, for your pertinent intervention. It enables me to make good my oversight, which pleases me. But it also obliges me to repeat my instructions to you, which displeases me,' he growled. 'I would appreciate it if you would swiftly finish the work necessary to convert the old Carmelite convent and lodge these people there in a decent manner,' said the Superintendent firmly. 'I will no longer tolerate the sight of these workers being housed worse than animals, and within a few leagues of my chateau! Damn it, Monsieur Le Brun, how many times do I have to reiterate the value I attach to the living conditions of everyone who is in my service!'

Gabriel gazed at the Superintendent with silent admiration.

'I shall see that it is done, Monseigneur,' was all that Le Brun said in reply, his head bowed. 'I shall see that it is done.'

CHAPTER FORTY-TWO

François d'Orbay's residence – Friday 11 March,
eleven o'clock at night

S TANDING by the window of his large office, with his long,
sinewy hands clasped behind his back, François d'Orbay
watched the rain fall in large droplets onto the paving stones.
The downfall prevented him from having a clear view of the
courtyard, which was deserted and lit only by two storm lanterns
mounted on either side of the door. His visitor was late, but
curiously the wait did not displease the architect. He sighed and
took a few steps towards the centre of the room where he caught
sight of his image in the mirror hanging on the wall. His features
seemed harder, his face leaner. He stepped a little closer. *So, the
years are beginning to show*, he thought with bittersweet irony.
The silence, which filled the house, disturbed only by the pitter-
patter of rain on the roof and windows, seemed restful to him. He
left the room, crossing the salon and the entrance hall, and
headed in the direction of his children's apartments, groping his
way through the half-light from memory with one hand
brushing the wall. The sound of his feet on the tiled floor woke
the governess, who half sat up in her bed in the anteroom. He
gestured to her to lie down again and continued towards the door
of the room where his little boy and girl were sleeping. A weak
ray of light filtered through the shutters of the window, which

opened onto the garden, enabling him to find his way. He stopped for a moment at the head of the two beds, then knelt and pulled the covers up to the children's chins.

How often have I been able to see them sleeping like this? he thought. One year in Rome, another in London, all that incessant travelling: the years had passed so quickly, and the burden resting on his shoulders was so weighty. He was always in a hurry, suspicious of everything and everyone, always fearing betrayal and imagining the worst. God, how all-consuming this passion was! How many times in the past ten years had he escaped prison or death? How many times had he taken insane risks without informing his family, without his wife knowing what he was thinking when he remained silent for minutes on end? *But then again, I have been lucky*, he thought with a shiver. He closed his eyes to drive away the familiar faces of those not so lucky, and then opened them again. The two children were sleeping soundly. He gently lifted the little boy's inert arm, taking away the wooden horse he had kept close to him, and placing it beside the bed; he pushed aside the locks of hair, which trailed across the little girl's forehead. Then he stood up regretfully. The voice of his personal valet jolted him out of his reverie. He stood in the doorway, calling to him in a whisper:

'Monsieur! Monsieur! Your visitor has arrived.'

The architect sighed and turned to follow his servant. On the threshold of the room, he took one last long look before closing the door, ensuring that the latch made no sound.

Giacomo Del Sarto sat by the fire, stretching his hands out towards the flames whose light played on his face, emphasising his pale complexion. His black cloak was spread out over a nearby chair, and water trickled from it onto the ochre-coloured hexagonal floor tiles. He pointed to it in disgust as d'Orbay entered:

'All I did was step out of the carriage and take a few steps, and here I am, soaked to the skin. It seems that we are destined to meet each other only on stormy days!'

He stood up and they embraced warmly. Then they both sat down in silence as the valet left the room.

'Well,' began Giacomo Del Sarto when the door had closed, 'what is going on? I left Rome as soon as I received your message. I didn't think we would be seeing each other again so soon after our last meeting. You had me worried, you know. I don't like these emergency procedures.'

D'Orbay sighed and poked the fire.

'I had no choice. I needed your advice and there was no time to convene our Brothers. What's more, I don't think that would be wise in the current climate.'

Giacomo leant forward, his brows knitted.

'Things are that bad?'

'Alas, they are. There have been strange goings-on these last few days. There seem to be various influences acting upon one another . . . First, you should know that the lost documents have reappeared.'

The visitor almost shouted out in surprise:

'What? Where?'

'It is a curious story. It seems that our worst fears were well founded: the documents which as you know André had to abandon when he escaped, were indeed in the hands of Mazarin.

Fortunately for us, they remained unintelligible to him. The code was never broken. And I am convinced we were well served by the Italian's pathological suspicion. He dared not mention the secret to anyone in case they already understood it . . . In short, the dog died without knowing . . .'

'But the documents,' cut in Del Sarto, 'how were they released from Mazarin's clutches? Who has them now?'

'I am coming to that; this is where the story becomes intriguing. A group of zealots partially burned down Mazarin's palace to cover up a burglary. I do not know exactly what they were looking for, but I am now convinced that without realising, those criminals stole our documents and then lost them in their flight. They were found by a young man who by chance then crossed paths with Nicolas Fouquet and has since become his protégé . . . A young man whose identity I knew the moment I saw him, before I even knew his name, so striking is his resemblance to his father.'

Giacomo absorbed this and sank deeper into his armchair, clasping his hands.

'You have guessed too,' went on d'Orbay, getting to his feet. 'Yes, the young man who got his hands on the documents is André's son, Gabriel de Pontbriand. A curious irony of history, don't you think?' he asked with a slight tremor in his voice. 'Fifteen years ago the father escapes death by a miracle and loses the documents. For fifteen years we tremble, not knowing where they are, protected as they are only by the code which governs them. And then Providence, or whatever you like to call it, takes delight in plunging a second Pontbriand into this vipers' nest, just when we are almost at our goal . . .'

'Can we get them back from him, without telling him?'

'I fear, alas, that it will not be as simple as that. According to Barrême – who as usual said too much but at least thought to alert me when the young innocent came to him asking him to decode the papers – he saw the signature, which is not in code. He knows that this is the only thread linking him to his father. I could of course silence him,' he said in a sinister voice. 'The thought did cross my mind, I must confess. But I do not have the right. That is why I wanted to see you.'

'And what about Nicolas? We must not lose sight of the essential point. What does he say about this?'

D'Orbay shook his head.

'We have spoken of it. That is another reason for my bringing you here. The most recent information since the death of Mazarin seems to indicate that the young King is determined to abandon his games and his idleness in order to govern. He no longer wants a Chief Minister. This does upset our plans somewhat. We would have preferred to retain an easily manipulable monarch. That was our hope when we met in Rome, and it would have been simpler. Still, instead of prevaricating, I think we should hasten our plans in the light of these events. I have already given orders for the works at Vaux to be speeded up, and I have no difficulty in justifying that. The longer we wait, the less we will be able to impose our view on the King. Conversely, by acting swiftly we can take advantage of the fact that his resolve has not yet translated into actions. And we are more certain to succeed because, through young Pontbriand, we now have hope of recovering the key to the Secret, and of being able to read the document, which will soon to be on its way from Rome. On the strength of this additional trump card, Nicolas will be able to convince the King, of that there is no longer any doubt.'

He sat down opposite his visitor and gazed at him seriously.

'I believe we will have to act this summer at the latest, as soon as we have recovered the manuscript and the key which allows us to decipher it. But we will have to take risks. What do you think?'

'That is for you to judge, François,' replied Giacomo softly. 'First, try to recover the formula. For that, I think you will have to go to London as soon as possible,' he added. 'As to the rest, consult Nicolas. I will agree to whatever you decide.'

D'Orbay appeared relieved.

'That is what I was hoping to hear. I have to confess, the post horses have already been reserved as far as Calais. I will leave immediately. It is one more breach of our safety rules, but too much is at stake.'

The Grand Master nodded with a half-smile. Taking d'Orbay's hands, he clasped them tightly before getting to his feet to retrieve his cloak.

'I on the other hand shall stay here for two days. Long enough for a debate at the Sorbonne and a private consultation. Then nobody will be surprised by my visit to Paris.'

Six hours later, before the dawn lit the paving stones, which glistened with the previous night's rain, François D'Orbay was walking down the staircase, dressed for his journey. As he crossed the entrance hall, he thought of the little bodies slumbering behind the bedroom door and quickened his step.

CHAPTER FORTY-THREE

*Versailles hunting lodge – Sunday 13 March, seven o'clock
in the evening*

THE last rays of sunlight were disappearing above the forest,
leaving a few rosy streaks amongst the fat clouds massed on
the horizon. Lost in contemplation, Louise de La Vallière gazed
through the window of the anonymous carriage which had come
to fetch her from the toll-gate in Faubourg Saint-Germain. In an
effort to control the emotion which made her hands tremble, she
had spent the whole journey looking out at the countryside, as
the carriage brought her via the Meudon road to the marshy
valley where the Versailles hunting lodge stood. The young girl
frowned with disappointment as they rounded the final bend and
she spotted the building's rectangular mass.

'I'd imagined it would be bigger,' she murmured to herself.

Then she felt herself blush at her own audacity, and her heart
began to race again. She could see the fascinating image of the
King's face in her mind's eye; it had filled her dreams for the
past fortnight, ever since her presentation to him and the receipt
of that note. She had not dared reply but there had been a
second note, and a third . . . and now she was on her way to this
momentous meeting. '*I am hunting at Versailles that day and
dare to hope that you will consent to join me for supper there at the
haven inherited from my father which I cherish most particularly. If*

you do me this honour, you will find a carriage awaiting you at the toll-gate of the Abbey de Saint-Germain at five o'clock. There is no need to respond. Not daring to ask for a 'yes', even a 'perhaps' is enough to fill my heart with hope.' She recited the words of the message for the hundredth time. Everything, right down to the absence of a signature, touched her, moved her and thrilled her by adding to the romantic nature of the adventure. She felt fleeting remorse at not having spoken to Gabriel about these exchanges, though she had found him anxious and curiously distant during the past few days. He had refused to answer her when she questioned him about this silence.

The carriage's final jolt as it stopped at the end of a little road lined with cypress trees brought her back to reality. As she stepped down from the carriage, she noticed that it was now completely dark.

'Take care, Madame, the ground is uneven,' said the manservant who lit her way.

The cold made her shiver and she pulled her stole up over her head, holding it tightly about her shoulders. At the end of the pathway, a lantern hinted at the lodge's contours. As she began to walk along the earthen path, Louise imagined she was dreaming again as she had as a child. She had walked just like this, or even run, towards the prince who would tear her away from her life in Anjou, carry her far away from her family, far from the burdensome reality whose boredom she could not share with anyone except Gabriel, her confidant and playmate.

'You're a boy,' she would say. 'You can leave, run away, fight, become a buccaneer . . . But I have nothing to look forward to.'

How she had wept when he disappeared without trace!

The lodge was quite distinct now, its rows of red brick interspersed with white stone from the quarries nearby.

'My God, it's a far cry from Amboise,' she murmured as she stepped onto the paved terrace that led to the entrance.

The hunt had been disappointing. They had tracked a young stag all day, only for it to escape in the end, toying with the hunting party and leaving them exhausted and robbed of their victory. Furious, the King had abandoned the hunt there and then, working off his anger by riding his mount at breakneck speed through the woodland which sloped down towards the valley. The musketeers had difficulty in following him and were dismissed at the gate, the King demanding that his carriage be readied without delay, and that he be left alone. The coach left shortly afterwards with the entire retinue, but without the King, who had discreetly remained in the apartment which had been appointed for him on the upper floor of the hunting lodge. An hour later, the sovereign's anger had abated only slightly. Still in his hunting clothes, having merely scrubbed his upper body with cold water and exchanged his leather baldrick for an indoor jacket of purple silk, Louis XIV was still wandering about his office, his heavy boots echoing on the wooden floor. The creaking of carriage wheels and the neighing of horses drew him to the window, which overlooked the surrounding woodland and the track that led to the back of the lodge to facilitate secret arrivals. Narrowing his eyes to see more clearly, the sovereign suddenly made out the bright patch of Louise's gown. She was walking quickly, scarcely lifting her skirts whose hems concealed her feet giving the impression that she was moving without touching the ground. The King observed the graceful silhouette with a satisfied sigh as its features gradually became clearer. She looked up as she approached the building, and he smiled, knowing that she could not see him. He realised that it was the innocence and dignity that emanated from her slender neck, her narrow, almost triangular face, and her large bright eyes that was so moving. Tearing himself away from his contemplation of her as she reached the front steps, the King of France automatically glanced in the mirror as he left the room. He saw the reflection of a young man of twenty-three, whose eyes still burned with the embers of rage, now softened by a roguish glint.

The King wiped his mouth, drank a mouthful of wine and looked up at Louise.

'Do you like the quails? And the wine? It comes from the vineyard at Vougeot. Monsieur de Condé did me the honour of giving me several cases because I was weak enough to tell him that it was to my taste. But you are not eating anything,' he added, serving himself again from one of the numerous dishes lined up between them on the pristine tablecloth.

'The Prince de Condé?' murmured Louise.

The King merely smiled.

'Such is my cross, Mademoiselle. Everyone thinks they can interpret my words and imagine that they please me by repeating things which once solicited a word of appreciation from me, when that word may have been spoken simply by chance . . .'

Noticing that the young girl was blushing, the King pulled himself up:

'Look here,' he said, reaching into his shirt for a small key that was attached to his neck by a golden chain, 'do you know what this key is, Mademoiselle?'

At the young girl's stunned expression, the King continued:

'It was given to me by a loyal friend, who was delighted to be able to bring me a gift of cocoa transported back from the Indies alongside a cargo of spices. He had a hermetically sealed box made, and locked the cocoa inside it. Then he gave it to me, making me promise always to carry the key about my person for fear that someone might rob me. So I am in charge of the cocoa, and nobody can get to it without my permission . . .'

He was trying not to laugh.

'You will note that I accepted it because he is a very dear friend. And I like the idea because it makes me think of him.'

He fell silent for a moment and considered the young girl's astonished expression.

'What do you think, do tell me! Do you think I should give it up, take the key from my neck, and hand over the burden to someone else? Don't be afraid, speak: the King demands your advice,' he said with mock-severity.

Louise now gently raised her eyes.

'Not at all, Sire, I think you should keep it. Just make one or two copies of it to enable others to share the cocoa.'

'How right you are,' commented the King with a smile. 'But you have listened enough. Tell me about yourself.'

'About myself!' cried the young woman. 'But Sire, there is nothing to say. I was born seventeen years ago in Amboise, I had a happy childhood thanks to the generosity of your uncle, God rest his soul, and I owe it to his protection that I was chosen as a companion for your future sister-in-law. There is nothing else to say. I have neither a cargo of cocoa to deliver to Your Majesty, nor witty conversation with which to entertain you . . .'

Louise broke off anxiously. The King had suddenly got up from the table, throwing his napkin onto his plate. Seeing that he was still smiling, she regained her composure and stood too, amazed to see him walk round the table and personally draw back the chair behind her. As she was curtseying, he took her hand without a word and led her towards the garden. The clouds had drifted away, and stars were now twinkling in the darkness.

'I love this soft, damp air', said the King of France. 'It brings back the taste of my childhood. For me this is a place of repose, and also a dream, the dream of something different,' he said thoughtfully as he gazed up at the sky.

All of a sudden she shivered, and he asked anxiously if she was cold. She shook her head, but without listening to her he rushed inside, leaving her dazed and alone, only to return a moment later carrying a silk shawl.

'It was given to me by the Venetian ambassador to support the countless unlikely tales he told me about his compatriots' exploits in China,' commented the King in a low voice as he placed it around Louise's shoulders. 'Just think, the threads which cover your back have travelled thousands of leagues from China to Versailles,' he added, standing back to judge the effect of the silken fabric.

'Look, I am cold too,' he went on, holding out his hands to the young girl.

Crouching a few yards away in the shadow cast by the trees, a dark figure who had observed the entire scene watched the King and the young girl go back into the lodge, side by side. The silhouette remained there for a few more seconds before disappearing, swallowed up by the darkness.

CHAPTER FORTY-FOUR

Jean-Baptiste Colbert's residence – Monday 14 March, eleven o'clock in the morning

WITH his arms folded, Colbert hesitated for a moment before repeating his order:

'More to the left . . . further still!'

The docile workers carrying the heavy antique bowls moved them inch by inch along the wall of the entrance hall, opposite the stone staircase which led up to the first floor.

'There,' exclaimed the new Steward of Finance, 'that's better.'

He stepped forward and measured with his feet the space between each of the bowls and the black marble cabochons that separated the white marble tiles on the floor. Satisfied that the gaps were equal, he moved away again to enjoy the effect.

'Good,' he said, rubbing his hands and setting off upstairs two steps at a time. 'Now for the chest of drawers on the landing!'

Resigned, the workers followed in his wake.

'This has been going on for four days,' whispered one.

'He obviously never sleeps,' moaned another.

'Come, come, hurry up,' Colbert urged them, at the same time quickly scanning a document handed to him on the stairs by a secretary.

'Ah!' he broke off, examining a sheet from another bundle

his colleague had given him before leaving as swiftly as he had arrived. 'Time is pressing and my visitors will have arrived for the meeting. More's the pity,' he sighed regretfully as he glanced at the chest of drawers he had wanted to move. 'We shall continue later.'

As he walked back to his office on the ground floor, overlooking the garden, Colbert spent a moment enjoying the sight of the new interior: 'my' new interior, he thought. For several years, Colbert had been accommodated free of charge in this small private residence adjoining the Cardinal's. In the four days since he had become its effective owner – subject only to Parlement's ratification of the will – he had come to regard each room and each piece of furniture with passion. As though endowed with new energy, he had sacrificed some of his rare hours of sleep to undertake the total redecoration of the house to which, until then, he had paid scant attention.

Toussaint Roze – whom Colbert had appropriated without delay – stuck his head through the door of the anteroom.

'Monsieur Lulli is here, Monsieur,' he announced.

Without answering, Colbert indicated that his reflections were not to be disturbed. The visitor could wait. This was another rule the new owner had established.

'Where was I?' he went on softly, rubbing his eyes which lack of sleep made appear even heavier than usual.

Now that the first stage had been achieved, with Fouquet miraculously distanced from his dream of becoming Chief Minister, he would have to build upon that success. First he would feed the King's mistrust towards the Superintendent of Finance, started by the intervention of the Cardinal before his death: *Things are moving in the right direction*, thought Colbert. Next he would cut off Fouquet from his networks as much as possible: *That is today's task*, he murmured, glancing again at the list of names lying before him. *Once that is done, I must also think about keeping an eye on the King's volatile temperament*, he told himself thoughtfully. *And shed some light on that curious story of stolen documents the Queen Mother told me about. There is something about it that's being hidden from me, something that is not entirely above board . . . I don't know what part the Superintendent, the travelling entertainer and that scheming woman play in it, but I shall find out every detail in the end.*

A carnivorous smile twisted his mouth:

And then I shall think about my position, he concluded, ringing the bell which the Cardinal had used for so long. Toussaint Roze reappeared at the familiar sound:

'Why have I not seen the royal warrant for the Vice-Protector of the Academy of Painting and Sculpture? I spoke to Monsieur Le Tellier about it and he was supposed to be bringing it here.'

'I am expecting it this morning, Monsieur.'

'Good. I shall look at it over lunch. Now, send in whoever is waiting to see me.'

As Toussaint Roze closed the door behind him, Colbert glanced at the garden, musing that he would also have to redesign the copses.

'But plants grow so slowly; it takes too much time,' he grumbled in annoyance.

The sight of the walls enclosing the little park had made him think about the gardens at Vaux. His informers brought him regular descriptions, which made him so angry that he refused to read them.

The door opened again as he looked away from the scarcely flourishing vegetation.

'Monsieur Lulli, Monsieur,' announced Toussaint Roze, leaving them alone.

In came the Italian musician, bent double in a respectful bow. He clasped his hands and stretched them towards Colbert in an air of supplication.

'Ah, Monsieur Colbert, I am in despair!'

'Come, come, Monsieur,' urged the Steward, a little surprised by this attack of theatricality. 'What is the purpose of your visit?'

'With the passing of Monsieur Cardinal, Monsieur Colbert, I have lost more than a protector, a patron, and the source of my inspiration . . . The Cardinal, Monsieur Colbert . . .' lamented the Italian, whose interminable sentences and gabbled diction were further complicated by his pronounced accent.

Colbert raised a hand to halt the torrent of words.

'That is sufficient, Monsieur. I understand your distress and it is justified. I share it, as does the entire Kingdom. But for pity's sake, what is it you need? What is it you lack? What do you want?'

Thrown by Colbert's cold tone and directness, the musician was struck dumb for a moment.

'Well . . .' he began.

Colbert gestured that he should continue.

How I detest him, him and his kind, he thought as Lulli began a rambling discourse trying to explain that he wanted nothing for himself, *how gladly I would crush them; what the devil was the Cardinal thinking of, putting up with them? And what weakness on Fouquet's part to support them . . . At least the trade in paintings, of which the protectorship of the Academy of Painting and Sculpture will give me a monopoly, will enable me to earn some money! But this, this cheap theatrical whining. Anyway, since he's asking . . .*

'Very well, Monsieur,' he cut in. 'You wish to be Steward of Music? I have heard your request and I shall look upon it favourably when I speak to His Majesty about you.'

Colbert withdrew his hand in irritation as Lulli attempted to seize it.

'That will take a little time. I have to take the oath for my new offices. Besides, I have been charged with putting the Cardinal's affairs in order,' he said, puffing out his chest, 'and this will occupy my days to a large extent. But don't worry, I shall see to it.'

Lulli opened his mouth to thank him, but Colbert glared at him.

'Do not thank me, Monsieur, before anything has been arranged. Moreover I ask nothing of you except an assurance of your fidelity . . .'

Lulli nodded vigorously.

'Your *exclusive* fidelity,' Colbert concluded, looking him straight in the eye. 'We understand each other completely, do we not?'

Lowering his eyes, the musician nodded again.

Once Lulli had gone, Colbert allowed himself a small smile of satisfaction.

'One. A small one, but one all the same. The next one is more important,' he added greedily. 'You are to summon Molière as soon as possible,' Colbert said to Toussaint Roze, who had returned having shown the musician out, 'preferably before my imminent departure for Fontainebleau, where I am to join the King,' he added, unable to prevent himself assuming an air of superiority. Then the joyous but cruel gleam that had appeared in his eyes grew brighter.

'Is he here yet?' he asked, looking once again at his list of appointments, and at a nod from Roze, Colbert commanded:

'Show in Monsieur Everhard Jabach!'.

CHAPTER FORTY-FIVE

Fontainebleau – Monday 14 March, eleven o'clock in
the morning

FOUQUET detested his office. It was located in the financial administration building constructed under Louis XIII, which adjoined the Oval Court, a few yards from the main body of the Château de Fontainebleau. It was late morning, and he was coming to the end of some tedious signatures. The last document he had to examine concerned a decision the King had taken the previous day, to transform the Église de Saint-Louis in Fontainebleau into an autonomous parish and to allocate it to missionaries specialising in the care of lepers.

'Well,' thought the Superintendent, 'the King really does seem to be dealing with everything now. And here am I, transformed into a parish clerk!' Hearing the clock on the front of the nearby Albret residence strike eleven, Nicolas Fouquet broke off from what he was doing. The hour of his audience with Louis XIV was approaching, and he would have to set off without delay.

Louis XIV had come to Fontainebleau for the first time at the age of six, and he liked to return regularly to escape the burdens of etiquette at the Paris Court. This time the King had brought forward his visit, hoping no doubt to dispel the emotion and sadness of his godfather's death. He had even decided to take up residence there, despite the fact that a large proportion of the furniture which travelled with the King was still in Paris. He had arrived the previous evening and was already in his hunting clothes again. His gloves were folded and threaded through an impressive leather belt which displayed his favourite cutlass to good effect; it was with this blade, given to him by Mazarin on his thirteenth birthday, that he killed the finest stags in the nearby forest. As Fouquet walked into the room, preceded by the sovereign's principal valet, he stopped in his tracks, dumb-founded. There in front of him the King of France was dancing, dressed in all his hunting finery!

'Come in, come in, Monsieur Superintendent,' said the King, barely turning his head so as not to lose the thread of the figure he was executing. 'You see, I rehearse everything just like a strolling player. I am practising the "Ballet of the Seasons", so as to be ready for the celebrations I shall be holding here next spring.'

Not entirely sure how to respond, Fouquet gazed admiringly at the young sovereign's agility as he danced, the rhythm indicated only by the tapping of the dancing master's cane on the wooden floor.

'That will suffice,' said the King, extracting a fine lace handkerchief from his sleeve and mopping his brow. 'I must speak to Monsieur Superintendent – it is time to turn our attentions to matters of State.'

Louis XIV signalled to his dancing master and valets to leave, and sat down in his armchair.

As he stood before his King, Nicolas Fouquet did as

etiquette dictated and executed three magnificent bows, so deep that he swept the floor with the plume of his hat. From the King's response – a nod of the head – he knew that he was permitted to speak.

'Sire, I listened to Your Majesty at the Grand Council which followed the passing of His Eminence and I have asked to speak to you this morning about a matter concerning the management of the Kingdom's finances, which is worrying me. It is my duty to tell Your Majesty the truth about the past. Necessity forced me to deviate from the proper respect for prescribed forms and procedures in my management of the Treasury. Your Majesty will no doubt hear rumours of all this.'

Astonished by these unexpected confidences, Louis XIV looked searchingly at his Superintendent of Finance.

'Your Majesty should know,' continued Fouquet, 'that everything I did was in perfect agreement with and under the sole authority of Cardinal Mazarin. We took enormous risks in order to re-establish confidence in the State's solvency, in particular following the terrible liquidity crisis of 1654. Often, Sire, without Your Majesty's knowledge, I staked my own possessions in order to guarantee the King of France's signature. Today you are taking on the burden of the country's government. It was my duty to tell you the truth. I have come humbly to beg your pardon for the improprieties committed solely in the interest of the Kingdom's finances. My crime is that I have always sought to do my best to protect my King, and to respect the orders of the Cardinal your godfather to the letter,' ended the Superintendent, bowing his head.

Louis XIV seemed impressed by this admission.

'Indeed,' he replied, 'I have heard certain rumours of racketeering that implicate you. The service of the State as I see it demands extreme rigour. I expect exemplary self-denial on the part of my ministers. From now on, the Kingdom's interest must prevail over personal and family interests, Monsieur Superintendent.'

'Those are words which I gladly make my own, Sire. How many times have I uttered them! You know how much your dear godfather loved his family. In recent days, you will have been able to measure the consequences resulting from the greed of those close to him, at a time when it has become necessary to sell off inheritances.'

Fouquet knew he had struck home with this allusion to Mazarin's will. There was nothing the King did not know about his Chief Minister's financial abuses, and doubtless even less about Colbert's role in concealing the sources of the fortune belonging to the Italian's clan. He should have no difficulty imagining that Fouquet also knew Mazarin's affairs. Was this not the right moment for him to bury it all along with the dear Cardinal? Also, the King knew that Fouquet had never failed him. On the contrary, the King had benefited on numerous occasions from sums acquired thanks to his minister's financial agility.

'Monsieur Superintendent,' said the King, 'your course of action honours you. Let us forget the past; I grant you my pardon. In future, I ask that you adhere to the usual rules. Also, I order you from now on to put an end to loans at usurious rates, to cease the practice of excessive discounting of bills and to settle immediately all transfers and extraordinary arrangements.'

'Sire,' replied the Superintendent, relieved at these words, 'I promise that I will continue to serve Your Majesty with all the zeal and affection imaginable.'

'To provide you with a further indication of my trust,' said the young King in a softer voice, 'I command you to create a council for overseas trade, in order to provide the Kingdom with the means to fight off competition from certain of our neighbours. Along with Messieurs Aligre, Colbert and Lefèvre d'Ormesson, you shall be taking decisions which are of the utmost importance to the Kingdom's prosperity. Let us forget the past so that we may work for the greatness of France,' concluded the King, standing up as Fouquet bowed low. 'Monsieur d'Artagnan awaits me and I am in a hurry to hunt out that full-grown stag whose boldness my master of hounds so praises,' added Louis XIV as he strode out of the room to join his hunting party.

In the corridor Fouquet met Lionne, who immediately petitioned him regarding his gambling debts and asked him to grant a new deadline for payment. As magnanimous as the sovereign, Fouquet once again yielded to his request. It was the best way to align himself with this powerful member of the King's Council. Fouquet made his way back to his office with a light heart, and found himself face to face with Colbert.

'Monsieur Colbert, how pleased I am to see you,' he said cheerfully. 'His Majesty has entrusted me with creating and directing a council for overseas trade. I suggested that you should be a member, knowing of your taste for maritime matters. Despite the King's initial reticence due to the consider-able burdens currently resting on your shoulders, you should know that he nevertheless granted me this request. So we shall meet again shortly to talk about that,' concluded Fouquet, and he went on his way without giving Colbert another glance.

'How delightful,' answered Colbert darkly.

CHAPTER FORTY-SIX

*Westminster, London – Wednesday 16 March, nine o'clock
in the morning*

WALKING along the banks of the Thames, François d'Orbay turned off the path as soon as a bend in the river provided a glimpse of the Tower of London's distant outline. He plunged deep into the alleyways which led up from the muddy quays to the centre of the city, several times thanking heaven for his good knowledge of the city's landmarks. In fact the fog which had veiled the horizon when he awoke seemed to be growing thicker with every minute. Given the narrow winding streets, lined with tall wooden houses, he would have had little chance of finding his way without the help of a native. And in these troubled times, that was an extremely perilous proposition. Turning round, he tried again without success to make out the contours of the Tower which could guide him on his way. The few lamps illuminating the inn signs looked like yellowish haloes. Lowering his head, he quickened his pace.

Ten years had passed since their last meeting. He had been so young back then, almost an apprentice. So much had happened since. He felt suddenly apprehensive, as if the experiences he had accumulated during that period – the journeys, the encounters, the family he had created – might serve to emphasise how much their paths had diverged.

He was about to stop again, when the dark mass of the abbey suddenly loomed up before him. The fog obscured its height, concealing the greater part of the building, but he was over-joyed as he recognised the iron gate.

The fog may thicken all it likes, he thought as he climbed over it. *Now it is my ally*. He set off along the path leading to the church door, then turned onto the earthen track which forked off after a few yards and led towards the willows in the grave-yard. When he reached the curtain of trees he too vanished, swallowed up by the mist.

André de Pontbriand shivered, feeling the cold chill his feet. Hidden behind a tree, he was pleased to see François d'Orbay appear through the foliage. *Almost on time*, he thought. As he followed him across the little wooden bridge spanning the stream which ran alongside the tombs, he carefully observed his former pupil's movements, gait and moments of uncertainty. He smiled when he saw him frown as he searched for the designated tree, then crept after him.

François d'Orbay stood stock-still, gazing at the weeping willow. He was just bending forward to decipher the inscription on the tomb when a voice made him turn round.

'It is the tomb of John Donne. I am fond of his poems and I like to stroll here from time to time. Even if it is early in the morning and the weather is hardly welcoming . . .'

The emphases were the same and so was the slightly drawling intonation. D'Orbay stepped forward and embraced the man tightly.

'Let me look at you,' the man said as he stepped back, his outstretched arms still resting on François' shoulders. 'You still have the eyes of a child, but with a few small lines now, and an unfamiliar hard glint in them.'

François d'Orbay was so full of emotion that for a moment he could not speak. *How he has aged*, he thought as he took in the white hair, the almost translucent skin and the hollow cheeks. Even his blue eyes, which seemed larger now that his face was ravaged by fatigue, no longer shone with the same brilliance, as if all the life within the tall, emaciated body had taken refuge there in order to fight one final battle.

It was Pontbriand who broke the silence.

'Come, François, let us take a stroll. Walking is not easy for me, but I do not much care for standing still.'

Then, as d'Orbay noticed Pontbriand grimacing as he put his weight on his stiff right leg, he said grimly:

'That hasn't got any better either, has it?'

They slowly walked a little way together, along the banks of the stream. The visibility was better now, and d'Orbay had the feeling that he was walking beside a shadow. Only the old man's exhausted breathing gave him any substance.

'You know that poem by John Donne, François. How does it go? "Blood, suffering, sweat and tears / are all that the earth possesses . . ." Sometimes, I confess, I have the impression that it was written for me.'

André de Pontbriand now stood facing the almost invisible bulk of the abbey, his blue eyes seeming to see through the wall of mist.

'Fifteen years, François, for fifteen years I have been living like a rat. It is fifteen years since I saw my family, kissed my wife, took my children in my arms. Fifteen years during which I have vegetated like a hermit, for fear of compromising my Brothers. For fifteen years I have reproached myself for having placed our cause in danger and saving my own life without making good the damage I had done.'

When he turned back towards François, the younger man saw that his eyes were feverish.

'Is it not curious? I saved my own life, but only to live like a dead man, concealed and useless. All I have done is teach children from time to time, as I once taught you, never to see them again . . . And all this, only for our plans to fail one after the other,' he said, indignant, 'as they did again, here in England!'

'The conditions turned out not to be favourable,' François cut in briskly. 'The men were unsuitable: too divided, too ambitious.'

André de Pontbriand gestured listlessly.

'You don't have to humour me, for pity's sake. I know the truth: why hide it from each other? Our men thought that to kill a King would be enough to bring down the edifice of tyranny and change the course of everything, alter a country's destiny. But killing the King of England served no purpose, because he had a son and supporters who survived; worse, who found in his death a new energy to fight the revolution that had begun. And do you know why they won in the end, why this attempt to abolish a despotic order failed, why there is once again a King upon the English throne? Because that revolution was incapable of producing for all to see the proof of the purity of its intentions. All it had to show was the blood that dripped from a man's severed head. What a mistake: to believe that the murder of a King could replace the need to demonstrate why the monarchy should be overthrown . . . Oh, I quite understand the impatience of those who acted: it is not easy to possess the truth without being able to demonstrate it. But however tragic the prospect of having to wait, perhaps for centuries more, we must no longer allow ourselves to be blinded; we must no longer believe that we can triumph before we have rediscovered the key that gives access to the Secret.'

The old man's face tensed.

'I am more aware of this than anyone else. I have paid so dearly for it that my belief in its ultimate success is perhaps the only thing that still keeps me alive . . .'

D'Orbay frowned uncomfortably and laid a hand on the arm of the man whose voice had suddenly become faint.

'Enough of that. Tell me why you have come. You have taken a huge risk, leaving France and travelling to London. You have also risked giving someone else a clue that might lead to me, or identify us both and destroy my cover. It is not that I enjoy it, but my trading business has helped the passage of so many of our brethren that it cannot be considered unimportant. Your trip was planned in such a hurry, and doesn't even satisfy the minimum security requirements: that is not like you,' he concluded in a calm but questioning tone.

They were now facing each other, the old man taller than d'Orbay by almost half a head.

'Why are you here, ten years on, François d'Orbay? Why have you come to see old Charles Saint John, an honest merchant who's prospered through trade in the Indies?'

D'Orbay swallowed hard.

'To talk to you about old, bitter memories, master,' he began gently.

The man sighed heavily.

'I haven't come here to see Saint John, master. I have come to seek advice from André de Pontbriand.'

The old man leapt forward as though the embers of an inner fire had suddenly burst back into flame:

'Don't touch him!'

André de Pontbriand had listened calmly to d'Orbay's detailed account of their position. With narrowed eyes he had analysed the strengths and weaknesses of the situation, scrutinising d'Orbay's sentiments without revealing his own opinion at all. But the moment he heard about his son's involvement, that calm was suddenly shattered. He seized d'Orbay by the collar.

'Don't touch him, do you hear me? I want to see him. Bring him to me and I'll persuade him. I'll get that code back. After all, I am the only man who would be able to identify it and decipher it straight away. I want to see him!' he repeated, raising his voice.

D'Orbay gestured that people might hear them. Pontbriand conceded with a nod, but he wouldn't let go of d'Orbay's coat.

'It's not so straightforward,' the architect argued. 'As you said yourself, the risks are enormous and we have enemies everywhere. Our only chance is for him to know nothing about us.'

'Bring him to me,' repeated Pontbriand. 'I want to see for myself. And I've already waited too long. Cardinal Mazarin's gaols may not have finished me off, but my damaged leg isn't their only legacy. I didn't escape from that dog only to die here without having achieved a thing,' he hissed, his eyes glinting with anger once again. 'I have been living alone like an animal for fifteen years, François: don't you think I have the right make myself useful? And if that enables me to see my son, who was a child and still is in my memory, is that such a crime?'

He let go of the coat.

'I want to repair the harm I did when I lost the documents, preventing our Brotherhood from revealing the Secret it guards to the world. If it hadn't been for my mistakes, our Brothers might already have succeeded . . . And I need to explain to my son why he hasn't had a father for the past fifteen years.'

Seeing him sway, d'Orbay tried to support Pontbriand but was brushed aside.

'You were the pupil and I was the master. You still address me as such. But now I am no more than a dead weight, and you are one of the masters . . .'

Once again, François d'Orbay held out a hand to André de Pontbriand, who accepted it.

As they resumed their walk amongst the tombs, the sun appeared for the first time that morning, a pale aureole surrounded by white, only just visible through the wisps of fog.

CHAPTER FORTY-SEVEN

Château de Vaux-le-Vicomte – Wednesday 16 March,
five o'clock in the evening

Isaac Bartet knew everything. After all, that was his job. Many years before, he had entered the service of Cardinal Mazarin and served him as an investigator in certain delicate matters. For some time, he had also been secretly working for the Superintendent, thus playing a double game that relied on the fragile balance of gleaning information and giving it either to the Chief Minister or to Fouquet. He sat calmly in the small, half-decorated salon which separated the two wings of the Château de Vaux-le-Vicomte, awaiting the master of the house. Fouquet had asked him to conduct a full investigation into young Gabriel. The spy had worked as quickly and as efficiently as usual. He had discovered the young man's precise origins and his connection with Louise de La Vallière, although he could not state with any certainty that she was his mistress. Most importantly, he had discovered that Colbert's police, led by Charles Perrault, was keeping watch on the actor, suspecting him of being mixed up one way or another with the burglary at the Cardinal's residence. Thanks to his network of contacts, which extended all over Paris, the investigator had also solved the mystery of Gabriel's attackers. He knew that the zealots searching for the marriage contract between Anne of Austria and Mazarin were without doubt behind the fire in the Cardinal's library. Like the police, they too imagined that Gabriel was somehow involved in that affair. Isaac Bartet was delighted with his harvest of information and had decided to travel to Vaux in order to pass it on to Fouquet, and also to inform him what Colbert had been up to lately.

Meanwhile Gabriel was on his way back from a long walk around the estate, taking advantage of the few pale rays of sunshine that had pierced the clouds after incessant days of rain. The stay at Vaux had enabled him to take stock of the past month's events. He was well aware of the danger he faced by choosing to retain the papers contained in the red leather case, which he was now sure had been lost by the thieves who had targeted the Cardinal's library. The discovery of his own father's signature had haunted him constantly, and he was determined to unlock the mystery of the codes in the insane hope that it might help him track down the man he had missed so terribly since childhood. Deep down, the young man now sensed that André de Pontbriand might not be dead. His father's absence throughout his youth in Amboise seemed to Gabriel to raise a multitude of questions, as did the attitude of various family members when little Gabriel had asked them about his missing father.

Lost in thought, he extended his stroll as far as the mill-stream which flowed through the estate. As he passed the colossal statue that loomed over the gardens, he opened out of curiosity the access hatch to the ingenious system that supplied the various lakes with water. Continuing his exploration, he then descended the narrow iron staircase and inspected the works in detail. Gabriel decided that it would be the ideal hiding place for the red leather document case, which he no longer wanted to keep in his room at the chateau. *If I prise loose this large stone, there'll be enough space to store the documents safely*, he told himself as he examined the structure. He promised himself that he would return at nightfall, when the men working on the various sites around the gardens would have left. As he walked back to the chateau, the young man was dreamy. Since that morning, he had been thinking constantly about Louise.

Isaac Bartet was only too happy to bump into Gabriel, and at once decided to take advantage of the meeting to test him and observe his reactions.

'Did you have an enjoyable walk in the gardens?' Fouquet's henchman asked.

'Excellent, thank you,' replied Gabriel, surprised to be accosted in this way by a stranger.

'You are, I believe, secretary to Monsieur Molière?' Bartet went on.

'Indeed,' Gabriel replied, increasingly disconcerted.

'And you have been staying here for several days?'

Bartet's persistence was beginning to make Gabriel feel uncomfortable.

'Kindly excuse me, Monsieur, but I have things to do elsewhere, and what is more I don't really want to answer your questions.'

'That is a pity,' replied Bartet, not at all thrown by this. 'Doubtless you are unaware then that last night your master, the talented Molière, was in the office of Monsieur Colbert, for whom he now works? This will oblige you to choose your loyalties, young man. You do not know me,' added Bartet, 'but I know who you are. You should be aware that I work for Monsieur Superintendent. My name is Bartet, Isaac Bartet. So you can trust me, for the least that is said about me is that I am the best-informed man at Court!'

Gabriel was incredulous.

'Molière, working for Colbert!' he repeated. 'But that's quite impossible. At this very moment, he's writing a play for the Superintendent!'

'Dear boy, just because he undertook a substantial commission and showed loyalty in Mazarin's time does not prevent him from changing horses as the political wind changes direction. You seem very naïve. Colbert is powerful and liable to become increasingly so. Yesterday alone he turned Lulli and then your man Molière as though they were two pancakes!'

Gabriel was distraught. His future as an actor in a prestigious troupe was threatened. His childhood dream of treading the boards had suddenly been snatched from his grasp.

'And I have further news. Did you know that the King of France has a new mistress?' Isaac Bartet continued in a voice intended to be jocular, at the same time pretending not to notice that the young man was agitated. 'They had their first meeting yesterday evening at Versailles, in the utmost secrecy.'

At this announcement Gabriel turned pale, which of course did not escape Bartet's attention. He went on:

'I myself saw the young lady join our esteemed sovereign for an intimate dinner. That little La Vallière girl has a nerve! Only just joined the Court, but already she has scaled its summit.'

'Are you sure of what you are saying?' Gabriel growled, seizing the informant's arm. Bartet had not expected this reaction, but was delighted by it.

'Gently, young man, gently. Of course I am sure – I saw them with my own eyes! Are you by any chance jealous? Perhaps you are acquainted with Mademoiselle de La Vallière?' Bartet added. 'In that case, pray accept my apologies if I appeared to be unmannerly towards her . . .'

Gabriel pulled himself together and let go of the man's arm. Devastated by this twofold betrayal, he hurried through the great entrance hall and went to his room. He rummaged through his things to find the leather document case, all the while considering the consequences of what he had just learned. Through the window, he saw that dusk was beginning to fall over the immense building site of the chateau gardens. He opened the document case and looked again at the parchment bearing his father's signature. Tears formed in the young man's eyes. As he left his room and then the chateau, heading for the hiding place he had identified earlier, a dull anger simmered within him.

I am going to hide these accursed documents, he told himself, clutching the leather case to his chest, *and then this evening – whether she wants to or not – Mademoiselle de La Vallière is going to hear a few home truths!*

The full moon illuminated the chateau almost as if it were day. At the wind's caprice, the trees cast their moving shadows across the immense gardens under construction, whose subtle harmony had been conceived in Le Nôtre's imagination. Wearing a black felt hat and a warm, loose-fitting coat, Gabriel left the main building and strode towards the stables. A few minutes later he re-emerged, leading a magnificent bay thoroughbred firmly by its bridle. He make a slight detour to leave the estate, taking the earthen track that ran alongside the outbuildings to avoid the paved avenues, which he thought would be too noisy. On this clear, cold night, the smallest breath by horse or rider formed a fine cloud of vapour, which lingered in their wake as they rode to the gates. Once outside, Gabriel leapt astride the horse and galloped off to join the Paris road.

The cold which now whipped his face allowed Gabriel to recover a little composure as he galloped between the tall trees lining the road. Since he had learned of the meeting between the King and Louise, the young man's anger had not abated. He could not bear to think of them together in the intimate surroundings of the hunting lodge at Versailles. As an antidote to his burning rage the sharp cold was almost pleasant, as was the thought that he would be regaining control of his life that very evening.

After all, I can't stay locked away in that chateau when my future is being played out in the capital. And also, he told himself, *too many people seem to know more than I do. This may cost me my stage ambitions for the time being, but I won't rest until I have got to the bottom of all of this.*

Gabriel arrived in Paris very late and went straight to Louise de La Vallière's home. The young girl was getting ready for bed having spent a good part of the evening with Henrietta, her young mistress, who yearned for conversation and affection. Louise was tired out by the pace the King's future sister-in-law expected her to maintain. Gabriel found her dressed in a simple nightgown with a little lace collar. She was surprised and delighted to see the young man again, and threw herself into his arms the moment she opened the door.

'Gabriel, I'm so happy to see you,' she said, embracing him tightly. 'But what are you doing here at this hour? Where have you been for the last few days?'

Gabriel was unmoved by this welcome and pushed his young friend away a little roughly.

'I was worried about you,' he told her angrily. 'I was afraid you might have caught cold in the forest at Versailles, unless of course the King of France offered to keep you warm!'

The attack was so vulgar that Louise was dumbstruck. Gabriel carried on even more aggressively.

'You're not answering me. Do you imagine, you poor girl, that Louis XIV sees you as anything more than an additional partridge for his hunting table, which is by all accounts already extremely well laden!'

Thrown for a moment by the violence of this tirade, Louise smiled at the young man, who was a little baffled by this unexpected reaction.

'Are you by any chance jealous, Monsieur de Pontbriand?' she asked him with a hint of irony which failed to mask her emotion. 'I'm flattered. But tell me, what do you know about my dealings with the King that you should react like this?'

'I know what everyone in Paris knows!'

'Namely?' she retorted, with her lips pursed.

'Namely that, scarcely after her arrival at Court, young La Vallière lost no time in seducing the King, with the sole aim of satisfying her ambitions. Namely, that a romantic rendezvous recently took place at Versailles. Do you dare deny it?'

'My poor Gabriel, you clearly know nothing about Court relationships. How do you know that the meeting wasn't dictated by my position as companion to Henrietta of England? And anyway,' the girl added angrily, 'why should I have to account to you for my actions?'

Gabriel suddenly felt his anger dissolve. The quiver in Louise's voice, the tears she held back, but that made her eyes shine, her flushed cheeks: all these signs proved her sincerity.

'You do not know him, you cannot imagine how different he is from the impression he gives in public.' The young girl waved her hand helplessly and let out a sigh of dismay.

'Oh! What is the use of trying to explain . . . I do not know why I imagined that you . . . Is that all you came to say to me?' she concluded sharply.

Gabriel shook his head, then approached her and took her hands.

'Look at me, Louise,' he ordered her gently. 'Will you believe me if I tell you that I am simply afraid for you? I am not accusing you, I am not judging you. I will just be there.'

Louise stopped avoiding his gaze. Their eyes met for a moment in the silence, then Gabriel continued:

'There is something else. I found out this evening that

Molière has offered his services to Colbert. I thought that your proximity to Monsieur, who is so generous towards the troupe at the Palais-Royal, might enable me to find out more so that I can inform the Superintendent of Finance without delay.'

Louise was now smiling.

'So it might be useful to have a friend in high places? You don't sound so moralistic now!' she replied. 'Take off your coat and sit down.'

The young woman covered her shoulders with a white woollen shawl, and as she prepared some mulled wine with cinnamon, told Gabriel all she knew about the latest scheming at Court. Several times over the past few days she had in fact had the opportunity to overhear the King's brother's conversations. Gabriel was relieved to learn that Nicolas Fouquet had obtained the King's pardon at Fontainebleau, regaining his place in the forefront of the Kingdom's Government, but a confirmation that Lulli and Molière had rallied to Colbert's side worried him.

'Clearly I will have to remain in exile,' said Gabriel, conscious that Molière might distance himself from him for fear of arousing the suspicions of Colbert's police.

'You will certainly have to be discreet, and whatever you do, stay under Fouquet's protection,' Louise advised him.

'If anything happens to me,' said the young man as he was leaving, 'you should know that I have hidden documents of the greatest importance in the grounds of the Château de Vaux. They are at the bottom of the shaft, at the foot of the giant statue overlooking the gardens. You're the only one to know about this hiding place, and the existence of the papers! I cannot tell you any more for the moment,' he added. 'You'll have to trust me.'

The young girl stroked Gabriel's cheek affectionately.

'I'm so glad to have seen you this evening, and to have regained your trust, Monsieur Spy,' murmured Louise as Gabriel hurtled down the stairs.

A moment later he was galloping through the slumbering streets on his cold journey back to the Château de Vaux-le-Vicomte.

CHAPTER FORTY-EIGHT

*Paris, Palais de la Cité – Friday 18 March, four o'clock
in the afternoon*

S*TEWARD of Finance*: the title went round and round in Jean-
Baptiste Colbert's mind like a deafening litany. When he
had taken the oath a few moments earlier, the deceased
Cardinal's protégé had felt his heart fill with joy and pride as the
words spoken by the Parlement's president resounded in his
ears. *Steward of Finance*. Colbert was sitting on a gold-trimmed
red banquette in the great gallery beside the meeting hall, now
emptied of its crowd. Dressed as usual in black from top to toe,
enlivened for the occasion by a belt of watered silk, he tried to
hold on for a moment to his public recognition. Closing his
eyes, he tried to recall the exact feeling he had experienced, to
picture once again the faces of each of his assistants . . .
Footsteps striking the marble floor of the corridor and echoing
beneath the vaulted stone roof made him turn his head.

'There you are, Monsieur!' exclaimed Toussaint Roze,
waving his arms. 'I feared you had left alone, or in another
carriage.'

Colbert gave him an icy look.

'I was merely meditating for a few moments. Well, let us go
if we must,' he grumbled.

'The fact is, Monsieur Perrault is waiting for you, Monsieur, by the carriage,' Roze apologised as they headed for the door. 'And Monsieur Le Tellier has said that he would like to see you this evening, to discuss an important matter relating, so he told me, to the security of the State . . .'

Colbert did not respond, but his gaze clouded. What had he been thinking, summoning his investigator here at this hour? The presence of Perrault reminded him of the bad news of recent days, detracting from the dazzling success of his promotion.

'Did you flush him out?' he demanded of his investigator, without even greeting him.

Perrault stammered, holding open the door of the carriage for Colbert, followed by Roze.

'No, of course you didn't,' said Colbert as he warmed himself. 'But he cannot have flown away, damn him! That boy must be somewhere. So find him. Between that man Molière, who does not even know his secretary's full name, and you, who have no idea where he is hiding, what am I supposed to do? Look for him myself?'

Leaning out of the window, Colbert stopped talking for a moment and scowled at Perrault, who had not moved a muscle.

'I need results, Perrault. Quickly. Find that boy, find the papers, but for the love of God find something!'

Colbert angrily pulled down the curtain and rapped sharply on the carriage partition, signalling that it was time to leave. Perrault could barely swallow as he watched the carriage move off into the distance.

Colbert breathed deeply. The words and tone of voice he had used to reprimand Perrault had left a pleasant taste in his mouth. Not enough however for him to relax completely nor to restore his earlier feeling of satisfaction.

'I have yet to determine what is really on the King's mind,' he mused. 'I am not happy with the audience granted to Fouquet, nor this business of a council for overseas trade. I must know more.'

Suddenly, a broad smile lit up his ugly face.

Ah yes! Now there's an idea, he thought. *I'll find out more about the King's intentions and at the same time solve the problem in which Perrault has become mired, despite such a promising start.*

Looking pleased, he turned to Toussaint Roze who was sitting beside him.

'As soon as we get back, organise a meeting with the Cardinal's niece.'

'But which one?' Roze enquired fearfully.

Colbert sighed.

'Olympe, of course.'

Colbert settled down on the carriage's comfortable seat and closed his eyes to relive the moment when he had sworn his oath as Steward of Finance . . .

Roze, who sat with his hands resting on his knees, thought it best not to ask if the meeting was very urgent.

CHAPTER FORTY-NINE

Mont-Louis – Sunday 3 April, eight o'clock in the evening

COLBERT recognised the road which was taking him to Mont-Louis. But this time his visit was not undercover, unlike that of the night of 10 March. Having used Le Tellier as a go-between, he was on his way to meet the Archbishop of Paris, absent from the capital for almost ten years. Paul de Gondi's semi-clandestine return to the city and the prospect of their meeting titillated Colbert, who was now anxious to leave no stone unturned in his frenzied quest for support.

The former Fronde member had prepared his mission to Paris as soon as he heard that his enemy Mazarin was dead. As he still feared arrest, the Roman exile had deliberately asked the Superior of La Chaise for his hospitality, and it was in the latter's private apartments that he now awaited his visitor. Colbert took pleasure in imagining him gazing nostalgically through the window at the outskirts of the city he had been parted from for so long.

'Spring brightened up Paris this afternoon, Monseigneur, but I am sure the French sun is no match for the Italian one,' said Colbert with pointed irony as he entered the room.

Paul de Gondi turned calmly at the sound of the voice which had interrupted his reverie.

'Winter is at an end, Monsieur Colbert, and the sun now shines for everyone,' replied the Archbishop, not displeased with the direct tone their conversation had taken.

After the usual polite exchanges, the two men sat down opposite each other in the only armchairs the Superior's modest dwelling had to offer.

'My dear Colbert, I shall not prevaricate about the reason for my visit. The death of Mazarin opens up a new era for the Kingdom. It seems to me that the time has come to purge the past,' said the Archbishop firmly. 'There are many who demand my return to Paris and beseech me to occupy at long last the archiepiscopal throne which is mine by right!'

He's mighty sure of himself, Colbert said to himself, making an effort to look as if he was hanging on Paul de Gondi's every word.

'I would like to believe that I was unable to return to my dear homeland because of a misunderstanding between the King and His Holiness,' the Archbishop said in an increasingly confident tone. 'For my part, I have always been faithful to His Majesty, which is what led me to oppose the Cardinal's intolerable financial irregularities. Today, exile weighs heavily upon me. My dearest wish is to be able to return to Paris. I know the price of this request, and am willing to provide the King with several tokens of my goodwill.'

Here we go, Colbert said to himself, nodding his encouragement to the Archbishop.

'In short, Monsieur Colbert, I am firmly resolved to lay my rights to the Archbishopric of Paris at His Majesty's feet . . .'

Excellent, thought Colbert, remaining silent to allow Paul de Gondi to reveal a little more about his intentions.

'Clearly,' went on the former rebel, 'it would be appropriate, as a sign of his new-found trust, for the King to grant me the guarantees hoped for by an exiled former prisoner who is anxious to have the freedom to come and go as he wishes.'

'I hear you, Monsieur Archbishop,' Colbert said soberly. 'But you spoke just now of several tokens?'

Surprised by this decidedly cold reaction, Paul de Gondi reflected for a moment before continuing.

'If this comes about, my friends will be in your debt – and you are aware of the influence they wield in the Kingdom.'

This is more interesting, thought Colbert, picking up on the allusion to the zealots and to their previous unerring support of Fouquet and his family.

'And what else?' persisted the little man, keen to push his advantage further.

'I am coming to that, Monsieur Colbert. You are searching for some documents stolen from the Cardinal's palace, and you know that those documents are no longer in the hands of those responsible for their disappearance.'

Colbert started. *Cunning Archbishop*, he said to himself, astonished by these revelations. *Now I know what he's come back for.*

'But you probably do not know the exact nature of the stolen papers. I have a theory about them which I believe is extremely credible.'

'I am all ears, Monseigneur,' declared Colbert, suddenly amused.

'Mazarin threw me into prison at Nantes, and I shared a cell with a man whose real name I never knew,' explained Gondi. 'He called himself "Naum". We had time to get to know each other and I can attest that the man was highly educated and trustworthy. Several times I had the opportunity to test the quality of his reasoning and the truth of what he told me. Naum was ill. Sensing his end was near, he decided to confide in me. He told me that he had given Cardinal Mazarin some extraordinary documents in exchange for a large sum of money, by what means I do not know. He was arrested shortly afterwards, and was convinced that the Cardinal wanted to kill him. As he lay dying, the poor man revealed to me where he had hidden his money. In fact it was this little gold mine that enabled me to go back to Rome and live there after my escape,' added Paul de Gondi, clearly still pleased to have cocked a snook at Mazarin.

'But,' interrupted Colbert, 'what did these "extraordinary documents" contain?'

'According to him, they gave the formula that gained access to a text which was capable on its own of casting doubt upon the foundations of the State and of the Holy Church. I know little else. Naum was not a talkative man, particularly as his illness rendered him unconscious a good deal of the time. Surely this name, Naum, will not have escaped you in His Eminence's accounts?' Paul de Gondi asked with a small smile.

Colbert did not know what to say. He did indeed recall having noticed this peculiar name against some very large sums of money in the Cardinal's private accounts. In fact he had asked Mazarin for clarification, but had not received an answer.

The Chief Minister had merely told him to classify this sum under the heading 'Exceptional Service to His Majesty'.

It was all slowly becoming clear in his mind. The Cardinal's anguish when he learned of the disappearance of his papers must have been partly down to the loss of this Secret he had purchased at such a high price from Naum some years earlier.

The Archbishop knows a great deal more about this than he's letting on, thought Colbert, more and more convinced that Gondi was manipulating the networks of zealots from Rome, and was behind the burglary of the Cardinal's apartments too.

'Thank you for confiding in me, Monseigneur,' said Colbert, trying to sound flattering. 'As far as His Majesty is concerned, I shall be your faithful mediator. I know how much the Kingdom would stand to gain by welcoming back a man of your worth. I shall try to ensure that our conversation bears fruit.'

Paul de Gondi smiled at these words, thinking that his aim had been true.

Having taken leave of the exile at the door of the building, Colbert climbed into his carriage. As the vehicle moved off, he gazed at the distant outline of the capital and mused that the Archbishop of Paris's dream of a triumphant return to Court might come true after all.

CHAPTER FIFTY

'Look, Louise, the horse chestnut trees are in blossom!'

Leaning against the window of her carriage door, Louise de La Vallière bent forward to look at the white flowers that were illuminated by the last rays of sunlight. They had just passed the toll-gate at Vincennes and were now travelling through the outskirts of the city. Dusk had brought with it a cool breeze making the carriage's occupants shiver.

Spring has arrived, thought Louise, *my first spring in Paris.* She tried to imagine what the lodge at Versailles would be like in springtime. She could not help it, everything made her think of the King.

'Louise, are you daydreaming?'

Louise started in surprise, making her companion laugh. Aude de Saint-Sauveur, another of the maidens of honour attached to the household of the future wife of Monsieur, the King's brother, pointed towards the lights that had appeared to the left of the carriage.

'Look, daydreamer: there's the keep of Vincennes. And there,' she added, pointing to the left, 'that avenue of flaming torches leads to Monsieur Superintendent's house!'

Louise listened in amused silence, observing her companion's excitement.

'Pray God that this marriage takes place soon, so that we can celebrate too,' added Aude, as if Henrietta of England's marriage was also to some small extent her own.

Much good will it do her, thought Louise, gazing into space, *but the truth is, this is all she has, this life as a maid of honour.*

She felt herself blush at the superior tone of her inner voice and rearranged her necklace to disguise her lack of composure.

'We've arrived, we've arrived,' cried Aude, bursting with impatience.

The carriage made its way up the avenue, which was lined on either side by blue- and gold-liveried footmen, all of them carrying torches, whose light added to that of the nearby keep.

From the window of his office, Nicolas Fouquet watched his guests arrive thinking that he ought to have postponed these festivities. Coming only a month after the death of the Cardinal and the King's reorganisation, the event was taking place for no reason other than his wife's goodwill – and in spite of her pregnancy, which tired her and was sure to prevent her enjoying her guests. For the first time, the revels seemed futile to him. *Come*, he told himself, attributing his bad mood to having worked too many hours over the past few weeks, *I must join the guests and put on a brave face against ill-fortune.* But his mind was filled with thoughts of another celebration, the only one he was really looking forward to: the one to mark the completion of his chateau at Vaux.

Fouquet paused for another moment at the top of the grand staircase that overlooked the entrance hall. The guests had now all arrived and an uninterrupted tide was ebbing and flowing from the salons to the garden, where two chamber orchestras were playing.

At least the weather is on our side, he thought to encourage himself. And, taking a deep breath, he plunged into the crowd.

Louise was bored, yet she had barely been there for half an hour. She had to admit that she was not in the mood to enjoy herself, however splendid the evening and however prestigious the list of guests. The opening display of Roman candles had entertained her for only a moment. Tables groaned under plates of meat and pyramids of vegetables, but even the most exotic fruits did not tempt her. And the little animals – monkeys and brightly coloured birds – which mingled amongst the guests had merely drawn a smile. Aude had vanished without her noticing, and Louise now found herself sitting on a bench seat next to a pillar, topped with an antique bust carved from black marble.

'Are you missing your actor friend, Mademoiselle de La Vallière?'

The ironic question made her jump for the second time that evening, and looking displeased, she turned towards its author.

There in front of her stood the master of the house, Nicolas Fouquet, wearing a slightly mocking smile. Surprised, Louise got to her feet and curtseyed, at the same time thinking that the gibe had been only partly incorrect: she was indeed missing Gabriel, despite that absurd jealousy . . .

'Youth is inconsistent, don't you think?' went on the Superintendent. 'You are bored in Paris while he is bored at Vaux, if I am to believe what I see. If you were there you would see him moping about with that languid air of his, fretting. He daren't give too much away because he has been well brought up, but he's as easy to read as an open book, even though he's an actor.'

Detecting a glimmer of wariness in Louise's eyes, Fouquet came closer.

'Don't worry, Mademoiselle. When he placed himself under my protection, Gabriel did me the favour of confiding in me to the extent that I know what unites you, that is to say his name, his parentage and his youth. I only wish him well. But apart from the dangers which surround him, making it preferable for him to stay away from Paris, I fear that Monsieur Colbert's manoeuvring with regard to that ungrateful wretch Molière may have considerably damaged his professional situation. I don't yet know what is afoot that should make his activities so interesting to such powerful individuals, even if he is Gabriel de Pontbriand. But I shall find out. From now on, he had better be careful.'

A note of urgency entered his voice.

'That applies to you too, Mademoiselle. It is said that the year 1661 is a perilous time for newcomers to Court. Take care,' he urged her, his tone serious. 'One is not always aware that one is playing a dangerous game until one steps on a nest of vipers . . .'

Perplexed by this enigmatic phrase, Louise looked at him questioningly.

'What do you mean, Monsieur?'

'Monsieur Superintendent!'

As he was swallowed up by a group of guests, Fouquet gestured vaguely to Louise that he was unable to answer that. She watched him move away with an unpleasant feeling of apprehension in her heart.

Why did he say that? she wondered, knitting the slender eyebrows which arched above her large blue eyes. *And what exactly does he know?*

She had no time to arrive at an answer before a hand was laid on her bare arm, making her jump for the third time that evening.

'My dear, how nervous you are,' said the voice of Olympe Mancini softly.

Louise bowed, trying to suppress the blush she could feel rising in her cheeks.

'What do young girls dream of?' Olympe continued, sitting down beside her. 'Shall we talk for a while? You are young and new to these surroundings; I should like to talk to you as I would to a friend. The Court is a cruel world and above all a world that is difficult to understand, full of codes and manners which set traps for the newcomer. It is best not to venture into it alone; it would be far too easy to believe that the moon is made of green cheese . . . or of charming princes,' she commented with a feigned air of detachment.

Louise's mistrust sprang into life. She could feel Olympe's eyes on the back of her neck, on her cheek. She must not allow her feelings to show.

'People are like seasons,' went on Olympe, 'ever changing and unpredictable. It is better to start from the basis that one has no friends apart from those with whom one shares a common interest. I know this must seem sad and cynical to your childish heart, but it would be wicked of me not to put you on your guard.'

Louise felt Olympe's cold fingers on her wrist.

'I can be your friend; I have to be your friend. A friend who is extremely dependable, faithful and useful. A friend capable of keeping your secrets and protecting them. Believe it or not, they do not interest me,' she said, her voice suddenly curt.

Louise listened in silence as the words accumulated, adding to her feeling of unease. She took a deep breath and turned to face Olympe.

'That would be a most precious friendship,' she replied slowly, making an effort to control her intonation. 'I fear I do not have the means to afford it.'

Olympe hesitated for a moment before replying.

'Do not be foolish. What interests me is what you see, what you hear, no more. You will talk to me, and that is all.'

'Secrets are like perfumes,' said Louise, pulling her hand away. 'They cannot bear to be spilled . . .'

'Precisely!' Olympe exclaimed, her voice almost menacing and tinged with the fear that her prey was about to escape.

'. . . and besides, I cannot answer your proposition on my own. Do I have your permission to put it to His Majesty?' Louise enquired, fleeing without waiting for an answer, as though frightened by her own boldness.

'Damn her!' swore Olympe between her teeth. 'She will pay for this.'

Louise ran towards the garden and came out onto the terrace, almost knocking over a servant carrying a salver. The cool, flower-scented air filled her lungs. She realised she was trembling.

The festivities were coming to an end. Guests were leaving the house in small groups, travelling back down the avenue where the footmen had once again taken up their positions. The cold air slowly reclaimed the deserted grounds. Jolted about by the wheels as they trundled over earth that was still muddy from the previous day's rain, Louise drew her shawl more tightly about her shoulders. Aude was already asleep beside her, her head slumped to one side and threatening to fall onto her shoulder at every jolt. The shrill grating of the wheel hubs resounded in Louise's ears. She tried to relax, but was unable to forget her encounter with Olympe. The woman's words seemed to stick to her skin like the over-sweet juice of those grapes she had once pilfered with Gabriel: *What a long time ago*, she reflected . . . She shivered again as she recalled the threats barely veiled by Olympe's honeyed words; she had made it known that she was aware of the bond uniting Louise with the King, and that people with evil intentions could take offence at it and seek to harm her. Olympe had hinted that she needed protection, and that it would be so easy for her, so innocuous, to ensure the recognition of powerful people by telling them what the King said, and what his concerns were.

Louise wondered if she had been right to say no; perhaps she should have held her tongue. Whatever the answer, the lightning bolts that issued from Olympe's eyes as she had fled left her in no doubt that there was no way back.

'Tomorrow, we shall see tomorrow,' Louise murmured again, feeling sleep overwhelm her.

A moment later, as the coachman urged the horses along the road to the Paris toll-gate and the Vincennes keep had already vanished over the horizon, there was only silence and darkness inside the carriage.

CHAPTER FIFTY-ONE

THE last guests had left the Superintendent's house. The servants were all bustling about, moving back furniture and clearing away china to remove all trace of the buffets laid out in the house's numerous reception rooms. Nicolas Fouquet had no desire to go to bed, particularly as his wife's pregnancy meant that pleasures of the flesh were out of the question. He had brought François d'Orbay and Jean de La Fontaine to his office to sample some port wine he had ordered by the case. The conversation was relaxed and merry. After weeks of uncertainty about the Cardinal's health, then the establishment of the new governmental structure imposed by Louis XIV, the Super-intendent had the feeling that things were settling back to normal. His approach at Fontainebleau and the sovereign's pardon seemed to have dispelled all the suspicions that Colbert had been working perfidiously to instil for months.

'Did you see him when he was taking the oath?' said La Fontaine, 'He was all puffed up like a bullfrog trying to make himself as big as an ox.'

The comparison made Fouquet burst out laughing.

'Well observed, my dear Jean! The frog who tries to puff himself up like an ox, that is certainly an idea which might lend itself to one of those fables you are so good at! It is true that the snake featuring on good Monsieur Colbert's arms has seemed very flat for some weeks now,' added the Superintendent. 'I must say, since my appointment as head of the council for overseas trade, the dear man hasn't missed an opportunity to reaffirm his loyalty to me. I have to listen to his honeyed compliments every time we meet.'

'Monseigneur, beware of snakes which appear to be asleep in the sun,' d'Orbay went on, savouring his port. 'Those creatures are more treacherous than frogs!'

'You are right, my dear d'Orbay.'

The Superintendent sank back into his armchair, thinking of Mademoiselle de La Vallière's gentle beauty. He regretted not having been able to continue his conversation with her.

'I wonder what Olympe Mancini wanted with young La Vallière.'

One might have thought François d'Orbay could read Fouquet's mind.

'Nothing good, no doubt,' replied La Fontaine. 'The poor little thing looked extremely uncomfortable when Olympe was gripping her arm.'

The Superintendent's eyes were closed and he seemed not to hear what was being said around him. At last he sat up and began speaking again.

'I have to leave for London in a few days' time to settle some highly important financial matters. In my absence I am counting on you, Messieurs, to see that our projects at Vaux continue apace. My dear Jean, you will need to reprimand Le Brun; he hasn't delivered the tapestries he promised, and a large part of the chateau's decoration is being delayed as a result. And you, d'Orbay, your task is to supervise work in the gardens: I have the impression that the supply of water to the lakes is falling behind schedule. Damn it, one can't keep using wintry weather as an excuse in April! One other thing – please see to it that the plants and species I showed you are planted so that they mature by the summer,' finished Fouquet, exchanging a look of complicity with his architect.

As soon as he heard of the Superintendent's imminent departure for the English capital, François d'Orbay had an idea.

'Don't worry, Monseigneur, I shall personally ensure that we double the size of the work teams and motivate everyone to make up for the delays that have built up over the winter,' said the architect. 'I was at the site again yesterday and I promise you that they are making good progress. What worries me at Vaux, if I may make so bold, is something else.'

'What do you mean?' the Superintendent asked with a frown.

'It's young Gabriel, whom you have taken under your wing. I have the feeling that he is quite miserable.'

'Are you sure?' Fouquet queried, realising that d'Orbay was trying to send him a message without alerting La Fontaine. 'What has happened?'

'It's probably down to Molière's betrayal, which has deprived him of his theatrical dreams. But I imagine that he is also unhappy to be so far from Paris. What can one say, Monseigneur? At his age, the joys of the countryside are soon exhausted! You should let him have a change of air,' the architect added subtly, his eyes suddenly brighter.

'Why don't you take him with you to London?' La Fontaine suggested to Fouquet.

This suggestion was exactly what the architect had been hoping for. He could already imagine his old master's joy at rediscovering his son.

'An excellent idea!' said the Superintendent with a laugh, delighted at d'Orbay's shrewdness. 'I shall take the young turtledove to London then. But I cannot guarantee that the Thames fog will bring back his smile!'

CHAPTER FIFTY-TWO

Palais du Louvre, Colbert's office – Friday 15 April,
six o'clock in the evening

WITH his hands clasped behind his back, Colbert had been pacing about gloomily for almost twenty minutes, mechanically following the border which ran around the edge of the large Gobelin tapestry laid on the floor in front of his desk. Seated on either side in two bright-blue wing-back chairs were the King's brother, the Duc d'Orléans, and Olympe Mancini. Both of them were equally preoccupied, and the Duc d'Orléans was fiddling with the green ribbons adorning his white silk jacket with podgy, be-ringed fingers.

'All the same,' he went on plaintively in his falsetto voice, 'all the same, when I abandoned my plan of going hunting with my brother today, I was expecting other news; news more in accordance with our hopes . . .'

'I'm pleased that you speak of "our" hopes, Monseigneur,' Colbert interrupted, still pacing and taking a deep breath to mask his irritation. 'First because that word flatters me, unworthy as I am of the way you generously associate me with your worries. Second, because I see that we have arrived at the same opinion by differing paths. You believe that Mademoiselle de La Vallière is encouraging your future wife's complaints about you, and might do you the disservice of conveying these calumnies to the King. I fear this too, and the fact that it wounds you upsets me. What is more, you think that this young girl is uncontrollable. I am convinced of that too. These young women of the Court often have their heads turned. So much the worse for her. We gave her an excellent opportunity,' he added, turning back to Olympe, who was silent, 'yet she did not wish to take it. So much the worse for her. But I have to say,' he added, finally ending his circular walk and turning his gaze upon Olympe, 'that I fear something worse.'

'I can confirm that I saw her speak at length to the Superintendent at Saint-Mandé,' declared the young woman, as though prompted.

'And she even uttered the name of that young man Gabriel,' cut in Colbert, 'whose propensity to find himself amongst known conspirators against the State is beginning to disturb me, all the more so since he disappeared without trace just after a private meeting with . . . Superintendent Fouquet! You are right, Monseigneur.' He raised his voice. 'This has gone on too long. We have discussed the facts, tiresome facts. We must now act. Immediately. We must put an end to this. My men have been instructed to find Gabriel and to get hold of . . .'

Colbert broke off, signalling that a full account would take too long.

'Well, that's another story. Anyway, they are trying to find him. Meanwhile, no one must be allowed to reach the King through Mademoiselle de La Vallière. She must be put out of action,' he concluded grimly.

The King's brother was still for a moment.

'What exactly does that mean?' he asked anxiously.

'It means,' said Colbert, approaching Olympe, 'that the messenger who offered security will now deliver the opposite.'

The prince frowned, dumbfounded, making Colbert smiled.

'You were not yet born, Monseigneur, but you will certainly have heard about what happened to your mother the Queen, may God watch over her.'

When the prince did not react, Colbert continued in a professorial tone.

'When your father Louis XIII, King of France, discovered that she was informing her Spanish relatives by letter about what he had said and done, he wanted to dissolve the marriage contract and send her away. She was fortunate in having the active support of the late Cardinal Mazarin, God rest his soul. Well, what has happened before may happen again. Except that Mademoiselle de La Vallière will not have an advocate of the Cardinal's stature to defend her!'

'Imagine if she was conspiring!' the King's brother exclaimed enthusiastically, suddenly catching on.

'Indeed,' Colbert encouraged him. 'Anyway, I have found this conversation most constructive,' he said for Olympe's benefit.

Olympe got to her feet and bade the two men farewell with a curtsey before heading for the door.

'So you think the problem will soon be resolved?' the prince asked.

'I do not think; I know,' replied Colbert reassuringly. 'Monseigneur, the greatest virtue of women like Olympe is that they understand without having to be told explicitly, or in any great detail . . . they just go where their hatred leads them. She's so practical, as many women are.'

The King's brother merely nodded.

CHAPTER FIFTY-THREE

G ABRIEL was waiting by Fouquet's side in the ambassadors' stateroom. As he looked up at the lintel of the imposing mantelpiece, supported by two bearded giants, he stifled an exclamation of surprise.

'Look at that!' he said, pointing to the coat of arms carved into the stone.

Fouquet smiled and looked up.

'Why are you surprised, young man?'

'Er . . . well, it's in French, Monsieur Superintendent,' Gabriel said, showing him the motto. 'It says, *honni soit qui mal y pense!*'

'That hadn't escaped me,' Fouquet said phlegmatically. 'Particularly since it's the heraldic motto of the King and his family. In fact it's one of the things his opponents and his father's murderers held against him . . . Anyway, you are amazed by everything; I have a schoolboy for a secretary,' he chided Gabriel affectionately.

The doors opened to admit the royal entourage, led by the King of England, Charles II. Gabriel was fascinated by the force of character emanating from the King as he slowly mounted the purple-draped dais making his way towards the throne, above which hung an escutcheon embossed with the lions of England.

'How young he is,' thought Gabriel, 'almost as young as the King of France. Almost as young as I am.'

Protocol followed its course, with the King receiving the homage of his Spanish, Austrian and French visitors. They all glared at each other, each trying to determine the real reason for these ambassadorial visits, which were ostensibly out of courtesy towards the new young monarch so recently returned to the throne. Gabriel imagined this was the reason for the perceptible tension in the room, for its ambient chill and austerity. Unless it was the weight of suspicion, he mused, observing the large number of guards around the dais who watched the visitors attentively, scrutinising their garments for signs of possible weapons.

'Gabriel, Gabriel.'

The whispered call made the young man turn just as Fouquet, having approached Charles II, was bowing and handing him a letter from the King of France.

At first all Gabriel could see was a large silhouette in the corner by a side door, a few yards to his right.

'Gabriel,' the figure persisted, still in a low voice.

I've heard that voice before, thought Gabriel, moving slowly towards it while trying to keep one eye on Fouquet.

'Who's that?' he asked, also softly.

A hand gripped his wrist and pulled him roughly into the shadow by the door. Gabriel could not suppress an exclamation of surprise.

'Monsieur Barrême!'

The mathematician gestured to him to keep his voice down, and drew him out of the room.

'Sh! No names. Be quiet and follow me.'

'But what are you doing here?' replied Gabriel without moving. 'And where am I to follow you to?'

Barrême turned round, looking angry.

'Don't you ever stop asking trivial questions at inappropriate moments? I noticed that tendency the last time we met.'

Gabriel still didn't move.

'In Heaven's name, Gabriel,' Barrême continued, his tone more urgent. 'We only have a little time before they notice your absence. If you want to know what was in those papers you showed me . . .' he added, lowering his voice even more.

Gabriel glanced into the stateroom and saw that Fouquet was still talking to the King. He hesitated for a second, then signalled to Barrême to lead the way.

'What a strange character,' he thought as he followed in the fat man's footsteps.

CHAPTER FIFTY-FOUR

T HE man who called himself Charles Saint John could bear it no longer. He could neither concentrate on the thick book of accounts for his modest trading company, nor watch the comings and goings in the street as he usually did when he could not focus his attention on the task in hand. Ever since Barrême had told him that they would be there that afternoon, the tired old man had been in a sort of frenzy.

'I haven't seen him for fifteen years. What is he like? How will he react? What does he think of me? How can I explain those fifteen years of abandonment?' he kept asking himself. Over the years he had become resigned to never seeing any member of his family again.

Charles Saint John's two-storey house stood in a labourers' district. The ground floor was permanently filled with stacks of merchandise from the various maritime trading companies he did business with. Two clerks were in charge of the stores and checked everything that passed through. This line of business was an ideal cover for the old man, allowing him to make numerous journeys without arousing the least suspicion, and it was also his sole source of income. He lived on the upper storey, which was simple and comfortable. Next to his bedroom he had set up an office which also served as a library. Over the past fifteen years he had built up a substantial collection, mainly of poetic works. He had also made his own attempts at writing and had kept several manuscripts, but he had never dared to have them published.

When he returned to the window again, he saw a carriage stop outside his house. The coachman jumped down to unfold the three steps which enabled travellers to descend more easily, then pointed in the direction of the trader's house. The old man's heart began to pound. Barrême was first to emerge from the vehicle, swiftly followed by Gabriel. The man waiting so impatiently at his window did not immediately react, as if he were dumbstruck by the sight of someone who was no longer the little 'Cherubino' he remembered. Ashamed at this hesitation, he felt beads of sweat appear on his brow as he said to himself:

'Gabriel . . . My little one!'

'Where on earth are you taking me?' said Gabriel, grabbing the fat man and looking up at the modest trading house he was about to enter.

'You are nearly there, so just be patient,' answered the mathematician, pushing him inside the room where customers were received. 'Go upstairs. *Someone* is waiting for you,' he added, pointing to the stairs.

Gabriel went upstairs alone. When he reached the first-floor landing he tensed, fearing another attack. As he approached the half-open door, a voice called out:

'Come in!'

The young actor was taken aback, but responded to this invitation and entered the office where a white-haired man stood with his back to him, his arms motionless. Slowly, almost theatrically, the figure turned to face his visitor. Gabriel looked silently at the man and was first struck by the light of the pale-blue eyes. The young man began to feel awkward, and decided to say something:

'Monsieur . . .'

'I am pleased to see you. I never believed that this moment would come,' interrupted the old man, walking slowly towards Gabriel as if approaching a bird that he didn't want to scare away.

As the man drew nearer, Gabriel was overcome by a huge wave of emotion. 'That voice,' he said to himself, looking closely at the old man, 'and now those eyes, this face . . .' He took a step back. 'Who are you?' he asked almost inaudibly.

Without answering, the man came nearer still, then raised an arm and took Gabriel clumsily by the shoulder.

The young man could feel his fingers trembling.

'How tall you are now,' said the man softly.

Gabriel noticed his eyes grow misty.

'You can't be . . .' stammered the young man, realising in a flash just as the man who had pretended to be Charles Saint John took him in his arms.

'My child, my dear child, I have found you at last,' rejoiced André de Pontbriand as he embraced his son.

A host of images flashed through Gabriel's mind. He was so emotional and stirred up that he could not immediately answer his father. His father remembered from his childhood, for whom he had wept so many times in those lonely nights in Amboise, about whom he knew nothing, and whose strength and counsel he had so missed. Here he was, behind this old man's mask. He recognised him without really knowing him, this familiar man who was at the same time a complete stranger.

Some seconds passed in silence. André de Pontbriand remained there, with his arms wrapped around his son, as if he were seeking to make up for all the years of painful separation. Then he loosened his embrace and stepped back to take another look at his child, this man with the strong face, whose cheeks were bathed in tears.

'But what are you doing here, using a false name? And why did you abandon us, and allow us to think you were dead? I should at least have an explanation before I accept your embraces!'

With a bitter smile, André de Pontbriand looked at his son's clenched fists and the fire in his red-rimmed eyes. Now that his initial astonishment had passed, Gabriel's emotions were turning to anger. *He is so like me*, thought his father.

'You are right, my boy,' he answered sadly. 'I sacrificed you to a cause that is greater than all of us. In my heart I carry the responsibility for my exile like a wound which will never heal. You are a man now, and you have a right to know the truth. Do not judge me yet! I shall answer all your questions. But before I do so, may we sit down?' he went on, indicating the part of the room which had been furnished as a sitting room. 'I shall have some tea brought up. You see, after all this time

I have allowed myself to be seduced by English habits!' he added with false levity.

André de Pontbriand took a sip of his tea, then began his account of the past fifteen years.

'First of all, I have to tell you that, since the age of twenty, I have had the honour of serving a noble company of men as your grandfather did before me, and his father and grandfather before him. There are just fourteen of us spread out across the world in order to protect a Secret of incalculable value. This sacred cause brought me here to London, and subsequently prevented me from rejoining you. The announcement of my death was designed to protect you from danger, after our cause was betrayed. Just so that you know, the man who betrayed us called himself Naum. Fifteen years ago he received a large sum of money from Cardinal Mazarin in exchange for a document on which my name appeared. The document, which he stole from me, is the key to the Secret, without which no one can access it. Fortunately I had taken care to encode it, having been initiated by your grandfather into the mysteries of the art of cryptography. The Cardinal's police had identified me and were searching for me, and the stakes were so high that I had to go into exile and cut off all links with my past. You see, my dear Gabriel, to save the honour of the Pontbriands and to preserve your integrity, I took the terrible decision never to see you again; I melted into the skin of Charles Saint John.'

Gabriel shivered as the veil which had shrouded his childhood was partially lifted. His head swam.

'But why?' he demanded, bewildered. 'Why?'

'Let me explain, and please give me time,' cut in his father. 'We have both waited so long . . .'

The old man told him all about his life in London, his new profession, and his journeys to trade in far-off places. Then he asked his son about the rest of the family.

As he listened, Gabriel gazed intently at the room in which he was sitting, trying to record each sensation, smell, sound, each detail of the furnishings. How many times, in dreams, had he visualised his father walking through unknown and always fantastical settings. The ordinariness of this interior both fascinated and moved him.

Gabriel's flight to Paris to escape his uncle's authority and join Molière's troupe made André smile, happy to discover his son's bold nature. The conversation lasted a long time, for the two men had fifteen years to catch up on.

In turn, the young man gave his father a detailed account of the incredible discovery and the peculiar chain of events which had taken surprising directions finally leading him to London. When he heard the names Nicolas Fouquet and François d'Orbay, André de Pontbriand smiled again. Gabriel questioned him several times about the Secret and about this mysterious company of fourteen members, which intrigued him. But he was frustrated by his father's responses, which were mostly cryptic. He wanted to know more.

'Don't torture me like this, my son,' André said with a laugh after a little while. 'Only initiates may know the rules of our company and the nature of the text we protect. You are already in sufficient danger and you know too much. My faithful friend Barrême told me about the bundle of papers you showed him.'

He fixed the young man with his steely gaze.

'What have you done with those papers?'

'I have them here in London, in my baggage,' replied Gabriel.

'My carriage is at your disposal. Go and fetch them and come back to dine with me. We still have so much to talk about.'

Only too happy at this prospect, Gabriel stood up to leave, impatient to get to the bottom of the mysterious tale.

'Hurry back,' the old man could help saying. 'And take great care.'

CHAPTER FIFTY-FIVE

WHEN Gabriel returned to his father's house, he found him still in his office on the first floor. He looked tired.

'My son, I am so happy that you were able to come straight back,' André de Pontbriand declared.

'Here you are,' replied Gabriel, holding out the red leather case bulging with the notorious papers. 'This is what I found on the floor of the prompter's box at the theatre.'

'Let me see,' said André, putting on his pince-nez. 'Sit down, my son, this will probably take a little while.'

André de Pontbriand minutely examined the parchments contained in the document case one by one. As he read them, he sorted them into separate piles on the large mahogany table he used as a desk. Gabriel watched his father admiringly, taking his time to rediscover the man by observing him closely. Little by little, he noticed expressions or family traits that brought back vague childhood memories.

'There we are,' the old man said at last, rubbing his eyes. 'As you see, I have sorted the papers into three categories. That', he said, his voice filled with emotion as he pointed to a sheet lying on its own, 'is the document sold by Naum to Mazarin. On the back is the coded despatch note followed by my signature, which you recognised.'

André de Pontbriand slid his trembling hand over the document. Gabriel gazed in silent amazement as his father battled with emotions that threatened to overwhelm him.

'If you knew how important this piece of paper is to me,' said the old man barely audibly, letting the document slide slowly from his grasp. 'And beyond me, for the future of the world! And you have brought it back to me . . .'

Tearing himself away from his memories with some difficulty, he silenced Gabriel, who was about to ask another question, and turned to the rest of the papers.

'This here,' he went on, indicating the second pile, 'is an infinitely simpler form of encryption, known as Italian code. For years it was accessed quite easily by all those associated with the Court, but it hasn't been used since it was broken during the Fronde. It is known to have been the code used by Anne of Austria for her secret correspondence. At first sight I think I can identify these as official deeds. I will need a little time to get to the bottom of them and discover their contents. And those over there are financial papers, written in such a way as to prevent them being accidentally read by some junior employee. It seems to be some kind of hidden accounting that shows the various manipulations undertaken by His Eminence to increase his own wealth. Look at this one, for example,' said André, showing one of the documents to his son, 'It reveals the shadowy arrangements that were devised for the purchase of the Montereau and de Moret toll houses by third parties in the Cardinal's pay.'

'Now I understand why Colbert and his henchmen are so fiercely determined!' Gabriel exclaimed.

'Whoever lost or hid this leather case in your theatre must have known perfectly well what they were looking for,' André went on. 'But let us return to the documents in the Italian code,' he added, turning to the second pile. 'Allow me a few moments to translate these deeds. I think they might well contain an important State secret.'

As his father opened drawers and took out strange little rulers covered in figures, and then busied himself copying them onto the documents in question, Gabriel reflected that he had been entirely unaware of the explosive nature of the writing case.

'Now I understand why the whole world seems to be against me', thought the young man, even more impatient to know the truth.

'Well, Monsieur de Pontbriand, you have been sitting on a bomb!' exclaimed the old man after a long period of silence. He was evidently satisfied with his work. He stood up and walked round the table to show the document to Gabriel, who seethed with impatience as his father read on, looking more and more astonished.

'First of all, we have here the official deed of marriage between Anne of Austria and His Eminence Cardinal Mazarin! Do you know what that means, my son? If the Fronde members or those in their service had been able to get hold of these parchments, I believe the Kingdom of France would have exploded, with incalculable repercussions. What is more, this code is child's play for anyone with a little knowledge of the cryptographic art!'

Gabriel could not believe his ears. The rumour had spread all over Paris, it is true, but nobody had imagined that proof of the marriage between the King's mother and the Chief Minister could be so easily accessible.

'But that is nothing compared to the letter attached to the deed.'

Gabriel was in a state of high excitement.

'What does it say? Who sent it?'

'Anne of Austria, my son, sent it to Cardinal Mazarin. And its content is incredible: this letter, Gabriel, dated 1638, twenty-three years ago, is from a young mother writing after the birth of her child to the child's father . . .'

'Mazarin was the King's father?'

His head was spinning.

'My son,' said André, 'now you know enough about the affairs of the Kingdom to appreciate the importance of these papers. They would be capable of unleashing a civil war . . .'

'But what are we to do with them?'

'We will have to act with extreme caution. I imagine Colbert is actively searching for them. Your life and mine would carry little weight in comparison,' he concluded sombrely. 'You said you would be in London for a few more days. First, I shall take the necessary steps to reassure my Brothers about the fate of our company's papers. As I told you, I am not worried in that respect. The codes have not been broken; they are indecipherable to everyone except me. One day I shall explain to you how I can be so certain,' added André in answer to his son's questioning look. 'As regards Mazarin's secret accounts and the proof of his marriage, you shall take those papers back. I imagine that the private residence in which the King of England has accommodated you is the best-guarded place in the Kingdom. Before you leave, we shall discuss what to do next.'

Gabriel found his father's cold determination suddenly reassuring. He realised just then how much he had missed this paternal protection.

'It is getting late, father,' said the young man, seeing from the clock that it was half past eleven.

'And you must be hungry! I could eat a horse,' added André, leading Gabriel to a downstairs room where a cold meal awaited them.

'I am delighted by what you said just now,' said the young actor, attacking a magnificent slice of lamb. 'I shall pray that the return of these compromising papers enables you to come back to Amboise soon,' added the young man, suddenly overcome by a tide of emotion which he vainly attempted to suppress.

At these words, André de Pontbriand was unable to stem his tears.

'That is my dearest wish,' he said. 'You cannot imagine how transformed I am by the happiness of seeing you again. This evening, I can hardly feel the aches and pains that have been bothering me for several months. It is as if some of your strength and youth has been passed on to me!'

The conversation continued between the two men, both eager to find out about each other and make up for lost years. Gabriel kept trying to persuade his father to talk about the precious text to which several generations of Pontbriands had dedicated their lives. In the end he appeared to sink into deep thought.

'What are you pondering all of a sudden?' asked his father after a moment's silence.

'Didn't you think to make me part of that line too? If this secret is so important, why didn't you want me to be one of those men charged with protecting it?'

'Believe me, my son,' André told him, 'if I don't tell you any more about our family's secret this evening, it is only to protect you. Please don't be impatient!'

When he saw Gabriel's sombre expression, the old man leant towards him and looked him right in the eye.

'Do you want me to tell you the truth? For years I hoped that the line would be broken. For years I have lived as a recluse, licking my wounds, hating my destiny and hoping beyond hope that you would escape all this. I hoped that my generation would end our quest, and that you would be freed from it . . . That's why I was so overwhelmed when I learned what had happened, that you had found the documents . . . Do not think badly of me,' he added, his voice suddenly tired. 'Come. You want me to prove what I say? Well, I am going to tell you a secret that is worth more than gold. Listen carefully, Gabriel, for very few men have heard what you are about to hear. I am going to read you a translation of the text which was lost for so long, and which you found. That way, you will already be one of us.'

He went away to his office and returned a moment later with the document.

Gabriel listened in astonishment to what seemed to him to be a long succession of plant names and expert dosages. André de Pontbriand smiled when he had finished reading.

At one o'clock in the morning, after talking at such length with his son, the old man decided to go to bed. He suggested that Gabriel should spend the night with him.

'You can sleep in the armchair in my office,' his father added. 'Then we can look at the documents again tomorrow morning.'

Delighted, the young man bade his host goodnight and went to settle down for the night. He couldn't sleep, and kept turning over in his head the strange phrases spoken by his father. It was very late when he finally fell into an uneasy slumber.

CHAPTER FIFTY-SIX

London — Saturday 23 April, four o'clock in the morning

THE sound of furniture crashing to the ground suddenly awoke Gabriel, who at first did not know what was going on.

'Help!'

His father's muffled cry left the young man in no doubt, and he swiftly snatched up his sword which lay on the ground beside the armchair where he had fallen asleep. In a single bound, Gabriel was in the corridor. It was so dark that he had to grope his way through the unfamiliar house. As he reached the door to his father's bedroom, a faint glimmer of moonlight illuminated André de Pontbriand's inert body sprawled across the bed. At that same moment, a man knocked into him as he ran from the room.

'Stop right there!' roared Gabriel.

The only response was the menacing glint of a blade, and the fight began. As he defended himself against his assailant, Gabriel realised that the man was not alone, for he could hear a huge commotion coming from down below. Charles Saint John's trading offices were obviously being systematically searched. Driven by rage, the young man fought harder still against the thug who had just attacked his father. Leaping deftly aside to evade his adversary's blows, he found himself first on the staircase, then a moment later in the large room where clients were received. Everything had been turned upside down. The bales of precious fabrics had been torn open, and chests full of spices emptied. In the adjoining room, several men carrying torches were in the process of emptying the cupboards where the merchant kept his accounts.

'You're done for!' he cried, launching himself in the direction of the shadowy figures.

Oblivious to the danger, the young man found himself fighting four against one. He had forgotten none of the lessons he had received from his uncle at Amboise and wielded his blade with rare dexterity, skilfully parrying the four villains' attacks. He was wondrously agile. He dealt one of his adversaries a deep wound in the shoulder. Then, with a masterstroke, he plunged his blade deep into the heart of another, who collapsed without even finding the strength to cry out.

At a brief command from the wounded man, the three survivors fled through the window they had broken to get into the house. For a moment, Gabriel thought of pursuing them through the darkened streets, then changed his mind as he remembered his father lying upstairs. The young man seized a torch and rushed to the bedroom where he had surprised the attacker a few minutes before. As he approached the bed, Gabriel paled. There was a small patch of blood on his father's nightshirt, just above his heart.

'They've killed him!' he gasped as he saw the old man's livid features, and his head began to spin. Distraught with grief, he gazed at the body of the father he had miraculously redis-covered only a few hours before.

Gabriel forced himself to be calm. He would have to return to Fouquet immediately and place himself under his protection. He rushed into his father's office to gather his things, and in particular the precious documents which he would now have to protect. Before he went downstairs, he stopped one last time in the bedroom where the body of André de Pontbriand lay.

'Father, I shall do my utmost to be faithful to you,' murmured the young man, his eyes brimming with tears as he took one last look at the father whose life still remained so full of mystery.

Before Gabriel left the house, it occurred to him to search the man he had killed as he lay there in a pool of his own blood.

'Who are these villains, and who are they working for?'

The discovery of a letter in his victim's inside pocket provided the young man with his answer. The letter was signed by Charles Perrault, chief of Colbert's police. The men had been instructed to follow *young Gabriel during his stay in London, and at all costs and by any means necessary to retrieve any documents in the said actor's possession.*

The young man felt a wave of anger sweep through him.

'So, it was Colbert himself who killed my father,' he told himself. 'Colbert is going to pay for this with his life, even if I have to sacrifice the remainder of mine!'

The rest of the missive provided him with additional information: *'At the end of your mission stop at the coaching inn in Beauvais, and send me a letter informing me of your return to France. Whatever happens, await me there.'*

In a flash Gabriel made up his mind not to waste a moment

longer in London, but to set off in pursuit of his father's murderers.

I'll send Fouquet a letter telling him that I've returned to Paris, the young man said to himself as he left his father's house, *then I shall head for Beauvais!*

Pain and grief had given way to cold rage.

CHAPTER FIFTY-SEVEN

On the road to Paris – Sunday 24 April

GABRIEL did not spare his horses. Leaving London, the young man headed straight for the coast and succeeded in obtaining a passage to France just as the ship was about to sail. After taking advantage of the crossing to rest and sleep, the Pontbriand heir disembarked at Boulogne and hurried to the first coaching inn to obtain a fresh horse. He chose a sturdy one so that he would be able to gallop all the way to Beauvais without losing any time.

Throughout the journey, Gabriel thought constantly of the events of the past hours. The image of his father's corpse kept coming back to haunt him. He now had only one aim: to avenge his death, first by catching the fugitives and making them pay and then by confronting their master. *I'll do whatever it takes to make Colbert pay for this!* the young man told himself over and over again, intoxicated with grief.

Reaching Beauvais at last, Gabriel had to skirt the magnificent, four-hundred-year-old cathedral to reach the coaching inn nearby. There were few people there at that time of day.

'What can I do for you, Monseigneur?' Scipion Carion asked as he greeted him, bowing low.

The landlord of the post-house was short and plump, but his cheery face inspired confidence.

'I've arranged to meet some friends,' said the young man, anxious not to arouse suspicion. 'They may be waiting for me already. And I'm hungry and thirsty.'

Scipion Carion took him by the arm and led him to the inn's dining room, so that the traveller could satisfy his appetite. Gabriel followed him but remained on his guard, discreetly scrutinising the customers seated at their tables.

'You'll find the best cook in Beauvais at my inn. Madame Carion herself does all the cooking here,' the man announced proudly, showing Gabriel to a table next to the window.

Eyeing the other guests, Gabriel suddenly straightened up and reached for his sword.

'You!' he cried, lunging at three men who were seated at the back of the room.

The three companions, clearly taken by surprise, then charged at the young man with their swords in their hands. As they began to fight, the innkeeper cried out:

'For pity's sake, Messieurs, spare my family! I have only this inn to provide for them! I beg of you, do not break anything!' the poor man pleaded as weapons clashed and plates flew off the tables.

Once again, young Pontbriand's agility unsettled his opponents, who were as taken aback by his bravery as they were by his surprise appearance.

But despite his dexterity, Gabriel now felt he was in trouble, and when he received a light wound on his shoulder he decided to run for it. Jumping out of the open window, he found himself once again in the courtyard of the coaching inn. The three men immediately rushed out of the inn in hot pursuit.

'Careful, he's dangerous!' one of them shouted as he set off after the fugitive.

They caught up with their quarry in front of the cathedral and the fighting recommenced on the steps of the great building.

Backed up against the heavy wooden door, the young man thought he was done for. Then he remembered his father, whom he would never see again, and rage lent strength to his arm. He ran one of the attackers through with his sword, and the bloody corpse toppled down the cathedral steps. *It's a good thing there's nobody around,* thought Gabriel, anxious to extricate himself as quickly as possible. He killed the second attacker by piercing him through the eye. Anger gave him the power to finish the job with a thrust through the heart of the third. He too fell to the ground and lay still.

That's that then, thought young Pontbriand, wiping his bloody sword on the torn clothes of his last victim. *But there's no time to lose. I must hurry before these villains are discovered.*

As he dashed away from the cathedral, keen to return to Paris as quickly and discreetly as possible, Gabriel felt a kind of intoxication overwhelm him.

This is only the first step, he told himself, inspecting the wound on his shoulder. *Now it's between you and me, Colbert!*

CHAPTER FIFTY-EIGHT

Paris, Julie's lodgings – Wednesday 27 April, eight o'clock in the morning

G ABRIEL had arrived in Paris three days earlier and taken refuge at the home of his friend Julie. The actress lived alone in a modest attic room, not far from the Palais-Royal theatre. The young woman had greeted the fugitive with surprise and emotion, extremely happy to be reunited with her confidant who had disappeared so suddenly from Molière's troupe. The young man told her nothing of his adventures, but began his stay by sleeping for almost twenty hours at a stretch. When he awoke, the anger generated by the sight of his father's corpse had still not left him. He was more determined than ever to assassinate Colbert. So as not to worry Julie, he invented a scenario in which he had played the hero, forcing him to hide in Paris for a few days. She believed him or pretended to, happy that this conjunction of circumstances obliged him to stay with her. She didn't ask how long he would be staying; in fact she did not ask him anything at all. And on the second evening, on her return from the theatre where she was still playing in *Dom Garcie*, she invited him into her bed. The comely actress no longer made any secret of her feelings, and these had not escaped him. He in turn was not immune to her charms and willingly tasted the pleasures she offered, even if they did not ease his grief.

Each day, when Julie had left for the theatre, Gabriel prowled around outside the Palais-Royal or Colbert's house, trying to work out the best way to kill the man he now regarded as a personal enemy. Gabriel's blood boiled at the sight of the walls and the courtyard glimpsed through the doors as they opened for a moment to allow a carriage – perhaps Colbert's own carriage? – to pass through. Standing patiently in the cold, hidden in the shadow of the carriage entrance, he noted the times at which the servants entered and left; the guards' movements; in short, all the details which might feed his hunger for vengeance.

On this sunny morning he was still in bed, with his arms wrapped around Julie, when someone knocked at the door.

'Open up, Gabriel! I know you're in there!' said the voice on the other side of the door.

The young man leapt out of bed and seized his sword.

'Don't open the door,' pleaded Julie, frightened by the sudden awakening and pulling up the coverlet to hide her breasts.

'Open up!' the voice persisted. 'It's François d'Orbay.'

Reassured, Gabriel opened the door. The architect smiled at the sight of the young man, stark naked, brandishing his sword.

'Well, my fugitive friend, it's quite clear you have nothing to hide! Get dressed,' said d'Orbay, paying no attention to the young girl who had now vanished beneath the bedclothes, 'then come down and join me in my carriage. I have to talk to you – by order of the Superintendent of Finance!'

Gabriel closed the door again and rushed around to gather up his clothes which were scattered all over the room.

'Don't worry,' he said kindly to Julie, kissing her on the forehead. 'He's a friend of Nicolas Fouquet. I'll come back as soon as I can.'

The young girl looked at him with rather a sad smile.

'Go,' she said. And then, more softly: 'Farewell, mysterious Gabriel.'

A heavy carriage with six horses was waiting in the street. The curtains were drawn, so it was impossible to see inside. The architect was leafing through a newspaper as he waited for Gabriel.

'I am delighted to see you again, Monsieur de Pontbriand. We were extremely worried when you disappeared from London!'

'But I left a letter explaining everything to the Super-intendent!' replied Gabriel sitting down opposite d'Orbay. 'My hasty departure was for pressing, personal reasons which I cannot reveal to you, Monsieur d'Orbay.'

'I know!' François d'Orbay cut in grimly, laying a hand upon his arm, 'and I share your grief. Believe me . . .'

'You can't know!' the young man interrupted.

Astonished by this harsh reaction, François d'Orbay smiled and went on softly:

'Listen to me and don't interrupt, Gabriel. Charles Saint John – or more precisely André de Pontbriand, your father – was one of my friends. I knew him a long time before you were born. His violent death has caused me great pain, particularly since I saw him only a short time ago, in London. I have a general idea of what happened. I asked that you should be watched from a distance and . . .'

He stopped for a moment and clenched his jaw.

'Anyway, my men arrived too late to prevent it. They saw you running away, then lost track of you during the Channel crossing. I didn't realise what had happened next until later, when I heard through my sources about the deaths of three men at Beauvais. It wasn't very difficult to work out. It was a rather more delicate task to find you in Paris. But believe me, the only reason I've been searching for you since my return is that I feared for your life. I have to say your hiding at the home of that young actress was ideal from my point of view, and from yours, if I'm to believe what I saw just now,' the architect grinned knowingly. 'If Isaac Bartet hadn't spotted you prowling around Colbert's residence and then followed you here, we would still be wondering if you were alive!'

Gabriel frowned at François d'Orbay. He did not understand exactly what game d'Orbay was playing and decided to give nothing away until he knew exactly how much the Superintendent's close colleague knew.

'I don't know what you're planning, but I must urge you to be extremely careful,' went on d'Orbay. 'Monsieur Colbert doesn't take kindly to his men being murdered!'

'I want vengeance – I want to punish that man Colbert for his crimes. If as you say you were a friend of my father, his cowardly murder by Perrault's henchmen cannot leave you unmoved. For several weeks I have been at the centre of an intrigue over which I have no control, and which I still don't fully understand, but whatever the dangers, I cannot allow the death of a Pontbriand to go unpunished!'

'Steady now! Gently, young man. You want to kill Colbert, is that it? Don't you think that's a little presumptuous on your part?'

Faced with the boy's stubborn silence, d'Orbay went on:

'Your father and I shared a commitment to the service of a cause that is greater than we are. Perhaps he talked to you about it. In fact it is in our struggle and the nature of the documents that fell into your possession that you will find the source of your misfortunes. If you truly wish to be faithful to the memory of André de Pontbriand, you should talk to Nicolas Fouquet himself before you commit an act of folly for the sake of honour.'

Gabriel said nothing. He did not know what to do or how to react, and at the same time had the disagreeable impression that d'Orbay knew much more than he was giving away.

Understanding his unease, François took a letter from his glove and handed it to Gabriel.

My dear François,

Thanks to you I have just been reunited with Gabriel. What joy! He has gone to fetch what we have been hoping for, and I am using his absence to write you this letter, filled with a father's emotion and gratitude. If destiny should strike me down I am counting on you to take care of my cherubino.

Your friend,

Charles Saint John.

Gabriel paled as he read this posthumous message.

'Very well, Monsieur, I believe that you knew my father, but this note doesn't free me from the need to avenge him. As you know the details of what happened you should also be aware that I found a document on the body of the man I killed in London that directly implicated Colbert. Colbert is the one who directed the assassins.'

He was now almost shouting.

'I am going to kill Colbert. I want to avenge my father!'

D'Orbay's tone turned icy.

'And we shall avenge him, believe me. But not now. And not in this way. Do you think Colbert is so naïve that he neglects to be constantly on his guard? He has you watched, you disappear, and his men are murdered. Would he then continue to act as if nothing had happened? I am sure that his guard has already been strengthened, even if the link has not yet been established between you and those men's deaths. Though in all likelihood it has. If Bartet found you, do you think it would be impossible for others to do so, too?'

Gabriel was silent, shaken by d'Orbay's arguments.

'Throwing yourself straight into the lion's mouth, alone, would not serve your vengeance and would compromise our plans. For pity's sake, go to Vaux and see Fouquet. I promise you that Colbert will still receive his just desserts.'

Gabriel nodded.

'Very well, I shall follow your advice and go to see the Superintendent, but do me the kindness of telling me everything you know about my father, and about the mystery surrounding his life which seems, alas, to have also been the cause of his death!'

Relieved, d'Orbay sighed and laid his hand once more upon the pale youth's arm.

'It's a long story,' he said, giving the signal for the carriage to set off. 'A long story. But Nicolas Fouquet should be the one to tell it. He alone has the right. He was chosen,' he added enigmatically.

CHAPTER FIFTY-NINE

Vaux-le-Vicomte – Saturday 30 April, three o'clock
in the afternoon

G ABRIEL watched the white pebble skim over the surface of the lake, then sink straight down beneath its dazzling surface.

The afternoon sun cast patches of golden light across the nearly completed gardens, emphasising the brightness of the chateau's pale stone façades. The scaffolding had disappeared, flowers and shrubs were gradually covering the bare earth, bringing the flowerbeds to life, and Vaux was slowly taking shape, little by little revealing its full majesty.

But all this was far from the young man's thoughts. All he could think about, obsessively, was the distance that separated Vaux from Paris, in other words from his father's murderer. Two days had elapsed since he had agreed to take d'Orbay's advice and follow him to Vaux. Two days, during which his appetite for revenge had continued to conflict with his belief that to mount a lone attack on the man who dared to have a snake for his emblem was a recipe for failure and suicide.

'Gabriel.'

The soft voice made the young man turn round. Dropping his handful of pebbles, he leapt to his feet to face the man who had called to him.

'Monsieur Superintendent?'

With his eyes lowered and his hat obscuring his face, Fouquet silently removed his dusty gloves and took off the travelling cloak he wore to protect his dark green doublet.

'I've just arrived from Paris,' he said.

Looking up, his eyes met Gabriel's.

'I must talk to you, my dear Pontbriand,' he went on.

At that very moment, the sun struck the chateau's front windows and dazzled Gabriel. He blinked and took a step back, temporarily blinded. In this moment of bedazzlement, he heard Fouquet's voice again:

'It's about your father.'

Gabriel's expression hardened.

'François told me about your conversation,' went on Fouquet.

He came closer.

'I can imagine your impatience, your rage, your pain. François shares them, as do we all.'

He had placed deliberate emphasis on the word 'we'.

'And we shall avenge your father.'

Taking him by the elbow, Fouquet led him slowly away.

'I met him only once a long time ago, and very briefly. To me he was Charles Saint John, not André de Pontbriand . . . And yet in that one meeting he talked to me in barely disguised terms about you and about what he called his "other dream", to distinguish it from the quest pursued by our Brotherhood. Despite his ardent desire to spare you the sufferings he had known, that dream was to make you his heir. I confess I did not immediately understand what he meant. He realised this and repeated the word "heir". He meant his heir to our project, and not only in the sense that you were his son.'

Fouquet paused to look Gabriel square in the face.

'That is a very special kind of inheritance, Monsieur de Pontbriand.'

The young man clenched his teeth and tears shone in his eyes.

'I shall be direct, Gabriel. We need you. The documents you miraculously retrieved at the theatre, then saved once again on the night your father was murdered; these documents which have placed your life in danger are of vital importance. They altered the course of your father's life, and yours for that matter. Now you have a chance to change that curse. If you entrust me with the documents, you will be carrying out your father's dearest wish . . . And you will succeed him.'

'But what are these accursed secrets which have torn my family apart?' demanded Gabriel.

'I shall tell you; you've earned that right many times over. But I want it to be your choice. Gabriel, there will be consequences if I tell you the story of this secret: if you hear it, it means that you have already accepted it and agreed to serve it. Once I've told you, there can be no going back.'

The Superintendent broke off for a moment and moved a little way away from Gabriel.

'Rest. And think. For once, time is on our side. We are alone until tomorrow. I am going to check on the construction work, and then we shall have dinner with La Fontaine. You must not let anything slip, I beg you. La Fontaine is a dear friend, but he is not one of us and must not find out what is at stake in this conflict. If you don't think you can manage that, do not come down for dinner; I will say that you are unwell. In that case I shall wait for you in my office at eleven o'clock tonight. If you join me there, I shall consider that you have accepted your inheritance and the burden of these secrets.'

Without waiting for a reply, the Superintendent of Finance left Gabriel and headed back towards the chateau.

Night had fallen over the Château de Vaux. Standing in his office at the French doors which opened onto the terrace, with his hands clasped behind him, Nicolas Fouquet gazed out at the inky sky dotted with stars. He smiled faintly in the silence as he listened to the sound of light footsteps on the wooden floor in the adjoining salon. The door creaked open softly, and Fouquet turned to see Gabriel standing motionless in the doorway. The light from two torches surrounded him with a luminous halo that emphasised the pallor of his skin. Dressed in a simple white nightshirt, he came forward with a spring in his step, looking Fouquet straight in the eye, and stopped in the centre of the room.

'I'm listening.'

'The night is warm,' answered Fouquet, pointing to the terrace. 'Shall we walk?'

The lights of the chateau were still twinkling in the distance. Setting off along an avenue lined with young poplars, the two men felt the warm breeze caress their faces as it rustled through the leaves.

'It's a very long story, Gabriel. It began more than one thousand six hundred years ago, by the Sea of Galilee in the Holy Land, at the house of a fisherman who hadn't returned home in years; not since he left to follow a prophet called Jesus. The man was called Simon Peter and his village was Capernaum. And this story began while he was busy re-reading the testimonies written by other companions of the master. There were four of these testimonies, four documents which the world would come to know as the Gospels. Four documents which would not have given rise to this story had Simon Peter had not been mad with rage, horrified by what he read. He took a terrible decision, the decision to rewrite part of those texts, to alter them. In fact it was quite a mundane thing: an act of censorship. Except that it changed the course of history throughout the world. Simon Peter cut the texts. He expurgated them and dictated a new version, the one we know. Then he buried the original texts in an amphora, and for twelve centuries no one knew anything about them. Until the crusades brought our knights to the Holy Land. Until a few of them, on the road to Syria, stopped beside the Sea of Galilee and sought refuge in a cave which had become accessible after twelve hundred years of erosion. Until they found the amphora in that cave. Amongst them was a learned man who knew Aramaic. Months later, in his monastery in Jerusalem, this learned man spent some time deciphering the texts, which were written on papyrus. Despite the terror which filled him as he read them, and after checking thousands of times that his eyes were not deceiving him, this learned man found the courage to reveal his discovery to the chapter of his order. That learned man was also a soldier. His order was that of the Templars. And these writings were then given a name: the Fifth Gospel. That is the Secret which your father bore. Like me, like others, he was guardian of the Fifth Gospel, willing to sacrifice everything so that this Secret should not fall into unworthy hands liable to misuse or destroy it. Its injudicious revelation could provoke a terrifying situation of murderous anarchy. Like others, your father had taken a vow to bear this Secret and to wait until the appropriate circumstances arose. Only then could it be revealed, to a man capable of comprehending its meaning and accepting this inheritance before his people, thus countering Simon Peter's rewriting.'

Stunned, Gabriel hung on Fouquet's every word.

'But where are the documents? Did I carry them?'

Fouquet smiled.

'No. By an incredible stroke of fortune, you carried the key which provides access to them. The knights hid it in order to protect the Secret. After translating the text, they copied it between the lines on each of the leaves of papyrus used by Simon Peter. Then they soaked the pages of this codex in a bath of special ink which rendered them unreadable. They had learned this art from an Arab scholar. All the pages of the codex are turned black on both sides. And only their immersion in a decoction of plants, prepared according to an extremely precise formula, can cause the ink to vanish and reveal the true text in Aramaic and in Latin. What is more, this operation has to take place at a particular time on a particular date, which only occurs once a year. The formula for this decoction is on the document your father encoded, and its history is almost as extraordinary as that of the codex itself. It was lost during the sacking of the

Templar's commandery by Philippe le Bel. No one knew what had become of it. As for the codex, unreadable as it was, it was carefully hidden in Rome. We were merely the guardians of a memory whose existence we passed on from generation to generation, ready to act if we picked up the trail of the formula. This we did at the height of the Fronde, a little less than fifteen years ago. The formula reappeared in the hands of a Genoese merchant. How it ended up there, nobody knows exactly. All we know is that during the pillaging of the commandery, one of our Brothers – on the point of being caught and murdered, and unable to communicate in any way with our Brotherhood – in an act of despair entrusted the formula to a servant who did not even know what he possessed. He ordered him to flee to Italy and to make contact with one of our people there. He failed to do this. Instead the wretch sought to turn what he possessed into money, without success; he died in poverty around 1350. It is probable that the formula lay for three centuries in a loft before the chance transactions of buying and selling caused it to be brought in a trunk to Genoa. The formula had been stored with other documents belonging to the Templars. Letters mainly, any objects of value having been destroyed. The Genoese merchant had known your father twenty years earlier, when they fought together in the French armies against the Habsburgs. They had remained in contact by letter and this merchant knew of your father's interest in the history of the Order of the Temple. He therefore offered to send him the documents, not imagining for an instant what they were. As for your father, he realised imme-diately. We had almost reached our goal. An extraordinary meeting of the fourteen members of our Brotherhood was hastily arranged, in Rome. Alas, when he arrived in Rome, your father revealed to his travelling companion, another of our Brothers, the subject of the meeting. Only your father's passion for the art of cryptography saved us then. In fact he only had time to encrypt the text in a code known solely to us. The very next day and one day prior to our meeting, the traitor denounced him and handed him over to Mazarin's agents in Italy. Although abducted and taken back to France, where he was imprisoned and tortured, your father said nothing. In the end he escaped, but he left behind the coded formula which was lost for fifteen years until Providence placed you in its path.'

'But what about the original of the formula?' Gabriel asked.

'He destroyed it when he realised he had been betrayed.'

The Superintendent looked away.

'This story is the curious result of man's desire to put everything in writing. Why did Simon Peter not destroy the papyri? I have never been able to explain to myself what held him back. If he had done so, nobody would ever have known anything . . .'

He sighed before continuing, an edge of tension perceptible in his voice.

'For four centuries we have waited and patiently prepared for our chance. Fortified by the possession of the codex, even though we could not make it readable to many people, we made preparations to reveal its existence in several countries, in the hope that we would eventually recover the formula. I was chosen by my Brothers to prepare for the occasion in France. In the meantime, the revolution in England almost presented us with our opportunity. Cromwell was our man: had he not been killed by the grain of sand in his kidneys, the face of the world and our destiny would have been different. But . . .'

Gabriel opened his mouth but Fouquet spoke first.

'Don't ask me to tell you the contents of the codex now. You will have to trust me for the moment, just as I am demonstrating my trust in you by revealing to you the very existence of our secret. The plants needed for the decoction are growing in the orangery and will be ready for the transmutation process in a few weeks' time; the location is ready too,' he said, indicating the chateau. 'Everything is now possible . . . if you place your trust in me.'

He approached Gabriel. Once again, there was a smile on his face.

'There, Monsieur de Pontbriand; you now know half of your inheritance. You know what gave meaning to André de Pontbriand's life. Do you want to know the other half? It will tell you how to become his son a second time.'

Gabriel smiled back at him. The men faced each other, two shapes surrounded by darkness.

'Speak, Monsieur. You cannot reveal the nature of the Secret to me, I accept that. So tell me, what can be at stake that is important enough to persuade a son to put off avenging his father?'

'Open your eyes, Gabriel: it is all around you. The stake is symbolised by these walls,' he added, making a sweeping gesture towards the rooftops of Vaux as they glistened in the moonlight.

Gabriel shuddered.

'It is almost time. Follow me.'

In silence, they left the poplar-lined avenue and walked up the hill through the trees.

'This mound was created using the earth removed to create the chateau's foundations,' said Fouquet, as they emerged at the top of the hillock. 'Look to your left, and you will understand.'

Fouquet watched him, smiling.

'Surprising, is it not? No one but d'Orbay and I have gazed upon what you see here. This is the true vista of the Château de Vaux.'

As far as the eye could see, the roofs Gabriel saw from above to the left and right seemed to stretch all the way towards the horizon, linking the chateau and its outbuildings in a compact unit and totally transforming the look of the edifice. What Gabriel was gazing at in wonderment was no longer simply the proud chateau of a great lord but a town, a new city.

'Vaux is the concrete illustration, the symbol of the word of which we are guardians. Like that word, it has two appearances: one obvious but deceptive, the one you see through the main gates when you look at the façade. And the other, hidden one, which reveals its true nature.'

Fascinated, Gabriel could not tear his gaze away from the sight.

'Now do you grasp it?' Fouquet went on. 'This Secret involves more than just you and me, and that is why you must postpone your vengeance: it involves the entire Kingdom, and even more than that. This Secret is the establishment of a new political order. That of a society of consent, not of fear; of choice, not of subservience. A society in which the sovereign will no longer reign in the name of a transcendent order, but in the name of the people who make up its population. A society in which the ruling principle will be equality, in which chateaux will no longer glorify one man alone, but will instead become houses for all.'

Gabriel was now gazing at the Superintendent.

'Vaux is the symbol of that. At its heart, beneath the cupola where the sun of our Brotherhood will soon shine, beneath the fourteen pillars symbolising the fourteen Brothers who have borne this quest through the ages, the codex, the Fifth Gospel, will soon lie. This dome was built in such a way that its positioning would be just right on the designated date, enabling the text to be revealed in the right conditions. And it is there that I shall hand the King the proof before which he will be obliged to bow, and to agree to re-establish his reign upon new foundations.'

Fouquet took a step forward.

'We chose the sun because it looks upon all men in the same way, granting them its light and heat equally. If you defer your rightful desire for vengeance, our plan will have more chance of succeeding. The choice is now yours. Your father's inheritance is now in your hands. Do you count yourself one of us, Gabriel de Pontbriand?'

Turning aside for a moment, Gabriel took in the formidable view that had been revealed to him. Then he looked once again into Fouquet's eyes. The wind had strengthened and was ruffling his black hair.

'I do,' he replied simply, opening his arms. 'But will you at least tell me the date chosen to reveal the text?'

Fouquet smiled, and his eyes took on a supernatural brightness.

'The seventeenth of August,' he replied. 'The evening of the seventeenth of August.'

CHAPTER SIXTY

'Do not move, Your Highness, I beg you, sit still!' said the painter in his heavy accent to Henrietta of England, the future sister-in-law of Louis XIV.

Positioned on a chair that was uncomfortable to say the least, and imprisoned in a ceremonial gown whose corset barely allowed her to breathe, she was clearly beginning to find the sitting tedious. Her future husband had insisted upon these long hours of posing for a painting by the talented and famous Dutch portrait painter, Rembrandt Harmensz Van Rijn. The artist, who was more inclined towards self-portraits, was finding the task extremely boring, too, but the substantial sum of money promised by the King's brother had persuaded him to accept the commission.

Louise de La Vallière was present on this morning, as she was each time, so that she could respond to her young mistress's every whim. A respectful but friendly relationship had grown up between Henrietta and the young girl from Amboise. They liked to entertain each other by making fun of old Rembrandt's mannerisms. They particularly made fun of his outfit, which comprised an over-sized cap, presumably designed to protect his bald head from the cold, and a thick indoor jacket spattered with paint. Louise smiled as she watched Henrietta, who was a little intimidated by the artist's barked commands. She was thinking of Gabriel. A laconic letter had informed her of his departure for London along with the Superintendent, and since then she had had no news. She missed their desultory conversations – more than she would have imagined.

But he must have come back from London, she thought. *The Superintendent has been back in France for several days . . .*

At that moment, Isaac Bartet came discreetly into the large salon, which had been transformed into a painter's studio for the occasion. Raising a finger to his lips, he signalled to Louise not to say anything, so that his presence would pass unnoticed.

'Come, Mademoiselle,' he whispered in her ear, 'I am on a mission for the Superintendent and I must talk to you. It is important!'

The spy in Fouquet's service led the young girl into the corridor.

'Whatever is happening, Monsieur?' Louise asked, intrigued. 'And first of all, who are you?'

The spy made a small bow.

'Isaac Bartet at your service, Mademoiselle. Don't be afraid,' he went on, seeing the young girl's look of suspicion, 'I am a friend and have only come to disturb you because I urgently need to place you on your guard: a great danger threatens you. Mademoiselle, I have very little time to explain the situation to you, So I would ask that you trust me, and that you don't interrupt.'

Louise nodded to the man to continue.

'I am in possession of a letter from Madrid addressed to

Henrietta of England that shows you in a very bad light. In this missive – which fortunately I was able to intercept, and of which this is a copy so that you may acquaint yourself with it in advance – you are accused of being in the pay of the Spanish court. The author even mentions your recent nocturnal meeting with Louis XIV, whose mistress you are said to have become with the sole intention of serving a cause contrary to the interests of France!'

'But that's all . . .' cut in the young woman.

'All of it is untrue, Mademoiselle. Of course. You know that, as do I. But this plot has been extremely well devised and I fear that other copies of the denunciation may have been sent elsewhere to guarantee the attack's inflammatory effect. The interest which His Majesty has indeed shown in you, together with your link with the Superintendent of Finance via young Pontbriand, are known and are of interest to the highest powers in the land.'

Bartet lowered his voice.

'As for that nocturnal meeting with His Majesty, I think you are aware that the walls of Versailles have ears and perhaps eyes. Even if your evening remained a chaste one, you will find it very hard to make anyone believe it. Do you not agree?'

Louise was devastated, not only by the accuracy of Isaac Bartet's information, but above all by this calumny, whose icy breath she felt on her skin.

'My God,' she exclaimed in alarm, biting her lip. 'What am I to do?'

'Protect yourself, Mademoiselle,' replied the spy. 'And I shall leave as soon as possible for Dijon in order to warn the

Superintendent about this plot. It seems to me that it is aimed directly at him through you.'

'Might I ask you to make a stop at Vaux to hand a letter to Monsieur de Pontbriand?' Louise asked.

'Be quick, there is not much time,' said the spy.

Leaving Bartet where he was, the young woman ran to Henrietta's boudoir and sat down at her work table to write a desperate appeal to Gabriel on paper that bore her mistress's coat of arms, briefly summing up the threats she was facing. 'Am in grave danger. Do not know what to do in your absence. I beg you to come to my aid!' She signed the missive 'Your Louise'.

She handed Bartet her letter, carefully sealed and enclosing the accusatory letter given to her by the spy. As she watched him stride away, Louise hoped with all her being that Gabriel would come and bring his answer in person.

'Who can I trust in this nest of vipers?' she wondered, devastated. Was it possible that people could wish her such ill? Again she tried to summon up images of her childhood to counteract the fear which was invading her. Images in which Gabriel was by her side . . .

On her way back to the great salon, Louise pinched herself and breathed deeply to make a little colour return to her features.

'Put on a brave face,' she murmured. 'Don't allow anything to show . . . And hope.'

Henrietta smiled, reassured to see her young maid of honour return. She raised a hand in her direction.

'For pity's sake! Do not move, Highness, do not move,' snapped the painter. 'Or your mouth will have the same rictus grin as one of poor Doctor Tulp's corpses!'

CHAPTER SIXTY-ONE

Vaux-le-Vicomte — Tuesday 10 May, six o'clock in the morning

IT was daybreak and an early ray of sunlight cast a red glow on the mahogany desk in Gabriel's bedroom. The lines of letters and figures in the coded document danced before the young man's eyes. 'The Fifth Gospel', he murmured again, as if uttering the words could give meaning to the impenetrable pages. He rubbed his sore eyes. At times, it seemed to him that Bertrand Barrême's appearance at the royal palace, his father, and the hours he had spent with him had all been a dream. Only the terrible burning pain that had gripped him when he discovered his father's death, which had been torturing him ever since, cruelly proved that it had all been very real. All that prevented him from yielding to despair were anger and a thirst for vengeance: a thirst that d'Orbay and Fouquet's revelations had not quenched, but only deferred. Exhausted, he went into the adjoining washroom. The sting of cold water on his face made him shiver. He washed his arms and chest and was drying himself vigorously when someone knocked at the door. Taking a moment to put his shirt back on, Gabriel opened the door and came face to face with Isaac Bartet. Without a word, Bartet handed him a letter. The young man was taken aback, but he smiled when he recognised the writing.

'Louise!' he exclaimed softly.

He broke the wax seal hurriedly and unfolded the letter. His smile froze. His fingers tightened around the paper and a sudden pallor spread across his tired face.

He looked up at Bartet, who stood there quite still.

'For the love of God! What is going on?' he demanded.

'Well, Gabriel?' said François d'Orbay sleepily, sitting up in his bed with a look of surprise. 'What is the meaning of this?'

The young man was clearly in a state of agitation. As he seized d'Orbay's hand, his voice trembled with emotion.

'Terrible danger . . . I must talk to you without delay . . .'

'What time is it?' asked d'Orbay, surprised to see only the faintest glimmer of daylight through the gap in the heavy curtains.

'It's very early, but I couldn't wait.'

D'Orbay was overcome with anxiety at the sight of Gabriel, who was barely dressed; his shirt was creased, his hair was unkempt, and his eyes were red from lack of sleep. Pushing back his bedclothes, he sat on the edge of the imposing canopied bed and grabbed his dressing gown while Gabriel paced around him.

'Come, my friend, calm down,' d'Orbay urged. 'Tell me what has upset you. I hope you have good reason for disturbing my slumber.'

'Louise's safety is at stake, perhaps her life . . .' cut in Gabriel.

D'Orbay frowned.

'You mean Mademoiselle de La Vallière?'

Gabriel's nod confirmed his fear.

So, he thought, *even after Nicolas put her on her guard. That child is playing a game that is too dangerous for her.*

Gabriel's fevered gaze made him sigh.

And this one, too. What have I done to deserve this, to find myself surrounded by all the most imprudent young people in the Kingdom? he thought.

'She sent me this letter this morning, via Bartet,' said Gabriel, reaching inside his shirt.

D'Orbay took the letter and read it swiftly.

'You're right, this is serious. Fortunately for your friend our spies are effective and this letter has fared better than the daily reports Bartet sends to the Superintendent. Fouquet sent me a concerned letter yesterday, telling me that nothing had reached him since he arrived in Dijon three days ago for his tour of inspection of the Duchy of Burgundy's tax collectors. I fear that I have now discovered the reason. The reports must have been intercepted by someone who knows that Bartet has discovered the conspiracy, and wants to prevent the Superintendent from intervening. To strike during his absence: that is cunning. It is fortunate that Mademoiselle de La Vallière thought it wise to alert you.'

D'Orbay handed the message to Gabriel.

'Very well, there's no time to lose,' he said after a moment's reflection. 'We must leave for Paris.'

Gabriel paled.

'Do you want to save your friend? Then go and get ready, and come back here in half an hour. I will have a safe-conduct pass drawn up, and a letter which I shall sign on behalf of Nicolas – we will have to get it to the King himself without delay if we want to forestall his reaction. The letter of denunciation is well crafted, and it will not be easy to prove the conspiracy. But a warning from the Superintendent saying that he should be on his guard will at least incline the King to check the information before he yields to angry impulse. I know His Majesty's hot temper only too well. We cannot risk awaiting the Superintendent's return. He will not be back here for four days, and that may be too late . . . This letter has to reach the King before these traitors manage to get their false messages to him! Go, Gabriel. Hurry. Get your things ready and come back immediately. Each hour that passes brings a greater risk to your friend. You shall go on ahead to reassure her and give her a copy of the letter in case some misfortune should befall us. Then hurry to Versailles. We shall meet outside the toll house on the Paris road. I shall join you by another route, in a carriage bearing Fouquet's coat of arms – we have to take all possible precautions.'

D'Orbay watched him indulgently as he sped off.

'A child. But an enigmatic child', he told himself as he poured himself a glass of wine from the carafe on his bedside table.

One hour later, wrapped in a travelling cape of simple grey woollen cloth, and with nothing on him or his mount to identify the Superintendent's household, Gabriel galloped away from Vaux by the southern gate.

'Hold on, Louise,' he whispered as he spurred on his horse. 'I am on my way.'

CHAPTER SIXTY-TWO

Hôtel d'Orléans – Wednesday 11 May, ten o'clock
in the morning

SLEEP had eluded Louise for a long time. Interminable hours had elapsed since Bartet's visit. Hours of anguish, in which the young girl expected to be arrested and exiled at any moment. Hours, moreover, without any word from the King of France nor a reply from Gabriel. Wide awake, Louise counted each second, each minute. She could not calm herself, incapable as she was of thinking of a way to save herself, and not knowing whom to turn to. And it seemed to her that the most terrible thing of all, after all these hours of waiting, was not to know her fate. Exhausted, she fell asleep at dawn and was still sleeping at this late hour of the morning.

She was awoken by the sound of gravel hitting her bedroom window and propped herself up on her elbows. Then she rose in haste, frightened, and ran to the window. Opening it a little way, she stuck her head out to look down into the courtyard, but could see nothing. She was about to close the window again when she heard her name being called, very softly.

'Louise,' whispered a familiar voice, 'Louise.'

Leaning out a little further, the young woman looked towards the dark corner at the base of the wall, where the voice seemed to be coming from. Straining her eyes, she could just make out the movement of an arm.

'Louise,' repeated the voice. 'Open up, it's Gabriel.'

The young woman's heart leapt and she rushed down to unlock the door, snatching up a dressing gown on the way and putting it over her nightdress as she hurtled down the service stairs. She paused for a moment at the bottom and then, reassured, opened the door that led to the courtyard.

'Gabriel!' she breathed, throwing herself into his arms. 'I was so afraid. Did you get my letter?'

He nodded, intoxicated by the fragrance of her blonde curls and the softness of her cheek in the crook of his neck.

Then Louise stepped back and, glancing swiftly to the right and left, took him by the hand to lead him inside.

'Wait Louise,' he said, his voice tinged with regret. 'We don't have much time. I still have to find a way of getting a letter to the King to warn him of this conspiracy. And all is not yet won. Our enemies are watching us, and over the past few days I have come to realise how determined they are.'

Rummaging beneath his cape, he withdrew an envelope and handed it to her.

'Don't be afraid,' he went on more gently, seeing fear return to the young woman's face. 'It's only a security measure. First thing tomorrow, find some pretext to go and stay somewhere safer, with the Queen Mother for example. And keep this letter with you. It is the copy of one addressed to the King from François d'Orbay. It bears Fouquet's seal, and you will only need it if we fail in our attempt to reach the King. In that unfortunate event,' he emphasised, 'give this copy to the Queen

Mother, and tell her all you know about these threats. And in the meantime, ask her if I may have an audience as soon as possible. It is very important,' he stressed. 'I shall explain later, but for now you should know that I have documents for her which are of the utmost importance. Come,' he said, stroking Louise's cheek as a tear trickled down it, 'try not to worry. We will succeed.'

'I was so afraid,' she replied, squeezing his hand. 'I was so afraid you would not come . . . All those days with no news. Where have you been since you came back from London?'

The shadow that crossed Gabriel's face made her shiver.

'You're not saying anything. What is the matter? You're making me anxious . . . Something about you has changed.'

Gabriel took her face in his hands.

'It would take too long to explain. I have found out more about my past in the last few days than in the course of my whole life. And the more I learn, the more obstacles are put in my way . . .'

'What do you mean? I don't understand any of what you're saying.'

'I found my father, Louise . . .'

A dazzling smile blossomed on the young girl's face:

'Your father! That is wonde . . .'

The pain which suddenly clouded Gabriel's features stopped her in her tracks.

'He is dead, Louise. He was murdered before my eyes. And I know who is responsible.'

Louise's voice was now no more than a whisper.

'My God, Gabriel, that's terrible! Who . . .'

'Our enemies are the same. But I shall avenge him.'

'These obstacles – do you mean his murderers?'

'There's more to it than that. There's more at stake in this sinister story than my own destiny or my father's. But everything is linked, Louise: the threats against you, my father's murder; we are all the playthings of a machination which involves the future of the entire country. A plot in which I must choose my role,' he added, as if talking to himself.

'I'm frightened, Gabriel,' answered Louise, pressing herself against him.

Gabriel closed his eyes and wrapped his arms tightly round the young girl's shoulders. They remained like that for a moment, in silence.

'It is nearly over,' Gabriel went on. 'Tomorrow everything will be over. Now go back upstairs. I have to go to Versailles.'

Louise trembled at the sound of this word.

'Yes, to Versailles,' Gabriel confirmed. 'The King is hunting.'

CHAPTER SIXTY-THREE

Versailles hunting lodge – Wednesday 11 May, two o'clock in the afternoon

'SUPERINTENDENT's service or not, I say again: you cannot pass!'

Leaning out of the carriage window, François d'Orbay slapped the flat of his hand against the embossed escutcheon depicting a squirrel that adorned the door.

'For the Lord's sake, Monsieur Musketeer, I shall give you one more chance to take back what you just said . . .'

'Whoever you may be,' interrupted the soldier, raising his voice, 'do not imagine that you impress me. The King is hunting, and he is not to be disturbed! Hey, young man,' he said in alarm, turning round suddenly, 'are you deaf? Where do you think you're going?'

Having leapt out of the carriage via the far door, Gabriel was already running towards the brick building.

'Guards, sound the alert,' roared the musketeer, setting off in pursuit.

The metal gate that protected the hunting lodge was set into a small guard post. All of a sudden three musketeers emerged from it and blocked Gabriel's path. The young man stopped in his tracks and hesitated for a second, just long enough for the soldiers to charge at him and seize him.

'Cowards,' yelled Gabriel, struggling as d'Orbay joined them breathlessly, followed by the musketeer who had sounded the alert. 'Three against one! I dare you to fight like men!'

'You are about to discover the price of your behaviour,' threatened the musketeer, seizing d'Orbay by the arm. 'Go,' he ordered the soldiers who were trying to bring Gabriel under control, 'take that madman away. Two or three days in prison will cool his ardour . . .'

Gabriel felt a terrible anguish grip his heart. To fail, so close to their goal! Clenching his teeth, he struggled even harder.

'We're going to have to knock him unconscious!' roared one of the musketeers.

'You are making a terrible mistake,' cried d'Orbay as the man dragged him backwards. 'We have here a letter of the utmost importance!'

'Help!' Gabriel shouted at the top of his voice. 'Help!'

'What is the meaning of all this noise?'

The man who had just spoken was standing on the other side of the gate, silhouetted against the light, in the middle of a group of half a dozen men who had just come through the door of the hunting lodge. With short, sharp movements, one finger at a time, he was adjusting his leather gauntlets, which gleamed in the sunshine.

Suddenly silent, the musketeer who had given the orders shaded his eyes against the glare.

'Well, are you deaf? Answer me! What is the meaning of all this shouting?'

'These two men are troublemakers, Captain . . .' replied the man, rather uncertainly.

'No, we are not,' chimed in d'Orbay, freeing himself from his guard.

Also blinking in the glare, he rushed towards the gate.

'Monsieur d'Artagnan, the sun prevented me from recognising you. I am François d'Orbay, Monsieur Superintendent's architect at his chateau in Vaux, and this lad is Superintendent Fouquet's secretary. He is carrying an urgent letter from the Superintendent to His Majesty. Look at our carriage,' he said, pointing to the coat of arms painted upon the doors.

D'Artagnan signalled to the musketeers to release the prisoners.

'They are zealous,' he grunted. 'Come, Monsieur, let me see this letter,' he said to Gabriel, putting his hand through the gate.

Gabriel frowned and rubbed his wrists.

'Indeed not, Monsieur. Monsieur Fouquet told me it had to be handed to His Majesty himself.'

Disarmed by such self-assurance, d'Artagnan smiled faintly.

'Well, my noisy young fellow, you are certainly audacious! You wouldn't be a Gascon, by any chance? Even a little?' he added, still reaching out.

Then he said more sternly:

'Hurry up, I can feel my patience running out, Monsieur .'

Gabriel did not move. He looked the musketeers' captain up and down disdainfully.

'I may only be from Touraine, Monsieur, but I know what "into the King's own hands" means. And the subject matter is too serious . . .'

'That is enough,' interrupted the man with the leather gauntlets. 'You have a letter for the King of France?' he said, stepping forward. 'Then give it to him and for pity's sake let me get on with my hunting.'

'Sire!' exclaimed d'Orbay, suddenly recognising Louis XIV.

Stunned, Gabriel spent a fraction of a second examining the features Louise had described to him. Suddenly he recognised the strength of character in the eyes and the thin lips, the carriage of the head that seemed to make him taller. Withdrawing the letter from his shirt, he knelt and held it out.

The King took it without a word. Anxiety clouded his eyes when he saw the seal embossed with its squirrel. He turned it over in his hands, as though hesitant to open it.

'Monsieur d'Artagnan, hold the hunting teams back. I need to get to the bottom of this.'

He gave his hat and cloak to a manservant, took off the gloves he had so carefully donned, then turned to go back into the hunting lodge. As his foot touched the first step, he seemed to change his mind and turned to d'Artagnan.

'This will take only a moment. And of course you will release Monsieur d'Orbay, who for love of me will forget to give an account of your musketeers' zeal to his friend, Monsieur de La Fontaine . . .'

The architect bowed.

'As will Monsieur . . .'

'Gabriel de Pontbriand, Sire,' replied the young man, bowing again.

CHAPTER SIXTY-FOUR

'READ it, Monsieur, read it!'

With a contemptuous expression, nostrils quivering, the King tapped his foot irritably on the parquet floor. Without turning round, he waved the flat of his hand in the direction of the two letters that lay on the gaming table in his office.

Colbert had just entered. Caught off guard, he took a few short steps forward and gingerly picked up one of the letters.

'And then explain to me what my police are doing, Monsieur!' growled the King without giving him time to read. 'What is the use of spies? What is the use of spies if the Superintendent of Finance has to warn me about the despicable manoeuvring taking place in my palace! Just imagine if the forgery had arrived and if, for one reason or another, Monsieur Fouquet had not been able to send me that young man, Gabriel de Pontbriand, in time; or if this letter had not reached me, as was very nearly the case! Just imagine: I might have believed that lie! I could have been deceived! I could have got it wrong! Listen to this, Colbert,' he went on more coldly: 'the King of France could have acted unjustly. And I had to interrupt my hunting and return here at the gallop, without even being able to change my clothes,' he added, pointing to his boots. 'No, this cannot be.'

When he heard Gabriel's name, Colbert could not hide his surprise. *Of course it would be him, impossible to track down and protected by Fouquet. And, as if by chance, busy trying to save that scheming girl.*

Fouquet, La Vallière and that young Pontbriand – those three are always thwarting my plans, he thought as his anger grew. *Pontbriand, at least I have his name. The game is by no means over . . . But I shall have to be canny. I must find those documents before they do, at all costs . Or if they have them already,* he shuddered, *I will have to take them from them. Gondi is not a man to talk for nothing. But first I must try to limit the repercussions of this letter fiasco.*

'Your Majesty's anger is justified, and I thank Heaven that a tip-off – I do not know its source – meant that Monsieur Fouquet could intervene in this fortuitous way. I for one was not even aware that he knew Mademoiselle de La Vallière,' he added in a tone of feigned ingenuousness.

The King raised an eyebrow but did not reply.

'Anyway, the most important thing is that this villainous conspiracy has been uncovered before any damage – even reparable damage – was done,' continued Colbert, rubbing his hands. 'I shall of course have this scurrilous letter analysed,' he said hurriedly, slipping the sheet into the sleeve of his jacket.

'Do it, Monsieur,' said the King without looking at him. 'Do it and find a culprit quickly, for my patience has its limits. I am aware of your efficiency and my godfather praised your net-works of informants as being more effective than those of the official police . . . The fire at the Palais-Royal was intolerable. And now we have absurd conspiracies against a young girl who has done no harm to anybody. And for what reason? Because she is presented at Court and my wife does her the kindness of addressing a few words to her at her presentation? But take note, Colbert: these wretches have pushed calumny to the point of depicting her in this letter as my mistress, citing as proof certain personal details which only a few people close to me know. You see here,' he said, 'what is said about the S-shaped scar at the top of my thigh, given to me by one of the first wild boars I killed . . . That is proof of the falsity of this letter.'

Colbert nodded and lowered his gaze.

'Anyway, that matters little. This has to stop,' said the King. 'Alas, it is too late to hunt today,' he added with a sigh, turning to look out of the window.

When Colbert had gone, the King remained in his office for a while, savouring the silence and the calm, and allowing the tension which had gripped him to abate little by little. To his surprise he realised that what upset him most was not that there *was* a conspiracy, but that the victim of that conspiracy was Louise de La Vallière: greater than the fear of being manipulated was the fear that this manipulation might force him to cut his still-tenuous ties with the young girl who caused this curious tight feeling in his chest. He recalled how he had learnt his lesson when he had tried to impose his passion upon the Court, believing that his love for Marie Mancini could be combined with the interests of State. Poor fool that he was, he had been cruelly brought down to earth. But he had only been a child then.

'It's different now,' he thought. 'Very different.'

He rang the bell-pull until a head appeared at the door.

'Paper, ink and a pen,' he ordered.

And when the servant looked puzzled:

'You heard me! I am not going to dictate, I intend to write. Go, and be quick about it.'

Quick. The word lodged in his mind. There was no more time to lose. Tomorrow she would have his letter. He would see her as soon as possible. And she would be his. *To hell with procrastination, now is the time for action*, he told himself, picking up the pen which the manservant had so hastily brought him.

'Bring a steed to my door,' he added as the servant backed out of the room.

A smile lit up his arrogant features.

'Because it is what we ardently desire.'

CHAPTER SIXTY-FIVE

Versailles hunting lodge – Wednesday 18 May, midnight

L ouise was not asleep. With open eyes she had watched the candle on the round table beside her flicker and die. Stretching out her arm, she could touch the hot wax that had trickled onto the base of the candlestick before the flame went out.

Now, motionless in the darkness, she allowed her eyes to grow used to the gloom, and saw the shapes of objects reappear: things that had disappeared in an instant when the room had been plunged into darkness. Through the half-open shutters, she heard the sounds of the night and the muffled clamour of the forest that reminded her of Amboise. A ray of moonlight slid fleetingly across the large mirror hanging above the fireplace. She followed it until it disappeared, obscured by the fabric of the canopy suspended above her head. She let her gaze roam over the fine linen sheets, over the bedspread that had half fallen to the floor. She felt a desire to seize hold of the hand that lay upon that sheet, to slip her slender fingers between those strong, powerful fingers which, even in sleep, were still clenched almost into a fist. She sat up to look at the face of the sleeping man whose back was towards her. Once again, she felt her heart pound and could not suppress a smile.

'My lover', she whispered, tracing the line of the man's ribs with her finger. 'My lover, the King of France.'

Suppressing the desire to laugh, she slid out of bed and ran on tiptoe to the window. Pushing aside the curtain, she looked at the leaves swaying in the wind, and the clouds lit up by the moon as it ran above the forest.

Now she could see things more clearly: the carafe of wine and the glasses, the chairs on which they had sat, her clothes too, she thought, treading on her abandoned gown where it lay on the carpet. As she walked past the mirror, she started at the sight of her silhouette before laughing at the prudish reflex that had made her instinctively cover up her breasts. Coming closer, she let her arms fall to her sides and smiled at her reflection.

'Here is the mistress of the King of France,' she murmured in a low voice.

The touch of her palms on her thighs made her shiver.

She turned back towards the sleeping King, towards his hands whose caress she could still feel on her back, on her legs. She reddened as she thought of the crude words he had uttered, the voracious kisses that were almost bites, the whirlwind which had swept her up when he laid his hand on her, the unknown fever by which she had felt herself carried, and swept away. She paused as she saw the sleeping man stir in his dream, waiting until he sank into calm again.

She would have liked to know what he was dreaming, but she no longer had need of his words, not for the moment, nor of any of those almost violent acts that had frightened and delighted her at the same time. 'Louise': he had spoken her name with a gravity she had never seen in him, and he had told her how much he had been afraid of losing her, but that she need not worry now, he would protect her, and no enemy could harm her; 'nor any so-called friend', he had added, returning momentarily to his customary haughtiness. She had tried to stop him saying that he found her beautiful, and had blushed and protested when he said it anyway.

Oh! If only this moment could last for ever! A week ago I was in terrible trouble, and now I am the King's mistress, she thought with fervour as she toyed with the ornaments on the marble top of the chest of drawers. *When I tell Gabriel* . . . Immediately she regretted her thought. The blood rose to her face. No, Gabriel must never know! Was she mad? Of course he had saved her, but . . . *in another life* were the words that came to mind. Gabriel de Pontbriand had saved little Louise de La Vallière. *But little Louise*, she thought, once again sliding pleasurably beneath the warm sheets, *little Louise is no more*!

CHAPTER SIXTY-SIX

Paris, Porte Saint-Martin – Thursday 19 May,
eleven o'clock at night

THE woman scowled at the moonlight which projected her shadow onto the garden wall. With her hand, she swiftly traced an inscription in the earth she had just turned over, then immediately wiped it away, muttering a few guttural words. Straightening up, she spat onto her hands and began filling in the hole she had dug at the foot of a shrub and into which she had slipped three shapeless packages wrapped in brownish cloth. Throwing in the last spadeful of earth, she gave it a few more blows with the back of her spade to pack it down.

Only then did she take time to breathe, hands on hips, before wiping her forehead with a cloth attached to her belt. Unconcerned that her hair was dishevelled and sticking to her temples, she picked up her spade and was heading for the half-open door at the back of her little house when the sound of a carriage on the uneven paving stones of the street made her freeze. She held her breath for a moment, just long enough to be sure that the sound of hooves did not herald a patrol of the militia on night watch. *No, it is only her. Right on time*, she grinned to herself, hurrying towards the house.

'I'm coming, I'm coming,' she replied furiously in response to the sound of banging on the door. 'Not so loud!'

The door creaked open. The silhouette of a woman could be made out in the gloom of the space that served as a living area. The wooden table and the two benches flanking it were only partially lit by the fire in the hearth. Above the fireplace and along the walls, strangely shaped bottles were arranged on shelves, separated by books of spells and wooden or metal boxes piled on top of each other. On the ground, patches of damp oozed through the ochre-coloured earthen floor.

Olympe Mancini pushed back the hood of her cloak and forced herself not to retch as the suffocating, sweetish odour hit her nostrils.

Her hostess watched her slyly in silence, still rubbing her earth-covered hands on the rag knotted to her belt.

'How may I be of service to you, Madame?' she began in as friendly a tone as she was capable of. 'Perhaps I can use my arts to unburden you of some inconvenience . . .' she continued, deliberately staring at the young woman's hands, which she kept crossed over her belly.

Olympe looked her up and down haughtily.

'That's not what I'm here for. I had thought your sorcery would be more perceptive,' she said maliciously.

The woman instantly shrank at the accusation.

'Madame,' she stammered, 'there are words . . .'

'You do not know me,' Olympe cut in, walking around the room and looking up at the collection of dusty flasks, 'I, on the other hand, know who you are, and the nature of your art. You are Catherine Voisin, witch, poisoner and abortionist! I am here in the name of interests which are beyond you, and which you could not even imagine. If you even try to find out more, I promise you that the Chief of Police will soon be taking an interest in the curious plants you tend by night in your garden.'

Catherine Voisin trembled.

'And the other packages you deliver for those extremely unorthodox nocturnal ceremonies.'

Olympe allowed her threats to have their effect before continuing, turning towards the woman.

'But if all goes well and if you manage to hold your tongue, you have nothing to fear. Abortions and Black Masses are of no interest to my associates. What does interest them, on the other hand, is to ensure an effective and undetectable means of cutting short the passage of someone they know through this vale of tears.'

Reassured that the conversation had returned to her trade, Catherine Voisin managed her honeyed smile again.

'Yes, yes, I see. Is it a man, strong, thin, a small woman?' When she saw Olympe's look of suspicion, she said, 'I have to know for the dosage; one does not kill a rat in the same way as a dog.'

Alone in the carriage with the curtains drawn, Olympe took the small glass phial from beneath her cloak. Holding it carefully in her gloved hands, she raised it to the level of her eyes and gazed for a moment at the turbid, milky-blue liquid.

'This time, Colbert will be pleased,' she thought. 'What a simple mechanism life is! And so fragile!' The clatter of wheels resounded in her ears as the carriage travelled through the darkness, while the face of Louise de La Vallière danced before her eyes.

CHAPTER SIXTY-SEVEN

Saint-Mandé – Monday 23 May, ten o'clock in
the morning

STANDING on the topmost white stone step overlooking the park, Nicolas Fouquet watched his children playing with hoops. His eyes followed their game as they ran about and tumbled, letting out shouts of joy and peals of laughter, and the Superintendent could not bring himself to return to his office. Distractedly, he picked a red flower from one of the majestic vases decorating the flagged area, and toyed with it, pulling off its petals one by one.

'Armand, let go of it!' shouted one of the childish voices, suddenly petulant.

Lowering his eyes, Nicolas Fouquet looked at the flower stem, which was now bare. With a sigh, he cast it to the wind and turned on his heel.

As the double doors opened to admit the Superintendent, his visitor turned away from his contemplation of one of the canvases hanging on the wall.

'Monsieur Jabach,' Fouquet greeted him, 'I very much regret having made you wait, all the more so since I abandoned you to a work unworthy of you. Your eyes will resent me for wounding them with so little refinement compared to what they are accustomed to gazing upon.'

The financier bent forward in an exaggerated bow, the fabric of his customary black garments pulled tight by the extent of the movement.

'Not at all, Monsieur Superintendent. This canvas is in fact very fine, and the scene . . .'

'The battle between the Horatii and the Curiatii.'

'. . . is handled with great skill. Incidentally, the hospitality of your house could change lead into gold,' smiled Jabach.

'Thank you for coming,' continued Fouquet, his serious tone indicating that he wanted to get to the point of their meeting.

'The honour is all mine,' replied the financier, pretending not to have understood that the time for civilities was over.

'Monsieur Jabach,' said Fouquet, showing his guest to a chair, 'I shall not beat about the bush. My clerks tell me that two bills drawn on your establishment for a sum of . . .'

He stretched out a hand to a file laid out on a small sideboard beside his own chair and briefly flicked through it.

'. . . two hundred thousand écus have just been rejected by your accountants. I am also informed that the file was immediately passed to one of the King's stewards, that is to say, one of my subordinates?'

Jabach merely blinked and pursed his lips.

'Monsieur Colbert, to be more precise.'

The Superintendent's voice became more terse.

'Doubtless this is a careless mistake compounded by a coincidence, but I am hoping for an explanation without delay,

Monsieur Jabach, in the name of the frankness which you so praised in my presence not so long ago.'

Jabach opened his hands in a gesture of helplessness.

'Monsieur Superintendent, I am your banker and through you the King's banker. Your account with me is important, you know that. But do not ask me to play according to any rules other than those of my profession. Politicians take risks, Monsieur Superintendent, and bankers manage them. The subtle distinction is important.'

Fouquet's tone turned icy.

'Meaning?'

'That I cannot pursue a loan without a minimum guarantee. Without it I would be the one taking all the risk . . . and I would have no chance of recovering the sum.'

Fouquet leapt to his feet, striking the back of his armchair with the flat of his hand.

'But the guarantees exist!'

'For you, Monsieur,' Jabach defended himself, 'but not for the Treasury. And whereas Nicolas Fouquet is a good customer and a good payer, the State – do not make me suffer for my frankness, Monsieur Superintendent – is an unreliable payer.'

'There's nothing new about that!'

'In principle no, Monsieur Superintendent, but over and above the principle, in finance, there are rules for large transactions. And in the absence of credit these make clear stipulations. Monsieur Superintendent, listen to me carefully,' went on Jabach, standing up too as if to parry the anger which had brought colour to Fouquet's cheeks, 'and remember our meeting! You talk of frankness: did I not warn you against the dangers of taking on risks which exceed your limits, in your own name? And all this for the benefit of a third party whose solidarity and gratitude towards you were not assured? You were the one who told me that you would make sure you were protected.'

'I can accept the vagaries of politics,' hissed Fouquet, 'but I will not put up with treachery! And since you speak of our past conversation, shall we make a new pact? Let's continue to play your game of truth. The decor of my office is less fitting than your gallery, but never mind, we must make do with what we have.'

Jabach's looked pained.

'Do you dare to claim that Monsieur Colbert's involvement in this matter is pure chance, and that it has nothing to do with your sudden revelation of the perilous nature of my pledges?'

Jabach shook his head.

'I did not say that your pledges were perilous, Monsieur Superintendent. I would not presume to judge your practice of using your own credit for the benefit of the royal Treasury. I will even say that, to my mind, it bears witness to a great deal of devotion and gallant spirit. I only said that even *your* credit, which I alone may judge, can have limits, and that those limits have now been reached. In this I have not betrayed you, not ever. As for the involvement of a third party in this affair . . .'

The financier hesitated.

'Well, all right, since we are playing let us play to the end: it is true that the information I received relating to the shipping companies your family has acquired, and to your investments in Brittany and the construction of your chateau at Vaux, did influence my opinion. That is true. But what was I supposed to do? Forgive me, Monsieur, but I return to my argument: politics is for politicians; I am merely a banker.'

The little man approached Fouquet, fixing his dark eyes upon him.

'I am beholden to no one, Monsieur Superintendent. What is more, I have no worth in that respect, since no one would wish to be attached to me or to one of my people, even as an owner. You think of power and, nobly, of serving the King. I do not have those preoccupations. I seek to survive. I have seen too many of my kind end up on the scaffold, Monsieur Superintendent, to be anything other than wary of flattery and promises.'

It was Fouquet's turn to look at him in silence.

'Not taking sides is in itself taking sides, Monsieur Jabach. Your reasoning is hollow. I pray only that Monsieur Colbert's promotion to Vice-Protector of the Academy of Fine Arts, in other words to all-powerful master of the Kingdom's art market, in no way influenced your decision.'

Jabach's eyes flashed.

'I should have added that I am not sensitive to insults either, Monsieur Superintendent,' he snapped, heading for the door.

'The traitor,' muttered Fouquet as he watched the little man walk pompously away. 'La Fontaine told me so often enough.'

He clenched his fists.

'I must act quickly; there isn't a moment to lose. I must have that credit. I shall deal with Jabach later.'

Anger suddenly gripped him again.

'Colbert's traitor!' he shouted out.

His voice echoed in the empty room.

The sound of someone crying made him turn round.

'Papa,' sobbed his youngest son, frightened by the noise, 'Marie-Madeleine has stolen my hoop!'

CHAPTER SIXTY-EIGHT

Dampierre — Tuesday 24 May, eleven o'clock in the morning

As soon as spring came round, Anne of Austria liked to withdraw to the Château de Dampierre. She delighted in long daily walks in the park, ending them in the magnificent rose garden. This year she was allowing herself a short siesta each afternoon, doubtless an indication of the fatigue which came with age. That morning, the Queen Mother was reading in her boudoir with the window open so as to savour the scents of the garden and enjoy the May sunshine. She was wearing one of the black gowns she had worn ever since the death of Jules Mazarin. With the coming of old age, the King's mother had rejected everything that might appear too ostentatious. The manner in which her son had distanced her from power caused her a great deal of suffering. She, who had held this dear Kingdom of France in her hands, missed affairs of State.

'Monsieur Gabriel de Pontbriand,' came the sudden announcement from one of the Cardinal's former servants, who had remained in her service.

The young man entered, sweeping the ground three times with the feather on his hat in an expansive, elegant movement which he had now perfected. He was dressed in an immaculate white shirt, and his favourite boots of fawn-coloured leather reached up to his knees, giving him a military appearance.

What a handsome boy! thought the Queen Mother, reaching out her hand to receive her visitor's kiss.

'Welcome to Dampierre, Monsieur de Pontbriand,' said Anne of Austria engagingly. 'You are welcome here as a friend. A recommendation by the charming young Mademoiselle de La Vallière is my equivalent of a safe-conduct,' added the King's mother, indicating an armchair covered in sunshine-yellow velvet.

Impressed by the sovereign's dignified and rather severe expression, Gabriel tried not to display any sign of his anxiety.

'Majesty, the generosity of your welcome warms my heart. I wished to meet you in memory of my father, André de Pontbriand, who lived in London,' Gabriel began, looking directly at the Queen Mother, who evidently wondered where he was heading.

'London is an extremely beautiful city,' interrupted the sovereign with a sigh, suddenly lost in her memories.

'Before he died, my father asked me to deliver these papers to you, so that they would not fall into the hands of anyone who might misuse them.' Gabriel reached into the leather satchel he wore across his body, and extracted a bundle of papers tied with a red ribbon.

Anne of Austria frowned questioningly. She slowly untied the ribbon and began to read without a word. Then she turned white and scanned each parchment feverishly.

'Young man do you know . . . do you know . . . But how did your father manage to procure these? Do you have any idea of the significance of these papers?' asked the Queen Mother, studying the young man's face.

'I do not, Majesty,' replied Gabriel, lying with aplomb. 'All I know is the myriad troubles which have afflicted me ever since they came into my possession. I have the feeling that those who seek these papers are willing to do anything to obtain them!'

'Who, other than you and your father, could have got hold of these papers, young man?'

'No one, Majesty, I guarantee it. No one!'

'How can you be so sure?' replied the Queen Mother, her face clouding suddenly.

Gabriel decided to risk telling Anne of Austria what he knew and the manner in which he had obtained the papers. He recounted in detail the attacks which had befallen him. He revealed the circumstances of his father's death, but without mentioning the assassins and their leader. He also omitted any mention of the other documents.

'I thank you for your frankness, my child,' said the Queen Mother when he had finished. 'The existence of these papers must remain forever secret. Your father no doubt paid with his life for possessing them. For your own safety, I advise you to forget all about this!'

Gabriel rose to his feet and bowed to the King's mother, moved by the sovereign's dignity and self-control; and she got up herself to accompany the visitor to the door, which was most unusual.

'My boy,' she said, her voice suddenly affectionate, 'I shall not forget what you have done. From now on you may consider yourself under my protection. Please tell Mademoiselle de La Vallière that I am infinitely grateful to her for sending you to me.'

'Dare I ask, Majesty, if in your kindness you might extend your protection to Mademoiselle de La Vallière? In truth I fear more for her future than for my own,' he replied sombrely. 'I have reasons to believe that powerful individuals, some of them close to you, are plotting her downfall.'

'Great heavens, Monsieur, what are you saying? Close to me, what do you mean?'

'Olympe Mancini, Majesty,' Gabriel replied quietly.

The Queen looked thoughtful.

'Very well, Monsieur. Your request is granted. I shall agree to what you have asked. It's the least I can do in consideration of what I owe you. But do you have no concern for yourself?'

Gabriel bowed again but did not answer. He left the room with a lighter heart, telling himself that he had been right to take this course of action.

Anne of Austria asked to be left alone. She walked slowly back to her armchair and picked up the bundle of papers. One by one, she read through them.

Everything is here! she told herself. *The dogs have been thwarted, thanks to the courage and fidelity of the Pontbriands.*

The King's mother got to her feet and walked towards the fireplace. The hearth was empty on this fine spring day. Anne of Austria rang for a servant and asked for a fire to be lit. She watched patiently as the servant laid the fire, then slowly approached and threw the documents into the flames. Then she took a few steps back.

As the deed of her marriage to Cardinal Mazarin and

her letter admitting the King's parentage burned in the fireplace at the Château de Dampierre, the Queen Mother wept silently.

CHAPTER SIXTY-NINE

*Château de Vincennes – Thursday 26 May, three o'clock
in the afternoon*

'Roses make loyal friends, Monsieur Colbert, and silent companions.'

Colbert attempted a gracious smile, and smelt the flower which Anne of Austria cut and held out to him.

'Loyalty is in fact a quality I'm extremely fond of, Madame,' he replied with a bow.

Slowly, Anne of Austria and the new Steward of Finance strolled through the gardens personally designed by the Queen Mother, which lay in the shadow of the tower containing her apartments.

'But one which has no place in this meeting which you have taken it upon yourself to arrange, Monsieur Colbert?' replied the sovereign. 'Surely you have not deserted your offices and come to visit an old woman just to gaze at flowers and stay silent.'

'Madame!' exclaimed Colbert. 'I am neither a flatterer nor a man of fine words, and it is not my habit to try to please anyone except my sovereign or the Cardinal – God rest his soul. Perhaps you are suspicious of me because you misunderstand my character. Then I shall come straight to the point. The reason I wished to see you without delay and without witnesses,

Madame, was to inform you of grave matters concerning State security and the instructions that were passed down to me by the Cardinal.'

Colbert paused, hoping to see anxiety or at least surprise in the Queen's eyes. He saw neither.

'The Cardinal, Madame, wished to reveal to me certain secrets, and shortly before his death told me that he was worried about the disappearance of documents that contained them. Must I be more precise, Madame?'

'Meaning, Monsieur?' said the Queen, with a hint of emotion in her voice.

Is it possible that Jules talked? she thought.

'Well, Madame, I have found those documents. I believe they were stolen from the Cardinal's library at the same time as other equally confidential papers, at the behest of certain individuals who wish to gain control of the Kingdom's political affairs, who act on behalf of highly placed persons . . .'

'And what else, Monsieur?'

'Roses are dumb, Madame. In their presence I therefore dare utter the name of Superintendent Fouquet, although in truth I am not yet in a position to prove it. I say "not yet", for the evidence is accumulating.'

'Now then, supposing you had such documents, Monsieur, would not your most urgent task then be to give them to me?' went on the Queen in a distant voice, trying to mask her suspicion.

Colbert hesitated for a second before replying.

'I have to say that it seems wiser to me to retain them in the first instance. With the sole intention, of course, of protecting them before handing them back to Your Highness as soon as matters are closed; and obviously with the hope that I won't have to use them to prove the Superintendent's criminal intentions . . .'

What hatred, thought the Queen, *and how fearlessly he lies . . . unless there were copies of the documents that young man Pontbriand came to give back to me. God in Heaven, I cannot think that that young man was lying. But if Fouquet . . .*

'The air is still cool, is that why you shiver?' enquired Colbert, sensing with delight that his poison was slowly being absorbed. 'Madame, what are your own feelings on this? Do you think that the Superintendent's defence will be difficult to dismantle?'

The Queen shivered again as she understood the nature of the trap. *Decidedly not*, she thought, *and without a doubt it is Colbert himself who is the traitor, master blackmailer that he is. My silence against his. I allow Fouquet to fall and he preserves my honour and my son's destiny.*

Faced with a lengthening silence, Colbert decided to go on the attack.

'I do not ask you for an answer, Madame. And please believe that my greatest desire is to be able to return those papers to you without delay.'

He is lying, thought the Queen sadly. *Whether I really believe Fouquet to be guilty of sedition or decide not to defend him for fear of Colbert's threats, the result is the same – he is the winner.*

She raised her head and glared at Colbert.

'I must thank you, Monsieur. It is indeed rare that one is given an opportunity to distinguish so clearly between two moral attitudes. You see, what has differentiated you from a man of honour is the fact that a man who can lay claim to that glorious title came to see me a little while ago, to hand me those documents of which you speak, without even asking for the smallest favour for himself. And yet he was merely a modest secretary, without position or power.'

With his jaws clenched, Colbert absorbed the blow and took his leave.

The Queen Mother shook with anger as she watched him walk away: 'Dear God, but the company of roses is sweet,' she hissed between her teeth.

CHAPTER SEVENTY

Vincennes, Anne of Austria's apartments – Friday 27 May,
four o'clock in the afternoon

ALARMED by the melancholy which had overcome Henrietta of England as her marriage to the Duc d'Orléans approached, Anne of Austria invited her future daughter-in-law and her retinue to spend the afternoon with her. Seated around the King's mother, the ladies were listening to Monsieur Lulli regaling them with one of his recent compositions on the clavichord.

'What talent!' exclaimed Anne of Austria, applauding vigorously when the musician had finished his piece. 'Your music is an enchantment for both the body and the soul. It has quite sharpened my appetite,' she said cheerfully, clapping her hands in the direction of the servants who stood on either side of the main door. 'Bring some hot chocolate with cinnamon; I wish to introduce these ladies to the divine cocoa beans given to me by Monsieur Colbert,' she added with dark humour.

Louise de La Vallière sat modestly in the background. She was hoping to take advantage of this reception to thank the Queen Mother for so swiftly granting the audience Gabriel had requested a few days earlier. Olympe Mancini was there too, in her capacity as steward of the Queen Mother's household. She was discreetly watching those assembled, and most particularly Louise de La Vallière.

She chose the end of the musical sequence as an appropriate moment to approach Anne of Austria.

'Madame, may I request the privilege of speaking to you for a moment?' asked Louise de La Vallière, bowing her head before the Queen Mother.

'Of course, my little one,' replied the sovereign, leading her affectionately towards a window bay.

'Majesty, a dreadful cabal has hatched a plot against me,' the young girl began, a little upset. 'People are attacking my honour for reasons I do not understand.'

Perhaps because of your relations with the King? thought the Queen Mother, without betraying what she knew. *After all,* she said to herself, *Louis has displayed good taste, the young lady is pretty; and what is more, she does not seem stupid. At least she will make him forget Marie Mancini!*

'I can assure Your Majesty of my devotion to the royal family,' continued Louise, 'and I beg you never to believe the ignominies which certain people seem to delight in spreading about me!'

'Your devotion to the royal family had not escaped me,' replied Anne of Austria, with just a hint of perfidy. 'Have no fear, Mademoiselle, I am aware of these base accusations and such gossip does not impress me. As long as you know your place, you will find a friend in me!'

Relieved, Louise curtsied respectfully and lowered her gaze to conceal her turmoil.

'Your chocolate, Majesty.'

Olympe approached, bringing the two women cups of the hot liquid. She handed the first to the Queen Mother, who took it with a smile. Then she turned and handed the second to Louise.

'No, no, please, you must have this one,' said Louise, pushing away the cup. She was most surprised to be served in this way, against all the rules of etiquette, by the steward of the Queen Mother's household.

'Come,' said Olympe awkwardly, offering the cup of chocolate once again, this time with a broad smile.

Louise took the cup and was about to sip it when the Queen Mother stopped her with a wave of the hand.

'One moment, my dear. Permit an old woman to indulge a whim! Your chocolate seems creamier than mine. May I ask for your cup? I have a guilty passion for frothy chocolate!'

Disconcerted, Louise obediently handed her the cup.

'But . . .' stammered Olympe, 'Majesty, you cannot . . .'

'What is the matter?' asked the Queen Mother sharply, staring at Olympe all of a sudden.

Although she said nothing, Olympe was obviously distressed.

'What is the matter with you?' asked the Queen Mother again.

Then, taking a step forward, she dropped the cup which shattered on the wooden floor. The chocolate spread over the ground in a star shape.

'Heavens!' cried Olympe.

'Come, it's not serious,' commented the Queen Mother coldly.

The sound of the cup breaking made Henrietta turn round.

'Look, you've made someone happy,' she said with a laugh.

The puppy given to Anne of Austria by the King to ease his mother's loneliness was indeed now lapping up the liquid, watched anxiously by its mistress.

Louise spoke again as Olympe walked away.

'Majesty,' she said with a bow, 'the fear which I have confided in you is my sole excuse for the lack of education I've shown in omitting to thank you once again for granting the favour of a meeting to my friend, Monsieur de Pontbriand. Your generosity . . .'

'Monsieur de Pontbriand is a true gentleman, Mademoiselle, and a charming boy too,' replied the Queen Mother kindly. 'It was my great pleasure to receive him. People who come with requests are many, but those who come to give something spontaneously are rare. I am therefore in debt to you and I owe you my thanks . . . What is more . . . Oh my God!'

Anne of Austria interrupted herself at the sight of her puppy, which had rolled over onto its back. Its limbs were trembling and there was foam on its lips. Before she could reach it, the poor little creature was dead, a bluish liquid trickling from its mouth.

CHAPTER SEVENTY-ONE

*Château de Vincennes – Saturday 28 May, ten o'clock
in the morning*

'Too hot! Still too hot!'

With a gesture of irritation, the King rejected the pail of water which the manservant was about to pour into the copper bath in which he sat.

'I told you to warm it! Warm it, you fool, not boil it! 'Sblood, I am not a pig to be skinned!'

The servant ran out as fast as his legs would carry him, the water slopping out of his pail leaving steaming trails on the stone floor. The King re-immersed himself in his thoughts. The dazzling spring colours visible through his bathroom window, the blue of the sky: everything converged to drive away his momentary anger.

Even the constant feeling that there was still work to be done to ensure the establishment of his authority could not dislodge his smile at the thought of Louise's face and the stolen moments they had shared over the past fortnight. Everything about her delighted the young King: her beauty, her passionate temperament, her lust for life, her spontaneity.

And I am going to be a father he thought, untroubled by the change of subject. *Anyway, here I am thinking about politics again*, he mused plunging his head beneath the water as if to drive away these notions.

When he opened his eyes underwater, the face of Marie Mancini came back to him, just as the scar of a poorly healed wound continues to remind its owner of its presence from time to time. Marie and Louise: Louis XIV consigned these two names to the inner recesses where he isolated those young man's dreams he no longer quite had the right to enjoy. As for the Queen, she had now deserted those inner recesses where, moreover, she had made only timid appearances. Visiting her in her bedchamber was a duty, and one which only the King's sensual nature and overflowing vitality rendered bearable. True, the news of her pregnancy had delighted him, but only as the announcement of a victory on the battlefield might. The glory he envisaged demanded an heir.

'It has to be a boy,' he sighed softly.

Then he spoke out loud:

'Come, some water.'

Footsteps heralded the servant's approach. Readying himself for a cascade of hot water, the King once again slid full-length into the bath.

'My son, I have caught you unawares and I beg you to forgive this intrusion.'

Recognising his mother's voice, Louis XIV suddenly turned over, splashing everything around him.

'Madame?' he demanded in astonishment 'Obviously the King of France cannot have a second to himself!'

'Come come, my son,' replied Anne of Austria with a smile, sitting down on the small wooden chair at the foot of the bath.

'True, it has not happened for a long time, but I can remember supervising your bath on several occasions, including those when I do not think you could keep your head above the water on your own.'

It was the King's turn to smile.

'Alas, I have not come here today to be moved by talk of times past. And the reason I have not visited your office for a private audience is that I need to be certain that our conversation remains confidential.'

The King sat up in his bath.

'You unsettle me, Madame. What is this about?'

The Queen saw from her son's frown that he was troubled.

'Don't worry. I have not come to reproach you for your conduct, or to talk about your wife.'

The King's expression became even darker.

'I have already informed you of my feelings on that matter, as did Monsieur Cardinal in respect of his niece, and I shall not return to them, however disagreeable I find the rumours which unfailingly reach my ears.'

'People often speak ill of others, Madame, even within the walls of my own palace,' grunted the King, adopting a tone which made it clear that he did not intend to talk about it any further. 'You have been the victim of sufficient slander yourself, I believe?'

Mother and son looked at each other for a moment.

'Indeed, my son,' went on Anne of Austria. 'People often speak ill, you are right. But there are more serious matters. People conspire. And attempt murder. Even within the walls of your own palace.'

The King shuddered at these words, which reminded him too much of his recent conversation with Colbert.

'What? What are you saying?'

Anne of Austria got to her feet and walked to the window.

'The truth, Louis. There has just been an attempt to poison one of the companions of your brother's future wife, whose marriage is to be celebrated in a fortnight's time. In my apartments.'

The King opened his mouth to speak but no sound escaped his lips. Suddenly it seemed as though the water around him had frozen. The Queen went on with her story without looking at him.

'The young woman escaped death by a hair's breadth – and she was saved by a miracle. How pale you are, Louis,' she remarked in an even tone, turning round. 'And I believe the name of the young person is not unknown to you: Louise de La Vallière.'

The King stood up and took the towel proffered by a valet.

'That's enough, Madame. Do not play games with me,' he said coldly. 'I hear what you are saying and what you are not saying.'

'Then act, Sire,' continued the Queen in the same tone of voice. 'Right now it matters little what attaches you to her, and what I condemn as a mother, a mother-in-law and a Christian. All that matters is that an attack on her is an attack on you, and as Queen of France I will not tolerate that. You must act ruthlessly, my son, and without delay. Personal morality demands that you do so to save this girl whom you have placed in danger; but above all, your royal dignity demands it for the sake of your public glory and your authority.'

Draped in his towel, the King gazed with newfound emotion at the austere, dignified form of his mother, hearing in the sincere tone of her voice that which had guided his entire existence.

'You are right, Madame,' was all that he said.

The Queen raised a finger.

'One more thing, my son, before I leave you to your duty. No one knows what has happened except those close to me and those who are guilty of the infamy. This should not deter you from taking action. The punishment will be understood by the guilty parties, and those who do not understand it will fear it, which is no bad thing. Through the offices of a young man whom I believe to be honest and who has rendered me a great service, I have acquired further information which you should also take into account.'

'Speak, Madame,' replied the King.

'The steward of my household, the Cardinal's own niece, Olympe, has for reasons unclear conceived feelings of hatred and jealousy towards Mademoiselle de La Vallière. She is the one who carried out the attempt, I am convinced of that. As for the leader of this conspiracy, I hesitate to grant credence to those pointing a finger at your own brother. I hesitate because then I would have to acknowledge my own guilt at having failed to turn him aside from his appalling deviancies . . .'

'Enough, Madame,' the King interrupted gently. 'I know my duty and I know the Duc d'Orléans too well not to be aware of his weaknesses as well as his good qualities.'

The Queen nodded silently.

As she walked past her son, she brushed his cheek with the

tips of her fingers, which were almost entirely covered by the lace of her oversleeve.

The King stopped her on the threshold.

'Just a moment: the name of the young man who has made such serious allegations?'

'He told me that his name is Gabriel de Pontbriand, and that he is in the service of Monsieur Fouquet.'

The King watched her leave the room in silence, then stifled a shout of rage. Louise! How dare they?! When he had even promised that he would protect her. How stupid he had been! His power was nothing. His mother was right – he would make them tremble! He would trust no one.

His pain slowly turned to anger, modified only by his surprise at hearing the name of that young man in connection with Louise's rescue.

'Pontbriand,' he murmured thoughtfully, 'and Fouquet again . . .'

Then the blood that boiled in his veins made him angry again.

'They will fear me,' he seethed, leaving the room watched anxiously by his servants, who dared not enquire if he needed anything. 'I shall crush them all! I am the King, I will have no more advice, no more help, no more support!'

Tears of rage burned his eyes.

'Their presence humiliates me, all of them.'

How he missed his godfather. Even his mother's face seemed like an attack on his power.

'Am I still a child, that she must open my eyes! My mother's counsels, the Superintendent's cleverness! To hell with my advisers! I am the King!'

Realising that he had spoken out loud, the King glared thunderously at his principal valet.

'Dress me,' he snapped. 'And send for Colbert immediately.'

CHAPTER SEVENTY-TWO

L OUIS XIV's rage had not abated. He strode up and down
his office, shouting at the Duc d'Orléans.

'Monsieur, my brother, I shall no longer tolerate conspiracies at the French Court. The era in which people
fomented their own underhand schemes in the corridors of this
palace is over once and for all. Do you quite understand me? At.
An. End,' shouted Louis XIV, 'and that includes blood princes.'

'But . . .'

'There is no "but"! Who do you take me for, that you dare
to attack those close to me? You are a subject of this Kingdom
like any other and I demand the same obedience from you and
the same respect for my person, in the absence of which . . .'
growled the King, angrily seizing his brother by the jabot of his
shirt to bring his face up to his.

The gesture was so violent that the Duc d'Orléans paled.

'You must understand once and for all,' continued the
sovereign when he had let go of him. 'By attacking Louise de La
Vallière, you attack me. If I allow myself to be scoffed at, the
State would suffer the humiliation. To achieve your aims and
conceal your involvement, you thought it a good idea to place a
weapon in the hands of Olympe Mancini . . .'

'But . . .' the Duc d'Orléans attempted once again.

'Monsieur, stop interrupting me at every opportunity,' the King snapped. 'The information given to me by the Queen Mother has been corroborated by the investigation carried out at my request by Colbert. You were wrong to believe that my affection for the Cardinal's nieces would extend to pardoning this crime. Olympe deserves death a hundred times over. But out of respect for my dear godfather, I have decided to grant her the favour of exile. She is to leave this very day for the provinces, where she will pray for the eternal repose of the Cardinal's soul, and spend the rest of her days begging for God's pardon.'

Cowed, and hanging his head low, Philippe d'Orléans said nothing but waited anxiously for his punishment.

'As for you, Monsieur, I am giving you one final chance to rehabilitate yourself in my eyes and to show yourself worthy of my father's inheritance. You will marry Henrietta of England as planned. You will control your impulses in order to lessen my mother's grief, and you will cease your mania for conspiracies once and for all!' Louis XIV angrily signalled the end of the conversation.

Unable to find the courage to reply, the Duc d'Orléans left the room. After all, he had emerged rather well from the affair and promised himself that, from then on, he would steer very clear of any kind of intrigue.

'Send in Colbert,' barked Louis XIV, returning to his work table and picking up a letter.

'Colbert,' ordered the sovereign in a voice still filled with rage, as the Steward of Finance entered and bowed almost to the ground. 'You are to go immediately and inform Olympe Mancini of the decisions I have written down in this letter. You will see to it personally that my orders are carried out without delay. She is to have left Paris before nightfall. Do you hear me?'

'I shall see to it, Sire,' replied Colbert, curious to find out the contents of the letter.

As soon as he left the King's office, Colbert stopped by a candelabrum in the corridor to skim through the document setting out Olympe's punishment. He went swiftly to the other wing of the palace, to the apartments occupied by the steward of the Queen Mother's household. Through the carved wooden doors, he could hear the young woman sobbing. 'No doubt the Duc d'Orléans has already notified her of her fate', Colbert said to himself as he entered the salon. When she saw him, Olympe exploded.

'I will tell everything! Don't think you can escape from this just like that! It's out of the question that I should be the only one to pay! You were perfectly aware of what was being plotted,' raged the young woman as she approached him, ready to pounce.

'Calm yourself, Madame,' said Colbert, with a tone of cold authority. 'You had a narrow escape, and your clumsiness could have cost us dear. How could you be so stupid as to risk your head like that?' demanded the Cardinal's former secretary. 'Poison is a subtle weapon . . . doubtless too subtle for you!'

'But . . .'

'No "buts",' went on Colbert. 'No one asked you to be so clumsy. Consider yourself fortunate to have emerged with your life intact. Exile is not death! But I warn you, death will find you in any exile if by some misfortune you feel the preposterous desire to blurt anything out! In a word, leave here quickly and quietly, before the King changes his mind and sends you to the scaffold!'

Sniffing tearfully, Olympe Mancini realised that she had lost. She alone would have to take responsibility for her actions.

'You say exile is not death! I want to believe you, Monsieur. But you do not know how miserable our provinces can be in the winter,' said the young woman, her voice sugary again. 'In order to guarantee my silence, would it not be wise to endow my enforced stay with the minimum of comfort conducive to meditation and silence?'

Evidently these Mancini sluts will never change' Colbert said to himself.

'We shall make ample provision for that, Madame, ample provision!'

CHAPTER SEVENTY-THREE

Palais du Louvre – Friday 10 June, ten o'clock in the morning

'FIFTY-THREE cannons of green cast iron, including four Swedish carbines and a culverin; one hundred and fifty-seven of iron, thirty-three of them mounted on bastions; two mortars in green cast iron and sixty naval gun carriages in service. This is very good work!' Colbert said greedily, looking up at Charles Perrault who stood in front of his desk. 'But how the devil did you manage to draw up this inventory?'

'To get onto the island, I took it upon myself to send a vessel to the Breton coast with ten barrels and a wine trader from La Rochelle on board. They passed through the security surrounding the Superintendent's estates with no problems, and the wine probably also helped to loosen several people's tongues later,' replied the Chief of Police with false modesty.

Colbert eagerly read more of the memorandum drawn up by Perrault.

'Seven hundred and sixty muskets from Sedan, eight hundred and ten from Liège, some carbines, eleven hundred and seventy grenades, ten thousand six hundred and seventy three cannon-balls of all calibres . . . My dear Perrault, your precision is impressive and . . . worrying,' exclaimed the former accountant. 'How can you be so sure of your figures?'

'My envoy in Belle-Île performed a fine trick. Under the

pretext of a trade in cast iron, he was able to bribe the accountant at the fort. The inventory included in this document is an exact transcription of the one sent last month to Monsieur Superintendent!'

'Excellent!' Colbert said simply, returning to his reading. 'And all of this is supposed to be just for equipping ships or for the defence of the colonial trading posts? I knew it! Under the pretext of maritime trading, Fouquet has in fact built up a substantial army, even though the Kingdom is at peace,' he said, laying the papers back down on his desk. 'The lands in Belle-Île which he so loves are not destined to compete with Amsterdam, as he maintains, but to serve as a actual armed base, even as a fortress for him if necessary!'

'I estimate the number of labourers currently working on the island's fortifications to be fifteen hundred,' went on Perrault, seeing that the Cardinal's former secretary had finished reading his memorandum. 'According to my spy, there never seems to be any shortage of money. As for the name Fouquet, it is seldom uttered. The inhabitants of the island talk of the Lord of Belle-Île, if anything! As for the men at arms who make up the visible troops, there seem to be around two hundred, according to a count carried out by our spy.'

When he heard this number, Colbert chuckled.

'I knew it, and now your report is here to prove it, Perrault. This man who wishes to pass himself off as a simple shipping owner, concerned with increasing his wealth and France's expansion as a trading power, is in fact preparing for something quite different.'

'You mean . . .'

'I mean that I now need further evidence of these felonies in order to construct a solid basis for a court case whose repercussions will surprise you,' Colbert went on confidentially. 'I trust you, my dear Perrault. I know of your devotion to the King and your unfailing fidelity. Because of this, I know I can rely on you for a mission which is, to say the least, delicate!'

Acknowledging the compliment, Charles Perrault bowed respectfully.

'This is a grim time. To my mind, the Kingdom is at great risk if we do not act. The moment is propitious, and I am told that the Superintendent of Finance is once again suffering from an attack of malaria. He has recently retired with his entire household to his chateau at Vaux-le-Vicomte. Find a way of discreetly entering Saint-Mandé and unearth everything you can to support your memorandum! Act alone and with discernment,' added Colbert with an enigmatic smile.

Taken aback by this request, but at the same time flattered by the trust it implied, Charles Perrault said nothing and withdrew, bowing to the ground.

Colbert was still smiling as he watched the Chief of Police leave his office. He looked out of the open window through which the warm sun shone into the room.

The squirrel is in the trap! All I need is for Perrault to bring me back a little more evidence, and the King will no longer have cause for delay. No, there is surely no escape for the accursed Fouquet. I have all I need to uphold a court case from which the Superintendent cannot escape! thought Colbert, tapping his fingers on the memorandum describing the weaponry stored on Belle-Île. *Particularly since I shall use an intermediary to buy back his office of Procureur. That manoeuvre will deprive him of his remaining influence over the judges! After that, and before I arrange for his arrest, I will have to brush aside any objections from the Queen Mother. That won't be the easiest task, but I have done harder things,* he said to himself. *Moreover, the anxiety which our recent conversations have caused her will play in my favour. Anne of Austria will sacrifice the squirrel with difficulty, but she would rather cut off one of her arms than allow the smallest risk of harm to her son. It really is a beautiful day,* concluded Colbert, standing up to take a closer look at the gardens of the Louvre and enjoy the sun's warmth.

CHAPTER SEVENTY-FOUR

Palais du Louvre – Sunday 12 June, eleven o'clock
in the morning

'COME on, come on, give it to me,' ordered the King in a voice that was both impatient and happy, and he stretched out his leather-clad arm.

'Is Your Majesty sure that his glove is properly in place?' asked d'Artagnan anxiously.

'My dear Captain, I am not made of china and I do not need to be so carefully protected!' replied the King disdainfully, stepping aside. 'So give it to me, Monsieur.'

At that moment Colbert was shown into the King's office. He recoiled instinctively when he saw the man who was approaching the sovereign.

The King's falconer also wore a protective leather glove, and he carried a gerfalcon on his arm. The nervous movements of its wings revealed a span of over a yard. The man stood beside the sovereign and then, pressing his arm against the King's, began to slide the clawed talons from his own leather gauntlet to Louis XIV's. Fascinated, the young King watched him in delight as he made whispering, whistling sounds to the bird of prey, whose head, covered in a black-leather hood, bobbed jerkily up and down. To Colbert, it seemed to go on for ever. Taking refuge close to the table where he had just placed a voluminous fawn-coloured satchel, the little man watched the ceremony warily. He could not help thinking that introducing this symbol of war and brutishness to this place devoted to intelligence, calculation and strategy was a violation.

The King was now walking around the room with his eyes fixed on the gerfalcon attached to his raised fist. An almost childish pride shone on his face.

'You shall tell the ambassador how much this gift delights me,' he declared to the assembled company without taking his eyes off the gerfalcon.

One by one, each of the men he passed let out murmurs of admiration, which seemed to delight him even more.

'We must have this scene captured by an artist,' said the sovereign.

When he noticed Colbert, he smiled at the uncomfortable look on the Steward's face.

'Well, Monsieur Colbert, see what the Turk has sent me! Is it not magnificent?'

Colbert tried not to close his eyes when the gerfalcon spread its wings and let out shrill little cries very close to his face.

'Indeed, Sire', he agreed respectfully.

'Is my gift by chance the cause of the anxiety which clouds your face?' asked the King.

Colbert was indignant.

'Not in the least, Sire, but I bear the weight of cares which I take seriously, particularly as they concern the Kingdom and Your Majesty.'

Louis XIV grew sombre as he was brought back to reality.

'You are right, Monsieur – work calls. I cannot reproach you for it, even if moments of joy are very rare . . . Well, serious matters, you say?' he went on, holding out his fist to the falconer.

'Extremely serious, Sire,' confirmed Colbert. 'Your Majesty knows that I would not dare to disturb the course of his diplomatic activity were it not for a matter of the greatest importance.'

The King smiled.

'It's all right, Colbert. The Cardinal did warn me: "a tireless worker, but as sad as a day without bread".'

Colbert suffered the gibe without flinching.

'Anyway, to work. Messieurs,' added the King, signalling to the throng to leave as a manservant hurried forward to free him from the laced-up leather gauntlet.

'Well, Monsieur Colbert?' said the King when they were alone in his office, now returned to its primary use. 'So what am I to fear?'

'A conspiracy, Sire, and a rebellion.'

With clenched teeth, Louis XIV stared at the map laid out on the table. It showed the painstakingly drawn contours of Belle-Île, surmounted by a network of defences and turrets. A port appeared clearly on the map, along with some roughly drawn boats. Written on each element of the fortifications were columns of figures listing munitions, weapons, and names. Furiously, the King lifted the map, pulling out from underneath it a map on a larger scale, showing Brittany as far as Nantes. Here too, the defences and available resources were indicated with the same precision. Colbert's voice cut through the silence, making him look up.

'Sire, I too would not have had any faith in these documents were I not certain of their provenance, and if they did not merely add a final touch to a host of weighty presumptions. But I had to face up to the evidence. Yes, Monsieur Fouquet cheats in his accounts, mixing his privy purse with that of Your Majesty, returning to his former methods when he sought to make us believe that the Cardinal, God rest his soul . . .'

At these words, he raised his eyes to Heaven and clasped his hands, a scandalised expression on his lips.

'. . . was solely responsible for them. Yes, Monsieur Fouquet uses his Breton possessions to transfer his resources to America and the Indies via trading companies. And as if all of this: theft, fraud, misappropriation of public funds, calumnies of all sorts, aggravated by the attempt, in his madness, to corrupt innocent or gentle souls like that young fellow Pontbriand or Mademoiselle de La Vallière, alongside whom his assiduous presence has been verified . . .'

The King blanched as he heard these words.

'. . . as if all of this, as I say, were not enough,' continued Colbert without betraying anything of his satisfaction, 'Monsieur Superintendent has added to these infamies the threat of rebellion against his King by establishing – doubtless in case his misappropriations were discovered – an armed refuge in Brittany, from which an insurrection could be launched.'

Out of breath now, Colbert fell silent. The King stood motionless and pale-faced. Stunned by the profusion of documents and facts skilfully engineered to mask approximations, half-truths and lies, the King felt a profound lassitude wash over him. *So I shall never be done with it,* he thought with sudden anguish. *I shall always have to be fearful of plots and conspiracies.*

Looking up, he saw Colbert's greedy expression and shining eyes.

'The proof is here,' insisted the little man with a theatrical sweep of his hand, indicating the mass of documents which had spilled out of his leather case.

'Very well,' said the King tonelessly.

He gave a long sigh.

'What is really needed is for the century to be purged,' he murmured.

The Steward looked up inquisitively.

'Lock your files securely in a chest,' added the King, heading for the door.

On the threshold, he seemed to change his mind.

'The Cardinal did not deceive me, Monsieur Colbert. I shall not forget that.'

Colbert gave a deep bow. By the time he straightened up, the King had disappeared. He then went to the table and began to fold the documents one by one before putting them away in his case. When he had finished, he looked around the empty room in satisfaction.

'Sad as a day without bread,' he murmured with a shrug of his shoulders. 'It matters not, if I achieve my ends.'

Buckling his case, he put it under his arm before heading for the door himself. As he emerged into the corridor, he glanced through the window and saw the King in the palace courtyard, surrounded by a crowd of courtiers who had come to see a hunting demonstration by the precious gerfalcon. The bird of prey was at that moment flying from the hand of the falconer, who had removed the hood which blinded it. In a flash, it swooped upon a dove which had been freed from a little willow cage and seized it in its talons with a shrill cry. The falcon was now wheeling in concentric circles, with the dove clutched in its powerful grasp.

Colbert frowned in disgust and continued along the gilt-panelled corridor.

'Purge the century?' he repeated in a low voice.

CHAPTER SEVENTY-FIVE

'BLAST that kitchen boy!'

For the tenth time that day, Vatel, the cook at Vaux-le-Vicomte, lifted the two-pronged fork he used to turn the roasts and poultry with disconcerting ease as they hung above the fire. In the darkness of the immense basement kitchen, his size was emphasised by his shadow, which danced on the walls in the light of the flames.

'How many times do I have to tell him? Don't stoke up the fire too high if you don't want the meat to crack and all its juices to dry up!'

Crouching behind their ovens, his kitchen hands watched anxiously as this new bout of anger developed.

'And these cakes,' he yelled even louder, moving his fat body swiftly towards the babas and choux pastries carefully set out in rows on long copper trays. 'This cannot be true. . .'

'Jesus, Mary and Joseph,' whispered the kitchen boy furthest away from Vatel.

'. . . Jesus, Mary and Joseph! You must want me dead,' said the cook unconsciously echoing the boy, although he had heard nothing.

Sighing, his face crimson with anger and from exposure to

the fire, Vatel yielded to a moment of discouragement. He mopped the sweat which was dripping down his forehead and into his eyes.

'Come on, you heap of incompetents!' he roared, rallying. 'We only have one more hour until the meal is served! The King, Messieurs, you are cooking for the King! Have a little pride in your work, for the love of God!'

This last despairing cry made Gabriel de Pontbriand smile.

Poor Vatel, he thought as he reached the main entrance, *can cakes really be the cause of so much torment . . .?*

Once again, he felt the apprehension that had scarcely left him recently. They were close to their goal, and if everything went as they hoped, the evening would mark the dawning of a new era. Feelings ran through his heart as fast as the white clouds rushed towards the horizon. Tonight would be the realisation of his father's dream.

The young man strode up the chateau's steps looking for Fouquet. From the top of the steps the sight was amazing. Everywhere he looked, Gabriel could see little figures running about, busying themselves with the final preparations for the celebration. Gabriel grimaced as he recognised his former companions from the troupe amongst those on the actors' platform standing around Molière, who was waving his arms about in anger like a miniature puppet. Gabriel had met him that morning during an inspection with Fouquet. The coldness with which the great author had greeted him had at first wounded him, then strengthened him in his conviction that Providence had sent him in the right direction. Closer to him, groups of workmen emerged from thickets behind which he could imagine the fountains and rockeries, waterfalls, statues and mechanisms. The musicians were setting up alongside the lawns, magnificently aligned with the view of the chateau in the August sunshine. Turning round, he saw the crowd of guests converging slowly upon the chateau, filing past the gilded gates embossed with the Superintendent's arms. His heart thudded as he narrowed his eyes to try and make out Louise's face in the coloured mass of gowns and suits.

The familiar voice of La Fontaine drew him out of his contemplation.

'Well, Gabriel? Is that an outfit in which to welcome the King? The whole Court is hurrying to our gates and you have not even put on your waistcoat.'

Gabriel looked down at his shirt and bounded towards the stairs.

'Curious child,' murmured the poet, watching him hurtle towards his room.

Gabriel rushed down the stairs four at a time, trying to attach the blue silk ribbon that held his collar together. Stumbling, he almost fell head first, bumped into the stone banister to the sound of rending fabric, and found himself sitting on the first-floor landing.

'Confound it, my sleeve!' he exclaimed as he realised that the seam of his coat had ripped. 'Too bad,' he added, getting to his feet.

A glance through the window stopped him in his tracks. There before him, less than a hundred yards away, the King had just emerged from his carriage. Standing there with a pommel-topped cane in his hand, dressed in a close-fitting suit of golden fabric and a black hat decorated with white feathers, the King of France was smiling at a compliment from Nicolas Fouquet, who was bowing respectfully before him. Seeing that the retinue was on the move, Gabriel ran down the rest of the stairs, emerged onto the rear steps of the chateau and circled back round to slip discreetly into the procession. Peering over the heads of the crowd of courtiers who followed the King, Gabriel saw Fouquet explaining the layout and construction of his estate, gesturing with his hands as he spoke. The windows revealed so much of the gardens' magnificence that the walls seemed almost transparent. Impassive, the King gazed at the chateau and its dome with such intensity that Gabriel's heart missed a beat.

Come now, compose yourself, he told himself. *It is not yet time. And what is d'Orbay doing? If everything is to go to plan, he will have to be there*, he thought, biting his lip.

'Gabriel!

'Louise! exclaimed the young man as he saw a hand waving at him, struggling against the tide of guests.

Pushing his way through, Gabriel managed to catch up with the girl and draw her out of the crowd.

'So here you are, master of a very fine chateau,' she laughed.

Gabriel could not take his eyes off her dazzling gown embroidered with gold, her sparkling eyes, her white skin.

'Go ahead and mock, you cold-hearted girl. It takes a

celebration for me to be able to see you these days. The Court has made you entirely its own,' he said mournfully.

'Come now, you're the one who's invisible!

'No one is more invisible than a man one never thinks about,' retorted Gabriel seriously. 'And you know very well that I am here if needed.'

The allusion brought colour to Louise's cheeks.

'That is true,' she conceded. 'But you're the one who fled Amboise and abandoned me. And I'm the one who came to find you again!'

This reversal forced a smile from Gabriel.

'Go,' she told him, as he turned his head automatically to see where the King and his host had got to. 'Don't make the Superintendent wait. And besides, I have to find my duchess!'

'We shall see each other later at the spectacle!' Gabriel called to her as she fled.

In the distance, the sun sparkled on the King of France's dazzling finery.

The last of the guests who had dallied in the groves to watch the fountains were only just returning to the salons where Vatel had laid the dinner tables.

Already, courtiers in their hundreds were thronging around the platters of ducklings and fattened chickens and roasted meats of every kind, accompanied by countless garnishes, baskets of fruit and spectacular cakes.

Cries of delight sounded from the neighbouring room, where the guests were being treated to their first sight of the colossal full-length portrait of Louis XIV, which Fouquet had unveiled on the King's arrival.

Seated on a dais and looking down upon the throng, the King responded with cordial nods to the guests who jostled for pride of place in his field of vision. The Queen Mother, seated by his side, seemed to be suffering from the heat; she refused the food and was frantically waving a Spanish fan in front of her pale, tired face.

Fouquet stood by the door, receiving the compliments of those who were returning from the gardens, their eyes filled with wonderment at the sights they had just witnessed.

'What luxury,' said a voice behind him.

Fouquet turned to see Colbert, a glass of red wine in his hand, leaning against a pilaster.

'What can one devise that is too beautiful to please a King?' Fouquet replied, his cool tone tinged with hostility.

Colbert raised his glass with a nod.

'Pray excuse me,' Fouquet cut him off icily, 'it is time for me to go and enquire if His Majesty is ready to see Monsieur Molière's play.'

Turning to leave, the Superintendent did not see the little man's gaze stab him in the back.

CHAPTER SEVENTY-SIX

THE muffled sounds of the festivities reached as far as the statue of Hercules. Huddled in its shadow, Gabriel leant with all his weight on the lever he had slid beneath a flagstone joined to the monument's plinth. He stopped for a moment to get his strength back, and turned to look at the flickering lights at the far end of the gardens. All the guests were now in the chateau. Looking upwards, he gazed briefly at the dark-blue sky. The clarity of the night, illuminated by an intense, whitish-yellow moon, was not marred by a single cloud. Tensing his muscles, he pushed down on the lever again. Little by little, the stone moved from its housing, pivoting with a muffled cracking sound to reveal the dark cavity leading to the network of channels which served the park's lakes and fountains.

Gabriel groped about to locate the iron rungs set into the wall. Then he went to fetch the torch he had carefully planted in the earth behind the plinth, so that it would remain invisible from the buildings, and began to climb down into the shaft.

Taking care to gain a secure footing on the damp, rusty iron, he felt the stench of the stagnant water catch in his throat. He slipped his arm through a rung and pulled his cravat up over his face to cover his nose and mouth, and then continued his descent.

He thought of Fouquet and d'Orbay. Everything now rested upon him. He remembered d'Orbay's solemn expression as he said:

'Nicolas wouldn't be able to get away for long. A prolonged absence would be too obvious. And the same is true for me, though to a lesser extent; Colbert's men will be watching us. You are going to have to go and fetch the formula from wherever you hid it on your return from London. And you'll also have to carry out the transmutation process. I will have prepared the necessary plants in the tower beneath the cupola. They'll be hidden beneath the supporting structure – I showed you where. No one will have access to the tower except the man responsible for the fireworks, and he is one of us. The risk of fireworks exploding will keep away any intruders, as will the guards posted on the stairs. At exactly ten o'clock the moon's rays will be shining on the cupola at the optimum angle. You must be ready. Then you'll go to Nicolas's bedchamber. He'll be waiting for you to make sure the operation is a success . . .'

Gabriel suddenly lost his footing on a particularly slippery rung and almost fell, only just recovering his balance in time. He paused for a moment to get his breath back, then climbed deeper into the shaft.

When he felt packed earth beneath his feet, he stepped away from the ladder and headed down the tunnel which had opened up before him. The sound of the water running through the conduits echoed in the enclosed space, making his ears buzz. He concentrated on counting the number of steps he took, forcing himself to space them evenly, and after a while he stopped and turned to face the brick wall on his right. Leaning his torch against it, he took the dagger from his belt and worked away to remove a brick that was at waist-height. It fell to the ground without a sound. Gabriel slid his hand into the cavity and withdrew a small box, which he slipped into a pouch that hung round his neck, then returned the way he had come.

'He's late,' grunted d'Orbay, his voice filled with tension.

Screwing up his eyes against the summer wind's caress, Fouquet turned to the architect and smiled.

'Don't be impatient. He will be here any moment now.'

Then he gripped d'Orbay's arm and pointed to a silhouetted figure running along beside the outbuildings.

'Look, there he is. Allowing for the time it takes him to climb up to the tower, he will be in place in five minutes.'

The Superintendent took out a small silver pocket watch and held it up.

'Twenty minutes to ten. Perfect.'

They fell silent. As they stood there on the terrace, their eyes once again swept across the vista laid out before them. The brightness of the moon, together with the lights from the party, combined to make the shadows of the groves and flowerbeds dance in the darkness.

The two men returned to mingle with the crowd.

A moment later, Gabriel emerged on the balcony of the tower. He glanced swiftly at the moon, then went back inside to examine the supporting structure and re-emerged a few seconds later with a black box clasped in his hands like some precious gem.

Everything is ready, he said to himself feverishly as he lifted the lid, revealing twelve separate compartments filled with powders of various colours. *All the components are here: the eight plants, the powdered gold, the water, oil and myrrh.*

Setting down the box, he picked up from the ground a telescope with a dial fixed to its end, and raised it to his eye. As he put it down again, he realised that he was trembling and mopped his brow.

He unfolded one of the papers he had hidden beneath the fountain, read the first line, then took a pinch of powder from one of the compartments and put it into a glass test tube to check that he had the exact quantity required.

His excitement mounted as he followed the instructions, and his heart beat louder and louder.

Finally, he poured the oil and water onto the plants and then he stepped back to consult the watch d'Orbay had given him. It showed one minute to ten.

Carefully picking up the vessel in which he had mixed the herbs, Gabriel held it above a copper basin. His eyes rested on the parchment that lay there just as the moon's rays illuminated it with their almost unreal white light. A breath of wind swept across his cheeks as his hands tilted the vessel and slowly spread its contents throughout the basin. The thick, turbid liquid covered the manuscript, insinuating itself between its pages whose texture seemed to absorb it. Gabriel closed his eyes for a second. When he reopened them, he peered into the basin to see that the document had soaked up all the liquid.

He touched the pages of the codex, which seemed once again dry, and cautiously picked it up. He hesitated for a moment, tempted to open it, and then changed his mind as he looked down and saw the first guests below him, escorted by footmen bearing lanterns, heading for the dais erected at the edge of the forest for Molière's play. Fouquet must have taken advantage of this moment to vanish on the pretext of making final checks, and the King would have withdrawn to rest in his apartments until the spectators had taken their places. Perhaps the Superintendent was already in his bedchamber.

Gabriel rolled up the codex in a length of white cambric, descended the twisting staircase as quickly as possible, and walked past the principal beam that supported the dome's colossal frame. He lifted the trapdoor and operated the mechanism which opened a secret panel on the private staircase leading from the Superintendent's office to his bedchamber. Stealthily, he crossed the space which separated him from Nicolas Fouquet, ears straining for the smallest sound. He felt for the lever that opened the hidden door, revealed in the near-darkness of the corridor by the thin line of light that surrounded it. The door swung open without a sound. Gabriel stood on its threshold for a moment, dazzled by the powerful light that blazed forth from the two crystal chandeliers and was reflected in an immense mirror of Venetian glass.

Fouquet's voice reached him before he actually saw the Superintendent, who was standing beside his desk.

'Come here, Gabriel.

He obeyed, carrying the wrapped package in his hands. Fouquet took it without a word and placed it on the table. He gently removed the fabric, spent a moment contemplating the cover page, upon which had appeared green and red ornamental swirls together with a sun with fourteen rays, and caressed its surface. Then he opened up the document.

Gabriel watched Fouquet's hands move over the text and then looked up at his eyes. His gaze was so intense that it seemed it might set fire to the pages he was examining with such care. The Superintendent murmured some words softly as he read on.

Finally he closed the codex and stood for a moment, gazing into space.

When he turned towards Gabriel, the young man saw tears shining in his eyes.

'It is all for the best,' was all he said. 'All for the best.'

Then, as though emerging from a dream:

'Did François show you the mechanism allowing access to the cavity between the two domes?'

Gabriel nodded.

'Then go,' said the Superintendent, almost regretfully wrapping the fabric around the parchment once more . 'Don't waste a second: put it in place and then join us at the play.'

Gabriel opened his mouth to answer but Fouquet was already at the door, having laid the package on the desk. Gabriel picked it up and left by the hidden door. It slammed shut, plunging him into darkness again. As he headed for the staircase leading to the dome, the young man felt his heart pounding furiously against the parchment he was clasping to his chest.

CHAPTER SEVENTY-SEVEN

Vaux-le-Vicomte – Wednesday 17 August, eleven o'clock in the evening

As soon as the King had taken his place in the front row, Molière stepped onto the stage dressed in town clothes and looking preoccupied. The theatre had been set up on the avenue of fir trees so that its audience would benefit from the coolness of the fountains.

'Sire, I am afraid we have run out of time. I hope His Majesty will forgive us for not being able to present the entertainment that was expected this evening.'

A murmur ran through the crowd of guests invited to this sumptuous party by the lord of Vaux-le-Vicomte. Louis XIV himself remained impassive as he sat beside the Superintendent of Finance, whose smile was surprising after the announcement just made by the great actor.

But this opening artifice, devised by Molière as a prelude to the entertainment, soon gave way to Madeleine Béjart, dressed as a nymph. Thunderous applause greeted the actress's appearance. The entertainment commissioned by Fouquet was the first of a new genre that blended theatre and dance. There were ballets by Beauchamp between each act of the play, which was entitled *Les Fâcheux*, and a suite by Lulli had also been included. The story lavishly praised the King's merits, and it was a complete success. A long ovation greeted the end of the performance. Molière was exultant. The King had applauded and laughed heartily several times during the evening, which reassured Fouquet who had been suffering from a fever since the morning. As the guests began to disperse along the avenues, a firework display lit up the park, beginning with a formation of fleurs-de-lys. An enormous whale was then seen approaching along the canal, to the accompaniment of trumpets and drums. Puffs of smoke escaped from the animal, and the whole Court gasped in astonishment.

'Sire,' Fouquet ventured, 'this feat of illumination was perfected by the great Torelli, whom I brought over from Italy expressly for you this evening.'

Louis XIV nodded, but did not answer. He walked beside his Superintendent towards the chateau. Fouquet had been particularly attentive towards Anne of Austria, providing her with a carriage and pair so that she would be spared any exertion. Still dazzled, the crowd moved silently back towards the main building.

'View it from this side, Sire', cried Nicolas Fouquet, pointing to the chateau's cupola.

At that very moment, the final, crowning piece of the firework display exploded from the dome's pinnacle, to everyone's great surprise. Countless fireworks now formed an arching canopy of light above the delighted and astonished crowd. The Superintendent was watching Louis XIV, who was still as impassive as ever, despite the magnificence of the spectacle.

Whatever can he be thinking? he pondered, stunned by the young King's lack of reaction.

Inside the chateau a final collation largely made up of sumptuous trays of fruit was being served to the accompaniment of violins. Conversation flowed, and everyone was full of admiration. Never had the French Court been invited to such a reception, and the splendour of the chateau and its gardens reinforced the impression of power and grandeur even more.

On the pretext of discussing some financial documents, Nicolas Fouquet contrived to be alone with the King in one of the salons. Gabriel, who was looking for Louise, observed the scene from a distance, as did Colbert, who had been busily spreading his venom amongst the guests.

'Sire, all of this is for you,' said the Superintendent suddenly, taking in the chateau and its riches with a sweeping gesture. 'I have no other ambition but to serve Your Majesty and to place my fortune at the service of the King!'

The young sovereign looked at him darkly before answering.

'It is all extremely luxurious,' he said, eyeing the furniture, the tapestries and the paintings which decorated the room. 'Extremely luxurious!'

'Sire, permit me to provide you with further proof of my devotion tonight,' went on Fouquet, mopping his brow; his fever was making him feel extremely uncomfortable. 'I am in possession of an ancient manuscript of extraordinary value. A manuscript which, if used unwisely, could imperil the structure and government of the Kingdom.'

The young King still appeared withdrawn.

'Nevertheless, were you to accept it, this precious document could serve to enhance Your Majesty's present and future glory. The document is incontestably of Biblical origin. It would enable the King of France to re-establish the legitimacy of his power, and at the same time guarantee the happiness of the people he governs.'

'Is it your opinion then that the King of France's power is not legitimate, Monsieur Superintendent?' enquired Louis XIV pointedly.

'Your Majesty is young; you wish to take the Kingdom's affairs in hand and give France a place in the world which she has never known before,' went on Nicolas Fouquet without acknowledging what the King had said. 'This is a worthy ambition, but times have changed, Sire. The aspirations of ordinary people are evolving too. Tomorrow, the people will wish to express themselves in one way or another, to participate more actively in defining their own destiny. And if we do not listen to this wish, it will then become a demand, a rage, a rebellion. It will imperil our country! I can offer you the chance to instigate a new era! You alone can provide the impetus needed, and become the leading figure in this change.'

The King was still looking at Fouquet distractedly, making him feel more and more ill at ease.

'Sire, will you allow me to show you this document so that you can judge its contents?'

The obstinately silent King stood before the Superintendent as though lost in his own dreams.

'Sire, do you hear me? I beg you to consider my words! The fate of the Kingdom is at stake!'

All at once the King came to life:

'The fate of the Kingdom? And what do you mean by that, Monsieur Superintendent: that of a people, a monarchy or a sovereign? I hear what you are saying, but I question why you devote so much attention to the "wishes" of the populace and so little to the interests of your King. In what way is it in my interest to consider the wellbeing of those who wish to damage my power? And in whose name am I to question a tradition of which I am merely the repository, as were my ancestors before me and as my descendants will be after me?'

'But there is only one interest, Sire, that of France, of which the common folk are the flesh and you the embodiment!'

An icy smile flickered on the King's lips.

'You sometimes talk like those Jesuits who surround me, Monsieur Superintendent. Personally, I would prefer fewer arguments and more proof of the care you say you are taking to ensure my glory and the success of my policies. Moreover, your argument gives me no reason to go against tradition based upon the Church's teachings.'

'This text is precisely that proof, Sire. I have in my possession a torch which can set the country alight, and undermine the foundations on which it rests. But I wish to use that torch solely to light your way and guide your steps.'

The King clenched his fist in a gesture of vexation.

'Guide, guide!' he growled. 'I have no lack of guides; I can't set foot outside my bedchamber without ten people offering to guide me! I want to be served,' he continued, raising his voice.

'But you cannot ignore the text,' said Fouquet in reply. 'It exists, and you must look at it. I am serving you by enabling you to discover it, before the world knows anything about it. You may then consider it and prepare to reveal it to the world. You will be the man who opens the eyes of the world! Sire, this document speaks the Truth, the only Truth that is . . .'

'The Truth, Monsieur Superintendent,' cut in the King, 'has no need of discovery. It is already in our possession.'

'But Sire, just imagine . . .'

'And no one,' the sovereign interrupted again icily, 'has an interest in seeing it called into question unless he wishes to open a truly terrible Pandora's box. I know how I wish to be served. And what I do not wish is that my Superintendent of Finance should seek to turn himself into a philosopher and exegete. Forget Biblical texts, Monsieur Superintendent. For pity's sake, devote more of your energy to enabling me to possess the means to stage receptions as fine as the one we have attended this evening.'

He thinks I am mad, thought the Superintendent, coming to his senses a little. *Or is it that I am no longer speaking clearly? Has my fever led me astray?*

'I hear nothing of what you say about this manuscript,' went on the young King. 'Or more precisely, I hear nothing but words which a less benevolent spirit than mine would readily accuse of heresy, sacrilege or lese-majesty. "A torch"? "Undermine the foundations" on which the country rests? Why not also speak of republics, Monsieur Superintendent?' raged the King, before struggling to regain his composure. 'I cannot listen to these kinds of ideas. But tell me, are you ill?'

Without waiting for a reply, the King walked a few steps away before turning round:

'Farewell, Monsieur Superintendent, it is time for us to

part,' he said in a voice that was strangely measured and solemn.

Crushed, and realising that he was going to gain nothing from the evening, Fouquet trailed behind Louis XIV, whose slow, formal walk to the door of the salon provoked a tidal wave of bows from the assembled courtiers.

Fouquet stood at the foot of the steps and watched the King of France's carriage move away. He was now shaking all over from the fever which had been with him all evening.

La Fontaine approached him.

'You look unhappy, and yet what a magnificent reception! It lacked for nothing! The Court will remember it for a long time, I can tell you!'

'Let us hope the King does too!' muttered the Superintendent, walking back up the steps of his palace.

CHAPTER SEVENTY-EIGHT

*Vaux-le-Vicomte — Thursday 18 August, two o'clock
in the morning*

PALE, haggard and dishevelled, Fouquet removed the ribbon tied around his wrist and threw it to the ground. The shivers that ran through his body betrayed the fever which still racked him. Gabriel was about to open his mouth to say something but Fouquet gestured to him to be silent. From the great entrance hall, guests could still be seen in the grounds, strolling around the lakes in small groups, the women with their shawls pulled tight about their shoulders. Servants passed amongst them and began to dismantle the buffet tables set up in the groves. Two lines of guests formed multicoloured columns in the pale moonlight, hurrying to the chateau's gates, and carriage wheels could be heard crunching over the gravel driveway.

The two men remained silent for a moment, watching. The clicking of footsteps on the flagged floor made them turn round. There stood d'Orbay, leaning against the doorpost, looking serious and tired.

Fouquet and Gabriel looked at each other but said nothing.

Finally d'Orbay approached them.

'Well, here we are,' he said, his voice faint and full of emotion. 'Mass has been said, Messieurs, and I fear that our dream will disappear with the dawn'.

Fouquet looked at the architect in astonishment.

'It was probably madness to believe in it, but anyway, we cannot go back. What has happened has happened. We have tried to be faithful to our ideal to the end, rejecting the risk of division and civil war amongst our people. And we have dealt with ingrates throughout. Worse, nobody listened to us. But what does it matter now? We have gone too far to retrace our steps. This evening, Messieurs, our boats burned along with the fireworks. The King may pretend to misunderstand; but he understands very well. He knows the risk.'

The architect looked at the cupola above their heads and reached up towards it with an open palm.

'It's there, just up there between the two ceilings.'

He lowered his gaze and looked coldly at Fouquet, who was still impassive.

'We must act immediately. A copy of the document must be taken to the Papal legate and to Parlement as soon as possible, and messengers will have to deliver it to all the provincial assemblies. Immediately afterwards, our troops from Belle-Île and Brittany will march into Rennes and Nantes, and then on to Angers, Orléans and Paris. Four weeks from now, Nicolas, when the explosion has resounded throughout the Kingdom of France, we can seize the reins of power.'

His eyes were fiery as he looked deep into those of the Superintendent.

'We must act, Nicolas,' he went on, more urgently this time. 'If we do nothing, we are lost and the Secret is lost with us.'

Fouquet shook his head.

'All is not lost François, I am sure of it. We must not yield to panic. The King did not reject my offer. He did not say no. He said nothing at all. I shall go and see him; I shall take the time to show him the document in detail. He will come to his senses. He will understand where the truth lies and will not resist it. He will meditate upon its meaning and acquiesce, I am convinced of it. We cannot risk a civil war. The King will be won over,' he insisted.

François d'Orbay sneered at him.

'I cannot stop you believing in your dream, Nicolas, but you are on the wrong track. I shall leave for Rome tomorrow, to request our Brothers' arbitration. At least place our troops on alert,' he tried once more. 'Send Gabriel with an order to mobilise.'

'Two weeks, François, give me two weeks. Between now and then I will win the King's consent. Go to Rome if you wish, but allow me that time.'

'Very well. Two weeks, but not a day longer.'

D'Orbay was about to continue the argument, but then let his hand drop in annoyance and turned on his heel.

Gabriel began to follow him, but Fouquet held him back. The young man watched the architect leave, closing the door behind him. When he turned back, Nicolas Fouquet was staring at the cupola and its foiled plans.

CHAPTER SEVENTY-NINE

*Vaux-le-Vicomte – Thursday 18 August, two o'clock
in the morning*

'To Fontainebleau!'

From her seat inside the carriage, Anne of Austria heard the order ring out in the darkness and realised that the King was in no ordinary mood. It was still stifling despite the late hour, so when Louis sat down beside her with sweat on his brow, she thought he was suffering from the heat.

A few minutes later, as the carriage travelled between the tall trees lining the road to Maincy, Anne broke the silence.

'How I wish that your wife could have accompanied us!'

The Queen Mother pursued what already seemed to be a strange monologue as there was still no reaction from the King:

'I am sure she would have adored Molière's play and admired the setting, despite her condition. What magnificent gardens!'

The King, who was not normally short of things to say in these rare private moments with the Queen Mother, said nothing. It was as if he were immersed in contemplation of the streets of Maincy, which echoed with the sound of horses' hooves and the jangling of the musketeers who made up his guard. His retinue seemed in high spirits, and it was clear that the evening had been well and truly celebrated even in the stables.

No one has escaped the Superintendent's generosity, thought the King.

Deep within him, a muffled anger was coming to the boil as images of the folly returned to him. *Why such excessive luxury?* wondered the sovereign, *and what does he hope to achieve by displaying such magnificence in front of the whole Court? Colbert is right*, he told himself again. That evening the Superintendent's words had seemed to him to be laden with threats. Behind this strange proposition that was supposed to make the French people happy, Louis XIV had a strong sense that his power was being called into question.

'Are you upset, my son? Did Vatel's cooking not agree with you?'

The King's mother wanted to be reassured by the faint smile which appeared on his lips, but decided not to continue the conversation any further.

Louis looked at Anne of Austria as she sat there beside him. Her face was marked by fatigue, and by the effects of the oppressive weather. They were no longer the unlined features he remembered from his childhood, but those of a woman sorely tried by years of power and intrigue. Without being aware of it, he had become an adult. And, in turn, he was soon to be a father. Did he not owe it to himself to prove his new status to the country?

'Ah, Madame, should we not make all these people return their ill-gotten gains?'

The Queen smiled as she finally understood the reason for her son's silence.

'A few days ago, I received Colbert at Dampierre. He had no

doubt come to test my feelings with regard to Fouquet,' she said gently. 'The Superintendent of Finance is certainly not without his faults, but he has succeeded in reforming the Kingdom's Treasury. As for his immoderate taste for luxury, he is certainly ostentatious, but in order for the people to love their King, should he not retain as security a few ministers for them to hate?'

'Madame, I am no longer a child and I no longer need to be advised on matters of State,' retorted the King in a tone that brooked no reply.

Silence fell again between the two travellers as the royal cortege reached the leafy outskirts of Fontainebleau. Gazing vacantly out of the carriage, Louis XIV glimpsed the roofs of the royal chateau. This sight reminded him of the ostentation of Vaux.

Had the Queen Mother not been dozing, she would have been able to hear the King of France mutter:

'He has stolen my dream. He will pay for this.

CHAPTER EIGHTY

Rome – Wednesday 24 August, eleven o'clock at night

FRANÇOIS d'Orbay entered Rome in a torrential rain storm. The architect was forced to stop to prevent his mount slipping on the uneven paving stones or, blinded by the lightning, rearing up and unseating him, and he found refuge beneath the arches of the Coliseum. He waited there, huddled against his horse's flank, as the raindrops hammered down on the stone and the earth, turning to rivulets on the unmade road surface which ran past the ruins of the ancient forum. A powerful flash of lightning zigzagged across the sky, fleetingly illuminating the silhouettes of the ancient buildings veiled by torrents of water. D'Orbay shivered: whether from cold or tiredness, he could not tell. Since he had left Paris six days earlier, he had taken only a little rest, changing horses frequently so as to arrive at his destination as quickly as possible.

He stroked the neck of his horse, which seemed agitated again. The animal tossed its head then seemed to grow calmer.

D'Orbay again pictured Fouquet's fixed mask. He could still hear the firm tone of his voice as he was preparing to leave:

'My destiny will be what it must be. We have to continue right to the end; we cannot deviate from our path. We trust in the King's loyalty to his people and in the power of the Secret. For my part, I will not be the initiator of a civil war.'

Everything had been said. He had hesitated for a fraction of a second, no longer, and in the look he had exchanged with the Superintendent, d'Orbay had seen the irremediable split which had thrown them onto either side of a crevasse destined to grow ever wider. Their two lives had for a long time existed together in the dream he had forged, but now they were moving apart, never to be reunited.

'Come, my friend,' said d'Orbay softly to his horse, 'the rain seems to be slackening off. We have to leave; we no longer have much time.'

François d'Orbay stood silently before his peers. He had finished his speech, and felt curiously lighter, as if once again he was sharing the weight that had accumulated on his shoulders and no longer bore it alone. And yet he had realised how desperate his course of action was with each successive sentence; he knew it could not lead to anything.

Giacomo Del Sarto gazed impassively at the architect.

'The risk is great and you were right to come and inform us. Nicolas must be allowed to pursue his logic to its conclusion; such is his judgement. Let us only pray that he has seen clearly. Out of prudence we should prepare for the possibility of failure . . . In other words, the possibility that we might have to use force, or even save what can be saved if we lose that battle too . . .'

D'Orbay searched the doctor's bright eyes for a trace of accusation, reproach or regret. And yet he saw none of these things. All he saw was the eternal flame borne across centuries by generations of men just like themselves, and the calm certainty that beyond the potential defeat of the present, others would emerge to take up their torches and wait in the shadows until the hour of victory tolled.

The hour which I shall not see, he thought suddenly.

Del Sarto was now listing the precautions they would have to take, the places, practices and identities they would abandon, the new, far-off horizons towards which the documents now concealed between the two cupolas of the dome at Vaux-le-Vicomte would travel, the means whereby they could hide their tracks from those trying to follow them, and the methods they were to apply that would dissuade those who had the upper hand from believing that they could push their advantage further.

The Brotherhood was in the process of returning to the silence of anonymity once again, d'Orbay was certain of it.

For ten, fifty, a hundred years? he wondered.

His chest tightened. He swayed, passing a hand across his forehead. Then he signalled to the speaker to continue and straightened up.

A hundred years. Perhaps a thousand.

Now that they were alone again, Del Sarto's anxiety showed. He had been observing d'Orbay too, and had detected the fissure which had opened up in the architect's heart.

'When are you leaving, François?'

D'Orbay shrugged his shoulders.

'As soon as possible. I have to see Gabriel as soon as possible.'

And pass the torch to him, he thought.

'That is good,' replied Del Sarto. 'Pray Heaven that young Pontbriand proves to be carved in the image of his father and carries out our plan as best he can. And what about your own family?' he went on, more gently.

The architect did not answer. Images of his wife and children passed through his mind. Where were they now? Asleep no doubt, in a house where the furniture was already packed up, the luggage ready. Ready to run away, without ever understanding, never asking questions. Without ever being given a reason.

'What did you say?' Del Sarto, thinking that D'Orbay had spoken asked in surprise.

D'Orbay shook his head.

'Nothing.'

Then it was his turn to look at the doctor.

'Farewell my friend,' he said softly.

When they embraced, an icy shiver ran through Del Sarto. *I hope to Heaven that I misunderstood*, he thought in a silent prayer.

CHAPTER EIGHTY-ONE

Vaux-le-Vicomte – Sunday 28 August, ten o'clock
in the morning

Hugues de Lionne was already seated in the imposing carriage which had been standing for several minutes at the foot of the steps of the Château de Vaux. Departure was imminent, and everyone was waiting for the Superintendent of Finance. The two men were leaving for Nantes to rejoin the King, who had recently decided to pay a long visit to Brittany. At last Nicolas Fouquet appeared, extremely elegant in a black silk outfit over which he had donned a comfortable cloak to ward off the autumn chill. With it he wore a soft, tawny-coloured felt hat. Before getting into the carriage, he took his wife in his arms.

'Supervise the wine harvest at Thomery, my dear. I'm sorry to leave so suddenly, but the King insists. I love you with all my heart.' The Superintendent tenderly kissed the woman who had just given him another child.

'Take care of yourself, my dear! Don't do anything rash – spare a thought for your children,' she answered simply.

La Fontaine had also come out to say farewell, and Fouquet took him to one side.

'My dear Jean, in my absence I'd be grateful if you could attend to a delicate matter. As you know, the sale of my office brought me one million livres, which I immediately handed to the King. Harlay, who organised the transaction, still owes me four hundred thousand livres and is slow in paying. I still have a few fairly substantial sums in the hands of reliable friends, but that will not amount to much if . . .'

'If?' La Fontaine asked anxiously, frowning. 'Is there something you are hiding from me?'

'Not at all! Some say that I will be declared Chief Minister, others that I will be brought down by a terrible cabal. But over the last few days I have felt that the King has been better disposed towards me. It appears that I have regained his trust!'

'Are you so sure of that?'

'You're too pessimistic, my dear Jean. Didn't you predict a short while ago that I was destined for the Bastille? You see, it did not happen. On the contrary, *He* has summoned me to his side in Nantes. Come, stop tormenting yourself and just help me get back what I'm owed!' urged Nicolas Fouquet, turning towards those still waiting beside his carriage.

'D'Orbay!' exclaimed the Superintendent, seeing his architect leap down from his horse. 'You are arriving just as I'm leaving!'

'I came as swiftly as I was able, Monseigneur,' replied François d'Orbay with a bow.

'Gabriel will be pleased to see you. If you can manage to track him down,' said Fouquet with a laugh. 'I tried to find him to say goodbye, but he had left already at dawn! Let us talk on my return,' he added quietly, taking d'Orbay's arm, 'we shall make whatever decisions the circumstances dictate! But I still have hopes of persuading the King during this trip.'

The architect smiled back at him with a mixture of affection and profound sadness.

The Superintendent climbed nimbly into the carriage and sat down opposite Lionne, whom he greeted warmly.

'I'm pleased to be making this journey with you, my dear Lionne. If it's not too much of an inconvenience, I would like to make a halt in Angers. My family originates from there, you know.'

'I'll be delighted to do so,' replied Hugues de Lionne amiably.

'Let's go!' shouted the Superintendent to the coachman.

With a crack of the whip, the carriage bearing gilded squirrels and the Fouquet coat of arms on each of its doors was finally set in motion.

As they trundled down the avenue, Fouquet caught sight of Gabriel in the distance. Realising that he had arrived too late, he was running towards the carriage. The Superintendent leant out of the carriage door and waved farewell to the young man. He remained in that position to watch the familiar sight of his chateau disappear into the distance. *It certainly has been my life's work!* he said to himself as he admired the building's imposing yet delicate proportions.

As he took his seat again, Fouquet shivered.

'Don't worry,' he said to reassure Lionne. 'It's the same every time I leave Vaux. I always have the feeling that I'll never see it again!'

CHAPTER EIGHTY-TWO

Nantes — Monday 5 September, eleven o'clock in the morning

FOUQUET was feeling relaxed as he walked down the great staircase of the Château de Nantes, where the King had just convened his council. The Superintendent of Finance was deep in thought as he returned to the sedan chair awaiting him in the courtyard.

The meeting had certainly gone well. It was the young monarch's twenty-third birthday and everyone had presented their compliments. Louis XIV had even kept him behind for a private talk after the other ministers had left, in order to discuss various trivial matters. The lord of Vaux had interpreted this as a sign, and had taken advantage of the opportunity to request a private audience with the King. This had been granted without him having to give the reason for his request, and a meeting had been fixed for that very afternoon.

I shall be able to convince him at last. He must have been thinking about our conversation at Vaux, thought the Superintendent.

The rumours about him were proliferating. He had objected when, in the course of a long conversation the previous evening, another minister had expressed anxiety about the air of agitation and secrecy that seemed to surround the King and Colbert of late. The Superintendent had dismissed this with a wave of his hand.

'My friends, there is nothing to fear,' he had said, 'if anyone should be wary of Louis XIV, it is Colbert himself!'

The Superintendent recalled these words as he prepared to climb into his sedan chair.

As for d'Artagnan, he had risen at dawn and had carried out to the letter the instructions received directly from the King.

'Tomorrow, at four o'clock in the morning,' the King had told him after summoning him the previous evening, 'you will send ten men to Ancenis, led by a sergeant. At six o'clock, a squadron of twenty musketeers will assemble in the courtyard of the chateau. Another will take up position by the gate on the city side. The remainder of your company will wait in the fields, in case they are needed,' Louis XIV had continued as d'Artagnan looked increasingly astonished. 'You will carry out the act at the entrance to the chateau. Afterwards, a carriage with iron-barred windows will await you. You will head for Oudon without delay. You will be expected for the night at the chateau in Angers.'

So, still feverish from the illness that had kept him in bed for five days until this royal summons had brooked no excuse, d'Artagnan waited from early morning onwards for the man he was to arrest at the chateau gate. The King's words went round and round in his head:

'You are going to swear to me that you will reveal nothing of this until you have fulfilled your duty! The copyist who worked on these instructions has been locked up for forty-eight hours, so any leak detrimental to the smooth operation of this plan will have come either from you or from me! Go, Monsieur – the Kingdom's future depends upon your skill tomorrow.'

All that was now needed before action could be taken was the King's final confirmation as he left the council. Le Tellier was to relay this to d'Artagnan, but he had been waylaid in conversation beneath the trees and d'Artagnan dared not disturb him, thinking that perhaps the King had changed his mind. But then, when he saw that the Superintendent was about to leave, d'Artagnan rushed forward.

'Monsieur,' he said, interrupting the conversation, 'have the King's orders of yesterday evening been changed?'

'Not at all, Captain!' replied Le Tellier brusquely.

The sedan chair had disappeared.

D'Artagnan ran to the chateau's gates, and the musketeers on duty there told him that the Superintendent had melted into the crowds and bustle of Nantes. Not knowing what to do, the captain rushed to see the King, who received him immediately.

'Sire, he has escaped us!'

'That is impossible,' said the King, pale with rage. 'He must be found; and I shall find him! Take fifteen men and bring him in. Search the entire city if you have to!'

D'Artagnan promptly ran off to search for the Superintendent. Meanwhile, Nicolas Fouquet was calmly travelling along, breathing in the cool, dry September air, on his way to lunch at his residence in the Rue Haute-du-Château. The crowds in the old city's narrow streets had slowed down his progress, and d'Artagnan's troops caught up with his entourage in the Place Saint-Pierre, not far from the cathedral. Fouquet stuck his head out of the door to see why his bearers had stopped and recognised the captain.

'What is going on, Monsieur d'Artagnan?'

'Monseigneur, I must speak to you,' the Gascon replied in a sombre voice somewhat lacking in self-assurance.

'Can't it wait?'

'I'm afraid not, Monseigneur!'

Nicolas Fouquet then emerged from the sedan chair and bowed to the captain. A ray of sunshine peeped through the clouds, forcing the Superintendent to screw up his eyes to see d'Artagnan properly as he dismounted from his horse and stood facing him.

'Monseigneur! In the name of the King, I arrest you!'

The Superintendent's astonishment was evident.

'Monsieur d'Artagnan, are you quite sure? Is it really me you want?' asked Fouquet incredulously as the captain took the warrant from the sleeve of his jacket and handed it to him.

As he read the document, his eyes clouded. Deathly white, he returned the document to d'Artagnan.

'I wasn't expecting this at all,' murmured the Superintendent. Then, regaining his composure a little, he raised his voice and addressed d'Artagnan.

'Captain, I bow to the orders and desires of His Majesty as I have always done. I am therefore at your disposal. But I beg you, do not create a great stir!'

CHAPTER EIGHTY-THREE

*Vaux-le-Vicomte – Wednesday 7 September, five o'clock
in the evening*

'At the Château d'Angers!'

'You heard me, Monsieur de La Fontaine. Monseigneur has just spent his first night as a prisoner at the Château d'Angers.'

'Angers,' repeated d'Orbay, 'his family home! That can have only one aim – to humiliate the Superintendent in order to break him!'

'As soon as I learned of his arrest, I could think of only one thing,' confessed Isaac Bartet as he finished off the glass of wine he had been given on his arrival, along with some bread and cheese – he had been galloping almost non-stop for twenty-four hours. 'To inform you, and then head for Saint-Mandé to try and protect what could still be protected. So, Messieurs . . .' said the spy who had remained faithful to Fouquet, getting up from his chair.

'But be reasonable,' said La Fontaine, 'you cannot leave like this! You can barely stand. Get an hour or two's sleep.

'Think about it,' replied Bartet. 'We haven't a moment to lose. That venomous snake Colbert has orchestrated this entire operation. He must have despatched his henchmen all over the place already!'

As the hirsute, mud-spattered Bartet galloped away from the estate, Gabriel returned from riding the most beautiful thoroughbred in the Vaux stables. Dismounting, the young man realised from his companions' expressions that the situation was grave.

'They arrested Monseigneur yesterday morning in Nantes and he's been imprisoned in Angers. He'll probably be taken from there to the Bastille,' Jean de La Fontaine announced sadly.

'But that's not possible!' Gabriel declared. 'It's a mistake! The King must be told! When he knows . . .'

'It was Louis XIV himself who signed the warrant,' replied d'Orbay. 'There's nothing more we can do for the moment. Except save what can still be saved.'

'I'm going to stay here to try and safeguard everything that will be vital for the trial which Colbert is sure to stage-manage,' decided La Fontaine.

'Good,' replied François d'Orbay. 'You should also look after the interests of our friend's wife and children. Like Bartet, I fear that the vultures will swiftly descend upon the Superintendent's carcass.'

'And what about me?' Gabriel cut in. 'What can I do to prove my fidelity?'

'Protect yourself by leaving here as soon as possible!' suggested d'Orbay, giving his best friend's son a look that was both affectionate and firm. 'Go up and pack your things without delay. When you get to Paris tonight you can collect the rest of your belongings from Rue des Lions Saint-Paul and . . .'

The architect fell silent for a moment.

'and . . . then we shall see,' he went on. 'Go – I'll join you in a few minutes to help you with your baggage.'

'And what about you? What do you plan to do?' La Fontaine asked as they walked back into the chateau.

'Oh, I know where my duty lies!' the architect answered in a strange voice.

Gabriel ran up to his bedchamber. He could not believe that the Superintendent of France, the most powerful man in the Kingdom and the master of Vaux, could have been arrested and imprisoned on the King's orders. He thought of his father as he climbed the stairs four at a time. *He would have been able to advise me.* Then Louise's image came to mind. *I have to talk to her. There's no question of my leaving Paris without carrying out my revenge. She will help me . . .*

A few moments later, d'Orbay knocked at Gabriel's door.

'I've almost finished,' he announced without turning round. 'I have very few things here, I must say!'

'I've just given the orders. An unmarked carriage will be waiting for you in half an hour's time, to take you to Paris.'

'And what then?' Gabriel asked. 'I thought I might go and see Louise de La Vallière and ask for her . . .'

'Sit down,' ordered François d'Orbay. The young man was somewhat surprised by the abruptness of the command.

'The situation is serious, as you will have realised,' went on the architect, sitting down beside him on the bed. 'Fouquet may not emerge from this affair alive, and with his demise the hopes of your father and of our Brotherhood will have collapsed once and for all. Last week in Rome, I reassembled our company of wise men and we voted on the Superintendent's last request. He asked for you to be accepted into our Brotherhood, should any misfortune befall him.'

'Me!'

'Yes,' went on d'Orbay with a smile. 'He considered you worthy to succeed your ancestors. I must now ask you an important question, Gabriel. Do you feel ready, in your turn, to agree to protect the Fifth Gospel? Are you strong enough to devote your entire life to it and, if necessary, to sacrifice your life to it, as your father did? Would you be able to accept that from one day to the next you might have to change your identity, your life, leave your country and your friends, with no hope of going back? Think carefully,' he said solemnly.

'I accept!' replied the young man after a moment. 'But what must I do now?'

D'Orbay sighed deeply and withdrew a document from his doublet, then handed it to Gabriel.

'In this envelope you will find everything you need to know about the Brotherhood and its rules. Learn all of it by heart and destroy this copy.'

Gabriel gripped it firmly.

'Now I will tell you what our companion wishes. You are to go on a journey, Gabriel, and you must leave immediately.'

'A long journey?

'Yes, a very long journey in fact,' confirmed the architect. 'You are going to travel to the New World.'

Gabriel's eyes widened in astonishment.

'Yes, you heard correctly,' resumed d'Orbay, 'you're to leave for the Americas! I was instructed to hand you this letter once you had accepted, and particularly if I felt that the situation endangered the safety of Saint Peter's Secret. Fouquet's arrest and the dangers you and I face here oblige me to urge you to accept. I hadn't imagined that events would be precipitated in this way, but you have to protect our Secret. Louis XIV now knows of its existence. He may attempt to seize it in order to destroy it. Do you understand now why I'm in such a hurry for you to leave here?'

'I'm ready!' Gabriel answered simply.

'Very well. And don't worry,' added d'Orbay. 'I have just sent a messenger to Nantes. You'll be expected at the port on Saturday to embark for the Americas. And someone will meet you on your arrival in New Amsterdam. As for money, you will never lack for it,' d'Orbay added mysteriously.

A shadow passed across Gabriel's face.

'But I can't leave as quickly as that. My father hasn't been avenged. Colbert has not been made to pay. I put off my vengeance, but . . .'

'I shall take care of it,' cut in d'Orbay. 'It is all in hand. Have no fear, the punishment is under way. Your duty is now elsewhere,' he added more gently.

Full of emotion, François d'Orbay embraced the young man in silence.

Gabriel suddenly had a premonition that he would never ever see him again.

'Why don't you come with me?' he asked.

The architect smiled sadly.

'My time spent serving our Secret is coming to an end. In the Americas you will find companions who are young like you. That is what our Brotherhood's organisation requires. You will discover this when you read the documents I have just given you.'

Without wasting any more time, the architect led the young man off to retrieve the codex hidden in the chateau's cupola.

'Here,' he told him, handing him the precious cargo. 'In this box you will find a letter of explanation from Fouquet, which I ask you not to read until you are on the boat. Then destroy it. When you've read it, you'll know everything about the Secret of the Fifth Gospel!'

As the servants were loading the young man's trunk, d'Orbay said farewell to Gabriel.

'Don't do anything reckless, my boy. This evening, you have become another link in an immense chain which must not be broken! Now go,' he said, with moist eyes, 'and remember, your father would have been proud of you!'

As the carriage passed through the gates of Vaux-le-Vicomte at top speed, Gabriel thought only of one thing: taking Louise with him to the Americas!

CHAPTER EIGHTY-FOUR

*Vaux-le-Vicomte – Wednesday 7 September, eleven o'clock
in the evening*

FRANÇOIS d'Orbay gazed at the ceiling of the great entrance hall, and at the secret panel hidden in the Gemini medallion along the cornice. He thought of the months spent plotting in the shadows, patiently searching for the signs that had convinced him there was a chance they could take advantage of the exceptional circumstances provided by Mazarin's death, Louis XIV's youth and Fouquet's talent. Where had he gone wrong? What had he not known or misjudged, that this opportunity should have ended in such total failure? Far from calming the dull anger which had brought tears to his eyes, the sight of the towers of Vaux, of its perfect vista, the finely wrought gates, the pale stone, the gardens and the cupola, seemed to him to be a monstrous catafalque, erected to bear witness to this failure for hundreds of years to come. For months, he had exhausted his eyes and his hands on this prodigious work, imagined the radiance of this communal residence, the town destined to spread out around the palace at the heart of the new capital of a Kingdom where men would be equals, a Kingdom at last in accordance with divine teaching . . . For months he had watched as the Superintendent's passion for Vaux grew gradually in his soul. A passion which he had orchestrated and staged in order to help Fouquet. And even Colbert and his miserable intrigues had not ruined that! *No, of course they had not*, he tried to reason with himself. *Besides, what does it matter?*

A sad smile lit his face for a moment with a feverish glint.

It matters for Colbert – his price has already been fixed. One wounds a man where he is most sensitive . . .

He then walked along the terrace in the hot summer's night. Not a breath of air disturbed the surface of the lakes, which seemed to d'Orbay like dark mirrors in which he saw his dream drowning.

Maybe it just wasn't the right time, he thought as anger yielded once more to despair.

Raising his head, he wondered where the codex was now.

'Gabriel,' he murmured.

Only that name still brought him a little comfort.

Standing on the chateau's main terrace, he closed his eyes and forced himself to control his trembling arm.

'Safe journey, my boy. And good luck.'

Down below, his children were sleeping . . . Closing his eyes more tightly, he banished the image that tried to force its way into his mind.

It is better this way, he thought with a flash of clarity, *yes, it is better this way, it gives them a chance. . .*

All he could feel was the coolness on his lips and a metallic taste.

The flame zigzagged through the darkness like a small sun.

The blast rang out in the night's silence, and its sound echoed for a long time beyond the groves of trees, a long time after darkness had taken possession of the paved terrace once again. In the shadow of the cupola, motionless, the body that had rolled to the ground still held in its right hand the wooden butt of the pistol.

CHAPTER EIGHTY-FIVE

THE moment he reached his lodgings, Gabriel wrote a note to Louise, begging her to come. He entrusted the note to the coachman, with the order to 'return only with Mademoiselle de La Vallière'. It was several weeks since he had lived in this room. As he re-entered it and saw his possessions strewn everywhere, he felt as if an eternity had elapsed. He was no longer the apprentice actor who had dreamt of giving magnificent performances to tumultuous applause. Nor was he the awkward, rootless young man from Amboise. He had been a spectator at the cruel comedy of power which crushes individual destinies and claims that it does so in the name of the State. He had known the immense happiness and devastating pain of finding his father and then losing him for ever, a father whose life had proved to be steeped in mystery. Now he was a member of a shadowy organisation, protecting a mystical secret whose purpose still eluded him. Gabriel reminded himself that he had weathered these ordeals alone. Indeed he felt stronger and aspired to prove worthy of his name and of the trust placed in him by his father. The idea of leaving for the Americas frightened him a little, but it also filled him with excitement. As he threw into his trunk the few things he would need for his journey, Gabriel began to dream of extraordinary adventures.

Louise arrived just as he was finishing a letter to his land-lady, enclosing the money he owed her.

'Louise – it's you, at last!' cried Gabriel, leaping to his feet as the young woman entered and taking her in his arms.

'Careful, you're hurting me!' protested Henrietta of England's companion, a little surprised by this welcome. 'I hope you haven't brought me here in the middle of the night, without a word of explanation, just to suffocate me in your arms the minute I get through the door!' she added teasingly as she pulled away.

'No! The situation is . . . is fantastical! But sit down,' said Gabriel. 'I have to speak to you!'

Louise took off her cape, whose voluminous hood, edged with soft fox fur, enabled her to hide her face.

'I'm listening,' said the young girl, treating him to her most winning smile.

Gabriel gave her an account of the last few hours and told her of Fouquet's arrest. Bartet's news had not yet reached Paris.

'You must find yourself a safe place to live,' Louise interrupted. 'You no longer have a protector. I shall speak to the King as soon as he returns to Paris, if you wish me to!'

At these words, the young man scowled. A dull anger rumbled within him.

'No, no, and again I say no! I do not need you to talk to your King about anything. What is more, it was your King who ordered the Superintendent's arrest. He acts for his own pleasure and in his own interest! When will you see him for what he really is?'

'Do not judge the King too hastily. He conducts matters of State on the basis of information which you and I are unaware of. But I am sure of his character. He would never allow an injustice to be committed against you. I shall tell him . . .'

'You will tell him nothing at all, for I must leave!' Gabriel exclaimed. 'Before he was arrested, Fouquet entrusted me with an extraordinary mission. He asked me to leave for the Americas to ensure that his affairs prosper there.'

'The Americas?' exclaimed Louise. 'But when do you leave?'

Gabriel smiled at the young woman's surprise and took her hand.

'That's why I asked you to come tonight,' the young man explained tenderly. 'We have known each other since we were children. Rediscovering you here in Paris in February was a shock, and I didn't fully comprehend its consequences. When I received your message at Vaux, informing me that you were in danger . . . While I was galloping to your rescue, I realised . . .'

'You realised?' said Louise, suddenly anxious.

'I love you, Louise! I love you! I have never loved anyone but you,' said Gabriel, kissing the young girl's hands.

Louise said nothing. She looked at Gabriel as he drew her towards him.

'We can leave together tonight,' he said suddenly, savouring the sensual pleasure of this sweetest of moments.

'Leave? For the Americas? What are you thinking of? Henrietta needs me and I can't just leave like that!'

'I don't think you've really understood me,' said Gabriel, gazing deeply into her eyes. 'I'm not just talking about a journey. I love you and I'm asking you to be my wife, and to come and live with me.'

'But I can't! I can't!' cried the King of France's mistress, drawing back.

'Open your eyes. You're dazzled by the splendour of the Court, but deep inside, you know. You don't belong to that world of intrigue!'

'My life is here, Gabriel! This world which you denigrate because you want to escape it is my world. I feel at home in it. I am loved and . . .'

'You think you are loved!' raged the young man. 'But what do you know about love and about the way people really feel at Court. It's just a masquerade!'

'I'm young, Gabriel. I want to laugh and enjoy myself. I want to go to parties and balls, and experience the heady atmosphere of the theatre. I want to be intoxicated by the salons, meet the most famous scholars, and be dazzled by the greatest works of art. I want to charm the most powerful men and I, too, want to savour the delicious pleasures of power. You don't seem to understand that my life is here! I didn't leave Amboise only to abandon everything all over again, just as my dream is becoming real! Gabriel, I . . .'

Incredulous, Gabriel watched as her eyes flashed with a brilliant light.

'Don't say any more,' he cut in, pushing aside a lock of her hair with the back of his hand. 'Don't give me your answer yet. Not tonight. From three o'clock tomorrow there will be a carriage at the Porte Saint-Martin. I shall wait for you until four . . .'

Gabriel's gaze, at once determined and sad, touched Louise deeply and re-awakened the attraction she had felt for him for so long. She had always called it sisterly affection, as if to hide its true nature. She approached Gabriel and pressed her slender lips to his, feeling his warm breath. He enfolded her in his arms and kissed her ardently, encircling her waist in an embrace which she resisted only for a moment.

Pale rays of dawn light played upon Gabriel's sleeping body. The sound of footsteps on the wooden floor awakened him suddenly.

'Louise . . .' he said, his voice still heavy with sleep.

In the doorway, Louise turned and placed a finger to her lips before continuing on her way.

'We shall meet again, Gabriel de Pontbriand,' she whispered as she ran down the stairs.

CHAPTER EIGHTY-SIX

COLBERT awoke with a start, his hands trembling, and cold sweat trickling beneath his nightshirt. He realised that he had cried out. Pushing back the covers, he peered warily into the surrounding darkness. He crossed himself furtively in the total silence and mumbled a few inaudible words, then placed his feet on the ground and groped around for his slippers. Pushing aside the bedroom curtain, he looked at the gilded clock he had inherited from the Cardinal.

'How absurd,' he said aloud, as if to reassure himself. 'It was only a nightmare! Well now . . .'

Before going back to bed, he hesitated for a moment. Although he was convinced that this was perfectly sane and reasonable, he could not bring himself to do it.

'Tantalus,' he murmured, his voice still shaking with emotion.

His nightmare came back to him. Once again he pictured himself tied up, consumed by hunger and thirst and incapable of taking sustenance, of gathering the fruits which hung above his head . . .

In the corner of the room, amongst dozens of boxes and packages received as gifts or stolen from Fouquet's residences and brought directly to his own domicile, a small package rested against the wall. Colbert picked it up nervously and, removing the hastily sealed wrapping, looked once again at the painting: the canvas, surrounded by a frame of gilded wood, depicted the torments of Tantalus.

'Accursed picture!' he shouted, throwing the canvas to the ground.

Ever since he had opened this package almost by chance two days before, sure that it would contain yet another act of homage to flatter his pride, he had not been able to rid his mind of its image. And now it had even provoked a nightmare in which he himself had been subjected to the same torture.

Anxiety gripped him again.

Could it be possible? he wondered, terrified.

Unable to rest, he picked up a day jacket that lay on a sofa and quickly put it on, then covered his bald pate with a little felt skullcap and opened the door of his bedroom. The corridor was even darker. Colbert bumped into a column and almost knocked over the vase placed on top of it. He stood still for a moment, waiting for his heart's furious beating to grow calmer.

'Onward,' he said, continuing his walk to the staircase which led to his office. 'I must be sure.'

In this room, files were piled up on tables which had been added as need dictated. Colbert had assembled here everything relating to Mazarin's succession which he did not wish to see in the Kingdom's inventories. Half opening the shutters to admit the first light of day, the little man was unable to suppress a smile. The presence of these documents reassured him. Each pile consolidated his power. One contained inadmissible secrets in personal files that had accumulated over time. Several hundred influential individuals were here, like animals on a leash. Two other more voluminous piles contained details of the double accounting of public financial operations which had necessitated the use of third parties.

As the icy hand of apprehension which had awakened him insinuated itself once more into his mind, Colbert tried to divert his thoughts by sitting down in front of the fourth pile. He hastily leafed through the documents he had been analysing over the past few days and soon found what he was looking for. Colbert now examined the pages more closely, hesitated, then read on with even greater concentration.

'Onward,' he quietly encouraged himself.

The sun's rays now shone with their full force upon the wooden panelling behind Colbert and the large mirror that hung above the fireplace.

Deathly pale, the Steward of Finance sprawled back in his chair, with his hands laid flat on the armrests, and gazed into emptiness as if hypnotised. Perfectly still, he waited for the silent minutes to pass, each one bringing him closer to the moment when the house would come to life again. The premonition he had now confirmed would then be given life, too. For a few moments longer he was the only person to have understood it, and in an almost puerile way he held back the news which devastated him, as if the fact that no one else knew it would make it any less terrible.

Everything was there right before his eyes, and so clear that he wondered how it had taken him so long to realise. This was probably due to the urgency with which he had had to cover things up and protect himself, before orchestrating the counter-attack and finally dealing the death blow to Fouquet having transformed him into the perfect scapegoat. With all his energy directed towards these goals, he had neglected to check that, in addition to acting as an inventory, these papers also provided the means to access the riches they described . . .

His jaw clenched convulsively: ten, twelve, perhaps fifteen million livres! He hardly dared add up the figures.

Suddenly shaking himself, he frantically moved the papers around. Bills, percentages, commission received, years of the Cardinal's fraudulent practices and scheming to divert the fruit of this secret toil to Italy and the Netherlands: it was all there, meticulously recorded – but totally inaccessible . . .

One vital paper was missing, the one that would enable him to decode the series of figures that concealed the third parties; the banking establishments and the names with which the accounts had been opened. Without this document, everything else was as useless as a bottle of water placed beyond the reach of a man who was dying of thirst.

Then the truth hit him: that was it, the missing document stolen from the Cardinal's offices, a document so personal that even Mazarin had omitted to mention it to him. The burglars had acquired the key to the treasure and had all the time they needed to calmly siphon off deposits carefully divided amongst the most discreet banking establishments in the whole of Europe.

Straightening up suddenly, Colbert turned towards another pile of gifts heaped on his desk which was more impressive than that in his bedchamber.

'That painting ... The coincidence is too great ... And there was another,' he moaned as he rummaged haphazardly through the mass of packages of all sizes, flinging away those which hindered his search.

Finally, as he lifted up a larger frame, he happened upon a package identical to the first. He stood rooted to the spot for a moment, then began to tear off the paper wrapped round it. When he saw the second canvas, Mazarin's former secretary blanched: it depicted a man on his deathbed, with his family praying beside him. Amongst the figures at the front one could easily make out a tearful son.

Colbert's face drained as put down the painting. It was then that he noticed a card stuck to the back of the canvas.

With trembling hands, he brought it closer to the light:

'*Blessed are the meek, for they shall inherit the earth*', he read. *Blessed are the pure in heart, for they shall see God.*'

Dumbfounded, Colbert turned over the card:

'*Cursed be the avaricious, for they shall not enjoy their ill-gotten gains; cursed be the hard-hearted, for they are destined to suffer. Consider your current fate enviable. The deprivation of unwarranted financial resources and personal suffering are merely warnings designed to temper your sense of victory, and to convince you of how dangerous it would be for you to continue your search for those papers illicitly owned for a certain period by Cardinal Mazarin. You would then expose yourself to a crueller fate.'*

Colbert almost suffocated as he finished reading. Threats, in his own home! And blaspheming the Scriptures!

The dogs he thought. *The accursed dogs: Deprivation of resources!*

He almost choked, then bent forward to look at the note again.

Personal suffering?

He was so lost in thought that he did not hear the door open.

'Monsieur,' called the familiar voice of his personal valet, breathless after he'd been searching for him, 'Monsieur!'

Colbert gave his servant an incandescent glare.

'What is it, at this hour?' he growled.

'A misfortune, Monsieur, a misfortune!' cried the valet.

A dreadful premonition rooted Colbert to the spot.

'My God, Monsieur . . .'

'Well, speak!' roared Colbert.

'Your father, Monsieur . . .'

Colbert collapsed into his chair, dropping the sheet of paper, which fluttered to the ground.

'He was found this morning, in his bedchamber. Dead.'

'Dead,' repeated Colbert in a daze.

Feeling faint, he put a hand in front of his eyes to drive away the words which danced before them: *cursed be the hard-hearted, for they are destined to suffer . . .*

CHAPTER EIGHTY-SEVEN

At sea, near Nantes – Monday 12 September, ten o'clock
in the morning

THE wind had got up during the night, forcing the ship to lower its sail for a time. Despite this it was making good progress, its prow gently cleaving the swell.

Gabriel reached the bottom of the companionway which led to the passengers' cabins. He paused for a moment to get his bearings in this still unfamiliar space, then continued on his way towards the aftercastle. There, at the foot of the steps that led to the bridge, he sat down, protected from the sea-spray by the sail chests.

He watched the sea foam spatter the boat's prow as she reared up before plunging her nose into the hollow of a wave. He was fascinated by the empty vastness of the sea; he had only ever seen the ocean once, and had not dared to do more than dip his bare feet into the water.

'Can you swim, Monsieur?' the captain had asked him during supper in his cabin the previous evening. 'No? Well, you would make an excellent sailor. I am suspicious of seamen who can swim – it makes them complacent about their ships!' he had exclaimed with a laugh, delighted with himself.

Gabriel had evaded questions about his final destination and the reason for his departure. He was a young man whose family wished to send away for a while. The pretext of an educational voyage had been well received, and the captain's ribald and benevolent smile seemed to imply that he had understood this to mean 'a moral scandal or duel'. In any case it was a better cover – more credible and much safer. When he arrived in New Amsterdam, he would still have time to decide what direction to take . . .

Taking off his gloves, Gabriel reached inside his cloak to remove the sealed letter which he had promised not to open until he was at sea. He looked at it quietly before making up his mind to open it. He felt that this act would erase a little more of this period of his life, people's faces, this whole mad year which had turned his existence upside down.

A pang of nostalgia and sadness filled him as he thought of those last days in France. He had spent the journey to Nantes thinking about Louise's absence at their meeting place at the Porte Saint-Martin, of that hour he had spent waiting in vain for her silhouette to appear in the doorway . . .

Once I have read and destroyed this letter, nothing will remain of my past life and nothing will link me to it. I too shall have disappeared, as my father did twenty years ago, he told himself, still hesitating. Then he quickly broke the blue wax seal and began to read.

My dear Gabriel,

When you read this letter, you will no doubt be far from Touraine. If it was given to you by François d'Orbay, this signifies that our quest has not been accomplished, but also that you have agreed to

467

become one of us, and to take up in your turn the torch which I bore. *Historical irony*: when your parents chose your Christian name, your father told d'Orbay it was because no destiny seemed finer to them than that of the Messenger, bringer of the divine word . . .

In the future, perhaps, it will be your task to complete our mission or to pass on the responsibility for it in your turn. Between now and then, you will have seen your Brothers disappear, and you will have had to leave others behind, without hope of return. I pray that these ordeals pass for you without leaving bitterness in your heart, the only danger we must fear. Gabriel, let your mission enter your heart, let your destiny merge with this collective, arduous task, which is so much greater than our individual existences. Such is the legacy that I am offering you. It is both little and much.

In the wooden box François gave you, you will find a translation of one of the documents stolen from Mazarin, which you were the bearer of. In it are passwords, contacts and addresses needed to access a part of the fortune improperly amassed by Mazarin and his henchmen. This treasure is now your responsibility. With you, it will be the most effective guardian of our Secret.

In your hands rests the fate of the Fifth Gospel, that is to say, the original version of the text of the holy Scriptures which Saint Peter modified, as I explained to you in the gardens at Vaux. You may now cast your eyes upon what has made thrones tremble, caused blood to flow and could still engender terrible misfortune if it escaped the hands of its guardians.

I imagine you at this stage of your reading, burning with the ardour of youth to seize upon this Truth: have you not yet guessed what its nature may be? Think, Gabriel: one may kill Kings, contest their legitimacy, whittle down their territory; one may intrigue to bring down a pope or to elect one. *Everything is conceivable in the realm of politics. But nothing can break the link by which the sacred legitimises temporal power and ensures its survival. And from whence comes this power that makes sovereigns 'God's lieutenants on earth'? From the latitude allowed on the subject by the Scriptures. 'You are my rock, and upon that rock I shall build my Church', said Christ to Peter; and also 'Do you love me? Then take care of my sheep.' Did these not seem strange, Gabriel, these phrases next to each other?*

If they did, you are now in a position to unravel this mystery: while generations have relentlessly sought to interpret it, you are about to understand it. Because you know that a pure, uncorrupted version exists.

An admirable fraud, in truth: for centuries men have slit one another's throats in the name of different interpretations, when in fact the source of the text to be interpreted was false . . .

Yet the teaching of Christ was extremely clear:

'Cursed be he who claims to settle the affairs of men in the name of my Father;

'Cursed be he who links the name of my Father with the quarrels of the Powerful. Let them build empires of dust but let them not place my Father's name on the pediments of their palaces of gold.

'He who tells you that he bears the sword, metes out justice to men and organises the life of the city in the name of my Father, in truth I tell you, he is a liar.' And again, 'Happy are those who have not the ambition of power; they shall be given a Kingdom at my Father's side.'

Those phrases are true. The previous ones, the ones which you know, are false.

The Truth is as simple as this: we have been asking for centuries why the question of political power is so absent from the Scriptures. It is because it was taken out. Christ's teaching is that there can be no political power based on spiritual Truth and that any attempt to link the power of the Church with the affairs of men, or indeed to legitimise the power of men through the spiritual source of his Church, is a heresy!

But better still, the teaching of Christ, this true text whose nature was confirmed to us on 17 August, tells us why this is impossible. Listen, Gabriel, listen to the message of Christ:

'Is there a hierarchy amongst the stars? And an order of precedence amongst the grains of sand? In truth I say unto you, that never does one grain of sand amongst the others imagine it can impose its truth upon the other grains of sand. All are equal and so it is with my Father's sheep. The law amongst them must be that of justice, and this justice, that of equality. Let he who reigns therefore reign through the power given to him by his Brothers: only he who chooses this way treads the road to my Father's house.'

What do you say to that, Gabriel? Imagine this news spreading through the Empire of Christians, imagine the crowds realising all at once that the sacred power of the King they obey is not only a lie but a fabrication ... Imagine them realising that they no longer owe their allegiance to the King or to the Pope. What would happen, in your opinion? That is why our mission is to find a man capable of orchestrating this revelation without opening Pandora's box. That has been my role, Gabriel: and now you have been initiated into our secret, in a more brutal manner than I was, or any of our Brothers. But necessity has demanded it.

Gabriel, I can imagine the look of fear on your face: but do you really believe that the truth is an easy thing to look in the face? If that were the case, the history of men would not be what it is. Such has been the terrible strength of Saint Peter: he knew that the content of the texts would never really be placed in doubt.

But be reassured: time will enable you to familiarise yourself with this scandal. You will learn to accept that there are eleven and not ten Beatitudes in the fifth chapter of Matthew; that Peter did not deny Christ thrice but four times, and that this fourth time was removed from the text which reached us; that he did not deny being one of Christ's companions, but instead denied altering the nature of the Saviour's message. You will learn to recognise between the lines the additions and the subtractions: the passages added and the passages suppressed.

This is what is contained in the manuscript which we have at last been able to decode.

Take the time you now have to assimilate this heritage. One day, perhaps months or even years from now, perhaps even after you are gone, during the lifetime of whoever succeeds you, this message will emerge again, and attempt to make its Truth heard without causing a cataclysm.

Take care of yourself, Gabriel. Now, as I leave for Nantes to attempt to save my mission, all my wishes go with you; I wish so much that you did not have to make this journey alone.

Farewell, Gabriel de Pontbriand. Be worthy of your Brothers, in the image of your father. I hope with all my heart soon to be able to return victorious, and to tear up this letter with my own hands.

Nicolas Fouquet.

Gabriel's hands were trembling so much that he could not fold up the letter. With the back of his sleeve, he wiped away the tears that filled his eyes. Then his chin dropped onto his chest. Motionless, he felt the crumpled paper between his fingers as though it were alive. At last he stood up, his curls flying in the wind which blew ever stronger, and headed for the ship's rail.

'Take care,' said a sailor who was coiling rope, his bare feet clamped to the deck, 'it's slippery over there.'

Gabriel walked past without seeing him and went on towards the bow. Before him, the foam of the waves formed a blurred horizon on which sky and sea mingled. The pieces of paper which he tore before flinging them to the wind whirled above the figurehead for a moment before swirling down and disappearing into the green water.

Gabriel remained there for a moment, gazing at the empty ocean. Then he returned to his cabin.

The box was there in his trunk, beneath his clothes.

The hull resounded with the waves that slapped against it, and the whistle of the wind in the sails sounded like shrill music. Gabriel seemed not to hear. His lips moved gently as he began to recite by heart: 'In the beginning was the Word, and the Word was with God, and the Word was God . . .'

CHAPTER EIGHTY-EIGHT

Château de Fontainebleau – Tuesday 1 November,
eleven o'clock in the morning

'A son! The Queen has given us a son!'

Louise was amazed to see the King of France open the window of the bedchamber where Maria-Theresa had just given birth, lean out and shout for joy at the top of his lungs.

'Come now, let's close that window! Your son and your wife will catch cold,' Anne of Austria told him gently, her expression radiant.

Obeying his mother just this once, Louis XIV approached the bed where the Spanish Infanta lay, exhausted by her labour.

'You have done good work, Madame! The child is magnificent. He shall be called Louis of France,' he said, gazing at his young wife with unusual tenderness.

Then the sovereign left the bedchamber so that the women could get on with 'their affairs'. Louise's gaze followed him as he walked away. When the door had closed, she stood still for a moment before she too approached the bed, her expression fixed, unable to take her eyes from the intricate little cradle in which the Dauphin had been laid.

Colbert, who was waiting with the principal ministers in the corridor, was first to congratulate the King. Then the monarch confronted the swelling ranks of courtiers. As he walked through the tide of humanity, Louis XIV remembered the events of this year, 1661.

At last, he told himself, watching men and women bow to him as he passed by. *At last I shall be able to show them what I am capable of!*